Call of the Forbidden Way

Call of the Forbidden Way

Robert Owings

COSMIC
EGG
BOOKS

Winchester, UK
Washington, USA

First published by Cosmic Egg Books, 2016
Cosmic Egg Books is an imprint of John Hunt Publishing Ltd., Laurel House, Station Approach,
Alresford, Hants, SO24 9JH, UK
office1@jhpbooks.net
www.johnhuntpublishing.com

For distributor details and how to order please visit the 'Ordering' section on our website.

ISBN: 978 1 78535 366 6
Library of Congress Control Number: 2015958688

A CIP catalogue record for this book is available from the British Library.

Design: Stuart Davies

Printed and bound by CPI Group (UK) Ltd, Croydon, CR0 4YY, UK

We operate a distinctive and ethical publishing philosophy in all
areas of our business, from our global network of authors to
production and worldwide distribution.

Prologue

On a remote Chilean mountainside, the parish Jeep slowed to a stop. Clutching his rosary, Father Clemente stepped from the vehicle, moving cautiously to inspect the unexplainable. A frightened man had come to him that morning from a nearby village, continuously repeating that none of the people who lived at the pagan commune could be found.

"Padre, come please," the man had pleaded with him, his voice trembling as he constantly made the sign of the cross. "Satan must have taken them. All gone—all destroyed."

A veil of heavy clouds was dissipating. In this region at ten thousand feet there was little but rock and stunted scrub covering the mountainside. Flames still flickered from the blackened hulks of several of the community's buildings. The trucks and cars that belonged to the members remained parked in their customary spots.

Climbing the stone steps of the main building that served as the commune's temple, Father Clemente saw that the doors were shattered and partially torn from their hinges. Just in front of the doors lay the body of Bacco, the large dog that had always played so gently with the children. He knelt and examined the dog, searching through the thick black fur for wounds. He found none. A lone crow sailed across the sky, its cry puncturing the silence.

Father Clemente had been here many times since the group had arrived from the suburbs of Santiago and founded their spiritual community some eight years ago. At first, he tried to warn them of their misguided ways and the dangers of ignoring the Catholic Church. He was deeply troubled that educated people would reject salvation through Christ. But as the years passed, he had come to know, respect, and love these people. Now this—as if some Biblical scourge had descended upon them.

For the last six months, the community's leaders had vigorously confided to the priest that a great danger was coming.

"Father, they are spirits—ones not of this world," Hernando, the commune's elder, had warned.

Hernando had implored him to pray with all his conviction—for them, for the people of his own parish, for all God's creatures.

Although somewhat troubled by their sense of urgency, Father Clemente had decided to dismiss their warnings as superstition. How like the simple country people of the Andes they had become, he thought. But now, something horrific had indeed occurred.

Father Clemente searched the rest of the compound, looking in vain for something, besides smoldering buildings and a dead animal, that might explain how twenty-eight adults and thirteen children could have suddenly vanished in the night.

Chapter 1

Just a Filmmaker

Carson Reynolds surveyed the landscape through the bug-splattered windshield, wondering why the Pine Ridge Reservation in South Dakota had been chosen for this event. The bland prairie lacked the dramatic setting of the Southwest that he would have preferred. The July sun beat down with little mercy on the litter-strewn parking lot of Big Bats store and filling station, their appointed rendezvous.

He felt somehow different being on this Lakota land. A strange, vaguely disturbing sensation stirred within; or was it just the climate change from California?

Lucas, his longtime soundman, sat beside him in the front of their rented van, reading an article on mountaineering in China while snacking on trail mix and downing gulps of Snapple. A sun bleached metal sign proclaiming, **Permits Sold Inside,** flapped in the wind.

Once again, Carson questioned whether he should be here. He had promised himself and others, especially Allison, that he would stop accepting documentary projects that were financially marginal. After all, his career was at a stage where he was supposed to be making respectable money and not just collecting awards for artistic achievement. He was hard pressed to justify taking on another documentary that paid little.

A dust-coated Chevy pickup pulled up next to Carson's van, once again disturbing the paper litter that occupied the parking lot. Out stepped Jimmy White Stone.

"Carson, you scoundrel, you made it," Jimmy called out, adjusting the heavy-framed eyeglasses resting on his nose. "I was starting to get a little worried."

"Sir James, keeper of the mighty pen of righteousness, good

1

to see you, my man," Carson replied, climbing out of the van.

The two men embraced. Carson pulled back to better take in his old college friend.

"Damn, how long has it been since we last saw each other?"

"About four years, I believe," Jimmy answered. "That night we had dinner together in San Francisco. That Vietnamese place on Valencia?"

Carson slapped his leg. "Mind like a steel trap. Never forgets the details."

Jimmy, a tall man with a lean build, dressed in a weathered corduroy sports jacket and faded jeans, looked all the part of the bohemian professor. Now well into his forties, he wore a braided ponytail streaked with gray. His expression conveyed his usual pensive mood, one that had become familiar over the years and that signaled a certain intellectual proclivity of Jimmy's that both attracted and annoyed Carson.

"Well, you must be doing all right," Carson said. "Every time I pick up a magazine, it seems your name is under the title of some article. Right? Read you in *Time,* the *Smithsonian, Rolling Stone.*"

Jimmy shrugged. "Yeah, I suppose being a journalist has worked. Or maybe it's just having an Indian slant on things that allows me to get in print. Hard to say."

"Don't be so fucking modest, you know you're damn good." Carson laughed, slapping Jimmy on the back while directing his attention to the young man emerging from the van. "Now, Jimmy, I know he doesn't look like much, but this is my dear associate and trusted soundman, Lucas."

"Welcome," Jimmy said.

"Thank you. Good to be here," Lucas replied, stepping forward, a crown of dreadlocks, gathered in a loose bundle, cascaded from a faded, backwards-facing baseball cap. "Hope we're not real late. We got kind of delayed at the airport getting all our gear through baggage claim, and then there's getting here.

Damn, this place is out there, dude."

"Don't worry, we won't start shooting until tomorrow, if then," Jimmy said casually as he studied the young man. "Besides, time moves at a different pace here than in the rest of the world. I only requested that you get here today so you could settle in. But let's go over to where we'll be filming, check out the generator we rented for your lighting. We can do some of the preliminary setup and planning. It's in sort of an isolated part of the rez, a special power spot."

"This project is so awesome," Lucas said, adjusting his baggy cargo shorts up to his waist. A down vest, cotton sweatshirt, and work boots completed his film crewmember look.

"Awesome?" Jimmy paused, surveying the rolling prairie. "Well, that's to be determined."

"From what you've told me, I still can't believe you talked your elders into letting us film this thing," Carson said.

"It wasn't easy," Jimmy said, narrowing his eyes craftily. "An intertribal medicine circle of this caliber is a major event. But it's imperative to capture this on film, a way to preserve what remains of the old ways."

"Well, we'll see what we can do," Carson responded. Despite the questionable monetary rewards, he felt honored to have been asked to make the documentary by a committee of Lakota elders. Jimmy, who had collaborated with him on films when they were both undergraduates at UCLA, had helped negotiate the commission. Carson was looking forward to working with his old friend once more.

As they rode through the reservation, Carson couldn't help but notice that conditions were far from romantic. Nearly every house or trailer beckoned for repair—cardboard patches over broken windows, blue plastic tarps wrapped over roofs, sagging foundations, and practically no evidence of anything having been recently painted. Carcasses of abandoned automobiles and trucks dotted the prairie. Many people suffered poor health, too, Jimmy explained—diabetes, tuberculosis, and alcoholism fed upon the community with little restraint.

Despite the apparent hardships, however, some young people strolled about with iPods and cheap new hip-hop-inspired attire. Expensive, late-model pickups sat in front of a number of homes, often alongside satellite dishes standing like great metallic mushrooms. To Carson the reservation presented a ragtag community caught in poverty and consumerism.

Early the next day, they drove out to the filming location, a flattened plateau at the end of a box canyon, surrounded on three sides by sandstone mesas. A band of rich green shrubs and cottonwoods ran around the plateau's perimeter.

Even though they had Jimmy's four-wheel-drive truck to haul the equipment, everything had to be carried up a footpath the last hundred yards. To power the lighting they strung large electrical cables along this path from a trailer-mounted generator stationed below.

While Lucas busied himself with the audio equipment, Carson took Jimmy through a refresher on running the second camera and the two-way radios.

"You don't need to worry about the battery pack; you'll get a warning readout in the eyepiece if it's getting too low," Carson explained. "Nearly everything is digital now. Not like the old days."

"Got it," Jimmy acknowledged. "Say, Carson, I again want to thank you for holding the crew to an absolute minimum. I realize having me on the second camera isn't how you'd prefer to work, but this is such a sensitive ceremony. We really need to be as unobtrusive as possible."

"No problem," Carson replied, giving Jimmy a pat on the back.

Later in the morning the medicine men began to arrive, amid great excitement from the growing audience of Lakota people who stood along the edges of the site. Jimmy had explained that hosting this medicine circle had charged the reservation with pride. Carson wondered if it was also a rekindling of old hope.

"What are they doing now?" he asked, watching the medicine men sprinkle water over each other and apply copious billows of smoke over one another's bodies from bundles of smoldering sage.

"Purification," Jimmy answered.

"Oh, fire and water, that's cool," Carson said, his eye locked on the camera's eyepiece as he filmed the scene.

Whenever he could free himself from the technical preparations, Carson took the opportunity to scan the gathering's array of faces. Many of the participants wore some form of traditional jewelry, moccasins or headgear, composed of beading, feathers, silver, and leather. They casually blended these items with everyday contemporary clothing: blue jeans, t-shirts with silk-screen prints of eagles or medicine wheels, fleece pullovers, and cowboy boots. But his eye was drawn to the quiet intensity of their faces, sculpted by age and a form of wisdom not acknowledged by modern Western culture.

In contrast to these medicine men, Carson's own appearance reflected mainstream America: khaki shorts and shirt, a safari vest. He looked as though he had stepped off the pages of a Territory Ahead catalogue. He found himself feeling self-conscious, hoping he wouldn't stick out too badly among these purpose-driven people of grit.

He edged over to Jimmy. "Colorful group you've got here, Mr. White Stone," he said.

"Thank you." Jimmy laughed. "We had some Hollywood costume people come in and create these outfits just for your film. Glad you like them."

"No, seriously, this is going to look good," Carson replied, sweeping his arm in front of the gathering of medicine men.

Jimmy turned to face him. "Well, that might be, but the film shouldn't be driven by just the visuals. These people aren't simply caricatures."

"I know, I know," Carson apologized without meeting Jimmy's eyes. "Just speaking as a filmmaker, that's all."

"These men have come from across the country, including a few from Canada, and that guy over there is from Mexico." Jimmy pointed. "There are about 140 of them. The majority of them are elders."

"So who are those young guys I see?"

"Apprentices who are especially gifted in medicine work," Jimmy answered. "You know, traditional healers. The guys who engage with spirit forces and such."

Lucas walked over and joined them, changing a set of couplings on the end of a cable while he listened.

"Care to explain anything else we should know about, like what to watch for as this thing gets going?" Carson pressed.

"Well, obviously nothing about this gathering is scripted," Jimmy said. "At least nothing has been revealed to me by my elders. I'm not sure they even know themselves exactly what's going to happen. Our charge is simply to film what unfolds here as best we can."

Jimmy pulled the thickly framed eyeglasses from his face, cleaning the lenses with a handkerchief in a concentrated manner. "Some of the language used in the singing might be of a special kind, perhaps known only to that individual medicine worker, a language given by the spirit world," he said cryptically.

"Well, we don't know Lakota from Latin, so it'll all be the same for us," Carson said, nudging Lucas' arm sportingly. "Right, my man?"

Lucas laughed. "Hey, whatever they say, I'll record it. No worries."

Jimmy paused, choosing his words. "I should let you know

that there's much more going on here than just this documentary. There're certain ..." Jimmy stopped. "Oh, never mind. Anyway, you're fortunate that most of the discussions will be in English. After all, it's the common language for Indians, too. So no worries, as Lucas so aptly puts it."

Around midday, with no discernable protocol as far as Carson could tell, men began to seat themselves on the ground, forming a large circle. An audience of three to four hundred Indians gathered behind, surrounding the medicine men. Carson, Lucas, and Jimmy positioned themselves between these two human circles, poised to move about as needed.

Carson was too busy panning to notice exactly how the ceremony began. But before long, someone was singing, and a large accompaniment of native drums and a host of supporting singers joined in.

To Carson, the songs felt haunting, a mixture of simple melody and indefinable melancholy, blended into a chant paced by primal rhythm. He focused his camera on the long-stemmed, leather covered pipes that began to be passed around the circle. The sacred smoke of tobacco melded with the scent of sage, leather, and sweat.

As the ceremonies progressed into the afternoon, the drumming intensified, penetrating into everything that composed the physical surroundings—people, cameras, rocks, sky. The trance inducing rhythm pulled at the confines of Carson's consciousness, teasing him to forget the demands of his camera. Various medicine men took turns leading the ceremonies with songs or dances, weaving their tribal tongues into an exotic spell over the plateau. While he could not understand the languages of the various ceremonial songs, Carson felt shaken to his core, as though his soul was loosening from its mooring. He had to truly concentrate to even stay focused on his job.

The ceremonies ran late into the night, resuming the next

morning. Carson spent some of those early hours filming various medicine men in interviews with Jimmy and meeting many of the honored guests. With little time for sleep, he began to run on adrenaline, fully aware that he was documenting something extraordinary. But by the third and final day, exhaustion was over taking him.

"Everything about this gathering has been going very well so far," Jimmy said before they started that morning. "And there have been serious concerns that it might be quite the opposite. It even appears the spirits are well pleased by our filming or otherwise they would have caused trouble."

"That's cool." Lucas laughed. "Don't want any of those dudes pissed off."

Jimmy took off his glasses again, wiping them nervously. "Well, sometimes you can only know that for sure if you make it home safely."

Shortly before dusk, the drumming suddenly stopped. With little said, those in the audience gathered themselves and silently walked away, vacating not only the plateau but also the surrounding area. Meanwhile, the medicine men gathered in small groups for prayers and once again smudged themselves with sage smoke. There was little sound other than the distant rumbling of departing cars and trucks.

"What's up with those people leaving?" Carson asked Jimmy through the two-way radio.

"The medicine men will do something special tonight," he answered, "a closed session, no audience."

"Oh, okay," Carson said, preoccupied with preparing for the night's work. He had little more than an hour before dark to make lighting changes, swap battery packs, load new video, do sound checks, and inspect cables. He longed to sleep but readied himself for this last push.

The special, closed ceremony began shortly after dark. Carson could discern little difference between this one and all the others—there was drumming and singing, only no dancing. But after about a half hour, the drums fell silent and the medicine men sat in quiet meditation.

Carson took the opportunity to check his equipment. Everything appeared to be functioning properly. He spoke softly into the two-way radios, checking in with Jimmy and Lucas. All was in order.

Suddenly there was movement; a handful of medicine men began moving around the circle, passing out small, leather pouches, amulets and feathers to the other attendees. They spoke softly among themselves, apparently exchanging some form of blessing.

The medicine men returned to their meditation.

Carson briefly moved out of filming range. "I hope they do something with a little action soon," he whispered over the radio. "This sitting in silence stuff is about as riveting as watching snow melt."

"Yeah," Lucas replied. "Jimmy, how much longer will they do this?"

"Until it's no longer time to do it," Jimmy whispered back.

Carson resumed filming.

Charlie Singing Wolf, a Blackfoot from Saskatchewan, finally broke the silence. "Brothers, we have made the prayers and sung the songs. We have shared much of our ways here; the medicine has been strong. Now it is time to speak of the great struggle."

His words took on an ominous edge. "The battle for the Great Mother is soon to come. More and more of those who wish to do harm are gathering; some even now walk upon Her bosom's surface. Others are hiding in Her belly while the rest continue to gather, hovering above. She is calling Her children to come together and defend Her life. It is by Her breath and blood that life flows to all Her creatures, to all plants and trees, to the rocks and mountains, to the rivers and oceans. She is in great danger. Those who wish to abduct Her are powerful beings. We must join with Her allies in this great battle. Is it not so?"

The hairs on the back of Carson's neck stood up. Without really understanding what Charlie Singing Wolf meant, he intuitively sensed the graveness of the man's prophecy. His hands began to tremble, causing the handheld camera to shake. He had to force himself to keep steady.

Charlie went on. "As you all must know, it is for this purpose that we have gathered here. Many of us have been receiving messages that speak of such things. And it is not just Indian people. We have heard it is the same for others from many parts of the world. Those of you who have met with the traveling ones from Tibet, those they call lamas, have privately spoken of these things. My own granddaughter has recently returned from a conference in Nepal. She tells me that there the Hindu medicine women, the yoginis, are preparing for this time. And my friend Ralph Wetspoon, a university professor from Vancouver, a member of the Gitksan tribe who went to Siberia last summer, tells me that even there the Tungus people, our old relatives, are talking this way."

The elder nodded, indicating he was finished.

An old Crow medicine man Carson had learned was from Montana began to speak. "I, too, have heard these things, Charlie Singing Wolf," he said. "This past fall, I was invited to go with some of the Christian people from my tribe to a gathering outside New York City. It was one of those events they call an ecumenical council, which is supposed to welcome many other ways of knowing spirit. You all know about those gatherings?"

Snickers emanated from the circle.

"One evening, after the regular program, I spoke with a woman from Haiti who practices the voodoo medicine, and also with a medicine man from the west coast of Africa. Our conversation turned to this matter. They, too, prepare for this crisis; they know of it in those lands. Of course, I only spoke of this among such medicine people, not with any of the others attending, and certainly not with those Christians from my own tribe."

"But there are some Christian whites who know of these things," interrupted the young Zuni, Luther Redbone, whom Jimmy had interviewed the day before. "I know a couple; they're Episcopal missionaries who work in South America. They visit my pueblo on occasion, and on their last visit they spoke with me about these things. They are the ones who told me that the curanderos in the Amazon are doing medicine work to defend our world from this danger."

"Enough, we agree that this threat is real," said Owl Eyes, the old Nez Percé medicine man with the commanding presence whom Jimmy had introduced Carson to that morning. Carson had somehow suspected it was Owl Eyes who had been silently in charge of the proceedings throughout the entire three days. While filming, Carson had observed the other medicine men watching this man, as if getting instructions from him. And on the breaks, Owl Eyes had been often sought after by other medicine men, always appearing to be in deep conversation with his peers. Carson clearly sensed that whoever the man was, he was a person of high authority among the group.

Owl Eyes reached into his medicine bag and tossed something that resembled sand toward the center of the circle. "The words of Charlie Singing Wolf and the others are true. I know it is so because in a dream I had this winter, I was visited by Wounded Paw, who told me of this danger."

A murmur spread among them. Carson wondered who or what Wounded Paw could be.

Owl Eyes lifted his hand, signaling silence. "This time we must not fail as we did when the whites came to this land. These powers that threaten us are far more dangerous. And even the white people will have to learn their forgotten ways of spirit if they wish to survive. With our people and allies, we must combine our powers in this struggle. We must unite these powers, weaving a giant blanket to cover the Great Mother. This is how it must be. Tomorrow we return to our homes. If the spirits allow and we have the courage, we will meet again." The drums began once more.

The Indians' prophetic words caused Carson's stomach to tighten with an indefinable fear. But the sensation didn't last; his rational mind regained control and began putting his thoughts back in order. "Whatever these Indians mean, they're only speaking metaphorically," Carson told himself. "And your job, Mr. Filmmaker, is just to document this stuff, not interpret it."

He immediately felt better, reassuring himself that he had his role in the world and the Indians had theirs. Redirecting his attention back to the job, he checked his camera.

"Goddamn it," Carson sputtered in disbelief. The camera wasn't running.

"What's the matter?" Jimmy White Stone whispered, appearing beside him.

"I can't believe it—I don't think I got any of their talk. Somehow the camera stopped. Thank God you were filming."

"Nope," Jimmy said flatly.

"What?" Carson hissed.

"No way, my friend; that stuff wasn't for the cameras. I turned mine off. I guess the spirits stopped yours. Believe me, it's better for you this way. I would've been very worried for you if you'd left here with that footage."

Lucas ran over. "Carson, man, you aren't gonna believe this, but somehow my equipment wouldn't record any of that stuff."

Fear once again pulled at Carson. "Evidently, it wasn't supposed to," he replied, shaking his head in resignation.

Jimmy White Stone nodded and returned to his camera.

Rain clouds gathered on the fourth morning, erecting dark walls in the western sky. Carson and Lucas hurriedly packed, throwing their gear into the rented van for the return drive to the airport. Carson was looking forward to getting home, to his own bed—to where he belonged. He felt more than weary, and a strange dream from the previous night still churned unresolved in his mind.

"So, Carson, about ready to get out of here?" Jimmy White Stone called as he strolled toward them, adjusting the thick eyeglasses on his nose.

Jimmy had been busy all morning, helping the various visiting medicine men with their homeward departures. Many had left before dawn. When Carson learned of this, he half wondered if they had done so because they thought they needed to slip away unseen by evil spirits.

"Well, Jimmy, quite an interesting soirée you girls throw," Carson said, attempting to be more lighthearted than he felt. "There's going to be some brilliant footage to work through."

"I knew you two would do a good job for us," Jimmy said, handing them each a small leather pouch decorated with beading and fringe. "My brothers want me to thank you and Lucas for keeping the space sacred for their work."

"What's this?" Lucas asked.

"These are medicine bags for you to take with you, to keep you safe on your journey home, as well as to keep in your home for protection. It's one of the ways we wish to thank you. But don't open them until you're home, and keep the contents in the pouch."

Carson nodded in appreciation. "It was an honor to be asked here. Thanks for these gifts."

The three of them stood together in a moment of silence as a brisk wind swept through, signaling a change in the weather.

"So when do you want to fly out to California and start adding the audio? And who's going to do the narration?" Carson asked.

"Oh, I've got several people I'd like to use," Jimmy said confidently. "I'll let you know in plenty of time. But first I have to write an article about this gathering for *Tribal College*. After that, I'll get started on the audio material for you."

"I still wish we could have got that footage from last night's little powwow," Carson grumbled, heaving the last duffel bag of cables into the back of the van.

"White folk." Jimmy laughed.

After a round of good-byes, the filmmakers drove off the reservation, joining the two-lane highway that would guide them back to a more familiar world. Carson eased back in his seat, glad to have Lucas at the wheel.

An hour later and miles away from the Lakota nation, a violent thunderstorm beat down upon the highway, whipping sheets of angry rain against the windshield. Carson, overcome by fatigue, fell into a restless sleep. The troubling dream from the previous night presented itself once more.

The large beast called to him, beckoning him to come, come inside a hidden place, there among the remains of so many who had lived long before, there, surrounded by knowledge that was forbidden and dangerous.

Chapter 2

Bear Dreams

Six weeks later, Jimmy White Stone was sitting in Carson's living room. He had flown to California to view the footage and start adding the narration, bringing drafts of text and a selection of musical feeds.

Their phone conversations since the filming had been charged with creative excitement. Word of the medicine gathering had spread across much of the Native American community and Jimmy had been asked to do an additional article, this time for *Native Peoples Magazine*.

Having already done the preliminary editing, Carson was anxious to show the product to his friend. Both men realized that they were riding something extraordinary with this film.

Yet Carson was troubled. Ever since returning home to Santa Cruz, he had been emerging from sleep exhausted by something possessing his dreams. Regaining a full sense of normality seemed to take half his morning. Privately, he feared his condition was somehow connected to filming on the reservation.

"So, aren't you gonna show me some of the footage tonight?" Jimmy asked, relaxing on the sofa shortly upon arrival at Carson's.

"No, let's start fresh in the morning," Carson answered. "If we get into it now, we'll be up half the night, and I'm already pretty shot."

He pulled out a bottle of Scotch, poured glasses for them both, and quickly downed a large gulp. Bringing the bottle with the glasses, he walked over and handed Jimmy a glass before taking his seat in the overstuffed club chair.

"Been working too hard?" Jimmy asked.

"No, maybe just drinking too much. Feels like I need to wash something away."

Jimmy remained silent, peering at Carson.

"In truth, Jimmy, I need to ask you something, man," he said, leaning forward and looking directly into Jimmy's eyes.

"Ask," Jimmy replied.

"All right, I got something my mind can't seem to let go of." He paused, taking another generous swallow of Scotch while fiddling with the bottle's label where it sat on the coffee table. "What was all that talk about on that last night of the medicine circle, the stuff you said the spirits didn't want me to film?"

Whatever meaning that night held, something had been eating at him. Yet hearing himself ask the question seem to spawn an unexpected sense of relief.

"Well, you heard it as well as I did. What did it mean to you?" Jimmy responded.

"Damn, Jimmy, maybe you should've become a therapist instead of a journalist. What a total flip of my question."

"I'm not trying to be obscure, Carson," Jimmy responded. "I'm trying to get you to bring it out in your own words, to say what it is that you understood from that night."

"Now you sound like a goddamn lawyer," Carson muttered irritably, pouring himself another glass. "Look, something is bothering me around this thing, and you're the only one I know who can possibly help."

"I understand," Jimmy said, continuing to stare at him unmoved.

"All right, here's what I think they meant," Carson blurted. "They think something bad is going to happen, probably globally. Am I right? Like, what, nuclear war or a new plague? Or some unpredicted environmental crisis, like the ozone falling into the ocean and the ice caps melting? And they think they can see this thing, this coming crisis, and the rest of us can't, but they're going to try to do something about it. Am I right?"

Carson stopped, hoping that whatever impending global

doom loomed ahead, Jimmy would confirm that it was one of these usual scenarios.

Jimmy placed his drink on the coffee table, pausing for an awkwardly long time in Carson's opinion. Finally, he asked, "Anything else?"

"Jesus, does there need to be anything more? I mean, isn't any of that bad enough?"

Jimmy remained silent, apparently turned inward with his own thoughts.

The same fear Carson had experienced that night on the Lakota reservation began to creep over him again. He suddenly understood: there was something more. The medicine men had been speaking of the coming of something unimaginable.

For several minutes, both men sat in silence. Carson struggled with his realization while Jimmy, frozen as stone and eyes shut, prayed silently.

Eventually, Carson found the courage to speak.

"So, what is it exactly that we're talking about, Jimmy? I mean if we're all going to encounter some kind of Armageddon, I'd like to be in on what we're dealing with. Maybe stock up on a few extra batteries."

"I'm not sure I can really explain it to you," Jimmy answered.

"Well, try, for God's sake."

"I could say that there are forces from spiritual dimensions involved, but that's just too simple," Jimmy began hesitantly. "It's a very complex matter. It's not just spirits; these are other beings. You would have to learn much about other ways of knowing to comprehend what this means."

For a moment, Carson relaxed, reconciling that whatever this coming crisis, it would be dealt with by those people accustomed to such matters. It would have negligible impact on the everyday life of the modern world; that much he assured himself.

"Other beings?" Carson inquired sardonically. "Oh, you mean like UFOs and creatures from outer space? Or is it just all the weird people here already? I see plenty of that type on the streets of Santa Cruz every day. Is the great white buffalo or some such going to show up? Just what the hell do you actually mean?"

"Well, some of all of that, in a way. But again, it's not that simple," Jimmy answered. "Look, we could talk all night and you wouldn't understand any of it without having been initiated into this way of knowing."

There was a long pause. Carson replenished his glass a third time, his rational mind attempting to downplay it all as just some Native American hocus-pocus. In fact, he was even a bit embarrassed, thinking he had stupidly taken on someone else's drama without any real reason. Yet he remained curious and inexplicably troubled.

"Okay, Jimmy, I'm a reasonable man. I'll accept that this is outside my capacity to comprehend. But I have one last question, and after that I'll try not to harass you any further with my curiosity."

"What is it?" Jimmy asked.

Carson leaned forward. "So, old friend, just how do I get myself initiated into this way of knowing?"

Jimmy laughed. "I don't think you know what you're asking."

A bolt of anger surged through Carson, heating the back of his neck. He shook his head in agitation, downing another gulp of Scotch.

"Hey, of course not," he replied acerbically. "I'm just some dumb white bastard; what do I know? You guys want to keep all the goodies to yourselves, hey, fine. That's your business. Can't blame you; we stole about everything else from you. Better hang onto something, for Christ's sake. Still, if this thing is as big as it sounds, you're gonna need all the help you can get. Better sign up all the recruits you can. Myself, I'd be down at the mall right now trying to get people to enlist." Carson laughed caustically, attempting to release the building frustration of the past six weeks.

"I hear a lot of alcohol talking," Jimmy said. "We can speak more another time."

Suddenly recognizing his hostility and rudeness, Carson felt ashamed. After all, it wasn't Jimmy's fault that something was gnawing on his psyche, nor was it Jimmy's responsibility. This was no way to treat an old friend.

"I'm sorry, Jimmy. I'm being an ass," he apologized. "It's late and I'm about wasted enough, hopefully, to assure myself a regular night's sleep. Jesus, if I could just not have one of those dreams where that goddamn bear's talking to me again. What is it with that son of a bitch anyway?"

"Excuse me, what did you just say?" Jimmy asked, almost coming off the sofa.

"Jimmy, man, if I insulted you by calling some spirit a son of a bitch, I'm sorry."

"No," Jimmy interrupted, sounding alarmed. "Did you say something about a bear?"

"Hey, again, I apologize. I called it a goddamn bear because I may have had a bit too much Scotch, but no disrespect meant. I'm just a little ..."

"These dreams you have," Jimmy interrupted again, "a bear talks to you?"

"Yeah, and he's a big mother, too." Carson laughed, suddenly needing another sip of Scotch. "So what the hell does that mean, anything?"

Jimmy sat back slowly. Carson knew the look on Jimmy's face. The one that said he was going into one of those pensive modes, no longer really present. Jimmy could be that way for hours, just thinking, meditating, processing.

"I can see you're off in your thoughts, my friend. Care to share any of them at this time?" Carson said, hoping to break Jimmy's silence. "Well, I'll leave you to them."

Carson downed the last of his glass and staggered toward his bedroom.

Jimmy White Stone sat in silence.

The following morning, Jimmy was already up when Carson stumbled into the living room, fumbling with a bottle of Tylenol.

"Top of the day to you, Jim, me lad."

"I bet it doesn't feel like that for you," Jimmy said.

"I would be grateful just not to feel, period," Carson said, laughing through his hangover. "Coffee will be on in a few minutes. You hungry?"

"I'll take you out for breakfast if you promise not to order any alcohol," Jimmy replied.

"Promise—at least not until this evening," Carson said. "But I need to take a shower and down a couple of pills with at least one cup of mud just to get out of the house. When I wake up these days, it's as if my dreams are still running inside the back of my head. Meanwhile, I'm operating at half speed like some zombie."

"More dreams last night?" Jimmy asked as the two of them entered the kitchen together.

"Yeah," Carson said, locking his bloodshot eyes onto Jimmy's.

"That bear again?"

"None other," he answered.

Only the gurgle of the coffeemaker cut the silence.

"Pour us some coffee, Carson, I've something to tell you."

"I hope you like it black," he said, trying to steady his shaky hands.

"That's fine," Jimmy responded, avoiding eye contact.

They moved to the living room, Carson taking his usual seat in the large club chair. Jimmy followed, positioning himself back on the sofa. They sat quietly for several moments, sipping coffee. Finally, Jimmy began.

"Carson, things like this are very unlikely. I mean, it's really unusual, but sometimes the medicine has a way of going into others for whom it is not intended. I'm not sure, but I have a strong suspicion this might have happened to you that last night at the medicine circle."

Carson stiffened, a mixture of fear and anger brewing inside. "So, you're saying that some kind of spirit stuff is mucking with me?" Carson asked, rocking forward in the big chair. "Well gee, Jimmy, that's just fucking swell."

"Listen, I'm sorry for whatever you've been going through," Jimmy said with a sigh. "We knew the spirit energy would be very strong that night. In fact, the whole time you were there the medicine men had created a protective shield around you and Lucas so that your spirits would not be disturbed by being so close to the medicine."

"Well, if that was the case, it didn't work too well, did it?" Carson snapped. "Your shield must have had a hole in it. Where's your goddamn quality control with these things?"

Placing his coffee down on the table, Jimmy removed his eyeglasses and began cleaning the lenses with determined strokes. "Hey, Carson, I can understand this being very upsetting, but I'm trying to help."

"I suppose it's just one of those unseen professional hazards they never tell you about in film school. Or maybe I slept through the class on knowing how to check for malfunctioning protective shields. Do you have any suggestion as to how to turn this shit off? How I can get my life back?" He struggled to control his bewilderment and rage at the Indians.

"Carson, as I tried to explain, I can't be sure if what I'm saying is correct," Jimmy said hesitantly. "But if I am correct, well ... "

"Well, what?" Carson demanded, his voice starting to shake with emotion.

"Carson, there was no hole in the shield."

"So how did this stuff get into me?"

Jimmy shifted forward, clearing his throat. "Listen, I may have this all wrong. I really need to get one of the men from the medicine circle to confirm what I'm saying."

"But if you're right, if there was no hole, then what the hell's happening here?" Carson pleaded, his desperation growing.

"Carson, I am not a medicine man, okay? There's a huge difference between what these men know and do, and what I know and do. I'm closer to your world than theirs. I just happen to know enough through my culture to understand that it's real. I don't actively operate in it. I'm a passive participant, at best."

"I don't know why I'm even listening to this shit. I could do better with my kid's Ouija board," he said, clawing the arm of the big chair with his fingernails.

"I'm sorry, my friend, but if I'm correct, we need to address this immediately. Your life may be in very real danger," Jimmy stated, extending his arms toward Carson, beseeching his friend to take him seriously. "There wasn't any hole in the shield; it doesn't work that way. If you were reached by the medicine, it means you were somehow, well, chosen. It's a sign."

"Oh, great, Jimmy. And what if I don't want to be chosen?"

"I'm afraid that's outside my sphere of expertise. Either way, you stand to be at great risk. We've got to call in someone who can properly deal with this."

Carson shook his head. "I can't believe I'm continuing to listen to this. I mean, if you aren't knowledgeable in your own people's magic, where do you get off telling me that I need to be getting help from one of your medicine boys? How do you know you're anywhere close to right on this thing?"

Jimmy looked down at the table, cautiously rearranging the position of his coffee mug as though needing to find the perfect alignment for the handle.

"It's because of your dreams; the talking bear that comes to you," Jimmy said, pacing his words cautiously, needing Carson to heed them.

Carson fought a sudden wave of nausea. In the depths of his soul, he realized that Jimmy White Stone was right.

Chapter 3

An Undesired Outcome

Three days later, Carson and Jimmy were waiting in the San Jose airport to meet two men, from the medicine circle that had taken place some six weeks before.

Luther Redbone, the young Zuni medicine man, was first to arrive. Carson stood back while Jimmy greeted Luther as he came out of the passengers only gateway. Carson again wondered what he was doing by consenting to this arrangement.

Inside the airport, Luther seemed somehow more ordinary. With his long, jet-black hair neatly held in a ponytail, his linen cowboy shirt, a stylish black vest adorned with sacred symbols, and pricey, Swiss, hiking boots, he looked more like the poster boy for Indian chic than a man of magic. Aviator-style sunglasses hid his eyes but Carson could feel them locked onto him. Luther and Jimmy approached.

"Carson," Luther began, "nice to see you again."

Luther's words seemed too formal, too un-Indian or something, he thought. Also, he felt as though some unspoken exchange was underway between them, more Indian trickery, no doubt. Or, he wondered, were his reactions to Luther simply expressions of his agitation with this whole screwy Indian business?

"Yeah, thanks for coming," Carson responded with vague enthusiasm while wondering what now?

"Come on, let's get your luggage and go over to meet Owl Eyes' flight," Jimmy said, trying to rally camaraderie. "He'll be landing within the hour."

"I've got all my gear with me in my backpack," Luther said, continuing to look Carson over.

"Well, that makes things simple. Good!" Jimmy said cheerfully.

While waiting for the other flight to arrive, Jimmy busied Luther with news of their progress on the documentary. Luther seemed to express a genuine interest and for a while Carson was able to relax. But as Owl Eyes' arrival approached, he could feel his stomach ratcheting up once more.

As a cluster of people emerged into the waiting area, Carson spotted the elderly Owl Eyes. Carson watched him step away from the flow of fellow passengers momentarily, standing silently off by himself.

"Air travel causes a disturbance in his energy field," explained Jimmy. "He's collecting himself."

After a few moments, Jimmy and Luther approached Owl Eyes. As Carson watched, the three greeted one another without handshakes, soberly exchanging words beyond Carson's hearing. Jimmy pointed in Carson's direction and the old man looked over. He scanned Carson as though to take in his essence.

Carson thought that Owl Eyes looked awkward in his street clothes. He was wearing an old, white dress shirt buttoned up to the neck, a pair of ill-fitting dark brown pants, and worn tennis shoes. His gray hair hung in two braids beneath a sun bleached, nylon baseball cap that sported the AIM logo of the American Indian Movement. Carson guessed his age to be in the mid-seventies. He figured that Owl Eyes had once been a man of great physical strength, by the size of his physique and shoulders.

Jimmy waved for Carson to come over and join them. Ambling in their direction, Carson pondered how he should address this venerated man. He was preempted.

"My friend!" Owl Eyes exclaimed suddenly.

"Yes!" Carson responded forcefully, surprised to hear himself react in such a positive tone. Something inside him was rushing to engage with the old Indian.

"We have much to talk about, I believe," Owl Eyes said, smiling for the first time.

Driving away from the airport with his party in tow, Carson felt heartened. Owl Eyes had extended a promising feeling of support. Yes, it all would soon be better, he thought. These guys would straighten things out, free him from whatever it was that had infected him. Oh, these crazy fucking Indians.

Carson focused his attention on the road, hoping to beat the afternoon commute back over Highway 17. Jimmy sat in the backseat with Owl Eyes, chatting with Luther about everything except the purpose of their trip. Although Carson was preoccupied with driving, he couldn't help but feel that he was under observation. Having Owl Eyes sitting directly behind him was particularly unnerving.

"Do you have enough legroom back there?" Carson asked, tilting his head to address Owl Eyes. "I can move my seat forward or we can move you up in the front."

Also, he wondered if driving a Jeep Cherokee was in some way offensive to his riders.

"No, I'm used to this SUV," Owl Eyes responded. "My grandson drives one, took me to the airport in it. Has the Grand Cherokee model, the Laredo package, nicer than this one— leather interior."

He would be glad to get them to their motel. And from there, the plan was simple; they would all go out together for an early dinner and then return to Carson's house to interview him. If he were indeed "infested" by something, then these men could exorcise it away and that would be the end of it.

Imagining that soon all would be well, Carson consoled himself with thoughts of a couple of vodka martinis. He owed himself that much. These Indians owed him, too, but all would be forgiven. It would be over.

"Just wait in the car," Jimmy instructed Carson as they pulled into the motel parking lot.

Carson felt impatient, resenting not being more in control.

They were on his turf after all.

The three Indians strolled into the motel office only to return shortly and climb back into the car.

"We need to leave here," Jimmy said.

"What's wrong?" Carson asked, assuming something was amiss with the reservations he had made.

"Nothing," Luther answered with a big smile. "We just decided to make a little change. Let's go to your house."

"My house? As in, you want to stay there?"

"No, we'll stay at this motel, but we want to go to your house now," Luther insisted.

"Okay, but what about dinner? Aren't you guys getting hungry? I thought we were going to eat first," Carson said, growing concerned.

"We've changed the plan," Luther said.

"We eat later," Owl Eyes echoed.

Further discussion seemed clearly out of the question. Carson resigned himself to the change and started the engine.

Walking through the house slowly, the medicine men proceeded to absorb the atmosphere. He followed along behind them as they ran their hands across his furniture, opened closets and cabinets, picked up books and framed photographs from his desk. They pulled back his shower curtain, opened his refrigerator, felt along the edges of his windowsills. On a shelf in the dining room, Owl Eyes paid particular attention to the leather medicine pouch that Carson had been given upon leaving the Pine Ridge Reservation. Without picking it up, he placed his hands over it several times.

Finally, the two medicine men concentrated their survey on the place where the dreams took place. Carson found observing these men, standing in silence in his bedroom, unsettling.

When at last they returned to the living room, Carson remembered his role as a host.

"Can I give you guys something to drink?" he offered. "I've

got about everything: wine, beer, hard stuff, juice, colas, coffee, or just water, if you prefer."

"I'll have some red wine, if it's open," Luther replied.

"Jimmy, what about you and Owl Eyes?" Carson asked.

"I'll join Luther with the wine," Jimmy answered.

"Bourbon. Straight," Owl Eyes said.

"Bourbon, straight up, no water, no ice? Man after my own heart. I think I'll do the same," Carson said.

"No! No alcohol for you," Owl Eyes stated flatly.

Carson was taken aback. Drinking had become his only escape during the last six weeks. How could they deny him this?

The four men sat in the fading light of evening enjoying their beverages, while Luther entertained them with a story about his dog, Tweeko's, love affair with his neighbor's goat. They laughed hard as Luther imitated some of the lovesick wails his dog would make over the beloved goat—which turned out to be a billy by the name of Roosevelt. Carson tried to laugh, too, occasionally sipping from a glass of unsatisfying grapefruit juice.

"Coyote medicine is working around your house, Luther," Owl Eyes teased his young colleague.

"Yes, it's shameful," Luther responded. "But Tweeko sure likes it!"

Their laughter settled into silence, closing the portal to the profane world. Owl Eyes motioned that he wished to go out on the patio. The others followed. He sat down on the tiled surface and began to pull out objects from a bundle he had brought. Luther sat down next to the elder Owl Eyes and then looked up at Jimmy, giving a nod.

"We need to leave them in private for a while," Jimmy explained to Carson. "They have to prepare themselves."

Carson dutifully followed Jimmy back inside to the living room, where they sat quietly. He felt uneasy. Soon drumming, then softly sung chants came from the patio. Carson looked over to Jimmy for some sign of reassurance, but Jimmy's eyes were vacant, as though he were far away. The scent of burning sage drifted into the house. When the drumming stopped, Jimmy motioned for Carson to follow him back out to the patio.

Once Jimmy and Carson were outside, Luther approached. He smudged them with smoldering sage while whispering a prayer.

"Come here, Carson," Owl Eyes instructed. "Sit across from me; Jimmy, you here beside me. We'll form a small circle."

The two men did as requested, sitting on the patio tiles. Luther began drumming. The three Native Americans seemed to fall quickly under the spell of the drum but Carson, in his anxiety, remained fidgety. Yet when the singing commenced, he noticed that he felt lighter, as though his body were expanding. His skin felt warm and electric against the night air. Just as the singing and drumming were flowing into a timeless resonance, Owl Eyes signaled for it to stop.

"Carson," Owl Eyes said. "Jimmy White Stone has told us that you have dreams where a bear comes and speaks to you. Is this so?"

"Yeah, I suppose," Carson responded hesitantly. "I don't know how else to describe it, really."

"What does the bear say?" Owl Eyes continued.

"That's sort of the weird part." Carson hesitated. "Well, it's all weird actually. But these dreams feel different from most. They're sort of an abduction or something. I mean, I know that sounds weird, too, but—"

"Just answer as directly as you can," Luther interrupted.

"Okay. This bear, and it's a really big bear, tells me I have to come with him. At least I think it's a him. He stands up on his hind legs and talks to me like he's a person. I don't know if he's speaking English, or bear talk, or what, but I can understand him."

"Come with him where?" Luther asked.

"To where he lives," Carson said.

"Does he show you where he lives? Do you go there with

him?" Luther probed.

"No, I don't think I have yet, although I can kind of look around him and see something that resembles a cave. There are lots of white sticks inside."

"Does he say why?" Luther pressed, careful to make no expression or gesture that might influence Carson's descriptions.

"Kind of, but I don't get it," Carson responded. "He wants to show me something, or maybe it's more like he has something to tell me, or teach me. I don't want to go with him because I have my own things to be doing. But the bear keeps insisting, keeps telling me I need to come with him. Even after the dream is over, I'm left in this struggle for what feels like the rest of the night. I'm trying to get away or back home, while I can still feel this bear beckoning me, even if later I'm dreaming about something else."

"And this happens every night, this dream with the bear?" Owl Eyes inserted.

"I can't remember when it hasn't occurred. Seems he's always there. When I wake up in the morning, I can still feel the dream, like it won't let me free to be back in my own world. Hey, maybe this winter he'll have to hibernate and we both can get some sleep," he remarked, needing to inject humor.

The others remained silent, expressionless, and serious.

"Think hard about this," Owl Eyes said. "Does this bear warn you in some way?"

"Like how?" Carson said, tossing his arms up to convey his frustration.

"By saying that you must come with him to avoid danger or sickness," Luther suggested.

"Oh that, sure. He's been saying that from the beginning, but I think that's just a trick to get me to follow him. You see, I know that if I go with him, he'll try to take me over. I will have to become something different—not a bear maybe, but something other than who and what I am."

The medicine men reflected silently for some minutes on what they had heard. This only added to Carson's anxiety.

"If this is some spirit guide or something from your world, I would really appreciate your taking it back to where it belongs," he blurted out. "I mean, I was only out there to make this film for you guys, not to get involved in your religion."

"What else happens in the dream?" Luther said, ignoring Carson's plea.

Carson sighed. "The main theme that plays out every night is that I'm supposed to join the bear in his cave, to respond to his calling. Then I get glimpses of really weird things, lost worlds or something, maybe sort of like science fiction scenes. There seem to be lots of white sticks all around. But all that stuff gets blurred in my memory when I wake up. The only really clear thing I can remember is the bear itself. And, oh yeah, something I almost forgot, seems that one of his paws is hurt, like he got injured in a fight or something. Yeah, he's wounded."

Owl Eyes and Luther immediately looked at one another. Carson observed their exchange, his concerns growing by the moment.

"So what do we need to do here, fellows?" Carson began, trying to get things quickly resolved. "How do we get the bear to go away? Maybe all this bear needs is just some medicine to fix his paw. Mercurochrome or something!"

Carson began to laugh. But within seconds tears were running down his face as he choked with sobs. Suddenly, the last six weeks of psychological exhaustion was out. And worse—he knew the bear was not going away. Jimmy reached over and embraced him. The two medicine men sat quietly waiting for Carson to regain his composure.

"Carson, I have things to tell you," Owl Eyes said. "Are you ready to listen?"

Regaining control, Carson looked at the old man.

"This will be difficult for you to accept. It's not your way of knowing," Owl Eyes began. "That night, in the land of the Lakota, we called our spirit guides. The medicine was extremely powerful. We covered you and the other man with our spirits to keep you outside the power. But medicine has a mind of its own. For reasons that only the medicine knows, it entered you. It is strange to me that someone not of our people would have been chosen in this way. Why it has done this is what you must learn. It haunts you now in the form of the bear with the injured paw." Owl Eyes paused. "Do you understand so far?"

Carson nodded numbly; still hoping it all would just go away.

"It is more than just medicine spilling into you. This has meaning. You are being called to answer. It means you must!" Owl Eyes said pointedly.

"And what does that mean? How am I supposed to answer some dream?" Carson asked wearily.

"It is not the dream you must answer, but the spirit who comes in the dream, the talking bear," Owl Eyes explained. "There is one who walks this world who is known as this spirit. It is he who calls you, and you have already seen him in his spirit form. You must go to him. He will guide you. His name is Wounded Paw."

Carson looked over at Jimmy White Stone; could this really be happening?

"There is such a man, Carson." Luther confirmed. "He lives in the Nevada desert."

"He alone can tell you why he had his spirit guide enter you, Carson," Owl Eyes said.

"What if I don't want to see him? Won't he just eventually leave me alone?" Carson asked, making one last attempt to hold on to his world.

"Possibly, but to ignore a spirit calling is dangerous. You should answer," Luther said. "Besides, there are others," Luther said, giving Jimmy White Stone a hard look. "Others who may have heard the bear calling you and who may try to find you, possibly harm you."

"He doesn't mean me, Carson," Jimmy said. "He means spirit energies, ones that are opposing our work."

"Our work?" Carson asked, bewildered. "And just what is *our work*?"

"Luther, tell him what he can understand of this," Owl Eyes instructed.

"Carson, you may not want to understand what I'm about to tell you, much less believe it to be true. Still, it's what we know as the truth. Try to listen as though it's the truth for you as well. Perhaps in time you'll be able to see things this way."

Luther collected his thoughts, touching an amulet that hung from his neck while uttering a short prayer under his breath. Then he gave a quick glance at Owl Eyes and began. "For ages beyond what the modern Western world has recognized as human history, people from all across Earth have been connected to spirit forces who also dwell here. This is the old way of being, staying in harmony with the forces of spirit. There are many forms that spirit comes in. This much I believe you must already know about us, yes?"

Carson nodded, passively acknowledging Luther's words.

"Those of us who work in these old ways, the medicine ways, we have a responsibility for keeping things in balance and alignment. That responsibility includes protecting Earth, the Great Mother, as She protects us. Are you with me so far?" Luther asked with a gentle smile, his first facial expression since the questioning began.

Carson shrugged, still struggling with the concept of having to go to Nevada to meet with the bear spirit medicine man.

Luther spoke on. "When I talk this way, I know my words sound simple. So, what I just told you is the simple version of our work, the one that is easier to accept by those outside our culture. But there is more to what we do, and that is not a simple matter."

Luther took a moment to observe Carson's reaction, making

certain to maintain eye contact. "Much of our work, the medicine work, is spent trying to come into an accord with these spirits— making amends for our bad deeds or seeking their help and blessing. Yet not all spirits work for our well-being. Sometimes, the interests of spirit beings are not aligned with ours. Your world would recognize such times as plagues, famines, or perhaps extremes of weather that threaten life. There are also imbalances that work directly through the acts of people, such as wars, political persecutions, and the stealing of others' land or resources. None of this is new; such things have gone on throughout time. Those of us who work with the medicine know that conditions are never stagnant; something is always going in or out of balance, and sometimes very badly. Do you follow me?"

Carson nodded again.

"Good." Luther paused, allowing Carson a moment to take it all in. "Now, this next part is going to sound very strange, perhaps, but just try to keep an open mind. Besides those spirit beings who dwell on the planet alongside all the animals, plants, and people, we believe that there are also spirit beings who come here from other places, from other worlds, or out of other dimensions. You see, spirit beings can go anywhere. This may sound very weird to you, like science fiction; or you may think we're all nuts. But this belief that spirit beings come here from other places, other worlds, is a long-standing wisdom tradition among many Native Americans, as well as in many traditional cultures across the world. If you don't believe me, ask any anthropologist at some university about what I just told you. Or go online and see how many cultures from around the world believe their ancestors or spirit guides came from the Pleiades, or some other star system. These beings have often been spiritual teachers, bringing their guidance to this planet. Some believe that Jesus and the teacher called the Buddha came here from these other worlds. Spirit beings have continued to appear here across the ages, including during these times. But others, well, they bring trouble. Sometimes they get involved with what is out of balance, either by causing it or making it worse. It's all much more complicated than that, of course, but just try to realize that this is part of what medicine workers must deal with. Do you follow?"

"Okay," Carson replied dryly, privately wondering if Native Americans had created the profession of medicine worker as a kind of benign placement for their mentally unstable.

Luther sensed Carson's resistance but continued. "Now we're facing a new type of imbalance, one that has never before occurred while humans have walked this world. A time is soon coming when outside forces will try to prevail here and take the Great Mother, to absorb Her life forces. These beings are from someplace far beyond this planet. As they increase their presence here, they will probably become more visible. But so far, only medicine workers have seen them. They appear as kind of a luminous energy field—beings that are unlike anything known in your world. The closest comparison might be mythological creatures out of a movie, but with a presence that is all too real. We feel certain that they're not here for our benefit. In fact, it appears they may intend to eliminate humans as a life form, perhaps other life forms as well. Trying to keep this from happening, Carson, this is our work!"

The four men sat silently reflecting on Luther's summary.

Owl Eyes spoke. "Carson, the medicine has reached out to you. I believe it may be because you have some connection to our work. Go to Wounded Paw; he will have the answers you seek. We will not speak more of this tonight."

Owl Eyes turned to Luther and gave another invisible signal.

They were finished. Luther patted Carson on the back as he stood up. The two medicine men packed up and walked back inside the house.

"So, what now?" Carson whispered to Jimmy.

"They will tell you in the morning," Jimmy said.

"Hey, Jimmy," Luther called out to them. "Let's go eat."

Chapter 4

Wounded Paw

"Carson, you know either of us would be happy to drive for a while and give you a chance to rest," Jimmy said, leaning forward between the front seats of the Cherokee. "You've been driving since we dropped Owl Eyes off at the airport this morning. Maybe you should save some of your strength."

"No thanks, I'm good," Carson replied, his eyes locked on the shimmering asphalt ribbon that sliced the desert floor. He needed to be driving, to keep his mind engaged, to have a modicum of control.

"Let him do what he feels is best," Luther said blandly from the passenger seat, knowing that stronger forces were now in charge of them all.

Jimmy sat back, allowing Luther to direct things. They were on their way; the encounter with the revered one loomed ahead.

In the two days since they all sat on his patio with Owl Eyes, Carson had tried to maintain a positive attitude. His inner voice struggled to convince him that all would be well; release from his strange dreams was nearly at hand. Still, he couldn't help carrying a brooding resentment for having been pulled into this whole affair. Why couldn't he just have his own world back? And now this, a road trip to the middle of nowhere, to see another old Indian.

To distract his mind, he turned his thoughts to Allison, his on-again, off-again, long-term, semi-official girlfriend.

She was, once again, perturbed. Their relationship, which had always been in a state of flux, was being further stressed. Allison was supportive of Carson as long as he was willing to drink less, get into therapy, take Prozac, spend more time with her—and, in general, grow up. She was convinced that this adventure to

Nevada was only an excuse to put off facing his real psychological problems, as she had so clearly expressed in last night's fight in his kitchen.

"So, let me get this straight, Mister Peter Pan," she began, leaning back against a counter, her arms crossed in exasperation. "You're going off to the desert tomorrow to play cowboy and Indians so you'll be able to sleep better at night? Yeah, I've heard that's the classic remedy. Should do wonders for you."

"Well, I'll admit it sounds pretty strange," Carson said, shrugging his shoulders with implied innocence.

"Strange? Strange and you seem to go hand in hand these days," she said, shaking her head and pursing her lips.

Carson tried to reassure her. "Just think of it as an extension of my making the documentary. It's no big deal, and I should be back by tomorrow night."

"Whatever, Tonto, knock yourself out." She smirked as she clutched her car keys, indicating she wouldn't be spending the night. "But this isn't how to get a film completed in a timely and lucrative manner. Besides, they aren't paying you enough for this documentary anyway."

For a moment he wondered if Allison were right.

Her words burned in his mind as he now drove across the desert. What was he doing, really? No, none of this made sense, and he ought to listen to her more. After all, she seemed to manage life so well, always seizing success with apparent natural ease.

In the last two years she had become the organizational and marketing force behind his work, transforming his career from that of a struggling artist-filmmaker to a quasi-viable business. She had worked tenaciously on his behalf, seeing to it that his talent was noticed and well marketed. When potential projects materialized into actual film commissions, it was Allison who had seen that the proper contracts were in place and that the production budgets were adequate. And once he had a completed film, it was Allison who ensured that it got into the appropriate distribution channels. He owed much to her, yet she had never once asked him, what it was about making documentaries that fed his soul.

The afternoon passed into evening as they drove, now deep in the wastelands of Nevada. At the outset of the trip, the three of them had been talkative, but their conversation waned the further they advanced. The growing silence intensified the uncertainty of what was to come. Uneasily, Carson sensed a growing force, pulling him more strongly by the minute into a strange realm.

Suddenly, Luther pointed ahead. "Turn north at the next road."

Carson felt his stomach tighten.

"Start slowing," Luther commanded.

"What road? It's all sagebrush."

"Just up there," Luther said. "About a hundred yards."

Carson slowed the vehicle, turning left on a barely noticeable dirt road with no signage.

"Man, Luther, you sure you know where this goes?" Carson asked.

"It's a back way into the reservation," Luther said decisively. "Otherwise, we'd have to drive about a hundred miles around, to come in the main entrance. Besides, this brings us in close to where Wounded Paw lives. We'll be less noticed by others this way. It's best."

"How is it you know this place so well?" Carson asked.

"I've been here before," Luther replied. "When I was a teenager I came here to be an apprentice for a year or so. And I've been back several times for additional training."

"So you're one of those, are you?" Jimmy said with a hostile tone. "Son of a bitch, I should've figured."

"One of what? What the hell are you guys talking about?" Carson interjected, alarmed by Jimmy's tone.

Jimmy leaned forward, speaking directly into Carson's ear, while keeping his eyes locked on Luther. "You see, Carson, as in most professions, all medicine men are not created equal, so to speak. And evidently, Luther here is one of those considered to be 'marked;' they have special talent. They're usually noticed at a young age by elder medicine men, then selected to undergo special training—training that can be very dangerous."

Luther continued to look straight ahead, ignoring Jimmy's embittered tone.

"I didn't realize you knew so much about this side of our work, Jimmy. I'm impressed. I guess I shouldn't underestimate your intellectual side."

"It's not my intellectual side," Jimmy countered. "I lost a cousin on one of those trainings. He was only fourteen."

"I'm sorry, Jimmy. I know there are some aspects of our culture that you must consider cruel. No one would challenge you on that. And I, too, have lost dear ones in this work. But it's not a choice; you should know that."

"I don't know much about your work, Luther," Jimmy responded. "But I do know there's a difference between a healer and a sorcerer. And once one has crossed onto that path, it's a different kind of medicine, engaging in powers that aren't suited but for a very few, if any."

"Yes, it often seems that way to me, too, my friend." Luther paused. "But then, as I said, for those of us who go there, it's not a choice."

"You better know what you are doing here. Carson doesn't deserve to be subjected to such dangers."

Luther turned to face Jimmy, his face stern and determined. "And you know that neither myself nor Owl Eyes would have insisted on bringing him here if we thought there was a choice in the matter."

"Oh, this is just great," Carson blurted. "Now I learn more scary shit's involved, as if alien spiritual beings weren't enough. Now we're dealing with some kind of sorcery? Why don't I just pull over and let you guys scalp me and be done with it? This is way too messed up!"

"Take it easy, Carson," Luther said calmly. "I'll be taking care of you, as well as you, Jimmy. Just trust me, will you?"

Carson caught a glimpse of Jimmy White Stone's face in the rearview mirror. He was biting his lip and nervously drumming his fingers on his seat back. Seeing Jimmy, a Native American, struggle to cope with the mysterious elements of these old ways allowed him to feel less an outsider. Yet witnessing Jimmy's change in demeanor only amplified his anxiety.

Luther began singing a native song under his breath, a soft monotone chant similar to one he had sung that night on Carson's patio. The three men retreated into a temporary peace, choosing to focus on the more immediate challenges of the dirt road as it wound up through the hills. A range of jagged mountains stood before them, providing a citadel for whoever lived within its massive walls.

"Jesus, guys, how do people live out here?" Carson asked.

"Not easily," Luther answered dryly.

Carson wondered if the reservation were one of the miserable dumping grounds selected by the federal government in the nineteenth century, or the tribe's actual traditional homeland.

"There's a pass that will take us through these mountains, and then we're almost there," Luther directed.

Carson drove on. The road climbed steeply as it snaked along the edge of the mountainside, past immense, precariously perched boulders that threatened to crush their vehicle at any moment. They crested the pass and began an equally hazardous descent, winding down into a landscape that appeared completely uninhabited.

"Okay, Luther, either these people know how to be invisible, or I think we're lost," Carson said.

"No, it's just that they have very large yards," Luther responded. "We'll come to another road up ahead. Turn right there."

Carson wished that they were lost, that they could turn around and leave before it was too late. He made the turn and drove on as Luther instructed. Still there were no signs of habitation. Large sagebrush dotted the desert floor. Birds darted alongside the SUV, striving to catch the numerous insects disturbed by the automobile. Occasionally a lizard or a jackrabbit scampered across the road. Large black locusts streamed continuously along before them, seemingly oblivious to the oncoming vehicle.

"We're on a remote part of the reservation. Only Wounded Paw and some of his assistants live out here. Slow down, we're almost there," Luther said.

Rounding a rocky outcropping, they arrived at a small cabin that looked as though it must surely be abandoned. A few equally dilapidated outbuildings and one lone cottonwood tree made up the supporting spread.

A young man was standing out front as if he were a sentinel. Another man was sitting on the steps leading up to the weathered wooden porch. Under the porch roof, in a large wooden chair that could serve as a pauper's throne, sat an old man. Even though the twilight dimmed his vision, Carson could sense the old man's gaze locked upon him. The unsettling fear he experienced in his dreams stirred within.

Luther opened his door and stepped outside, motioning for his companions to join him. They walked slowly toward the old medicine man, stopping just before the worn steps. Luther made a sign with his hands before speaking.

"Wounded Paw, we bring one who hears you in his dreams. Allow us to join with you at this time," Luther said.

The old man made a gesture with his hand and Luther

nodded.

The man sitting on the steps got up and walked inside, returning in a moment with a bundle of smoldering sage and a lit pipe from which he blew smoke onto the three visitors. Despite being only early September, the desert night was rapidly cooling. A chill ran through Carson as Wounded Paw's scan raked over him, penetrating into his soul.

When the purification was complete, the man with the pipe said some words in a native tongue that sounded familiar but equally incomprehensible to Carson. Then the man withdrew into the cabin. Carson and his companions continued standing before the cabin in the encroaching darkness.

From behind them a sudden cry shattered their concentration. Carson and Jimmy turned reflexively in the direction of the sound. Somewhere, hidden in the darkness, a man was singing a haunting medicine song similar to the ones that Carson had heard on the Lakota reservation. Carson and Jimmy exchanged a glance, then regaining their composure, turned to face the cabin again. The old man's chair was empty.

"Luther," Carson whispered, needing an explanation as to what was happening.

"Silence!" Luther shot back. "You're safe for now."

Drumming began inside the cabin, its rhythm merging with the wailing song resonating from beyond. Goose bumps broke out over Carson's body.

"Now, listen carefully," Luther began in a low voice. "We're all going inside. I don't know exactly what will happen in there; these things have their own course. But here are the basic guidelines. You are not to speak unless directly asked a question. Understand? Carson, this is not a typical house. Don't let that distract you from what you're here for. Concentrate on what you're instructed to do. While it may become frightening at times, be assured that Wounded Paw will not allow any harm to reach you tonight. Jimmy and I will be there in the room with you. Just follow his instructions. Don't try to resist; that's where trouble may find you."

Luther turned to Jimmy. "This may be an encounter with spirit medicine that's beyond anything that you've imagined. The best way for you to handle this experience is to call on your ancestors to make you strong. This medicine is very old, very powerful. Be brave, my brother."

Luther started up the stairs before either of them could register protest. Jimmy gave Carson a quick look and followed after Luther. Carson felt his legs begin to move forward. With no choice, he climbed the stairs and entered Wounded Paw's domain.

At the room's far end, a small fireplace provided the sole source of light. Dancing silhouettes flickered against the dimly lit walls; it was too dark to see much of the room's trappings. Wounded Paw was seated next to the hearth. Beside him, beating out the drum's trance-inducing rhythm, sat the man with the pipe. Luther and Jimmy sat across from them. Carson started to sit down with his comrades but was immediately directed to sit in the middle of the floor. As his eyes adjusted, he began to make out animal skulls peering at him from every direction.

Luther leaned forward, speaking just loudly enough for Carson to hear above the drum's resonance.

"You're to lie down with your head near Wounded Paw," Luther began. "When you're comfortable, close your eyes. He wants you to travel with him."

Obediently, Carson did as instructed. He wished he could have had an opportunity to speak with the old man first, or at least get a good look at his face. He settled upon the dark rug, which felt like fur. The drumming continued. As he closed his eyes the weariness of the day's long drive immediately began to take effect. He felt himself drifting into a dream state.

The experience felt different from his troubled dreams. There was a kind of acceptance, as though he might be revisiting some past-life connection. Now engaged with the dream state, Carson watched himself going down into a cavern, passing numerous objects, including the mysterious white sticks that now appeared strangely familiar. Something told him to keep his vision focused upon the path ahead. Responding to a beckoning call, he entered a large chamber and was greeted by a great bear.

"Welcome," the bear said. "I'm glad you came to see me at last. We have much to discuss."

Carson nodded in acceptance, approaching his mysterious host. The fear experienced in his dreams now replaced by wonder.

"Why am I here?" he asked, engaging the bear in telepathic dialogue. "What is it you want of me?"

"It is not what I want," the bear responded. "It is what needs to be attended to."

"I don't understand," Carson said.

"You may in time, if it is to be," the bear answered. "But for now, you only need to accept that I'm here to help teach you. You have been asked to walk with me and learn something of my ways. About this, the medicine has been clear."

"What's wrong with your paw? You appear to have hurt it," Carson said, noticing the bear moved with a limp when walking on all four paws.

"An old wound from long ago, a reminder that I must travel the medicine path cautiously and accept the wounds that come with it," the bear replied.

Carson indicated that he understood, though the bear's words were perplexing and troubling.

"I have visited with your soul for some time now," the bear continued. "You have become ill by being in contact with the medicine. That may soon change. You have been called. By coming here, you answered part of that call. Now you must decide whether to continue or not. Either choice has its dangers. If you refuse the medicine, it may decide to leave you. However, it may not. Your illness may become worse. Whichever path you choose, I'll assist you as best I can. But your decision should not come from what you call your rational mind. Your choice must come from the heart. At this time we do not know if you have the capacity for this work. If so, it must be developed and nurtured as you learn. I will help guide you in these matters. This much is enough for now; you have heard my words."

The bear paused, then resumed speaking. "Now, listen well. I'm going to retrieve your soul from the realm of the medicine and place it back in the container that you recognize as your body. Then you will sleep. In the morning, we will talk as human beings and you must tell me if you wish to follow the call of this work. If not, I will attempt to help release you from the medicine's further calling."

A warm energy began to gather within Carson. A deep sense of well-being filled him. Forgotten memories of his early boyhood days, charged with the joy of discovery, coursed through his mind, taking him back to a time when the world seemed wondrous and nurturing.

Then the bear indicated it was time to depart. Carson was guided out of the depths of the bear's cavern, out of the dream-state world. He emerged back into his body, slowly becoming aware that he was lying on the furry rug. He was weary but felt at peace. The journey was over. Within moments, he was overcome with heavy sleep.

"Hey, Carson, wake up man, the morning's getting away," Jimmy White Stone teased, prodding his slumbering friend. "You're living up to our stereotype of the lazy urban white man."

Carson gradually pulled himself up to see Jimmy, Luther, and Wounded Paw's two assistants looking at him. The scent of coffee punctuated the air. He slowly sat up, allowing his eyes to scan the room's exotic collections of bones.

The dark interior was more like a cave than a place for human habitation. The room contained few of the artifacts normally associated with modern culture. As Carson was to learn, it wasn't that Wounded Paw opposed such things, but rather he didn't require them.

Apparently understanding that Carson could use some psychological support at this point, Luther sat beside him, casually chatting about the cabin as if he were a realtor.

"This cabin was built well over a hundred years ago, by a white prospector, before the land had been zoned into the reservation," Luther began. "The building was never intended to last beyond the needs of a temporary shelter, but in the desert things have a way of enduring far longer than would be expected. There's no electricity or running water. Some limited repairs have been made from time to time, to keep out the occasional rain and snow, but overall the place seems to hold together by forces of its own."

Carson's eyes wandered the interior, taking in its many unusual objects. The furniture consisted of a couple of worn wooden chairs and a long, high table that ran most of the length of one wall. An overturned wooden bucket constituted another table, anchoring one of the corners near the stone fireplace. Stacks of old blankets lay along the floor, for sitting. Luther explained that these had been acquired years ago as payment when Wounded Paw performed healing work. Two small windows pierced the walls, but they were mostly covered by faded weavings that were badly frayed. Two kerosene lamps stood ready to be put into service.

As Carson gazed about the room, he felt a heightened sense of well-being. The myriad concerns that had plagued his life from the psychotic dreams seemed to be gone. He felt renewed.

Coming to his feet, he looked about for Wounded Paw. The old man was not among them. Jimmy handed him a cup of coffee. As he sipped, he began to study the collection of objects that adorned the room. Last night he had not had the opportunity to take in the many strange things, chief among them the giant bear skull. He also attempted to recall last night. He was certain that something important had happened, but his memory felt fuzzy. Did these Indians realize what had happened to him?

"Where's Wounded Paw?" he asked.

"Come, have some more coffee and a bite to eat, Carson," Luther said. "You'll see him soon enough. Let's get you fed and cleaned up a bit. Then you can try to explain your bad manners, falling asleep on us last night and leaving Jimmy and me to do all the unloading."

Luther's lightheartedness made Carson feel as though everything was now all right. Maybe it was indeed all over.

They sat in a back room that served as the kitchen, where an old wood-fired cook stove provided an additional source of heat in winter. A small table and cabinet counterbalanced the kitchen space, serving to house the few basic pots and dishes. Carson was hungry, readily consuming coffee and corn bread smeared with strawberry jam.

"You see how simply people can live when you come to a place like this," Luther said, his hands busy braiding a leather strap. "But notice I said simply, not easily. Wood has to be found and hauled in for the stove, as that and the fireplace are the only heat in winter. All the washing is performed outside in a galvanized tub. And when you feel the call of nature, you'll find a dilapidated but fully functioning outhouse around back. Most importantly, there's a good well here with clean water year round."

Sipping coffee in the light of day, Carson was thankful. He'd come through the exorcism and could return to his previous version of psychological well-being. Someday, if he were ever interviewed about the making of the medicine men documentary, all this would make a wonderful anecdote.

"Well, Carson, if you're finished with your latte and French pastries," Luther teased, offering him another piece of corn bread, "I'll show you around a bit and tell you more about Wounded Paw, given that the medicine has invited you here. It's a rare privilege to be here, even for Indians, but then most would be too frightened to come. Jimmy, I'm sure you realize that you're having a rare opportunity to observe one of our culture's most restricted chambers. I know I can trust you to preserve its integrity and that nothing about this visit will appear in your writings."

Luther led them back into the main room, where Carson had slept and undergone last night's ritual. Various containers were scattered throughout, each the reservoir of assorted objects of nature. These composed much of Wounded Paw's pharmacopoeia. The large buffalo skin rug, where Carson had slept, anchored the center of the floor. As Luther explained, the rug was a gift from a visiting medicine man from the plains. Native drums were stationed about. Strings of beads hung over nearly everything. Baskets containing assortments of feathers and shells crowded the remaining surfaces.

"You may come back here and look more if you like, but let me show you the other room," Luther said.

The cabin's third room was modest by the most Spartan standards—a small bedroom outfitted with a humble dresser and single cot. A few cardboard boxes served as the remaining furnishings. When the old man did supposedly sleep, Luther explained, he retreated to this simple place.

Wall spaces were adorned with weavings or paintings applied directly to the wall surfaces. Carson wondered if Wounded Paw had made them himself. They depicted scenes of otherworldly beings and realms. He also noticed that there were no mirrors anywhere in the house.

Most intriguing for Carson was the vast collection of bones, horns, antlers, claws, and teeth present throughout the cabin. The entire gamut of North American wildlife seemed to be represented. Antlers of numerous deer, antelope, and moose jutted from every direction, met by the horns of bison, bighorn sheep, and even a longhorn steer. Claws of eagles and mountain lions joined with fangs of snakes and teeth of wolves, alligators, and bears. Luther gladly identified the origins of the many objects, along with their significance. The shoulder bones of a huge Kodiak bear rested along the top of the long table. Several buffalo skulls looked out upon the room, their vacuous eye sockets still reflecting the unforgivable slaughter their herds suffered under modernity's conquest of the West.

Commanding attention above all else was the skull of a giant bear. It was stationed on the barrel table beside the chair where Wounded Paw had sat.

"I see that bear skull is fascinating you," Luther said, moving alongside Carson. "It's to the spirit of this great bear that most of Wounded Paw's prayers are addressed. No one is ever allowed to touch it; no one dares."

"Glad you warned us," Carson responded, sharing a look with Jimmy.

"I must tell you a little story," Luther continued, suddenly with a lighter tone in his voice. "Wounded Paw has been offered better housing on several occasions but has adamantly declined the offers. Once a Bureau of Indian Affairs agent paid him a visit here, to explain that federal mandates would not allow him to continue to live in such substandard housing. But the agent had hardly finished his words when he heard his car engine start. Rushing outside to investigate, the agent noticed that his car keys were still in his pocket. Perplexed, he proceeded to put his keys into the ignition and succeeded in turning the engine off. But as he was walking back toward the cabin, jangling the car keys in his hand, the engine started again. Frightened and confused, the agent climbed back into his car, not wanting to suffer a mechanical breakdown out in the middle of nowhere. He drove away and was never heard from again."

Carson enjoyed this insertion of jest for an instant but quickly sensed that Luther had shared the story as mere fact with no humor implied.

Luther led them outside. Wounded Paw's two assistants were seated on the porch.

"Perhaps I should introduce these men since you didn't have the chance to talk last night," Luther began, placing his hand on the shoulder of the one who had played the drum the night before. "This is Joe Buck."

Carson nodded a friendly hello to Joe Buck but was met with a blank stare.

"And this," Luther continued, pointing to the younger of Wounded Paw's assistants, "is Sydney. That's all the name he wants you to know him by."

Both assistants remained silent.

"Nice to meet you, Sydney," Carson said, wondering if either of these men understood English.

"Once I saw a documentary you made," Sydney replied abruptly.

"Oh really? Which one?" Carson said, amazed that one of these men would have had exposure to his work.

"It was on prisoners, concerning their views of social mores, although they didn't phrase their perspectives in such sophisticated terms."

Carson had not expected a tribal man working in the old ways to have such an extensive vocabulary.

"Where did you see it?" Carson asked, imagining it might have been in a prison setting from the young man's past.

"My sociology professor showed it in class one day," Sydney answered.

"You don't say," Carson said. "That's neat. I didn't know it was being viewed by any schools around here."

"No, this was back East."

"Sydney attended Yale," Luther added matter-of-factly. "I

understand he was Phi Beta Kappa, thinking of going on to study medicine there but deciding to come back here instead."

There was a tone of pride in Luther's statement, as if Sydney had outwitted a nemesis and somehow avoided a great mistake. Carson peered at the obviously intelligent young man, trying to fathom how he could make it from the environs of a reservation school system to Yale, and then turn away from such an opportunity to take up life in the barren terrain of Nevada.

Curious, Carson asked, "So, what made you decide not to become a doctor?"

"Oh, I'm becoming a doctor, just not the Western med school variety."

"I see," Carson said. "Guess you didn't care for the Western version?"

"No, I've no qualms with that, it was more that I was becoming progressively bored with the system's educational potential. The pedagogy is simply not engaging enough to hold my attention. Not to mention its naïve dismissal of the influence of spirit in the overall approach to health. It's nothing like the opportunity that I can have by being here."

Jimmy White Stone gave Carson a look, conveying that it would be useless for him to pursue the issue.

"When you've finished, go wash up, Carson," Luther instructed. "We have a little walk ahead of us."

It was midmorning by the time they left the cabin. There was still no sign of Wounded Paw. Joe Buck, the older of the two assistants, led the way as the five men hiked up into the mountains behind the homestead. They were within the shadows of the north side of the escarpment. The air still gripped the morning's coolness.

Along the way they occasionally passed unusual petroglyphs on the rock walls. These figures looked more complicated and detailed than those Carson was familiar with in photographs, or the few he had seen in person once in Arizona. Given that the cuts in the stone had crisp edges, Carson assumed that these must have been carved recently. He wanted to stop and examine them but had been told before departing the cabin that there would be no stopping or talking until they arrived at their destination.

About forty minutes later, the group arrived at a large cliff ledge that overlooked the valley below. Carson was grateful to be stopping; he wasn't used to the pace or the demands of the climb. The back of his shirt was wet from sweat and his breathing was heavy. Joe Buck approached Carson and produced a water canteen from his jacket.

"Drink!" Joe Buck said, passing the water to Carson.

Carson took the canteen and drank. The water had a bitter, metallic taste. He tried to give it back to Joe Buck.

"No, you keep it. Stay here and wait for Wounded Paw. Then you go home."

Joe Buck signaled to the others to follow him, leaving Carson alone.

He sat down on the ledge and surveyed the desert valley below, wondering why the others had left and what they might be doing. A large hawk was circling in the distance, effortlessly gliding on invisible thermals. With the sun now peaking over the summit, the temperature was rapidly rising. His thoughts turned to going home, to being back in his own world, back in his own life.

As time passed, he lay back on the stone surface and closed his eyes. Lists of things that needed his attention began to crowd his mind. He looked forward to telling Allison that the crazy dream stuff was finally behind him. They could get on with their lives. Perhaps their relationship would even start to improve. He thought about taking Ben, his son, on a camping trip to Yosemite before the season turned colder. Since the divorce he liked to think he made more of an effort at being a father, something

Maggie, his ex, had often accused him of doing poorly.

The wait dragged on. Carson was becoming bored and annoyed—Indians just didn't understand the value of time. He suspected that whatever remained of this visit, some further mumbo jumbo might be required.

"Fucking Indians!" he eventually blurted out loud.

"Yes, those words bring back some happy memories," a mildly craggy voice said. "Very enjoyable times with certain women."

Carson sprang up and spun around to find Wounded Paw standing behind him.

"Don't get up, I'll sit down beside you," Wounded Paw said, moving slowly without making a sound. "How are you feeling today?"

"Fine! And I want to thank you for whatever you did last night. It really helped. I can't remember much of what happened, but I sure slept well afterwards. I'm feeling like my old self again. And hey, I'm sorry about that Indian comment. It just sort of slipped out; just impatience, I guess. This whole thing has been pretty weird for me, you know, being dragged into this and wondering why it just wouldn't end."

Wounded Paw grunted a response, indicating understanding and perhaps empathy. But he wasted no further time listening to Carson's lament. The old man began singing a medicine song. The feelings conjured by the singing transported Carson to the previous night and the words of the bear. The matter was again at hand.

Wounded Paw stopped singing, the only sound a distant trace of wind as the two men peered over the desert below.

Now we'll speak together as men," Wounded Paw began. "I know that you have not sought to be here, that this world is strange and frightens you. Much of your world is strange and frightens me. Fear is common to all life. Only fools and idiots are free from fear, but there are ways to rise above the choking power fear exerts. I'm not expecting you to stand outside the touch of fear, but if you will allow, I can help teach you ways to conduct yourself when fear grips you. It cannot be done, however, unless you want to take up this path."

"Wounded Paw, sir," Carson stammered. "I wish to say how honored I am that you are even addressing me about this so-called choice. But do you really believe that this is right, my trying to work with you and your medicine friends? It's something that I don't have the least bit of knowledge about. I feel like I'm not supposed to be mixed up in any of this stuff. And even if I wanted to be, just how does a person like me bring anything that could possibly be of any use to you? Frankly, with all due respect, I think the whole idea is way off. And if we all hiked up here this morning for this, well, I'm sorry. No, if we tried this medicine thing with me, we'd probably only end up wasting each other's time."

Satisfied with his analysis, Carson looked over at Wounded Paw, certain that he would be excused from any further involvement.

"I'm sure you are most correct, Carson," Wounded Paw said slowly. "Let us, by all means, not waste time. Come, walk with me down to the cabin and join your friends. You will want to be getting home, I'm sure."

Carson was surprised by Wounded Paw's lack of resistance. The matter was finally settled. Someday, he would recall this entire affair as an extraordinary adventure, one that he could turn into a great dinner-party story.

The two men began their descent off the mountain, back to the cabin.

"Do you have any children?" Wounded Paw asked, pretending he didn't already know the answer.

"Yeah, I have a thirteen-year-old son," Carson said. "My work takes me on the road a lot, so he lives with his mom most of the time. But we see each other regularly when I'm home."

"What's his name?"

"Ben. Benjamin," Carson said, enjoying thinking about something more normal. "Neat kid—we have a good time together. Naturally, we have some different ideas about music, if you know anything about what kids are listening to these days."

"Sounds like my grandson," Wounded Paw said, chuckling.

"Oh, you have a family? Somehow I figured you to be a lifelong bachelor."

"My daughter's boy," Wounded Paw said laconically.

As they were passing the petroglyphs, Carson suddenly stopped. He felt he had earned the right to inquire about the curious symbols cut into the rocks.

"These are some pretty incredible carvings," he said. "Would you mind telling me something about their meaning?"

"Do you think that's wise? We wouldn't want to waste time," Wounded Paw said abruptly, a hint of sarcasm in his voice.

Silence hung between them. Carson wondered if he had offended the old man. So what if he was mad?

"These images are spirit helpers," Wounded Paw began slowly, pointing to one grouping of figures that looked like kachinas but with wavy, energy-like lines coming off their hands or heads. "They assist those spirits on the left there. They are here to guard this world against those spirit energies shown over there on that rock."

As Carson followed the descriptions, he turned to view the other images indicated by Wounded Paw. His eyes locked on large beings with strange proportions and large eyes. These figures also had wavy, energy-like lines coming from them, but these came out of their eyes or mouths. Weird, insect-like creatures flew among them while some other ominous creatures moved along the ground. Whatever these figures represented, it was clear that their intent was hostile.

A virulent bolt of energy struck Carson's gut. He staggered and sank to his knees. The shock was quickly replaced by a profound sense of loss, a remorse spanning back what felt like millennia. A vision of an unimaginably horrendous future churned before him—one that he somehow sensed had already begun to unfold.

His mind was suddenly swept away from the petroglyphs' threatening images, catapulting him into alien worlds populated by strange beings that appeared to be an evolved amalgam of man-like animal, insect, and god. Some called to him as if he were an old colleague, while others went about their tasks. Although the experience was only a glimpse and lasted but a few moments, these realms, these beings felt real—their existence irrefutable.

Carson suddenly recalled his words to Jimmy White Stone only days before: "Just how do I get myself initiated into this way of knowing?" He understood—he was receiving his initiation.

Slowly coming back to ordinary consciousness, Carson felt Wounded Paw helping him back to his feet. The old man was softly muttering a prayer in an ancient tongue, while making gestures around Carson's body with a bundle of eagle feathers.

"I think we might have more to talk about," Carson stammered.

"I know, Carson. The medicine knows. Now you know. Your heart has begun to grow. Come, we have much to do. You have been called to the medicine road."

Chapter 5

A Work in Progress

Father Clemente sat in the archdiocese courtyard, staring vacuously into the koi pool. In the two months since his devastating discovery at the pagan commune, no acceptable explanation had been established for what had happened there. Nor could the Chilean authorities find a trace of the missing people.

"My son," the smiling monsignor called, making his way across the courtyard. "I understand you're still obsessed by this trouble of yours."

"Monsignor," Clemente said, quickly rising to his feet. "It's good of you to grant me this audience. I pray you know I wouldn't take up the Church's time if this were just about me."

"Yes, yes, I'm sure," the monsignor replied, gesturing for the priest to sit back down. "And I know you've been deeply perplexed by this incident, but really, my son, there's nothing more you can do. These people had their own misdirected ways and probably did this themselves for reasons that would never cross your mind. You must let this go and turn your attention back to your parishioners, not these vanishing pagans."

"Yes, I'm sure you're right." Father Clemente smiled weakly. "However, there have been other rumors in my region about a coming peril. These are coming out of the indigenous communities and sound similar to what the people at the commune were saying."

The monsignor turned his head away, sprinkling fish pellets onto the koi pool. The surface churned in a golden-orange chaos as the hungry fish snapped up the food.

"Frankly, my son, I'm worried about you," the monsignor said. "I know you love your people, as a good priest should, but you've always been a bit too sympathetic toward native beliefs.

Perhaps you've been up in those hills too long and a change from there would do you good. Maybe even spend some time back at the seminary to clear your mind of this matter, bolster your faith."

Father Clemente remained still, watching the fish devour the last of the food and calm return to the pool. "Yes, perhaps you're right, Monsignor. I'll consider your offer."

"My son, it was not an offer; it's a directive."

The monsignor rose, kissed the priest on the check, and departed for his office.

Father Clemente peered into the koi pool's harmonious little world, weighing the schism that pitted his vows against his inner beliefs.

Driving back to California that afternoon, Carson wasn't in the least clear as to what he'd taken on. The drive home was paced by long periods of silence, interrupted by questions directed at Luther.

"Luther, are you sure that I've got to come back out here?" Carson pleaded again. "Why can't you send somebody to Santa Cruz to teach me whatever I'm supposed to do?"

"Did Wounded Paw offer that as an option?" Luther asked, trying not to express further frustration with Carson's carping.

"He just said I was to come back—to work with him."

"Did he say anything about someone coming to see you in Santa Cruz?" Luther pressed. "If so, I didn't hear anything about it. That means you're to come back here. Why are you trying to complicate what's clear and simple?"

"Clear and simple?" Carson snapped. "Maybe to you. I've got a life to live and work to do—your documentary just to name one matter at hand."

"You'll find a way for it all," Luther replied, sounding confident and nodding his head with an affirming gesture.

"Don't be so insouciant, Luther," Jimmy White Stone

protested from the backseat. "The man's trying to come to terms with a very troubling situation."

"Insouciant? Really, Jimmy, is that an old Lakota word?" Luther laughed. "Yes, Carson has some adjustments to deal with, and I know they're difficult. But it is what it is. Medicine is not for the meek. Our friend here will just have to find a way to manage under the circumstances." Luther shrugged his shoulders, signaling he was powerless to change things.

Two weeks later, Carson was back at Wounded Paw's, accompanied by Jimmy White Stone, who had agreed to lend support. The night before they left for Nevada, Luther Redbone had phoned from his home in New Mexico, extending his prayers and encouragement. Carson appreciated the call but took little comfort from it. An uncertain and baffling obligation awaited him the next day.

That weekend was the first of many visits to come. The subsequent trips he made by himself. Over the winter these usually became arduous journeys, negotiating snow and ice along I-80 over the Sierras.

In these early days, Wounded Paw limited the depth of his teaching to a neophyte's understanding, concentrating on building a student-teacher bond. They would talk for hours and take long walks in the hills behind the cabin. Sometimes Joe Buck and Sydney joined them. In truth, Carson was greatly relieved that this initial training avoided any reference to the dreaded alien spirits. And although the threat was always in the back of his mind, he took solace in this unexpected reprieve. He felt as though he were a boy again, on adventures with a wise grandfather, who was exposing him to the hidden nature of the world.

Through these visits, Carson learned much about Earth and the spiritual forces that inhabit it. He was guided through exercises of listening to wind and animals, feeling the textures of rocks and brush, learning to smell various qualities of dirt and water, reading the sky for signs and moving through nature as a participant rather than a trespasser.

"Do you like this reservation, Grandfather?" Carson asked one day while on one of their walks. Recently he'd begun to call the old Indian by the name Grandfather, as a sign of respect.

"This isn't the true home of my people." The old man paused. "But this place is good. It has much power. It's not an easy place. Places of power are usually not easy places for people."

"But the government says you guys own this, right?" Carson replied.

"Carson!" Wounded Paw exclaimed with surprise. "You cannot own a place, you only spend time there. We can say this is our land but that does not mean we own it. It owns us; we are the children of this land."

These talks had become routine as Wounded Paw gradually introduced him to the ways of the medicine. At first, Carson had struggled to make these teachings fit into his modern worldview. But over time, Wounded Paw led him past the limitations of empirical logic and the need to always have sensible answers. Gradually, Carson opened to an entirely different way of learning.

As they were wandering in the hills just after Thanksgiving weekend, Wounded Paw suddenly stopped and turned to Carson.

"My son, you better plan to spend a couple extra nights on this visit. Snow will block the roads for a few days starting tonight."

Carson looked up at the clear blue skies. While the air was chilly, there were no indications of an impending snowstorm.

"Why do you say that?" Carson queried. "The weather is supposed to be clear for the next five days."

"Well, your weathermen don't always get the best information." Wounded Paw smiled. "You see those antelope over in that thicket?"

"What antelope? What thicket?"

Wounded Paw pointed to a clump of scrub trees, bunched along the side of an arroyo some two hundred yards away.

Carson peered hard at the location, gradually spotting a small herd of antelope whose colors blended perfectly with the environment.

"Wow, damn good eyes," Carson whispered.

"They only gather like that at this time of year when there's going to be a heavy snow," Wounded Paw explained.

"Oh, so that's why you believe it's going to snow?" Carson replied.

"No," Wounded Paw announced bluntly. "These animals told me a while ago. They said to get ready for heavy snow tonight. I just came by here to thank them."

The old man walked about forty yards in the direction of the antelope, stopped, and called out a song to the animals, giving thanks to them.

Carson awoke the following morning to find two feet of snow covering the ground at Wounded Paw's cabin.

Carson's frequent visits to Wounded Paw created a backlash in his private life; he had much less time for Allison. She, too, had become busier. A successful real estate broker, she had been asked to join Dream, Dare, Develop, a training company that traveled western states conducting sales and marketing seminars for realtors. She was gone nearly three weeks a month. When she was home, she had that much more to do. Opportunities for the two of them to be together had become rare.

With the arrival of the Christmas holidays, the pressures surrounding their relationship intensified.

"Since you only came over for an hour on Christmas afternoon, I trust you've planned something special for New Year's Eve," she chided, holding her wineglass alongside her face, as if it were a vestige of royalty.

"Oh, I thought your sisters and their kids were still going to be here," he said, shuffling his feet on her kitchen floor.

"Carson, I thought I told you, they're leaving to go back to Phoenix on the thirtieth. Don't tell me you don't remember."

"No, no, I was planning on us all doing something, maybe having dinner at your place and I'd bring Ben over. We'd maybe go down to the beach and watch fireworks at midnight. Then I'd run Ben over to his mom's, and maybe you'd come back to my place."

Allison stiffened, her anger showing through her bristling body language.

"But hey, if I misunderstood," he quickly added, "and they're not here, well, that frees us up for doing something special."

"And just what might that be, this something special you're so thrilled to do with me?"

"I don't know," he said. "We could drive up to San Francisco for the night, maybe, something like that."

"Oh, lucky me, I'm practically speechless."

"Come on, now," he countered. "We've both been so busy we've hardly had time to see each other, much less work out New Year's plans, for Christ's sake."

"Perhaps I'm overreacting," she said, suddenly changing her demeanor and replenishing her wineglass. "I realize that I shouldn't have agreed to have my family here for the holidays. But you sure as hell weren't going to go with me to Phoenix. Besides, I thought you'd spend more time with us."

"Well, given my difficulties with your family, I try to limit my time here. Look, Sharon and her husband's politics are somewhere to the right of the Nazis, and Maureen can't talk about anything but her kids or shopping. Sorry if I don't get particularly jazzed by their company."

"Oh, is that it? Or are you afraid they might ask why you prefer spending all your time hanging out with Indians rather than with me?"

"Like you're ever here that much anymore."

"As though you'd know," she snapped, downing the contents of her glass.

On a frosty afternoon in late January, Carson stood on a rock cropping beside Wounded Paw. The temperature was barely above freezing but the sun was bright and reassuring. It felt good to be back with his teacher, his first visit in nearly a month.

"So, Carson," Wounded Paw began. "Where do you think you are?"

"I'm not sure what you mean. With you, I suppose."

"And where's that?" Wounded Paw insisted.

"In the hills, on your reservation," he answered doubtfully. "Nevada, western part of the United States, North America, third planet from the Sun?"

Wounded Paw shook his head in benign disappointment. "Your answer shows you still think in the same way. You aren't fully focused on our work. Wake up! You're in a place of spirit. You should know that by now."

"Yes, Grandfather, I do," he replied, embarrassed by his continued shortcomings.

"On the medicine road, you must see the world as a place of spirit first, not just a place with a made-up name like Nevada or the United States. Do you see the difference?"

Carson nodded in acceptance.

Wounded Paw continued. "Your culture believes the home of spirit is in some magic place that floats above, a place you call heaven, a place you call the kingdom of God. Is this not so? But we know spirit is everywhere. We don't die and go to the home of spirit; we live with it here, every day. Spirit is something that you can touch and not touch, see and not see. The earth is spirit. You cannot separate spirit from the physical world. It is more real than anything, but sometimes it does strange things, brings strange times."

In the evenings, they would sit by a fire and Wounded Paw would reveal experiences from his life, much of which seemed beyond what any human would ever encounter.

"One day, this was many, many years ago, I was struggling to persuade this spirit to vacate my patient's body," Wounded Paw said, sharing yet another of his experiences. "The poor woman was near death already and the spirit that was feeding on her would soon have to find someone else to feed upon. So I asked the spirit if it couldn't find a better way to exist than preying on helpless people." He paused, leaning forward to sprinkle a mixture of tobacco and dried sage on the giant bear skull, while whispering a prayer. "And the spirit told me it did not like feeding on people but didn't know how else to live on this planet. You see, it had been left here many ages ago by its kin."

"No, no I don't see," Carson responded. "What do you mean by a spirit that was left here?"

"Spirits such as this one are known as parasites," he answered. "You see, there are many types of spirit beings here. Some do harm, but they can also have their own troubles."

Carson struggled to comprehend. Every time he got closer to thinking he understood Wounded Paw's world, something more unfathomable, more uncanny, dissolved his grounding.

"I still don't get it," Carson protested.

Wounded Paw whispered some words in prayer, speaking to an unseen presence. "I promised to help this spirit get home," he said softly. "In exchange, it stopped feeding on my people. So the parasite spirit left and the woman recovered. That's all."

Carson shook his head, questioning as he often did both his and the old man's sanity. "And just how did you do that?"

"I arranged for his passage, to get him home and off Earth. I got him back to his kin."

"Okay, but just how?"

"There were some other spirits visiting at the time, and I asked them if they could do this. And fortunately, they knew where the parasite came from and how to transport him home."

When these talks took place inside the cabin, Carson sensed that the animal skulls were also listening, or that they were even speaking through the old medicine man. When the pair sat outside by the fire pit, Carson felt as though *others* stood in the darkness, just beyond the light emitted by the flames. This unseen presence always seemed to exist around Wounded Paw.

Gradually, Carson's training enabled him to accept that there were various kinds of spirits, not just human or animal ones, but spirits representing consciousness outside any known life forms. The difficulty here wasn't so much in accepting their presence, but rather in discerning just who they were and where they came from.

"Grandfather, when will I start to understand about these spirits I feel around you? I don't really see them or have contact with them, but when I'm with you, I can tell they're there. Or should I not get any closer?"

"They're only strange because they're unknown to you," Wounded Paw replied. "For me, they're old friends. This world would be poor without them. With more practice, you'll gain contact with many spirits. Or perhaps this might be achieved with the help of another teacher."

Over time, Wounded Paw taught Carson more about these spirit beings. He gave instructions as to which spirits to befriend and which to avoid, which to follow and which not to trust. Wounded Paw showed him not only how to navigate in such domains but how to conduct himself appropriately. There were definite protocols and etiquette to follow in dealing with spirits.

"This is Blue Metal Woman," Wounded Paw announced one night as the four of them sat outside by the fire pit, mumbling a greeting in a native tongue Carson couldn't understand.

"Say hello to her and tell her you're honored by her presence," Sydney whispered to him.

There was a long silence as Carson's eyes darted back and forth from Wounded Paw to Sydney, to Joe Buck, to the dark void on the other side of the fire.

"It's rude not to greet her," Joe Buck said, tossing some copal incense onto the fire and gesturing homage toward the invisible spirit.

Carson cleared his throat, recovering from an awkward mixture of fear and embarrassment.

"Greetings, Blue Metal Woman," he proclaimed, his words coming forced and superficial. "I am honored to be in your presence."

Joe Buck and Sydney snickered at his performance, but Wounded Paw remained silent.

"You guys are pulling my leg, aren't you?" Carson said.

"No, she's there all right," Sydney said. "You just haven't developed our way of seeing. You must learn to use a different kind of light; it's a kind of *dark* light. I know that sounds contradictory, but that's how it works. This will become easier when you start to work with peyote medicine. In time your old vision blends with the medicine vision and you won't even think about it."

The reference to peyote was worrisome; he chose to ignore it. Knowing he wouldn't gain further satisfaction for the time being, he continued. "And why is she here tonight? Is she here to help us with the trouble we face?"

"Assuredly, in her way," Sydney replied, providing none of the specificity Carson needed to hear.

Hoping to gain some sense of the spirit's relevance, Carson asked, "What's Blue Metal Woman doing?"

"She visits us. She's one of the main teachers for Joe Buck. Blue Metal Woman came here from another star place."

"Okay, I'll just have to take your word on that," Carson replied, trying to stay in sync with the three Indians. "And why does she have the name Blue Metal Woman?"

"That's her familiar name; she looks like blue metal. She's very beautiful and smart. Blue Metal Woman has other names, but those are sacred. Only those initiated to work with her are taught those names."

Sydney rose and addressed Blue Metal Woman with words of veneration in his native tongue, then sat down in silence. Joe Buck started a soft chant to honor the visiting spirit and was joined by Wounded Paw and Sydney. Carson observed tears slowly rolling down Joe Buck's face. The song finished, and the four men sat in silence with only the sound of the fire's soft hiss.

"Carson, listen well," Wounded Paw instructed. "When you have an encounter with an entity, it requires careful and humble acknowledgment on your part. Later, when you have developed more skills, you'll have to pay close attention to what these spirits say or do. This is one of the ways they teach you. And at the close of any encounter, always make a gesture of thanks for the privilege of their teaching."

There were many more lectures to come on appropriate etiquette and rules of engagement with spirits. In his mind, Carson likened this training to a bizarre course on cosmic diplomacy.

Ultimately, the old Indian was determined to teach Carson that entities were vital beings with whom he must align himself. Some of these spirits would become his guides and allies. And with time and training, Carson gradually began to gain an ability to visualize the presence of certain spirits.

"Who's speaking to you now, my son?" Wounded Paw asked after their nighttime drumming had stopped.

"It's a magpie, Grandfather," Carson answered. "He's telling me it's good to move away when certain dangers get too close."

"Did he come to you or did you ask for him to appear?"

"He just sort of showed up. And I can see him in that same strange way I saw you as the bear spirit last summer."

Wounded Paw whispered some words to the giant bear skull

across from him, and then returned to Carson. "Does magpie speak of other things?"

"Not much; he complains about the lack of berries these days."

"Oh, I've heard that before. He's right, but magpie always complains about something. Did you thank him for appearing?"

"Yes, and I asked if he had come to teach me something. That's when he told me about moving away from certain dangers, but he hasn't said which dangers."

"Magpie's usually not very clear about things other than food," the old man said. "Be sure to acknowledge him properly before he departs from your vision and ask him to come back and warn you when that danger he speaks of is approaching."

With the passing of the months, other entities appeared for Carson, usually in the form of various animals. It was Carson's obligation to acknowledge their presence and, more importantly, be prepared to befriend them and learn from any teachings they might share. As their work progressed, Carson gradually began to build a small pantheon of power animals.

It was early September as they walked up to the place in the hills where the two men had spoken just over a year earlier.

"How many spirit animals have come to you by now, Carson?" Wounded Paw asked.

"Let me see," he said, stopping to wipe the sweat from his forehead. "There's ground squirrel, antelope, jackrabbit, turtle, magpie, and your bear spirit if I can count that."

Wounded Paw turned to look out over the desert expanse as if he were watching for something. "I feel the coming of fall. There is change in the air."

"Yeah, it's already chillier at night," Carson replied.

"It's not just the seasons," Wounded Paw said, smiling at his student. "There's change with you, too. Of those spirit animals, only the bear knows how to fight danger," Wounded Paw continued, sniffing the wind as an animal might. "Those others, they either escape or try to hide."

"Is that bad?" Carson sounded alarmed.

"You've made some progress, but in the future you will need to call upon more powerful spirits. These spirits that came to you, they all have their teachings and value, but we're not preparing to do regular medicine work. I've strived to keep you on the safer side of this work for now. But a time is coming soon when you must have more powerful spirits or allies working with you. Yes, that time is soon—time for a change in the ways you learn."

Chapter 6

Peyote Path

"Hey, I brought you guys some good stuff from civilization," Carson yelled to Joe Buck and Sydney through the SUV's window, waiting for the cloud of road dust to blow past. "I got this beautiful wild salmon at the market this morning. Hope that's all right—or were you planning something special for tonight, like grilled dog?"

Wounded Paw's two assistants strolled over to give a hand with the unloading. Gusts of wind whipped through the cottage compound, speeding the change in temperature as the afternoon turned into evening.

Carson always brought food and supplies when he came. Over the past two years, the drive from Santa Cruz to the Nevada reservation had become a familiar, eight-hour commute. Originally, Carson had planned these visits around his work schedule. But as his apprenticeship continued, his priorities shifted and now he arranged his work schedule around the days and weeks he needed to be with Wounded Paw. The old Indian never bothered coordinating anything; he just seemed to know when they would spend time together.

"Well, Carson," Sydney began, "if you're really set on some dog, I think Joe Buck here can arrange something for you. His specialty's marinating one of those plump golden retrievers; you know, the kind you see riding in the backs of Volvo station wagons with red bandanas around their necks. They're real tasty cooked up slow over mesquite, with a few twigs of sage and a little crushed garlic."

"Perhaps on another occasion, fellows," Carson said, laughing. "Besides, fish should always be eaten while fresh. But I do appreciate the gracious offer."

Entering the dark cabin, Carson looked about for Wounded Paw. Evidently the old man wasn't around. While this was not unusual, Carson felt disappointed by his absence. Back in the kitchen, Joe Buck was already busy building a fire in the wood stove. Sydney quickly joined alongside, lighting the kerosene lanterns. Carson judged they were ravenous.

"When was the last time you guys ate anything?" Carson asked, opening the beers he had brought and passing them around.

"Maybe day before yesterday," Sydney answered, unaffected. "We were fasting and then things got very busy—the Visitors!"

A chill shot through Carson, the Visitors—the threatening alien spiritual forces he was being trained to combat. The familiar anguish that now shadowed his life returned.

"Thanks," Joe Buck mumbled, taking a beer and downing half the bottle.

Joe Buck seldom drank alcohol. He looked exhausted. He quickly turned back to the stove to oil a heavy cast-iron skillet.

Carson glanced at Sydney to see if he could glean any information from the bright young man's face.

"Ah, salmon, one of my favorites," Wounded Paw said, suddenly appearing in the doorway. He looked calm, but then he always did. "My son, I knew you would eventually serve some good purpose."

Carson turned to greet his teacher. These initial moments of reengagement were a mixture of joy and consternation. He cherished his time with the old man, the exposure to the teachings and their wisdom. But the purpose of his presence here always carried a reminder of the peril ahead.

The four men stood in the kitchen avoiding conversation, instead concentrating on the sizzle of the frying fish. Sydney toasted tortillas on the back of the griddle in between constructing an awkward salad, consisting of the fresh greens Carson had brought and canned yams. The aromas of salmon, beer, and wood smoke melded, teasing their hunger.

Joe Buck slid the fish onto plates, and in moments the four were eating. The Indians made no effort to converse, seemingly absorbed in replenishing their bodies. To Carson's knowledge, this was the first time that they had directly engaged with these alien spirits.

Carson pondered whether to ask. He needed to learn what had happened yet dreaded to hear about it. No, he thought, I don't want to hear about it, not now.

He decided to entertain them with stories about the film he was making, a documentary on the lives of women long-haul truck drivers. He rationalized that his anecdotes would provide his colleagues with a break from their intense spiritual work. At least he could be of service at this level. The Indians continued to eat in silence, giving no sign that they were listening or objecting to his tales.

After dinner, Wounded Paw said, "Let's go to the other room and talk, Carson. I know you're tired, but it's important to share some words."

In the front room, a lone kerosene lamp burned, illuminating the walls with distorted shadows from the animal skulls and horns. Wounded Paw sat in his place by the hearth. Carson eased over to his usual spot on a stack of blankets; close but not too close to the giant bear skull.

"Now listen, my son," Wounded Paw began. "We've had many talks. But there are things you are yet to learn. My ways come out of an old lineage. There have been many traditions in this world; most are no longer even traceable. On occasion, you may stumble upon some of these traditions, or the residue of their teachings and knowledge. In our spirit journeys here, you've had visions of exotic worlds and other times from long ago. We've spoken of your visits to these ancient cultures, what you call past lives. It's sad that there are fewer of these traditions in the world now, but perhaps that's how it should be; it's not for me to say. I'm from an old way; you're not. Don't let this deter you, Carson. What you must come to realize is that the path of spirit moves in one direction. It doesn't go back to dwell in the past. It goes forward, toward that place your culture calls the future."

"The future?" Carson questioned, once again failing to grasp the point.

"The path on which things are moving," Wounded Paw continued. "Your world would call it the direction of time, or something like that. When it comes to these matters, we speak a different language. We have another understanding of time than that of the white man. One day I may show you more about this. But for now, just understand that the universe does not run backwards. And, more significantly, know that this thing you call time is moving at an increasing speed. Everything is moving faster! Even light moves faster. You must come to understand this."

"I know you're telling me something important, Grandfather, but I don't think I fully get it."

"Do you think I teach Joe Buck and Sydney how to become good Indians for some long-ago time?" Wounded Paw asked rhetorically. "These men are not here to learn to become spiritual antiques. It would be sinful of me to lead them in only those ways. No, the world has changed; it has always been changing. I come from a tradition that has undergone change. All do, or they perish. It's good to go back and remember the ways of our ancestors, to honor those traditions—but families, tribes, peoples, even nations must find new ways to exist as the medicine moves into new paths."

Carson shifted uncomfortably on the stack of blankets, anxious to learn the outcome of their encounter with the Visitors, hoping that Wounded Paw would reveal some triumphant prognosis. Instead, he felt that something more macabre, more challenging was about to be unveiled—a further threat to life and sanity.

"When you find questions that trouble you, and you have no answers," Wounded Paw continued, looking directly into Carson's eyes, "ask for guidance from the heart of the medicine. If your answer takes you in some direction that only wants to return to the past, it will probably be the wrong one."

"I will try to remember your words, Grandfather."

"Yes, perhaps," the old man replied, waving eagle feathers over the giant bear skull. "If we're to repel the Visitors in the coming struggle, it will require working with all of Earth's forces. Embrace the whole, the light and the dark, the good and the bad. This is the way of the medicine. Remember this."

Wounded Paw leaned forward, whispering a prayer to the silent bear skull.

"We were attacked yesterday for the first time," he finally interjected quietly. "They came here looking for us. Our work's attracted them. It happens that way. Perhaps they were even looking for you."

Carson's stomach tightened. He had prayed that this dreaded day would not have to come.

"Who are these beings, Grandfather?"

"Spirits," he answered casually. "Those we call the Visitors."

"What happened?"

"If I told you the details, it would make more danger for you. It's hard to hide you already. With the knowledge and power you gain, you will attract them."

"Can you explain more, Grandfather?" Carson persisted. "What should I become aware of?"

"Everything!" the old Indian replied. "First, there are common dangers that might appear as accidents, such as a traffic incident. Or a thief breaks in at night to rob you and you get beaten or killed. If you have medicine knowledge, you might know that some spirit energy sent this robber. But most of these things happen in subtle ways. You may develop an illness, or have something bad happen in your business that takes away your money or reduces your power in the world. These things happen all the time. But you're thinking, who hasn't had something happen to them? And yes, many times spirits have little or nothing to do with these matters; but sometimes they do, especially for those who work with the medicine."

"Well, why not just concede everything to the action of some spirit?" Carson protested.

"Because that would be mere superstition, Carson—or worse, just lazy. A medicine worker needs to know what events are caused by spirit actions and what events are not. That is part of knowing how to be in this world—how to be on the medicine road."

Carson looked down at the buffalo skin rug, recalling that first night he'd come to Wounded Paw's with expectations of being freed from his troubling dreams. His fingers combed through the fur as he questioned if he'd ever advance enough to understand these ways, much less do what was expected of him.

"Don't try to force these things to come clearly to your mind," Wounded Paw counseled, as though reading Carson's thoughts. "They'll happen on their own. You'll begin to make the connections. When this happens, don't ask whether Grandfather would see what you see. Remember to use your own eyes; besides, you're not Indian. At first, you'll see spirit actions in forms that you already recognize: strife between people, some bad news story in the world, or perhaps something unexpected and wonderful happening for someone. And after you begin to recognize that these things come from spirit actions, you will, with time, begin to see those spirits themselves. They'll reveal themselves to you. The medicine will show you. But first, you have to develop certain abilities, or all of this will remain invisible to you. And it must happen gradually. If you see them before you're ready, that can be very dangerous, especially with the harmful spirits. I must rest now."

Over the coming months, Carson's sense of foreboding grew. He agonized over whether a time would come when he, too, must face the so-called Visitors. All the while, Wounded Paw called forth protection for all of them. He taught Carson a ritual to use at home for this purpose and another to use before he traveled anywhere.

"Dad, this is plenty weird," Ben, his son, said as Carson walked around his Cherokee, smudging the vehicle with a smoldering sage bundle. "Are you sure the Indians said to do this?"

"Yeah, I suppose it looks weird. Doubt there're too many people in Santa Cruz who're doing it," Carson replied. "Never saw it as an add-on feature at one of the car washes. But hey, you said you wanted to help me get ready for this trip, and this is part of what I need to do. Besides, it's not that much different than what lots of people do when they get their cars or boats blessed. Just a little added protection—spiritual air bags!"

"Can I try it when you're done?" Ben asked, jumping up and walking toward his father with a hand out.

"Tell you what, Ben. I'm sort of done with the Cherokee already. Why don't you bring your bike over here and I'll show you how to smudge it."

"Really? But don't tell any of my friends or Mom, or I'm not doing it."

"Promise. Now go get it."

Ben returned in seconds with his mountain bike, ready for the protective coating. He leaned the bike against a small tree just off the driveway.

"All right, first you need to clear your mind," Carson said, editing the ritual to suit his son's curiosity. "Now, close your eyes and try not to think; just be present with where you are at this moment, maybe just notice the sounds around you. And when you feel you're ready, open your eyes."

Ben opened his eyes within a few seconds, looking up at his

dad with a mischievous smile.

"Now think of any words you wish to say that would protect you and your bike. Then when you're ready, just walk slowly around the bike. Oh, let's see, for a bicycle like this, I'd say three times, letting the smoke touch as much of the bike as you can. While you're doing this, say or think those protective words."

"And that's it?" Ben asked. "What about that water stuff you sprinkled on the wheels? And I saw you fling some on your steering wheel too."

"Okay, okay, you can do that too. Sprinkle your tires, your handlebar, and even the seat if you like. All right?"

"Dad, this is really weird, but it kind of feels, I don't know, like some secret cool stuff."

"Well, it kind of is. Besides, it sure won't hurt anything to give it a try," Carson said, giving the boy a pat on the back.

"So what's in the water you use?"

"It's just a kind of tea, adding sassafras leaves to distilled water and letting it steep. When it's cooled, I stir it with an antelope horn that one of my friends, Joe Buck, gave me for just this purpose," Carson answered, trying to be forthcoming without allowing the deeper nature of his work to leach over and touch his son's life. "So, you ready to put some mojo on your bike?"

By the time winter set in, Wounded Paw deemed Carson ready to begin sessions with one of the sacred medicines—peyote.

Carson understood that this phase of working with peyote would come. He viewed it with uncertainty and troubling apprehension. His psyche was fragile enough already; could he handle this?

Although on occasion he shared a hit of marijuana with Lucas, in a social context, he didn't have much familiarity with drugs. He had experimented with LSD one summer in college but never considered that hallucinogenic substances could be capable of doing much beyond altering one's interior landscape—and sometimes in frightening ways. Until beginning his work with Wounded Paw, he had never considered working with a mind-expanding substance in a sacred manner, the way the Native Americans did.

What had not been announced was exactly when this peyote session would take place. Carson assumed that he would be well informed in advance, but the unexpected was often the norm with Wounded Paw. And so it was, just after Carson had completed a long drive over the Sierras on an icy Interstate 80, Wounded Paw proclaimed that tonight was the time.

"Here, chew this," Joe Buck said bluntly, handing Carson a cactus button from the power plant.

Even though he had been coached on what to expect, those lessons now seemed distant, suddenly just another discourse among so many. His confidence was shaky at best.

Carson placed the peyote button in his mouth and began to chew. Within moments his mouth was filled with its bitter flavor. He decided to focus his attention on the comforting flames in the cabin's hearth, taking reassurance from their heat and light.

Joe Buck carefully observed his chewing, monitoring him the way a mother would a child required to down an unpleasant serving of vegetables. Sydney sang a native chant while rocking back and forth. Wounded Paw, fully engrossed with calling the names of various spirit helpers, appeared to be withdrawn. Carson wished the old man would extend some form of acknowledgment as reassurance. But each man had his own task to fulfill; serious work was at hand.

Assured that Carson had been properly dosed, Joe Buck moved to his usual place and began drumming. Sydney continued to sing in his soothing, soft voice, while the old man directed his prayers to the giant bear skull.

Gradually, the effects of the medicine began to unfold. Time itself began dissolving, blending past and future into one, suggesting an alternative version of time's true nature. Carson remained aware of the men around him even though his mind flowed into ever-changing realities. Surges of energy pulsed through his body. He concentrated on following the calling of the great bear, who sang out to him through Sydney's song.

"Oh, you're back with me," the bear spirit said in a comforting manner. "You've been learning a thing or two, I see."

"Where've you been?" Carson asked. "This is the first time I've seen you since you brought me to Wounded Paw's. That was a long time ago."

"Oh, I've been around," the bear began, chuckling, "letting you learn from the humans. Letting you learn to teach yourself, as well. That's often the hardest method to master but essential to gaining true empowerment. But for now, you must rely on the wisdom of others to assist you; become strong through their support. Call on the power of spirit allies and ancestors to teach you. But be aware that sometimes other spirits may come that are too powerful for you. These encounters can be very dangerous if you have not developed the skills to engage with those spirits."

The bear's words melded with Sydney's singing, as if they flowed from a secret code imbedded in the song.

The bear spirit signaled farewell and Carson attempted to thank him, but his mind was already journeying to other realms. His body fell away as though it were nothing more than a cumbersome vessel that should be abandoned. Exotic, lost worlds opened before him, places that were oddly familiar yet phantas-magorical. He moved through a grand city that suggested ancient Babylon. Another metropolis emerged, this one located in a lush jungle environ, with buildings that blended the architecture of the ancient world with that of futuristic civilizations. Now and then he felt a connection with various past lives, recalling moments he had spent as a woman, a child, and someone quite old.

Following these encounters, his consciousness transitioned

into experiences of becoming various animals: scanning the ground through the eyes of a falcon as it circled the terrain, swimming through a stream as a trout, flitting among wildflowers with the wings of a moth.

"Know these worlds, know their many states of mind," the voice of the bear spirit called out to him. "Let the many be with you, and you with them. Know that all of this comes from the great source beyond and below, so great that we see only the smallest pieces of it. Know that there are worlds within worlds, flowing out of even more worlds. Become someone who can walk in these worlds. It's from knowing how to participate in such realms that one achieves the power of the medicine. You must learn these things, and more. One day, another will come to teach you more of these things. Now, let your heart grow."

The bear's words drifted through Carson's consciousness as the multitude of worlds continued to unfold—each one evolving from the previous one like a fractal, each revealing a network of relationships among them all.

The Indians spent much of the night in prayer and song. Occasionally, Carson tried to pray as well, but beyond the prayers for his own son, his effort lacked the grit of full compassion carried by the others. Despite having learned the words to a number of the songs, his condition was too taxed to participate. He recalled Wounded Paw's cautioning him not to become consumed by the exotic glamour of these realms, seduced by the depth of their intelligence and splendor. But gradually he surrendered the remainder of the night to the magical beauty contained within the medicine worlds.

Other nights with the peyote followed over the winter and early spring. Carson was never sure whether his visits to Wounded Paw's would entail imbibing the powerful entheogen or not. One thing was certain, however; with each passing session, there was an increased sense of urgency.

The Visitors came again that spring, though fortunately for Carson, not during one of his trips to the reservation. All the same, he noticed a marked change with his friends—they seemed to be guarded in their conversation while he was present. Sydney's effervescence had become subdued. Wounded Paw's time was dominated by long periods praying in front of the giant bear skull. But witnessing Joe Buck sing his death song during his last visit, a preparatory ritual undertaken when times seem particularly threatening, unsettled Carson the most. Things were different now.

Throughout this period, editing on the medicine circle documentary continued. A tribal association from Oklahoma had donated a portion of its casino profits to ensure the film's completion. Carson took this as a sign that he was somehow gaining power with his greater personal challenges associated with the film. Jimmy White Stone visited often during these times, helping with the final edits and always bringing improved versions of narration or new musical tracks.

Other work needed his attention as well. The filming of the women truck drivers would wrap up soon, requiring many hours in the editing room. Meanwhile, Allison was negotiating a very substantial project for him that was tentatively slated to start early the next year. She was still determined to make him into a successful businessman.

All the while, Carson somehow managed to make time for his son, trying to ensure that despite all his endeavors, Ben was not shortchanged of his father's attention.

Given all that he was doing, Carson was too preoccupied with the gravity of his spirit work and the demands of his professional and private life to notice that a radical change was imminent.

Chapter 7

Rhiannon

"Here we go, drink this," she said, in that self-assured manner that he found so annoying.

Carson reached out hesitantly for the potion, knowing it contained transport to uncharted worlds.

Rhiannon smiled, lifting a small glass to her own lips. She downed its contents, a dark brew made from tropical roots and leaves, allowing a soft moan to escape as she finished.

Carson followed, his taste buds searching for some category to describe the mysterious elixir—a concoction suggesting a combination of old-fashioned cough syrup and fermented diesel fuel. His confidence in her was shaky, but Wounded Paw had been emphatic that she was the person with whom he must work in his next phase of development. Nevertheless, Carson took little comfort in being placed under her tutelage.

He washed down the entheogenic tea with a small swig of water and sat back against the cushions. They were suspended in that ambiguous period, poised at the threshold, waiting for the psyche's gatekeeper to slip away and leave the doors of perception open for the Ayahuasca, the South American potion they had drunk, to do its work.

"He Ma Durga, Om Namaschandikaiye, Jaya Jagatambe He Durga Ma," Rhiannon chanted softly. This was but one of the many Sanskrit mantras she had learned from the seemingly endless list of ashrams at which she had studied.

Carson closed his eyes and leaned back against the wall. It had been less than two months since he had first met her. Rhiannon simply arrived one day at Wounded Paw's, apparently unannounced only to Carson.

"Hey, someone's coming," Carson announced as a crimson Toyota pickup came into view, headed toward the cabin and trailing a large plume of dust.

"Yes, we know," Joe Buck replied without looking up as he drew water from the well.

"Who is it?"

"She's a friend," Sydney answered, steadying the large galvanized pail used for the washing.

Something about this sudden arrival spurred a feeling of annoyance within Carson.

"Well, shouldn't we go say hello or something?"

"No, Wounded Paw will speak with her alone. We've got chores to finish. And I'd like to complete them sometime today if you can stop spilling so much water," Sydney said, giving Joe Buck a look. "Besides, you'll meet her soon enough."

Carson busied himself with helping Joe Buck and Sydney, until he glimpsed Wounded Paw and a Caucasian woman walking around the side of the cabin, deeply engaged in conversation. More troubling was his inability to stop staring at her.

She was a striking woman who carried herself with grace and power, evoking self-confidence and an alluring femininity. Her hair, a mass of dark auburn curls, was coiled on top of her head. He gauged that those locks must come down to her waist and guessed she was in her early forties. While she moved with a vivacious energy, there seemed to be a kind of wisdom emanating from her that exceeded her years. She presented the embodiment of a mythic Celtic queen. Her presence both attracted and frightened him.

"Come over here, my son," Wounded Paw called. "There's someone you must meet."

He walked toward them, trying to remain unaffected by the woman's presence.

"So, this is Carson," the old Indian said to the woman.

"Hello, Carson." She extended a hand. "I've heard some

intriguing things about you. My name's Rhiannon."

What held his attention was the light that glowed within her green eyes. It was evident to him that she was someone who had medicine knowledge.

"Nice to meet you. Guess I'm the only one who didn't expect a guest to arrive."

Shaking her hand caused an unsettling feeling to flow over his entire being. And there was something about her voice, as if he had known her.

"I suspect you didn't, but I prefer not to think of myself as a guest." She smiled.

"Rhiannon and I must speak now," Wounded Paw said, dismissing him. "You can talk more later, after your chores."

The old Indian and Rhiannon strolled off slowly, continuing to speak softly between themselves. Carson studied her, trying to use his acquired medicine skills to decode her. But the more he tried, the more she psychically evaded him, passively shape-shifting into various iterations of herself. But underlying all the anxiety she generated within him was the sudden distressful realization that she was going to be the architect of his future.

And despite his numerous protests, there was no changing what had been decided.

As Wounded Paw had explained, Carson was not an Indian — nor was he to try to be one. It had never occurred to him that his experiences with the Indians were only to serve as an intro-duction to medicine ways. Now he found that his path lay with this strange new teacher, utilizing her skills to further his devel-opment. Just how that was to be achieved remained unresolved. Wounded Paw was pushing him out of the nest, passing him over to the control of this woman, who contained the energy of the yoginis, the renowned goddesses of the Asian subcontinent.

The only predictable aspects of this strategy were that it would be difficult, at best, and by no means safe. As Wounded Paw often told him, undertaking medicine work of this caliber, work that directly engaged the reified energy of powerful spirits, was always dangerous. And having a noble cause or pure heart provided no safeguard to those on such a path. The process, with all its unknowns, would require trial and error—and some of those in the work would pay dearly for their errors.

Further complicating these grave circumstances, Wounded Paw had prophesied that certain people would inevitably emerge, seeking to suppress the medicine workers. To underscore such dangers, Wounded Paw only needed to remind Carson of what had happened to a Jewish medicine man known as Jesus.

At first, Carson's resistance to Rhiannon came from the realization that he would no longer be spending time with the old man he had come to love. Instead, he was now meeting with Rhiannon at her cottage, outside the remote community of Bolinas in west Marin County, about an hour's drive north of San Francisco. Her place was nested inside a large redwood grove, with enough clearing to allow an extensive garden of exotic plants and herbs. Here she maintained a botanical kingdom that helped supply the pharmacopoeia with which she worked. Carson was reluctantly impressed by her knowledge. She was a present-day incarnation of an archaic healer, midwife, good witch, and alchemist.

Tonight was not their first session together. They had met at her home on two previous weekends to journey with the medicine. The purpose of these sessions was to accelerate Carson's shamanic development, to propel him to a level of competency as a medicine worker—preparing him for the inevitable confrontation with the Visitors, by finding the critical source of power that so far had eluded him.

Yet from the beginning, there were problems. In their two previous sessions, they had taken different mushroom medicines at Rhiannon's directive, psilocybin on the first weekend and amanita on the second. Carson went into these sessions intending to get a deeper sense of Rhiannon, but somehow she seemed to evade him. In fact, he had little time to reflect on her. Both in and out of the first two sessions, she busied him with information. Rhiannon vacillated between being a harsh taskmaster and the all-loving womb of life. She continually exposed him to samplings from her knowledge: the religions and mythologies of the world's ancient cultures, implications of the hidden functions of DNA, the effect of astrological transits on world politics, the mysteries of plants, the esoteric potentials of yoga, various interpretations of UFO phenomena and her commentary on philosophers and sages from across the ages.

This overload of information, compounded by her rapid pace, was a radical departure from the teachings of Wounded Paw. Carson needed more time to examine and digest her ideas. Rhiannon's methods seemed to lack structure. Although he found her knowledge impressive, he was intimidated by her power, her confidence. His attitude oozed with resistance and Rhiannon seemed to know it. He put up numerous defenses, questioning her abilities and methods and privately accusing her of being pretentious, or worse—self-delusional. At the crux of his discomfort was fear. Simply put, Rhiannon scared him.

Feeling vulnerable at the outset of that first mushroom session, Carson turned inward, calling upon the more familiar spirits of his power animals. He questioned the appropriateness of his asking for guidance from Native American spirits alongside Rhiannon's cross-cultural practices.

"Remember to stay open to any spiritual energies that appear before you," she whispered as yet another directive.

"I'm working with my own already, thank you very much," he replied.

"Oh, is that so?" she countered. "In that case, may I meet one of them?"

Carson found her request invasive. Those beings were sacred to him, bonded with him at the most intimate spiritual level. She had no business connecting to his guides and allies.

"Uh, I don't think that's a good idea," he said.

"I don't mean to interrupt your session, Carson. I'm trying to gain a sense of your spiritual practice, to get in tune with your spiritual allies—who and what they are."

Carson chose to ignore her, instead asking his power animal spirits to shield him from all the strange energies connected with Rhiannon and her macabre deities.

"Very well, don't!" Rhiannon blurted, suddenly sitting up.

She had read his thoughts; Carson was embarrassed and angry.

"Listen," she said. "Let's just try to do what we can tonight. If you can allow that much!"

"That's what I'm here for, I suppose."

"Really?" she snapped in a sarcastic tone.

The exchange created an awkward void that dominated much of the remaining session. Little, if any progress was made that night.

In the second session, they had fared little better. Rhiannon decided to go at the core of his resistance, to break it down and dispose of it once and for all.

"So, how are you feeling?" she asked, her words coming smoothly.

"Very out there," he answered slowly.

"Uh hum, and do you think you can follow some navigation from me?"

"Is that really necessary right now?" he objected, feeling a growing sense of paranoia.

"Carson, why do you want to resist me so much?"

"I don't know. Maybe you distract me too much. Maybe I just don't like you."

"I don't believe that's true," she said. "Ask yourself the

question and tell me what answer comes to you."

Carson sighed heavily, unhappy at having to undergo this exercise.

"Because I feel like you have too much power over me!" he exclaimed angrily.

"What else?" she pressed.

"Because if I go down this path with you, I won't be able to ever go back to who I was."

"And is that so bad?"

"I don't know, goddamn it. This whole medicine world is too much. I don't know why you people won't understand that I'm not supposed to be like you."

"And how do you know you're not supposed to be like us?" Rhiannon fired back.

"I don't, I don't!" he shouted, suddenly sitting up, his mind swirling under the mushroom's influence. "I don't know who I'm supposed to be anymore."

"Good, Carson. Good for you," she whispered to him. "That very question, who you're supposed to be, that's the one you have to work on. That's one of the keys for you. We'll talk more about it at another time."

While the medicine had worked its powers well, Carson's attitude had not improved. He wondered if Rhiannon were abducting him into some hell of her own making, for some purpose that he would never learn until it was too late. Compounding these difficulties was his growing attraction to her. He argued she simply wasn't right for him; and that wasn't his fault, after all!

Bolstered by what he saw as an obvious case of irreconcilable differences, Carson departed the next day for Wounded Paw's. He would argue his case, convincing the old Indian that this arrangement with Rhiannon was not working, and he'd be released from her tutelage.

"I just can't trust her, Grandfather!" Carson exclaimed. "There are things about her path that are so outside of the ways you taught me. We're mixing too many medicines. It's crazy."

Wounded Paw listened, stone-faced, peering into the fire's embers as he sat across from the giant bear skull, his thoughts preoccupied with other matters. Carson knew these moments well; he could only wait until Wounded Paw was ready to speak. Despite the many days Carson had spent in this room, he never failed to feel unsettled by it. Being here always meant that he had crossed a threshold and was now inside the lair of the uncanny.

Finally, the old Indian spoke. "If she didn't hold the power to challenge you, she wouldn't be the right one. Yes, the mixing of many traditions can be perilous. But that's what these times require. We don't have the wisdom of one great path to tell us how this should be done. You all must wear the warrior's heart. And as you know, not all warriors come home."

Carson tried to console himself by acknowledging that, even Wounded Paw's Indian apprentices viewed his undertaking with foreboding.

"My powers to help you in these new ways are limited, Carson. I can send allies to protect you, but you're entering something that is beyond the experience of my tradition. Yet it must be so; the visions have been clear. That much I know with all my heart. Go back to her. She is the one who has been chosen to guide you now. The two of you need each other. I have seen this."

"Yes, Grandfather." Go back, back to Rhiannon, that madwoman? Did Wounded Paw truly know what he was talking about? Why was it necessary for him to be torn away from the Indians and forced to remain under her tutelage? Why couldn't she be more like this old man? Or was it that he had simply grown accustomed to Grandfather's ways? The thought that one could, in fact, become comfortable with someone such as Grandfather amused him momentarily. After all, even Wounded

Paw's own people believed that he had gone beyond the boundaries of what was considered appropriate spiritual work.

Looming above all these questions was the one Carson most dreaded, the one that had been there since that first visit to Wounded Paw—did he ultimately have what was required for such work?

"I'll do as you say, Grandfather," Carson responded. "Tomorrow I'll drive back to her."

Wounded Paw closed the matter with a terse directive. "You're in the service of the medicine now. Your personal feelings are not what this is about. You must stay on the path and for you that path flows through her. It has been shown. Behave like a warrior, nothing less. We will not speak of it further!"

Wounded Paw's stern rejection stunned and humbled Carson.

The following evening, Carson confessed to Rhiannon what he had done and struggled to apologize.

"I suspected Wounded Paw wouldn't allow you to continue with such a bad attitude," she said.

Carson laughed, smiling contritely.

"Carson, go home now; get some rest. We're both exhausted. Come back next weekend and we'll go at it anew. And remember—you don't have that much time to prepare yourself for this work."

Now, back for the third medicine session, Carson vowed to make a concerted effort to have their work succeed. His mind began falling through the familiar maze of geometric patterns.

"Jaya Mata Kali Mata, Uma Parvati Ananda Ma," Rhiannon continued to chant softly, occasionally smudging with sage smoke the various effigies and objects that comprised her altar's expansive pantheon.

Purifying her objects was no small undertaking for someone charged with a spiritual practice like Rhiannon's. Carson found her assembly of tutelary items confusing, if not overwhelming.

As far as he could tell, she had every global spiritual tradition represented in the assembly. The array included fertility gods from Niger; an antique Chinese quoin in carved ivory; several bronze Buddhist Taras; a full assortment of Egyptian gods and goddesses; stone reproductions of Aztec and Mayan gods; a collection of ancient goddesses of the Mediterranean, headed by figures of Demeter and Artemis; Black Madonnas and angels; and a multitude of Hindu deities. Scattered around these pieces were Buddhist rosaries, voodoo bones, decorative ears of Native American corn, rubber snakes, large crystals, and strategically placed tarot cards. The statuettes were joined by several paintings: a vibrant Virgin of Guadalupe, a Tuvan shaman on a flying horse, Lord Krishna sleeping on a lotus and spirit worlds of Amazonian ayahuasqueros. Mounted center stage at the rear of the enormous altar, in rich tones of vibrant red, was a frightening painting of the Hindu goddess Kali, wearing skulls around her neck and sticking out her blood-red tongue. Numerous votive candles, burning alongside smoldering incense illuminated the complex stage.

This ecumenical menagerie had initially amused Carson. He joked to himself that she was hedging her spiritual bets by embracing such an expansive pantheon. He also noticed on later visits that the pieces on the altar never seemed to remain in the same place, as if Rhiannon were constantly rearranging them, according to some spiritual pattern only she understood. Perhaps she was engaged in some kind of cosmic chess match, he thought. When he questioned her about it, she only responded with an unaffected smile, conveying that the matter was private. She did not need to justify her methods.

Rhiannon turned on the iPad with the selected music for the night's journey. Carson lay down on the floor among a group of pillows. It was his first time journeying with ayahuasca.

Patterns of candlelight danced across the ceiling. Carson suddenly felt chilled. He reached for one of several blankets that were close at hand and covered himself. Rhiannon crawled over from her altar and lay down next to him.

"Are you feeling anything yet?" she asked. "It's been almost a half hour since we drank the tea."

"Kinda," he answered, not wanting to share the truth with her.

Just speaking required extra effort. Carson's mundane consciousness was rapidly slipping away. As the transition progressed, he observed that his mind was not composed simply of his brain, but that it extended to include his entire body. His journey propelled him on paradoxical explorations—galactic expanses that would suddenly become subsumed within the infinitesimal strata of subatomic particles, only to open back into the vaster cosmos. Tremors of energy ran through his body as it sought to contain the information pouring into it. Closing his eyes, Carson fell into a world of multitudinous Ferris-wheel mandalas, each containing similar yet unique symbols that streamed past in patterns of some unexplainable order. Then he began passing into a series of chambers, as though he were entering through a magical ceiling. A Cheshire cat, whose body glowed with an oscillating light, guarded each chamber.

So far, Carson's body seemed to accept easily the ayahuasca without the nausea that Rhiannon told him often accompanied such journeys. Gradually, he was filled with euphoria. He journeyed into breathtaking worlds, unable to decipher whether they represented the past or the future—it didn't matter. Time itself was breaking down, dissolving away as mere illusion.

Carson found himself among archaic temples nestled in lush jungle gardens, viewing a stream of bizarre beings who inhabited these worlds. They all appeared actively engaged in various endeavors. For a period he rode through these domains on the back of a giant female snake, who was warmly greeted wherever she went. Carson marveled that when he engaged these beings in any form of communication, the messages were telepathically relayed. Regardless of species or life form, all thought was instantly conveyed without the slightest need for translation.

These realms felt different from those he had experienced under Wounded Paw. Carson pondered whether this was due to being in a new stage of his development, or to the absence of Native American guidance, or perhaps the alignment of the stars, to the change in medicine, or to Rhiannon. He struggled to retain the multitude of visions in his memory but, ultimately, the phantasmagoria overwhelmed his mind's capacity.

In the midst of his session, Carson tried to remind himself that he was not to become seduced by the bedazzlement of these worlds. Wounded Paw had warned of this temptation, on several occasions when they partook peyote, stating that such allurements could trap those who were unaware and prevent them from attaining the goal of the journey.

As the session progressed, new spirits continued to reveal themselves. Carson felt reluctant to engage with some of these new demigods, knowing that the portals Rhiannon was opening for him would include those that would challenge his limits. However, he knew it was necessary to acknowledge any spirit with whom direct contact was made. He suspected that many of these beings had been sent by Rhiannon, or perhaps might even be her in some archetypal form.

The music Rhiannon had chosen enhanced their journey; its potency was due more to its viscosity than to its melodic essence. Their souls moved upon energy streams driven by ethnic drums, while the droning of didgeridoos and sitars maintained them in suspended flight. The rich soundscapes propelled their psyches through primal realms, charged with sexual energy and hedonistic pleasure, to ethereal ones of purity and formlessness.

Arriving at one exceptional domain, Carson was suddenly overcome with what he could only describe as divine grace. Tears poured forth. As he sobbed quietly, Rhiannon reached over and gently held him, absorbing his release with a deeply comforting embrace. In the moment, she manifested the pure essence of the eternal mother.

But this reassuring experience was not to last. Carson began to have a growing awareness of Rhiannon's sexuality. Until this moment, he had resisted acknowledging her as someone he found attractive. Now, lying beside her, he could smell the natural perfume of her skin and hair. A growing desire to touch her teased him. He wondered if this, too, were not part of some scheme of hers, and possibly Wounded Paw's as well—perhaps a test. Trying to unravel the possibilities contained by the allure was too much to confront for now. He tried to shrug off the disturbing longing, chalking it up as just another absurdity of the situation.

A sudden movement from Rhiannon interrupted the spell. She rose to her knees and began making gestures with her arms, muttering another mantra under her breath. Her body trembled in spasms.

Only a moment before she had been holding him, intimately bonding in a state of loving support. Now, without a word of warning, she had catapulted herself upright onto her knees and away from him. She seemed to be entering a trance. Working with Indians had been bizarre enough, Carson thought, but at least they didn't suddenly shift into a state of madness.

Rhiannon's body stilled. She folded her arms in front of her in a position of prayer and muttered more unintelligible words. She then lay back on the mat and reached for Carson's hand.

"Carson," she began, "I'm asking you to focus your attention with me. Can you do that now?"

He lifted halfway up on one elbow, while slightly turning toward her. "If that's what I'm supposed to do, I'll try to follow your directions."

"I know you think I'm crazy," she continued. "What you think of me at this time isn't important. Perhaps you and I aren't really important. Work with me; you need what I can show you. I don't believe either of us has a choice in the matter. Certain forces are already at play. I know Wounded Paw has taught you that much. There may not be time to do what's required—but from now on, obey me!"

He lay back down as a wave of fear washed over his mind. The locus of his fear shifted to something looming in the near future, something nonhuman with powers beyond his comprehension.

"I'm sorry to be so resistant to you. Bear with me if you can."

"Carson, we don't have the luxury of doing this work at your pace, much less according to your sense of what's appropriate," she scolded. "Wounded Paw told me that you have been marked by the medicine. I trust him. Don't screw this up, for his sake. Do you hear me?"

"Yeah," Carson responded softly.

"And another thing, don't ever be timid in this work. Humble, yes. Frightened, sure. Confused, certainly. But never, never timid. Hold on to your soul at all times and honor the privilege of being an extension of the medicine. Just because you're only a human being, doesn't mean you don't have as much right as any other manifested form in the universe to be a participant. Be that gods or dust, it's all part of the Divine. In this work, timidity is the opposite side of the coin from hubris. Either will get you struck down fast and hard. And that would happen in a way that you don't want to imagine. Do you understand?"

Carson listened intently, partly out of fear and partly out of respect. Regardless of his ambivalence about Rhiannon's sanity, he had to acknowledge her intelligence. It was steadfast and lucid.

Lying on the floor mats, he turned to face her, feeling compelled to make eye contact. The candlelight flickered across her face. Her dark red hair shimmered with a life of its own. She seemed as much composed of shadow as of genuine matter. Suddenly his campaign of resistance could no longer hold its grip. He realized he must trust her.

"Finally!" she pronounced.

Carson laughed. Rhiannon did too. She gave him a hug. He relaxed for a moment, acknowledging the beginning of a new partnership.

Before Carson could speak, Rhiannon sprang again to her knees and emitted a powerful hissing sound. Her movements were fast and aggressive. She had instantly become something entirely other, something ancient and serpentine. Her glowing, snake-like eyes locked onto Carson's with hypnotic force. They burned an icy green, powered by a translucent fire deep within.

Carson was flooded with sensations, as if he were undergoing a succession of incarnations. He could smell the presence of wild animals. His nostrils twitched with the scent of blood, musk, dung, grass and water. He rolled up on his hands and knees, as if he were about to morph into an animal. Unable to remain kneeling, Carson lay back on the floor, as if pushed down by the sheer volume of information pouring through his being. From somewhere within the elusive vastness of the dark room, growls and groans sounded. He began experiencing being various animals, acquiring their gifts of speed or power as he transformed into their bodies, moving through the world as they did.

Gradually, his consciousness centered back to his human body and its more familiar realities. It was impossible to judge how long he had been in those other manifestations: other times, other realms, other lives. Exhaustion wracked his body. He could make out Rhiannon sitting across the room, her body undulating to the rhythm of heavy breathing.

Sweat soaked his clothes. The entire room vibrated in heat. Feeling dazed, Carson struggled to strip his clothes off. Luckily, one of the water bottles they had set out for the journey was within reach. Carson guzzled half of it down and gasped.

"Water?" Rhiannon's voice called.

"Yeah, you want some?"

"Um, I'll come over," she said.

She crawled over in the dark, extending an arm for the water when she was close. Carson handed over the bottle and listened while her silhouette drank.

"Who are you?" he asked.

She laughed. "I think what you really mean to ask is, *what* are you? No?"

"I guess so."

"Let's talk about that some other time, Carson. Are you all right so far?"

"Wow, how can I tell?" He laughed. "My body's generating such intense waves of heat."

"I know, mine too," she moaned.

She shifted her body to get more comfortable, moving into a position in which she was illuminated by candlelight. She was topless. Carson's gaze locked onto her breasts. As they passed the water bottle between them, he struggled to remain unaffected by her partial nudity.

Rhiannon seemed totally at ease, quietly swigging the water down while calming her breathing. Nudity, after all, was not an unusual state to progress to under the influence of the medicine. He could feel the heat pulsating from her body and knew she could feel his. Further, Carson clearly knew she was aware of his staring. This didn't seem to faze her.

"Catch your breath?" she asked.

"Some."

She reclined on the mat next to his. "Better lie back," she said. "There's more to come before we close the session."

Chapter 8

Holy Insanity

On Carson's next visit, he and Rhiannon sat in her garden casually chatting, once again psychically adjusting to each other's company. Now that his resistance had been cleared away, they both hoped he could more fully prepare for the intensified work that lay before him.

"You know, coming up here is not exactly convenient," he began. "I figured not having to drive all the way to Nevada and back would make life simpler, but ironically, it's the opposite. Seems that things are increasingly complicated."

"How do you mean?" Rhiannon asked.

"Well, Allison thinks we might be having an affair."

"Oh, I see," she said. "And what do you think?"

Her response caught him off guard. He found himself examining his thoughts around the question, wondering if it were only a matter of time. She looked at him steadily. Uncomfortable, Carson maneuvered the conversation to another subject.

"Has it ever occurred to you that I don't really know very much about you?" he said.

"So, what is it that you think you need to know?"

"Well, the basics might be good. Is there someone in your life? Have you ever been married? Do you have any children? Where were you brought up? Which schools have you gone to? Are your parents alive? What did they do for a living? For that matter, how do you support yourself? And how did you get involved with this stuff in the first place?"

"My, my, Carson. That's quite a list." She smiled, turning her head away from him. "Do you feel compelled to build your own personal profile on me? But since you've started this inquiry, is there anything else you feel you must know?"

"There is one item that I often wonder about."

"All right then, ask!"

Carson smiled. "Just what do you do on your day off?"

She burst into laughter. "That's one of the best questions anyone has ever asked me. Good for you."

"Well?"

"Actually, the less you know about me at this stage, the better for both of us. You may understand this one day."

Carson felt spurned. Yet he understood she was probably right. A certain teacher-pupil distance best served their work. If he got to know her better, any incipient projections would assuredly take root. This would only lead to further complications, and complications already abounded.

Rhiannon often wondered why the medicine had tapped this unlikely man for the work. She suspected it might be part of his karma, perhaps a past life that connected him to this path. Wounded Paw, in his usual laconic manner, had only shared that his medicine visions had informed him to call Carson, and that Rhiannon was to be involved in Carson's journey on this mysterious road. She resigned herself to the task out of respect for the old Indian and her own knowledge that the medicine works in ways that are often beyond one's ability to understand.

As their journeywork progressed, she remained steadfast in directing his development, navigating his psyche through an array of domains that she believed would further his growth. She focused on broadening his shamanic foundation, teaching him to draw power from various cultures and traditions that practiced the medicine. And although she believed her curriculum was the correct course, she fought to dispel her doubts in his ability to master it in time.

"You've got to round out your education. There's tons you should know," Rhiannon said, shaking her hands to express the importance. "You should have a more expansive view of Native American spiritual practices. Don't think because you've been in training with Wounded Paw that you've a thorough grasp of the field. On the contrary, his work is more centered on a kind of high wizardry than typical Indian practices. Do you follow?"

"No. What exactly do you mean?"

"I'm not saying you have to become an anthropologist. Just expose your mind to various beliefs and practices. And when you finish those books on North American Indians, which are easy enough to get through, I want you to start on these about the Aztecs, Mayans, and Incas."

"You're not serious." He halfway laughed.

"Of course not, none of what we're doing is serious," she said, tilting her head back as if speaking to no one.

Carson picked up a book, rapidly leafing through the pages. "So I'm just supposed to read this stuff and that's it?"

"Learn who these people were, what they believed, how they saw the cosmos and what their descendants do today," she implored. "At the worst, you might learn something. Is that so bad?"

"No, it just seems too late for me to be starting an extensive home-study program," he protested, throwing his hands in the air. "I'm always being told that the bad guys are coming any minute. It'll take me forever to absorb all this information."

"Yeah, I'm sure it feels just like that, and you've only started," she said, pushing another stack of books toward him. "When you finish those books on the indigenous practices of the Americas, you'll want to look at the impact of Christianity on those cultures, as well as the influx of Yoruba and other African influences on South America and the Caribbean."

"Hey, no problem, I'll be a fucking encyclopedia in no time," he mocked.

"Look, I don't expect you to remember all this material, but at least familiarize yourself with it." She paused, swirling her fingers through thick locks of her deep-auburn hair as she sought to find the right words that would motivate him. "Understand that I realize I'm subjecting you to a heavy load of work, but you'll need this one day. Hopefully, you'll be able to connect these seemingly disparate systems into a confluence—one from which you can draw power and knowledge."

"Oh God, this will take forever."

"Look, I realize this is a ton to go through, but it's needed," she said, gently placing a hand on his arm. "And when you finish those books, we'll begin deconstructing Christianity, looking at what was happening in the Middle East during the time of Jesus and how his teachings became institutionalized into Christianity, and progressing back through Christianity's often bloody conquests. You'll need to learn about other sects of Christianity: the early Eastern Orthodox, Coptic and Gnostic schools, the Cathars and the secret cults of Mary Magdalene. And as Christianity was spreading over Europe, the existing spiritual systems such as the Celtic, Norse and Germanic mythologies, the Mithraic cult and a general overview of old European paganism, all the way back to Ice Age shamanism. And all these were imposed on the longest worshipped being of the archaic world— the Great Mother Goddess. It's important that you learn about these other things because power is rooted in all the old ways. These are medicine ways that are imbedded in the collective subconscious, ways that can be drawn upon if you learn. Now does it make sense to you?"

"Well, when you put it that way, I guess I can see what you mean," he said. "It just seems too much to expect of me, I suppose."

"Take it a step at a time."

"All right, but remember, I'm a visual person, not a scholar."

"Well then, when you read about these things, try to visualize them. Use that inclination as a tool, imagining yourself in those cultures, in those times," she said, hoping she might finally be getting through. "Carson, this is a great opportunity for you. Imagine being in some ancient marketplace, hearing the people discuss their view of the world. What was the spiritual essence of early Islam, or perhaps more amazing, the quality of medicine experienced by the old Sufi mystics? Revisit the Old Testament and read about the early Hebrew prophetic shamans and then leverage that onto the mysteries of the Kabala. There're enormous fields of knowledge there. Then move to the Greeks and the numerous mystery schools that flourished across the Mediterranean and Mesopotamia. Do you see how all of this is part of the ongoing work of medicine knowledge?"

"Damn, nobody ever mapped out history for me like that." He shrugged.

"And that's just scratching the surface," she said. "In the ancient world, there's tons of this. Just wait until we get into the Egyptians, Babylonians and Sumerians. Then there's all of Africa with the various fertility cults, many of which continue to this day. Now there's a long-standing medicine tradition."

"Have some mercy, woman—just remember, I'm not a fast reader."

"That's all right," she said. "Keep in mind that the more you learn about these things, the more you'll see how all of these systems have been covertly influencing Western culture across the centuries, in disciplines ranging from philosophy to the arcane science of alchemy and sacred geometry. What I'm exposing to you is the old knowledge that has been long repressed, the forbidden knowledge of our culture. It was forbidden by the Church, by empirical thinking, by modern science, until just recently, and by most of academia. And the sacred medicine itself, which our society lumps under the label 'drugs,' has been forbidden by law. Wounded Paw speaks of the path to this knowledge as the 'medicine road.' I refer to it as the 'forbidden way.' Whatever it is, it chose to seek you and that's why you're here. You heard the call of the forbidden way."

For the following ten weeks, Carson was immersed in a continuous study program, feverishly working his way through the endless reading that lay before him. Reeling from the scope of it all, and knowing that all of Asia still waited, he needed a break. As they sat in Rhiannon's living room one afternoon, he pleaded his case.

"While all this religious heritage stuff is fascinating, do we really have time to be doing this?" he asked, nervously scribbling in the margins of a spiral notebook. "I mean, is this really going to get me ready in time to help with the Visitors?"

"In truth, I don't know. But you need to assimilate as much as you can. It may very well make the difference. For now, it's required of you."

"Required of me?" Carson shot back. "Do you have any idea how many times a day I've asked myself what the hell that actually means? And that doesn't even cover the question of whether or not any of what we're doing is real."

"Wounded Paw told you from the start that this work wouldn't be easy," Rhiannon said, repressing her frustration as she walked toward the window. "Doubt is one of the major obstacles that one must deal with on this path."

"I don't see you slowed down by it."

"I have my days," she said, turning back to face him. "But that isn't the issue; the peril is festering just beyond us. It's almost palpable. Soon you'll encounter it, too!"

"Just what does that mean?" he said, alarmed.

"Your skill level's growing." She paused, examining her thoughts. "Those who oppose us are surely aware of you. Opposite energies attract; soon you'll be directly challenged."

"You mean attacked?"

"Yes, attacked," she said with authority.

"Really attacked?" he asked nervously. "What does that mean? Do you think I'm ready?"

"It depends."

"What about you, wouldn't they have already attacked you?"

"That's already been happening at a low level. So far, I've managed to handle it, though it's been gnawing at me like a cancer."

Fear began to twist in his gut. Why had he allowed himself to get into this mess? He suddenly remembered the look on the faces of Joe Buck and Sydney after their encounter with the Visitors—even Wounded Paw had been shaken.

"When did this happen?"

"It's occurred twice in the last month. Luckily, these weren't the kind of vicious assaults they have been known to unleash."

"What happened?"

"What came at me was a presence, not a full-on attack in any physical sense. It was more of a foreboding. Not like when they attack in a more intense manner, as when medicine workers can actually see them, which I haven't experienced yet. I'm told that in those encounters, the Visitors actually manifest in a visual form. No, my encounters felt more like premonitions of a struggle on the scale of some Biblical epoch."

"Whoa, hold it," Carson interrupted. "If this thing's that powerful, how did you get through such an encounter? What was it like?"

"I didn't try to confront it," she said, turning back around and looking out the window. "When something like that happens and you aren't properly prepared, the best tactic is to allow it to roll over you, like you're caught inside a giant wave in the surf. You don't challenge it; you experience it and tumble along with it until it passes. I took in the presence that came at me, measuring its power and acknowledging its intent."

"Yeah, but these are harmful energies, right? I mean, if they're something evil and dangerous, do they just roll past you? You said they attacked you."

"I'm afraid you have too simple an understanding. They begin by making their presence known, first by trying to defeat one's will. Also, these initial engagements allow them to scan for points of resistance. Then they know where the energy is located that opposes them. It's all very sinister and cunning, actually."

"Keep going," he implored.

"Well, you might think of it as cosmic gunship diplomacy. The initial awareness of their presence is intended to make you feel hopeless, so you give in. And worse, along with that feeling comes a kind of implied offer to join their side, even though you realize that they don't really need you."

Carson was perplexed. His inclination was to reduce it all down to a simple issue of right or wrong.

Rhiannon turned and faced him again. "So what do you think this is all about?" she asked carefully, looking directly into his eyes. "This saving the planet. How do you see yourself in relationship to this work?"

"I suppose as someone who's been invited to be a part of those resisting this alien threat," he responded.

"Meaning we're the good guys and they're the evil ones?" she asked.

"Well, I suppose so. If their intention is to eliminate our lives or subjugate us to some lower position, then, of course—hell yeah!"

"So that makes you some kind of noble warrior, does it?"

He was becoming confused. Why was she denigrating their work, their cause?

"What do you mean, Rhiannon?"

"Well, you must stop and ask yourself how the Visitors might see their role. They may be on some noble crusade of their own, perhaps to save their species, their way of life, their culture. From their perspective, *they* could be the noble warriors and heroes."

"Wait a minute. Where are you going with this, and why are we talking in these terms?"

"Because it's time to consider such matters, that's why. Previously, it wouldn't have been appropriate to bring up. You needed to focus on learning the work. But now you've reached a stage where you need to become more objective and impersonal, less anthropocentric in fact."

"Go on," he said, his mind churning with questions.

"When something seriously threatens us, we project negative associations onto whatever it is. We tend to call it names, classifying it as something evil." She paused, biting her lip. "And these reactions become even more pronounced when we don't know much about whatever it is, the thing that goes bump in the night, that which comes out of the abyss. But remember, whatever their motives, they're competing for the same thing we are—the right to sustain themselves using this planet. Don't get caught up with who shines in the light of righteousness. Whatever their motivation, they're not coming here to unleash suffering for their own amusement. No, it's much more primal than that; it's a matter of survival."

She again faced the window, her arms crossed as she stood peering out. Carson was preoccupied in thought, digesting her words, reflecting how elusive medicine knowledge could be. The more he learned and achieved, the more it expanded into further mystery.

Turning her head slightly in his direction, she said, "From the Visitors' perspective, it's reasonable to assume they're undertaking a necessary cause. Unfortunately, it happens to clash with our own need to survive, or at least remain the dominant species on the planet. Would we not do the same to some other life form if we found ourselves in their shoes?"

"Are you just putting me through another one of your exercises?" he interrupted. "Am I supposed to build some kind of empathy for these harmful forces?"

"Not empathy, but understanding," she replied, turning around fully to face him. "Learn your opponents' motivations and strategies. If you reduce your awareness to simply seeing them as evil villains, while imagining yourself as some mythic knight in shining armor, you'll seriously limit your capacity to meet the challenge. You have to become more sophisticated in your understanding to match up against them. Ultimately, both sides draw their powers from the same source, the Universe Herself. See if you can discover how the Visitors do it, how they get their strength, what they depend on."

"But why would the divine love of the Universe allow such a thing as this to be happening?"

"Father, why hast Thou forsaken me?" She sighed. "Worlds come in and out of existence every moment in the Universe. Unimaginable scales of destruction and creation are ongoing across time and space. Our world is but another in this cosmic process. The why of it all, well, that's one of the great questions, isn't it? We're privileged to know certain parts but not the whole. The Universe isn't some static structure that can be dissected according to rationality and the laws of Newtonian science, leading to happy answers that'll be constant for all time."

"Then why were any of us even born if this was going to be the result? It's not fair, not right."

"Because, my dear Carson, the Universe, or God, if you like, is a process, not a thing, a shifting mystery oozing with paradoxes. Things exist simultaneously in contradictory states of order and chaos. On one hand, there's structure, tightly responding to mathematics and hierarchy. And on the other, there's the irrational, the dissolution of logic and rule and the portal through which the Elusive Other arrives. Compassion and cruelty, life and death, destruction and creation, suffering and salvation, beauty and horror—they're all rising out of and collapsing into the same source. You and I are all of these things, as is everybody and everything. Understanding this is critical for you to go further in our work."

"But what you're describing is madness, some kind of holy insanity," he said angrily, standing up and walking across the room. "I can't accept it!"

"You don't have to accept it. I wouldn't for a minute require that you accept my perspectives on the cosmos. However, don't stubbornly turn away from what you find uncomfortable. Consider these things and examine them against what you've been learning. But remember, don't take too long."

Carson felt tormented, desperate to arrive at an acceptable understanding of what he had been doing for the past two-and-a-half years, since he began working with Wounded Paw.

Rhiannon went on. "And to be fair to your present opinions, yes, you're supposed to work for the survival of your species. Not because you're noble or heroic, but because nature designed you to strive for survival. It's your obligation.

"I know when you look at the cosmology that I've just described it seems terribly ironic, and yes, possibly mad. It's the Uroboros, the snake that devours itself. But that's how it is—a great cosmic game of stretch and fold, all across the Universe."

Carson was not satisfied; neither Rhiannon's theology nor her philosophy gave comfort. Yet he had to accept that much of his reading validated her perspective.

As the weeks passed, Rhiannon continued to march Carson through his schooling. They were presently immersed in studying Asia, with its plethora of religious traditions. The geographic expanse alone was enormous, ranging from Persia to Polynesia, Siberia to Sri Lanka. Rhiannon started with a sampling of some of the oldest cultures: the Harappans of the Indus Valley, Cambodia's Angkor Wat and the Australian Aborigines. She bore deep into Mother India, that great font containing the roots of Hinduism and Buddhism, the two ancient traditions from which she had acquired much of her knowledge.

He felt restless sitting in her living room one wet and chilly afternoon. Flames flickered inside her wood-burning stove; the mood of winter seemed a fitting complement to their work. They had spent many weekends together by now, reviewing his studies, with more to come. He wondered would this scholastic ordeal ever end?

"Lots of weird faces, lots of unpronounceable names—hope all this comes to some use. Frankly, I don't know if this has been the best use of our time," he complained.

"Maybe, maybe not," she replied.

"But, Rhiannon, come on. I mean, I'm covering half the planet's surface here, exploring all kinds of traditions and philosophies, from Shinto to Zoroastrianism to Tungus shamanism, Taoism to Jainism, Zen to Tantra. Not even to mention all the weird Hindu deities and Buddhist stuff. For Christ's sake, it's endless. I feel mentally spent—enough of these arcane worlds with their legions of gods and stages of enlightenment."

"So you think it's all right for you to arrest your ignorance at its current level, do you?"

"Oh, very cute," he whipped, slamming a book on the sofa. "I didn't say I was quitting. More like taking a break, that's all. I've been thinking that I'd like to forgo our next session and use the time to see Wounded Paw."

"I don't think that's such a good idea," she answered, inserting a stick of wood into the stove.

"Why not?"

"There're a number of reasons. I know you don't like hearing me veto your travel hopes, but this isn't the time to go out there. Those men are very busy right now and would do better without your interruption."

He felt hurt. He liked to think that he was always welcome at Wounded Paw's. And how did she know they were too busy to allow him to visit?

"Excuse me!" he scoffed. "I believe I can go there if I decide to. I haven't got any information that they're too busy to see me. Frankly, I'm not sure I believe you know what you're talking about."

"They're busy," she said firmly.

"Oh come on, Rhiannon, be real. I'm tighter with those guys than you are and you know it. I'm welcome there anytime."

"No, no you're not," she replied, turning to address him sternly with her eyes. "Carson, it's not that they don't want to see you. It's that this is not the time—neither for you or them. The days ahead will be grave ones. They're busy dealing with this from their position and they need to concentrate on matters in their own way—without distraction. They're preparing to enter into a period of seclusion. And furthermore, it's not at all safe to make such a journey at this time."

"How do you know all this, Rhiannon? I can accept that you may have some kind of telepathic communication with Wounded Paw, but this is awfully fucking detailed, you know!"

"Carson, don't go into that sarcastic bullshit of yours," she snapped angrily. "Just because your feelings are hurt that you can't go see 'Grandfather' doesn't give you the right to regress to your old cynical mode. Grow up and let them do what they must, and attend to what you should be doing here. Wounded Paw didn't call out to you in your dreams because he liked you or something. He's a medicine man, and when the medicine talks, he listens and does what he has to, as should all of us who are in this work. The medicine, for some reason that defies all human understanding, selected you to be a worker in this realm. And both Wounded Paw and I were directed by it to train you as best we could. Personally, I would never have tapped you for a candidate, but it's not my decision to make."

Carson bolted off the sofa, pacing angrily around the room as months of repressed frustration came to the surface.

"Oh great, Rhiannon. When you want to control me you pull out the 'I'm psychic' card, claiming that you've some special esoteric information and that I must do as you command or the bad guys will get me. Well, fuck you!"

She stood up, stepping in front of him in a confrontational posture.

"Would that help? Is that your problem?" she challenged.

Silence hung between them. Her retort brought to the fore what he had been repressing. His tongue froze; no words would come to hide the obvious. Too many images, too many desires, too many needs overwhelmed him.

Chapter 9

Night of Storm

Rain slashed against Rhiannon's cottage, driven by gales sweeping in from the Pacific. Against the storm's cold, the wood-burning stove radiated reassuring warmth, and an assortment of altar candles washed the room in soft illumination. Carson was grateful to be inside, within this sanctuary, this gateway to so many strange worlds.

Due to numerous holiday related family and business obligations, this was their first session together in three weeks. Carson was hoping to rekindle their recently achieved teamwork, to demonstrate he could manage his frustration.

However, he was unsure of Rhiannon's state; she seemed uneasy. He suspected that the powerful storm pounding the coast was no coincidence in her mind. She had secluded herself within the cottage, immersed in puja—various rituals and prayers—preparing for what was coming. These prolonged meditations were critical for her drawing in protection and strength. She had instructed him to get lots of rest before coming up this weekend, to be extremely careful on the drive up and to take nothing in the profane world at face value.

Earlier, as he had packed for the trip to Rhiannon's, the phone rang.

"Carson, is that you?" a distantly familiar voice inquired.

"Speaking," he replied.

"It's Luther Redbone. How are you?"

"Hey, Luther, good to hear from you, man."

"Yeah, well I didn't want you to think we'd forgotten about you, you know."

"Well, that's nice to hear."

He had not heard from Luther since that initial trip to meet Wounded Paw; more than two years had passed. While Carson had maintained contact with Jimmy White Stone, Luther and Owl Eyes had faded into the distance.

"And to what do I owe the honor of this call?" Carson asked.

"I wanted to tell you that all of us are thankful for your dedicated work on the documentary—and also for your courage in accepting the medicine's call. We know that it hasn't been easy."

Carson sensed more was coming. "I had a great teacher," he replied.

"Yes, you did. And now you're with another one," Luther added.

Carson made no comment, signaling his ambivalence over his forced separation from Wounded Paw.

Luther continued, "I wanted you to know that we're praying for you both, especially at this time."

"Well, I'll send prayers to you, as well."

"Thank you, my brother. And, Carson, be strong. Heed what this woman tells you, especially at this point. She's very gifted."

"Seems I don't really have much choice in the matter."

"You will someday—be patient."

"So what do you hear from Wounded Paw, if I may ask?" Carson pressed.

There was a prolonged pause. He could feel Luther crafting his words.

"He's all right," Luther answered. "Very busy, as are all the medicine people right now. Our reservation is very quiet today; nothing's open. In a few hours we'll be going down into our kiva, to unite our spirits. May you be safe."

He thanked Luther and they said their good-byes. Carson didn't know whether to take comfort in this support or to feel worried, sensing that Luther may be preparing for a confrontation with the Visitors. And what might that mean for all the others, himself included?

A few minutes later, he was on his way to Rhiannon's. The three-hour drive would get him there by late afternoon. His mind was already preoccupied with the coming weekend's work, which would again include the taking of a holotropic sacrament. And there was Rhiannon—he was anxious to see her, despite the difficult nature of their partnership.

Driving down the side of Mt. Tamalpais, on California's scenic coastal Highway 1, meant he would soon be at Rhiannon's cottage. The narrow, two-lane highway had been carved out of the mountainside, leaving little provision for shoulders. A vertical rock wall rose massively on his right; a sheer drop-off to the ocean hundreds of feet below bordered on the left.

His thoughts wandered back to Luther Redbone's call, wondering what he and his people would be doing tonight. Carson wished he was a part of some culture that supported this work, not floating in modern America alone, with the exception of Rhiannon—the only person from his own 'tribe' who knew what he was doing and why; a woman who was both his tormentor and solace.

Suddenly, a logging truck that looked as if it should have been relegated to the scrap yard years ago appeared in his rearview mirror. Within moments, it was thundering down behind him, within feet of his rear bumper. Alarmed by the truck driver's dangerous behavior, he guessed that the old Peterbilt's brakes must be failing. He sped up to widen the space between his SUV and the metallic beast. But when he heard the driver downshift and accelerate as he came through a curve, Carson realized that the truck had no intention of slowing.

Racing to stay ahead of the old rig, Carson glanced between his rearview mirror and the winding road. Coming out of a hairpin curve, he spotted a fire-trail turnoff just ahead. With a frantic jerk of the steering wheel, he aimed for the marginal dirt roadway, skidding to an abrupt stop in a cloud of dust and gravel. The demon truck blew past, angrily grinding its gears as it raced on down the highway.

Carson sat for a long time, his hands trembling, fighting off a cramp in his right foot from the tension of his rapid braking. He got out and limped around to stretch it. The air was cold, fed by a sweeping bank of dark winter clouds. In the brisk wind, the sweat that had sprung from every pore chilled his skin.

Wishing to put the ordeal behind him, he mustered his wits and maneuvered his Jeep Cherokee back onto the highway. Shaken, he drove on. In another twenty minutes, he thankfully pulled onto Rhiannon's property.

As they sat in her kitchen, Rhiannon made tea from one of her numerous blends, adding to the brew something extra of her choosing. Carson knew better than to ask what it was, knowing that his question would only lead to a lengthy explanation on her pharmacopoeia. Once the tea had steeped, she poured two large cups. They sat mostly in silence, sipping the warm beverage and listening to the wind build outside.

Carson decided not to tell her about his near fatal encounter. He simply didn't have the energy to listen to her version of what it might have meant. If it weren't that they were scheduled to do medicine that night, he would have been assuaging the ordeal with a comforting bottle. Yet his mind continued to replay the scene from the road, trying to decipher it. How could such a heavy truck hold the road like that? He wanted to believe the incident reflected nothing more than the actions of a maniac truck driver.

"I hope you've kept up with the reading over the holidays," she said. "What I really hope is that you'll soon find that power source you must have. Do you feel any closer to that?"

"You know I don't, at least not that I realize," he answered.

"Well, as before, this will be the purpose of your journeywork tonight."

"Yeah, I know. Destination to nowhere, yet again," he said, throwing his hands up to indicate how futile his efforts felt.

"Damn you, don't you dare feel sorry for yourself. That's shameful, not to mention that it puts all of us at greater risk," she said forcefully, leaning toward him with a fierce emerald light burning in her eyes.

"You're right, I didn't really mean that," he apologized, avoiding her gaze.

"Look, you're making progress, even though you've not achieved certain levels," she offered. "The medicine can suddenly burst wide open for you. That could happen at any time. You have to keep trying, keep asking for this. Do the best you can. The medicine will do what it will do. Trust until then."

Privately, Rhiannon was less optimistic. She could feel the inimical threat building. The signs had become clear. She could no longer wait for Carson to resolve his frustrations with her or their work—time was running out. He would have to learn to find his power or quite possibly perish trying. When he arrived today, she immediately recognized that he had been targeted by something, even if he didn't realize it. Rhiannon's only reassurance was that he had somehow managed to arrive at her house alive.

But his thoughts were not on finding his power; they were on Rhiannon and his need to understand her better, to learn who she really was or how she became who she was.

"You know, you continue to mask so much about yourself, especially about how you got involved with all of this stuff to begin with," he said, pausing to study her face. "I've tried to respect your request for privacy in this matter, but it leaves me at a kind of disadvantage."

"How do you mean?"

"Well, you know all kinds of things about me and my life, but I know hardly anything about you. It's kind of unfair; you're in a position of privilege. So I imagine you as having some kind of special background, say a mother who was a famous witch and a father who was a great wizard, like in *Harry Potter*."

Rhiannon laughed. "Oh yeah, that's exactly how it was." She laughed more. "Okay, I'm sorry. I haven't been evasive about my life just to annoy you. I guess I see where you're coming from, but my childhood was not exotic. Someday, I may be able to share more about myself. But I'll tell you a little about my upbringing, if that'll help you become more adjusted to the medicine."

"Can't wait," he said.

"Well, my father was an electrical engineer, worked for Bell Labs and General Electric. He was all about empirical science and the practical application of technology. My mother was a professor of political science. For her, life was all about politics and the effects of economic structures on people's lives. Had she been born at an earlier time, she probably would have been a Marxist."

Rhiannon looked straight ahead, her words coming with effort, her voice tight and shaky. "While you wouldn't say they were atheists, they gave little consideration to anything spiritual. You might say they were too rational to bother with any nonsense like God. If you couldn't measure it with scientific instruments or argue about its political utility, well, it just wasn't worth wasting time on. And as it turned out, that's sort of how they dealt with me."

"What do you mean?"

"Oh, it wasn't that they were bad parents or anything like that. We were just oil and water. From my early childhood, I was always living in a world of magic, places that were inhabited by spirit beings and what Mom and Dad labeled 'imaginary friends.' It all seemed perfectly normal to me. But naturally, they expected me to grow out of such things. You know, move on with my interests like regular kids. They recognized that I was quite bright and otherwise healthy and normal. And meanwhile, they had my older sister for comparison. She was a model child. But apparently, I failed to demonstrate adequately that I was 'maturing'—that I could distinguish between make-believe and appropriate reality."

"Sounds tough," Carson muttered, starting to formulate the picture.

"They sent me to a child psychologist for a while, but that didn't produce the hoped for results. So being pragmatists, they had to accept the 'scientific truth' about their daughter, which was that I was somehow 'different' and unlikely to change. In hindsight, I suspect it was too much for them. They slipped into more or less ignoring me. This only made it worse from their perspective, as it allowed me more time to dwell in my secret worlds, where I maintained an active relationship with an array of spirit guides. By the time I started high school, they had completely given up on me. Otherwise, I wasn't a problem child or anything. I made good grades and such. I was someone very different—from them and just about everybody else for that matter."

"Wow, it sounds like being some kind of orphan in your own home," he said, leaning across the kitchen table toward her.

"Well, I was all right with it, I suppose, although it was weird, realizing that they maintained a completely different relationship with my sister."

"Are your parents still alive?"

"My father died from a heart attack twelve years ago. My mother's not well and lives in San Diego with Hanna, my sister. Hanna owns an advertising agency." She paused, looking down at the table. "So, you see, I come from a very normal family, normal background. No witches or wizards—just me."

"But how did you get to where you are now?"

"When I got to college I began taking courses in comparative religion, psychology, Asian studies and such things. That really helped me gain an academic foundation for much of what had been my interests and predilections since childhood. Then, over the summer of my junior year, I went to India. That's when I really began to burst out of the constraints of my upbringing. I was finally able to go into states of complete spiritual immersion, working with different teachers and masters. Things expanded from there. I went to other countries, studied other mystery traditions, and met more teachers. There was no turning back."

Carson mulled over her story, trying to imagine what she would have been like at the time, and comparing her path to his during those years.

"And Wounded Paw?" he asked. "How did you first connect with him?"

"That's a whole other story, too complicated to go into now."

"I knew you were going to leave that out," he whined.

Rhiannon laughed. "I left a ton of things out, Carson. That is not by any means my complete biography."

They finished the tea and Rhiannon busied herself with preparing for their coming session, setting out candles, selecting music and concocting the mind-altering sacrament that they would soon imbibe.

Night was rapidly approaching. Carson decided to use this time to take a shower, hoping the hot water and steam would restore his sense of well-being. Given the stress of the highway incident, he questioned whether he should be taking the medicine tonight, suspecting that he would have difficulty staying focused on his purpose. Yet he knew they would proceed with the night's agenda, regardless.

An hour later, they sat together on the living room floor. In the dim light, he watched Rhiannon's face, her eyes closed and her lips moving silently as she whispered one of her mantras. He was having difficulty clearing his mind. Was that truck intentionally trying to … ?

Rhiannon had been adamant that he must be focused and

prepared tonight. Sheets of rain drove against the cottage.

"Have you pulled your protectors near?" she interrupted his thoughts.

"Well, let me see here," he gestured with his hands. "I've got the good tooth fairy on this side and Sparky the Wonder Dog on the other."

"Asshole," she said dryly.

"Yes, of course, just trying to relieve a little tension."

"This isn't a night to be cavalier about such matters."

"I'm prepared, okay?"

"We'll see. You weren't so casual when you arrived this afternoon."

Carson wondered if she somehow knew what had occurred on the coast road. The tension between them remained palpable, not a favorable condition for the demands of their work—and not tonight, especially given Rhiannon's mood and his earlier conversation with Luther. But it was too late to deal with personal issues; bigger forces were about to unfold.

Rhiannon handed him a small glass containing the sacred medicine, a blended tincture of mushrooms and selected herbs. They looked at each other in silence, whispered a prayer, and drank the elixir.

Filled with anticipation, they lay down on mats and covered themselves with blankets, their psyches exposed for the uncharted journey. The medicine's power quickly fostered their descent through domains of unfathomable geometric patterns. Among the surreal landscapes, Carson sought out the familiar spirits who had befriended him in the past. However, tonight his efforts seemed to yield little compared to previous occasions. He felt disconnected from his guides and allies, as if they were engaged in matters of their own.

Feeling alone and vulnerable, he reached under the blanket and located Rhiannon's hand. Her skin felt cold; there was no response. He gently squeezed, but still there was no reaction. In the flickering candlelight, he studied her ashen face. There was no sign of life coming from her, not even an indication of breathing. Given his own condition, Carson questioned his assessment. He was well aware that he was under the influence of a hallucinogen and might be deceived by his own perceptions. Then it hit him—she had left her body. He strained to fight off an urge to panic; his breathing tightened.

Suddenly, the entire cottage began to shake. He could hear various idols from her altar tumbling over, along with burning candles that rolled off in different directions, threatening to set the place ablaze. From the dark recesses of the kitchen and bedroom came the sound of things crashing to the floor. Everything was happening within a warped sense of distended time; his mind raced, while paradoxically the physical world seem to move in slow motion.

Then, just as quickly, the shaking stopped. He got up and began restoring the fallen candles, many of them still burning. He grabbed one just as it was about to ignite the altar cloth.

"Be careful where you step," Rhiannon called out. "There may be broken glass on the floor." She had returned to her body from wherever she had been.

"Jesus, that was no small earthquake."

"Did all the candles get picked up?" she asked.

"Yeah, and miraculously nothing's on fire."

"You were hoping I would say that it was an earthquake, weren't you?" she asked.

"Yes. But the freaked-out part of me suspects it might have been something altogether different."

"Carson, remember it's normal to be frightened; but don't be blinded by it."

"By the way, where were you when that thing hit?"

"We don't have time to go into that now. Whatever rocked the cottage was only the beginning, sort of a sonar-locating wave. I believe we're going to have what our Indian friends call Visitors.

And the bastards would choose to show up when Pluto is in opposition to Saturn!"

He recalled her lecture on the effects of astrological transits; Pluto and Saturn were two planets that did not bode well in this alignment. Their conflicting paths in the sky meant that any trouble afoot would only be amplified.

He shrank into himself. If he could only somehow return to the life he had led just a few years ago.

Rhiannon got up and walked about the cottage to survey the damage. Her attention was focused on the doors and windows. In a few moments she returned to her altar and went about restoring order as best she could, given the influence of the medicine. Finally, she lay down again on the mat. Carson lay back down with her, relieved to have her alongside him.

"We must regain control over ourselves. That tremor was also designed to disrupt our journey, our shielding. Go back into the journey and concentrate on drawing to you whatever forces you can. Hurry!"

She bent over him, placing her hands over his eyes. Her touch was reassuring. Carson relaxed, quickly slipping back into the realms of non-ordinary reality. Whispering a prayer for them both, Rhiannon nestled beside him and drifted away into her own exotic domain.

Again he beseeched protection of the guides and allies he had acquired through Wounded Paw. Remembering Luther's phone call prompted him to pray for the protection of others. As he started to include his son in his prayers, he abruptly stopped, fearing to name Ben as it might make his son a target.

He called in his power animals, prayed to ancestors from beyond memory, and even attempted to beckon some of the spiritual images from the menagerie of traditions that Rhiannon had introduced him to: Naga spirits, Kali, and Durga. Needing even further reassurance, he reached back into the bedrock of his own upbringing and prayed to Jesus.

Despite his best efforts, a rising paranoia tore at his resolve. He began once again to question Rhiannon's motivations. Suddenly, he was more than certain that she was abetting the Visitors, quite possibly about to surrender him as a sacrifice. *She was the enemy!*

"Carson, what's going on?" she interrupted. "I can see a field of fear around you that's directed at me."

"Stay the fuck away from me!" he demanded, trying to move further from her.

"I thought so," she commented quietly. "You're identifying the source of your fear as me. Now recognize it for what it is and calm yourself. Get a grip and then come back to the work. This is not the night to indulge your psyche's shadows. You have to move on. We're facing some serious forces here. Pull yourself together."

Her steady words and even tone helped. Realizing what had happened, he collected himself; the paranoia passed, and he redirected his thoughts back to the session's work.

The storm continued to unleash itself upon the night. Outside, frantic wind chimes clattered in cacophony.

Chapter 10

Onslaught

Some time later, Carson's attention was again drawn to Rhiannon. Beneath the blanket, she twisted and jerked beside him, mumbling as if in a bad dream. He wanted to help her but knew he mustn't interrupt her journey.

She was such a mystery, one he wanted to solve—to find the magic key that would open her, allowing him into her secret domains.

The room had grown cold. He crawled over to the stove and began adding wood to the dying fire. Just as the new wood began to crackle, something of considerable weight began to roll across the roof, pounding as if trying to break through the cottage's frail construction. He questioned what kind of animal would be doing such a thing.

"Shut the stove door fast!" she shouted.

Alarmed by her command, Carson slammed the door. In the next instant, the entire length of the stovepipe began shaking violently. Rhiannon sprang to the stove and held its door tight. He fumbled for an implement to serve as a weapon against the would-be intruder.

Suddenly all was silent again except for the sound of the storm.

"What the fuck is going on?" he whispered in a shaken voice.

She did not respond. A litany of mantras spewed from her mouth amid gasps of air. In the dim light of the stove, his eyes strained to see her. She appeared to be shape shifting, becoming something other than a mortal woman. Her arms seemed to be extending to an abnormal length, and her hair spread open like the hood of a cobra. She turned and peered at him with the other-worldly, snake-like eyes he had seen briefly in other sessions.

And in the next instant, she was somehow standing across the room at a window. There, in a language that was unrecognizable, she shouted commands to whatever loomed outside the cottage.

Drawn by her powers and his own curiosity, he struggled to his feet and moved toward her. In what appeared as a trance, Rhiannon ordered unseen forces to obey her will. Carson moved closer, positioning himself at a nearby window, reluctantly daring to see what stood in the darkness outside.

At first, he could make out nothing but the prevailing darkness, much to his relief. But her continuing actions indicated that indeed something was out there. She was still chanting at a fevered pace. Still he saw nothing. The slightest hints of predawn light were striving to break through the shroud of storm and night.

Then, over by the rhododendron thicket, he began to make out something. It seemed to undulate in and out of an undefined form. As best as he could determine, it might have been twelve to fifteen feet tall, robot-like, yet diaphanous. It seemed imbued with a cool, grayish light. Now other forms became visible; ones that were low to the ground and glowed with a dull amber light. They seemed to be prowling, possibly digging, as if they were a pack of meticulously organized wolves. Carson stood mesmerized, petrified in awe and fear.

All the while, Rhiannon held her ground, trembling and hissing out a string of incantations to ward off the ominous Visitors. Flashes of light shot suddenly through the cottage. Windows and doors rattled angrily amidst a renewed pounding upon the roof. Heavy thuds sounded on the outside walls of the cottage.

Against this onslaught Rhiannon prayed with verve, now shifting into English:

May the souls of all beings that have incarnated on this planet rise to combat thee.

May all the spirits who have been nurtured by those souls join to fight thee.

May the mighty forces held in Earth's sacred matter unite to shield our holy Mother.

May the planets that form the family of our Sun come to the defense of their sister.

May the One and the Many that create and sustain all life and being deliver us.

The storm raged on, making it difficult for him to see through the driving sheets of rain.

A chilling howl pierced the night. Carson recoiled from the window. Rhiannon staggered and swooned. He rushed to her side, catching her before she tumbled to the floor. Filled with rage and terror, he screamed out. "Whatever you are out there—fuck you all!"

His body was shaking. Tears filled his eyes as he struggled to remain standing with Rhiannon's limp body against his. Energy he had never experienced before suddenly rose up through his body and shot out to confront the Visitors.

Peering out the window again, he began to detect additional movement in the dark. Another tall being appeared among the apparitions—this one closer to the cottage. He watched, believing his death was before him.

In a flash of light, the second tall being revealed itself, rearing up on its hind legs—the apparition of a giant bear. It bellowed over the storm's chorus. It was the bear from his dreams, the spirit form of Wounded Paw, accompanied by various animal spirits.

Flashes of light fired through the dark in all directions. More forms began to appear, moving alongside the giant bear. Some resembled buffalos or wolves; others seemed more humanlike. And still others suggested strange, ethereal beings as if from mythology—attired in elaborate costumes and armor. His allies had arrived.

Then, as suddenly as it had begun, it was over.

The storm's fury softened, and the night's savage energy shifted. The attack had passed. For the moment, things appeared to be restored, falling back into what is taken from granted.

He pulled the still-unconscious Rhiannon back to the mats and laid her down. He began to attend to her. Heat pulsated from her body. He was amazed that she was even alive, that they both were. She continued to tremble under the psychic fever. He lifted her head to see if she could drink.

Rhiannon opened her eyes and looked up at him. She took small sips of water that he offered her. Thankfully, her eyes had reverted to their normal, beguiling green. Gradually, she pulled herself up and looked about the cottage, assessing that it and they were more or less still intact. Sweat streamed down her face and neck. He knelt beside her, continuing to help her drink.

"I'm burning up; help me get these clothes off," she said weakly.

"Sure."

She stripped off everything and sat limp on the mat, staring blankly at the wood-burning stove.

"Don't put any more wood in the stove tonight," she whispered.

They smiled cautiously. Carson made his way to the bathroom and returned with a towel, helping her dry off, his mind and body flooded with a thousand thoughts and needs.

"Can I get you anything?" he offered.

"What do you have in mind?"

"You tell me."

"No thanks, water is about all I can manage for now. If we can hang on 'til morning, you can pour me a bubble bath. How about that?"

"You got it."

She suddenly laughed. "Well, did we kick some ass tonight or what?"

Carson could only smile in return. The gravity of what they had just survived stilled his humor. Rhiannon looked up at him and began sobbing. She fell against him and wept deeply. Exhaustion settled upon both of them and they lay on the mats, surrendering to sleep as the approaching dawn restored the world.

Carson awoke first. His mind was already challenging the validity of the previous night's experience. Midmorning light flooded the cottage, allowing a full inspection of any damage caused by the storm, earthquake, or spirit forces. Rhiannon lay beside him, a still-life nude. Carson pulled a blanket over her and got up. First he looked outside to assure himself that the apparitions he had witnessed the previous night were not there in the light of day. Thankfully, nothing more than fallen branches and standing puddles remained as evidence of the night's ordeal. Birds were busily singing.

"Carson," Rhiannon called out, half awake.

"Yeah, I'm here."

She sat up slowly.

"Help me, will you? I have to go pee," she said.

"Sure, go easy."

She came to her feet and wrapped the blanket around herself. He steadied her.

"Can you get a fire going in the stove? It's pretty cold in here," she said, shuffling off to the bathroom.

The thought of opening the stove door was frightening. He slowly cracked it open, encountering nothing more than warm ashes. In a few minutes, the welcome crackle of wood restored a sense of coziness to the cottage.

"Would you mind cooking something for us?" she called. "I haven't yet regained my strength enough to deal with anything like cooking."

"No problem. Or, I could take you down to the village for a bite."

Carson was anxious to reconnect to the ordinary, to a world that responded to the ordinary laws of physics according to ordinary logic. He longed to be surrounded by ordinary people in an ordinary restaurant on an ordinary day.

"Thanks, but we shouldn't leave the property," she yelled from the bathroom.

"Why not? Are they still out there?"

"What do you sense?"

Carson paused, wondering if he had misread the conditions outside the cottage.

"It looks like the coast is clear, as far as I can tell."

"Right, that's what I sense, as well. However, we're both still very depleted. We need to remain in a secure place while recharging. If we were out in public and something came at us, I don't know how well we'd fare. You could suddenly choke on something in a restaurant or maybe be the victim of a freaky automobile accident. Know what I mean?"

As Rhiannon emerged from the bathroom, she looked at him soberly, making sure that he grasped the vulnerability that lurked were he to be complacent. He was already recalling yesterday's encounter with the logging truck.

"Yeah, right," he said nervously. "What would you like to eat?"

"Everything! There's all kinds of stuff in the fridge and pantry. Create us something, but make it hearty. I'm going to throw some clothes on and go outside for a look. I need to attend to some things out there."

"Are you up for that yet?" he asked.

"I'll be fine. But thanks for asking. Sometimes, when you aren't caught up with being an ass, you can be a surprisingly sweet fellow."

Carson explored the culinary options. Rhiannon's refrigerator contained a bounty, but much of it defied identification. Herbs, roots, and potions of special teas competed for space with the normal foodstuffs. Finally locating eggs and something that he hoped was cheese, Carson decided to make omelets using every ingredient he could find that smelled like regular food.

In the midst of his labor, he stole glances outside to check on her. She was moving about the yard and garden, smudging just about everything she came upon to purify and cleanse it, using a large smoldering sage bundle.

Soon they were feasting rapaciously. Neither spoke much; they were too occupied by the demands of feeding their overtaxed bodies. He was astonished at how good the food tasted. Rhiannon supplemented her meal with several homemade capsules of herbs and vitamins, along with an elixir that she had pulled from the back of the refrigerator. Carson washed down his food with two cups of dark coffee. At last, they were sated and the world seemed to be restoring itself to a condition of sanity.

"Say, you're a pretty damn good cook."

"Thank you. I would tell you my secret recipe, but in all truth, I'm not exactly sure about the identities of some of the things that went into the omelet."

"Well, if my taste buds are correct, I would never have imagined using one of those ingredients in particular. If you miss your period next month, let me know. I use that one to help certain clients become pregnant," she said, giving him a wink as she relaxed back in her chair.

"Oh Jesus!" He blushed.

"Listen, come outside with me; I want to show you something."

Carson suddenly felt weary. The meal had just begun to restore his blood sugar and the cottage now felt warm, snug, and most importantly—safe. He longed for a nap, or at least just to be numb for a while. Couldn't they remain inside a while longer? He thought of being home with Ben, perhaps watching a college football game with him and some friends, with no worries beyond the game's score. Obligingly, however, he put on his shoes and coat and accompanied her outside.

The crisp air helped confirm that he was indeed alive and of the world. They walked slowly over the damp earth, navigating around a number of large fallen branches from the redwood trees. At the edge of her garden, Rhiannon turned him around to face the cottage. His eyes were immediately drawn to the roof. Several large boughs were strewn upon it, including a big eucalyptus branch.

"Whoa, so that's what was making that racket!" he exclaimed.

"Convenient, isn't it?"

But Carson welcomed the tangible evidence.

"Sometimes you have to call a spade a spade," he said. "I mean, if it walks like a duck and quacks like a duck . . ."

"Idiot," she scoffed. "Do you think it was just coincidental that those tree branches landed there? I know all the plant life around here very well. You see that bough of eucalyptus? The nearest eucalyptus trees are over five hundred yards away, over there, to the east. The storm came in from the ocean, blowing continuously from the west. Admittedly, it was quite a storm, but it would have taken something more like a tornado to rip off that heavy branch and transport it over here, in the opposite direction of the storm's path."

In the light of day, Carson had been busily repressing the terror of the previous night. His brief reprieve was now over. His memory began replaying the events: the crazed logging truck, the helpless sensation of riding out the quaking of the earth, the unearthly sounds upon the roof, the rattling of doors and windows, the strange lights, and—most disturbing—the menacing being by the rhododendron that had nearly succeeded in vanquishing them.

"Come over here, there's more you need to see," she called.

She was standing closer to the cottage, with a grim expression. He reluctantly obeyed and went to her. She pointed down at several puddles surrounded by rain-trodden mounds of dirt.

"These pits weren't here yesterday," she began. "They're from digging, from last night. Someone who didn't know better might think they're the work of some animal. But I've lived on this property for years. I have never had animals come here and dig like this. Not to mention in the middle of a horrendous storm."

"Why were they digging?" he asked uneasily.

"They weren't simply digging, Carson. They were starting to tunnel—tunnel in under the cottage."

"Oh my God."

"I had shielded the cottage thoroughly, you see," she said. "Plugging all obvious portals; fortifying the walls and roof, doors and windows; even calling in special spirits to seal any cracks or vents that I may not have been aware of. It's not that ordinary doors and walls represent any real defense unto themselves. One uses them as defined boundaries, a kind of matrix onto which to project the shielding. It might sound ludicrous, but after last night, I think you can appreciate how important this function is. And shielding of this nature has to extend down into the earth, all along the cottage's foundation. They had probed all these and were next trying to go under-ground, seeking to find a way up from directly under the house, through the floor. Thankfully, I remembered learning from an old Naga cult woman, on the outskirts of Calcutta, to extend the shielding under the house, as well."

Carson started to feel sick. Whatever this force was, he was confronting something against which he ultimately had no chance. It would only be a matter of time.

"We were fortunate last night," she continued. "Our prayers were heard and forces came to assist us, but it was very close. I'm sure you realize that. It took an enormous amount of strength to hold them off—ours and that of our allies."

"Why us?" Carson interrupted. "I mean, if these energies are so strong, why don't they just come on down and take over or something? Why haven't they unleashed some kind of Armageddon?"

"Because they aren't that powerful, at least not yet," she said. "Besides, an Armageddon isn't in their interest. To replace what's been operating on this planet, with all its interwoven complexities and exchanges of energy, is no small undertaking. They would themselves become highly vulnerable if they simply tried to muscle their way in by using brute, military-like force. Part of the reason they need this planet is to have ready access to all of its preexisting energies.

"What do you mean?" he asked, pulling his jacket zipper up tight to his neck.

"Think of them as kind of parasite-like. They aren't here to destroy but rather to sustain themselves off all that already exists on the planet—plant, animal, and mineral, and all the relationships and networks of life and matter that have been created here across the millennia, everything from the energy of the Sun as it affects the planet to bacteria. They will only destroy what resists their access to it all, to taking over here."

"How can you be sure you understand their intentions so clearly?" he pressed.

"Come on, Carson," she smirked, placing her hands on her sides. "This is what the medicine has shown nearly all of us. You saw glimpses of this yourself that day at Wounded Paw's, by the petroglyphs, did you not?"

"Well, that's true," he recalled. "But all this was so new then. I wasn't very certain about anything, much less have any real understanding."

"Oh, I think you understood well enough," she said, shaking her head affirmatively. "No, their plan must be executed in certain precise stages if they're to achieve their goals. And if they accomplish these initial stages, it'll become progressively easier for them. As they establish themselves here, different energy fields that reside on the planet will realign themselves to complement the Visitors' growing influence."

"I don't get what you're talking about."

"I'm speaking of those vast energy fields contained in such materials as earth and water, or those that organize weather; the energy held in a mountain range, a river, an ocean or those energies that extend throughout the entire network of Gaia consciousness and Her surrounding solar system. Whether people realize it or not, our very being is tied to these fields of energy. We couldn't exist without them. If the Visitors are triumphant, these planetary energy fields will realign with the Visitors' consciousness. The Visitors will grow progressively stronger as they feed from the realigning energies. It doesn't always have to be humans who dominate the planet."

Carson sighed heavily, the previous night's exhaustion taxing his ability to absorb her explanations.

"Various aligning processes have been going on since the beginning of the universe," she continued. "Things may start out in apparent chaos and violence—say, something as cataclysmic as an exploding star. But as such cosmic events settle, patterns of coexistence come into being. Various energies start to come into alignment with each other—they're drawn to one another. What we call life is the product of such an alignment, as are our thoughts, the rocks and trees, everything here. All this is a storehouse of energy, held in relationships of coexistence, from subatomic particles to the solar system we share. Preventing a radical changeover in these relationships, preventing a realignment of energy, this is the core of our defense."

Carson suddenly found himself confronting an entirely new level of cosmic operations. "Why is it that just as I seem to get a grasp of things, the medicine work always adds another complex layer?" he complained.

"Our Visitor friends well understand what I just shared. If they're able to secure their colonizing strategy to a certain point, the momentum will begin to work automatically in their favor. When that happens, there's no stopping them by any forces we can muster."

Depression began to sweep over him, along with thoughts of his son, the world as he had known it; he felt the loss and he felt defenseless.

"So, want to hear some good news?" she inserted sarcastically.

"Can't wait."

"First, they have to get past us, the people and energies that oppose their designs. We, the energy workers, the medicine people, are the ones who can possibly generate enough resistance to stop them."

Carson looked at her with resignation. He couldn't see any way that they could keep up a sustained resistance against such a powerful adversary.

"We don't have a chance, do we?" he countered, turning away from her.

Rhiannon's face flushed with anger. She grabbed him by an arm and spun him around.

"It's not just you and me and a handful of Native Americans," she said, her voice trembling with emotion. "There're thousands of people around the world who are working with us. And after last night, I would think you'd realize that those who are joining in this cause are by no means limited to human beings, or even human souls. Other types of beings and allies are joining in."

She released him, turning aside to regain her composure.

"Does anyone in the government or the United Nations know about this stuff?" he asked.

"A few people, but they can do little," she answered numbly, peering vacuously at the ground. "It would only unleash pandemonium if it were made public. Besides, what would their response be? Military action as we know it would be meaningless. A threat of this nature can only be met on the psycho-spiritual plane, opposed by powers of the same ilk. The Visitors know that and that's why they're coming after the spirit workers first. If they can eliminate us, there won't be much left to oppose them, at least not from the human side. Perhaps the gods and spirits that reside on the planet might prevail on some level, but I doubt we as a species would have much presence by that stage."

"Well, somehow we did make it through last night," he offered, attempting to bolster himself.

"Yes, yes we did, this time," she said. "However, they'll be back. And when they return, they'll bring more force than before. We just barely held them off last night. Already, others have not been so fortunate. An entire medicine circle was wiped out in South America last month, no survivors. We don't know what happened. Only shreds of human tissue were found. There have been reports from Nepal of a group being destroyed there, but it's been hard to get anyone to talk about it. The Nepalese government has put it down to an attack by local Maoist guerrillas, but there was no previous guerrilla activity in that section of the country. A group of African bushmen who had gathered to resist the Visitors simply vanished while conducting ceremonies in the Kalahari Desert. Their relatives can find no trace of them, and animals won't go into the area where it occurred. The Australian government is trying to explain the mutilation of a band of Aborigines, who were somehow slaughtered while in the midst of their dreamtime journey. The authorities don't know it, but these men had assembled specifically to combat our delightful new friends. And last week, a Catholic priest, a renowned healer and exorcist, one of our key people in Eastern Europe, was found charred to death in the burnt-out hull of his car along a road in Hungary. The police said it must have been the result of a direct hit by lightning. Our colleagues in

Europe checked; there had been no lightning activity in the area for weeks. Others are simply missing; we don't know what may have happened to them. A Native American medicine man in eastern Canada, a Sufi mystic who lived outside Istanbul, a cell of Dzogchen monks from Bhutan, a famed witch doctor from Mali, a coven of witches in Brazil, and a child from Crete who had extraordinary psychic gifts—all gone."

"Christ, Rhiannon, is there any real reason to have hope?" he said, fighting to stave off his sense of futileness.

"Well, maybe," she answered cautiously. "In our favor, a number of us have made it through these attacks so far. And as depleted as it may leave us, we've tended to come back more empowered and informed for future encounters. Plus, more of us are working together in a kind of network, lending support where we can. Last night many others sent their spirit allies to join us. And with their help, we made it through, did we not?"

Carson was only too aware of last night's arrival of the giant bear and many other spirits.

"I'm sorry that this is how you came to learn about being a medicine worker, Carson. But there's no going back for any of us. Maybe we'll survive this and go back to something like a normal life one day. But for now, we must do as we must. Resolve yourself to that, and it may go easier."

"Well, I don't seem to have a choice, do I? I guess I've never had one since that night on the Lakota Reservation. And you know what's even weirder? I still have no idea as to why me. Why am I here in this thing?"

"I'm sorry. I don't have an answer for you. I know it must be frustrating. Perhaps you were a powerful medicine worker in other lifetimes and were taking a break from it in this life. You weren't intending to do this type of work in this lifetime, but due to these dire circumstances, you had to be pressed into service."

The concept of a past-life relationship spurred myriad thoughts and possibilities in his mind. Whether there was any validity to it, it made him feel more at ease as to how he had been so radically captured by the medicine's power. He turned to her, gesturing acceptance with his body language.

"Maybe I was a medicine worker in some other life. Who knows, really? There's not much to cling to, is there? I mean, it's all quite maddening. The deeper I go into this stuff, the more I question my sanity."

"Listen, if it makes you feel any better, you aren't the only one who's been pulled in. There are others who were living some form of a normal life and somehow got conscripted into this. Not all of them responded as fully as you have, while many others have become totally committed. And I don't know if you've even stopped to consider this, but most of us who have been involved for years in this spirit work were happily occupied in other ways, never imagining that one day we would be drafted into the battle royale against an invasion of alien energy. Most of my time was spent working with a clientele concerned about such things as personal health, career moves, lost pets, love affairs, dead relatives, and whether or not their little precious souls were on the fast track to enlightenment.

"Then one day it all changed," she continued, her voice becoming charged with emotion, clearing her throat as she strove not to weep. "I recall the day well. I was in my garden that afternoon, happily preoccupied with my plants, when a premonition started to unfold. Naturally, I didn't want to believe it. I resisted it, perhaps in the way you did the calling of the medicine. I tried to force it from my mind, but it wouldn't go away. The visions that were coming across held and, if anything, grew stronger. Ultimately, I had to acknowledge that whatever it was, I must face it. It wasn't long before it became a shared topic among my colleagues, as they too were picking up similar information. Fortunately, some of the elders from our field, like Wounded Paw, had foreseen this. Thankfully, they had already begun to align their work to give us a foundation.

"That was almost four years ago. My world changed from that point on. Much of what had been my previous life fell away—clients, friends, lovers and even the process of normal human existence faded into the past. Occasionally, some aspect of all that shows up, but it can never stay long. There's simply not a place for it. And yes, I miss it."

Carson felt ashamed of his self-pity. Rhiannon had allowed him a glimpse of her humanity, one that resonated with courage and self-sacrifice.

"Let's go inside," she said, breaking their silence. "I'm ready for that bubble bath."

Chapter 11

Confession

The rustling of leaves against the windowpanes melded with the hissing of the wood-burning stove. Carson and Rhiannon sat in the living room, occupied in thought as evening faded.

"Do you need to meditate longer, or may I speak?" he asked.

"Of course you may," Rhiannon said, smiling. "I wasn't meditating, just thinking about certain people. What's on your mind?"

"I would think that would be obvious."

"I meant specifically," she said.

"Well, if those mothers are coming back, what are we supposed to do next time? How are we going to stand up to them if they'll be even more powerful? And when might this occur?"

"It won't happen tonight; I can sense they aren't coming. So you can relax that much. But I want you to stay here through tomorrow night, all the same. Tonight we'll send help to colleagues in the way they did for us last night. Somewhere, others will be assaulted. Understand?"

"How do you know where and when this is going to happen?"

"I don't know exactly where yet, but I can feel the Visitors' forces building. They'll go after some of our brothers and sisters somewhere. It's going to happen tomorrow night, that I can say confidently."

"And can we send help to those people?" he asked.

"Sure, I'll show you how."

"And what about us?" he implored, his anxiety rising. "I mean, you know, next time they come back."

"That's part of what we'll attend to tomorrow night. Last night, your Native American allies saved you, in large part, bringing their power to tilt the scales. The Visitors have no doubt noted that. Next time, they'll attempt to overcome that type of shielding. Native American spirits are generally adequate for Indians, but you're not one, so it's not going to be appropriate for you. Despite how you may feel about your initial training with Wounded Paw, you're really not grounded in Native American spirits. I can see that; Wounded Paw knew it; the medicine knows it. You'll need to come up with something else in your spiritual arsenal, something that really matches your soul's resonance."

Rhiannon added another stick of wood to the stove, pausing to observe the smoldering embers. Carson wondered if she were reading them, perhaps channeling some message from the glowing patterns.

"Go on," he said. "I know you're trying to tell me something specific and you suspect I don't get it. So, tell me more."

"Very well," she said, clearing her throat. "You've been gaining strength and skill; think back to when you first started with Wounded Paw. Compare that to what you've become now. Last night, when my shielding began shattering, you stepped in and directly confronted the Visitors, projecting your emotions of fear and rage at them, cursing them. That was a form of initiation under fire; you crossed a threshold last night. You actually commanded reified energy for the first time!"

"Explain further," he said. "What reified energy?"

"Your allies, the bear, all those spirits that came to assist you last night. Those are the reified energies, sentient energies or spirits, if you like. You called for their presence, you implored them to be there and they responded."

He had not thought about last night in that way. A kernel of hope grew within him. Carson pondered if he could've truly gained such abilities?

Rhiannon smiled. "I think this deserves a toast. I'm going to open a bottle of wine, and we're going to drink to your accomplishment, my friend."

She got up and went to the kitchen, leaving Carson time to digest what she had said. In a few moments, she returned with two glasses of dark red wine and handed one to him.

"I've had this reserve bottle of zinfandel that one of my old clients gave me. I was saving it for a special occasion and nearly forgotten it. So, here's to you, Carson. May your skills and powers continue to grow. And may we have other special occasions."

"Thank you kindly," he responded. "But I owe it all to you and Wounded Paw, especially your patience with me."

"Part of my job, I suppose," Rhiannon said, raising her glass to him.

He drank the rich juice, savoring its subtle texture and complex flavors while reflecting on the meaning of his accomplishment.

"Thank you for this honoring," he stated, tilting his glass toward hers. "And hell yes, may there be other special occasions."

"Well, I figured you'd prefer wine to one of the usual tribal initiations that is called for upon such a rite of passage." She paused, repressing her laughter. "You know, penile mutilation."

"Oh, let's just stay with the wine, by all means." He giggled, downing another swallow.

For a short time, they laughed together, enjoying the moment before the inevitable return of their grim charge.

"But you, I mean, my God, Rhiannon," he said. "You were amazing. I might have done something, but it was nothing compared to that incredible display you put forth against those bastards. Do you have any idea what you looked like during those moments? You weren't real!"

"I only know what I felt," she said, looking into her wineglass. "I don't have much awareness of my body other than that it's becoming a conduit for the energies that surge through."

"You spoke in languages I've never heard. I finally accepted that I don't actually need to understand the words you chant. It's the same with the Indians. If I can just open to the feeling of the words, I can somehow get the meaning."

He took another slow sip of wine then continued. "And then, there at the end, you said that beautiful prayer. Do you remember that?"

"I'm not sure, Carson. I remember the feeling of the overall experience, but too much was demanded to recall many of the details. Last night, I put everything I had out there. If I had perished then and there, at least I would have gone out in the bliss of having my soul fully activated at the moment of death. I do hope those people who have been lost have had that much."

"I'm not sure I'm ready to be that generous with my life."

"That's fine, too," she said. "Let's hope it won't come to that."

"What exactly happened last night when you went unconscious?" he asked.

"I'm not sure unconscious is an accurate way to describe it," she began. "I left my body; there was simply too much energy coursing through me to continue to stand there and maintain the physical requirements of being human. I had to shift into another state of being, one outside my body that called for a merging with the dakini goddesses; you know, the female warrior spirits. So, I went out of my body."

He glanced over at her altar, now more mindful of the powers represented by her numerous images from Southeast Asia.

"I'm a little confused. What would have happened if I hadn't been there?" he asked, feeling a bit less heroic than he had moments before. "How would you have been saved? I figured I was the last man standing, or something, saving both of us."

"Well, it might not have come to my needing to be saved. Meaning, I didn't have to work harder to save myself because you stepped in to take over the shielding. So yes, in a sense, you did save me because I didn't have to. However, when I left my body, I merged with the goddess Durga; remember reading about her?

She's the Hindu warrior goddess who destroyed all those monsters and the buffalo demon. Durga is the quintessential Amazon and not one to remain behind defensive walls during a fight. So you see, I went on the offensive in her form, taking the battle to them."

"I'm missing something here," he interjected. "This is very confusing."

"What you may be missing is that with my transforming into Durga, I was no longer providing the shielding, the defensive energy protecting this cottage. Consequently, you were in a very critical position. Fortunately, you met the challenge; you confronted the Visitors with all the might you could muster. Your efforts also allowed those beings who were trying to assist us to finally break through the barrier that the Visitors had put up to isolate us. In an old-fashioned sense, you were rather heroic."

"But bottom line, I didn't really do as much as I thought," he said. "It was you and my allies who fought them off. Jesus, what a dumb fuck I am. And here I was, figuring I saved you or something."

"You're here, alive and kicking. I should say that's an extraordinary achievement unto itself. I didn't save you, and your allies were having serious difficulty breaking through to help. Time was of the essence and if you hadn't raised your power level to match the Visitors' attack at that critical moment, well, I might not be talking with you now, at least not as a living person."

Carson sat pensive, mulling over his actions during last night's assault, questioning whether she was praising or patronizing him.

"Well, that brings us right back to what I was asking about before. What about next time they attack? I may have gained more power and skill, but it sounds like that won't be enough."

"No, no it won't," she said solemnly. "And that brings us to one of the reasons Wounded Paw wanted me to teach you more than his ways. As I've said, those work well for Native

Americans, but you're not an Indian. Some white people can achieve the real essence of their practices, but not most, really, and in this case, not you. It served you well as an initial training, the beginning of your journey on the sacred medicine road. And as you'll perhaps one day reflect, that training served as the foundation for your path. I don't know if you realize what an extraordinary resource you tapped into through Wounded Paw; the power and the knowledge he holds is always there for you, no matter where the medicine road takes you."

She walked to the window, holding her wineglass up to the light, studying the color of the wine.

She turned around. "Unfortunately, our Western culture retains only remnants of its ancient religions and shamanic ways. It took fifteen hundred years of brutal suppression, but the Church succeeded in pretty much wiping it out. Consequently, in our time, we've had to beg, borrow and steal from the rest of the world, while digging back into our own tragic history to recover whatever we can."

While she spoke, Carson's anxiety deepened, questioning how he could cobble together enough knowledge and power before the next onslaught of the Visitors?

"So, as ridiculous as my hodgepodge collection of deities must seem to you, they have opened a connection to many spirit energies for me. Being capable of working with them turns out to be one of my birthrights, it seems. In return for honoring them, they've given me many blessings in the form of teachings and skills. It's from the sum of these that I draw for my work. It's the fountainhead from where my power comes.

"Wounded Paw, in his wise seeing, knew that your path lay outside his tradition. He probably knew this when you first started with him. That's why, in time, you were sent to me, to expose you to some of what I know and to help you find your own source of power. And that's the strategy you must pursue. You have to extend yourself to find that power, wherever it may be, going to where you must, learning from whoever can help you obtain it."

"Wait a minute, I don't think I follow where this is going. Does this mean you're getting ready to boot me off to someone else like he did?"

"Not exactly," she said. "I'll always be here to help you where I can. Yet if time permits, I'd surely suspect that others will come your way as helpers, teachers and friends. But the immediate issue isn't about your finding other humans to work with, but rather finding your own power source, so that you're capable of working at an intense level on your own."

Carson was bewildered. What Rhiannon was describing sounded lonely, possibly worse than living in fear. He felt desolate at the thought of having to leave her.

"Hey, don't look so forlorn," she said, interrupting his thoughts. "When you're empowered to work on your own, you'll be very pleased by the fact. You'll see."

"And just how do I find this power source? And how will I know it when it happens? How do I keep it? And after last night's attack, is this going to happen soon enough, for Christ's sake?" he asked, slamming a fist into his other hand.

"Slow down, I'll help you with all that. I'm not through with you yet."

"You're sending me away somewhere, aren't you?" he said with a tone of embitterment. "I can feel it."

"Well, goddamn, Carson, that's a stupendous insight." She laughed. "You have started to come into some gifts after all. Yes, you're right. I'm going to send you somewhere, but it's not to a physical place. I've gotten indications of a region that you're supposed to explore for this purpose."

"And when's this going to happen?" he asked coldly.

"It's part of the intentioned work I've planned for tomorrow night. After we extend our aid to our colleagues, I'll direct you to a place. Don't worry."

"Rhiannon, I need to say something about us." He hesitated, his heart beginning to race.

"It's all right, Carson," she said quietly. "I know already."

Rhiannon rose abruptly. "I'm going into the kitchen to fix us dinner. Come with me and pour us some more wine. Maybe we can enjoy the rest of the night together the way normal people do."

Surrendering fully to their exhaustion, they slept in on Sunday. After a late breakfast of homemade crepes, they went for a long walk along a trail that wound across the grassy mesa above town. Conversation was sparse, Carson pondering the future's plausibility. The sun's warmth contrasted with the cool air of winter. This reprieve from their intense work served as a reminder of the preciousness of the world. It was good to be alive.

Upon returning to the cottage, Carson suddenly had the impulse to drive the two miles into Bolinas or even the extra five minutes over to Stinson Beach. He felt the need to get a newspaper, see other people, walk into a bar and hear the sound of a television, watch dogs chase balls on the beach — anything to reconnect temporarily with the regular world for a while. He justified his idea by believing he would return for the night's session more grounded, refreshed.

"Say, Rhiannon, I need to pick something up in town. Won't be gone an hour. Want me to get anything for you? You know you're welcome to come if you like."

"I do have something I'd like you to pick up. It's called a book and it's on that shelf, just under the living room window. We have a little homework to attend to before you can go out and play with your friends."

"Hey, do we really need to do that right now?"

"No, *we* don't, but you do."

"I thought we were through with homework for the weekend."

"Carson, get real, you'll never be through with learning. Now, if you're a good boy, I may let you go home tomorrow." She laughed.

Carson resigned himself. "So, what's it that I'm supposed to be looking up, anyway?"

"Just information about the place where your astrocartography says your power source is located," she replied casually.

"My what?"

"The place your astrological chart says you're most likely to access high levels of power. I looked it up for you using your natal chart. You need to read about this region, so that your subconscious will be primed to go there in our session tonight. The book is a way to get oriented. It'll help with tonight's journey."

"And just where is my astro, whatever the fuck you call it? Let me guess—New Jersey?"

"It's astrocartography. I'll show you the computer printout. It's a map of the world, showing the paths of the planets over Earth at the time of your birth. You use it to trace places where your planets intersect. You'll see. And your power spot is not in New Jersey, no. It's in the Himalayas!"

Simply hearing her speak the name of the famed mountain range sent a jolt through him. He had never been there and had no plans to do so. Yet something about it had always drawn him, and not in a particularly comfortable way. Sometimes in his sessions, he had experienced visions set in what seemed to be the Himalayas. He had dismissed these as merely reflections of possible past lives and had preferred not to examine their meaning. Certainly there was something about the region that resonated with him, but the very thought of it troubled him.

He pulled the large coffee-table book Rhiannon described from the shelf and sat down among the floor pillows. The book was a photo-essay with exquisite glossy prints. It transported the viewer to breathtaking vistas of natural wonder, hidden within the mysterious veils of the Orient. The pages displayed an array of ethnicities striving to eke out a living in these faraway regions.

Carson turned the pages slowly, occasionally returning to particular photos and reading their captions more thoroughly. The images promised would-be travelers exotic adventures, amidst a culture that maintained a daily relationship with gods and nature spirits.

How was he supposed to find his power source from a book about a place to which he had never been? This was even less his world than that of Wounded Paw. At least he and the Native Americans shared a common language and lived in the same country. Despite Rhiannon's suggestion, his intuition told him that this was a place better left alone.

She came over and sat beside him, looking on as he explored the pages. Occasionally she inserted commentary about various tribal groups, along with anecdotes about some of the places she herself had been. But she mostly sat quietly, allowing him to soak in the book's contents at his own pace. When at last he closed the book, Rhiannon handed him a sheet of paper—a computer printout of his astrocartography. Placing it on the coffee table, he studied the ribbons of lines that indicated his preordained locus of power.

"See there, where those four lines intersect? That's the place," she said. "If it were safe, meaning no Visitors, I'd insist that you go there in person, but conditions don't allow for that."

Carson's gaze remained locked on the paper. The paths of planetary bodies were traced across a world map, in orbiting patterns similar to those of man-made satellites. Some lines ran in loosely parallel configurations, while others occasionally inter-sected at certain locations. To his uninformed eye, most of the cartography was meaningless. The glaring exception, however, was a spot over the eastern Himalayas where four lines inter-sected.

"Those lines represent a rare configuration," she began. "When planets form certain transits, specific potentialities manifest. What you have there is the meeting of four very significant forces that create great potential for you, auspicious ones for the nature of our work. When one is in a part of the world where these conditions occur, the potential to manifest the qualities of these planets becomes highly amplified. I've explained all of this to you before. Don't just sit here looking blank. You know what I'm talking about."

Carson tried to recall her astrology lectures. They had been just another requirement in her endless curriculum. He had given them little attention.

"Look at what you have in this location," she continued, pointing to the intersection of the four lines. "It's your Jupiter, Uranus, Neptune, and Pluto all meeting. Hello!"

He stared at the map with embarrassment at his lack of understanding, as if he were looking at something that would be obvious to everyone but himself.

"Well, I suppose this explains my occasional longing for yak burgers."

"Very funny. Now be serious."

"Okay," he began. "How am I supposed to go about this thing? If I can't travel to the place, how do I establish a relationship with the energy that this piece of paper says is there for me?"

"You project there. You send yourself there in your sessions, in your dreams, in your studies, in your conscious thoughts. You absorb the place—and more importantly, you allow it to absorb you."

"Now, wait a minute. That part I can sort of get. But what's the difference between doing that and working through something like Native American spirits? I mean, if it won't work for me to connect to a traditional culture in my own country, why the hell would it work in some place on the other side of the world that I've never been to? I'm not Asian. I would think you might've noticed that by now."

"I'm not suggesting that you go native, for Christ's sake. Astrocartography doesn't mean you're supposed to convert to another culture. While you may very well relate to that culture, discover a strong affinity for it, it doesn't mean you're to try to imitate people from that location. What if there were no people there? Say these lines crossed over Antarctica or the middle of the ocean? The energy is still located there, whether or not humans are there. In fact, you can readily become distracted from the energy's essence by getting bogged down in the human culture of the region. The point is to gain benefits from exploring whatever emerges for you there, be it the culture, the land, or just a sense of power."

"Then I don't see why you had me look through this book."

"Because it infuses you with imagery. It's a tool to help you make the connection. It's simply a device to help get you there. Use those images as temporary road maps, that's all. And don't get swallowed up by that 'mystic of the Orient' stuff. This process will be more akin to a prospecting mission. Go for the essence, not the trappings."

After a late lunch, they ventured out to clean away the debris left by the storm. The freshly dug holes had drained, leaving only a couple of inches of muddy water in the bottom. Going to each hole, Rhiannon purified the scarred pits with fragments of animal bones, seashells, sprigs of cedar and sand that she had gathered from the base of the Egyptian pyramids. When they were done, Carson was directed to shovel earth back into the holes while she whispered mantras.

Next, she instructed him to get a ladder from her garden shed and sent him up on the roof to remove the fallen tree limbs. She remained on the ground and chanted while he labored to drag the branches to the roof's edge and pitch them off. Finally, only the large eucalyptus bough, whose presence defied logic, remained. Carson was hesitant to disturb it. For a prolonged moment, he just stood looking at it, posturing as if he needed to catch his breath. Rhiannon looked on, waiting for him to free the roof of the last vestige of the storm.

"Is something wrong?" she asked.

"I'm not sure. Want to make sure I can move it safely without tearing up your roof."

"Oh, I didn't think about that. If it's too large for one person, I could come up and help. Or I could wait until later in the week and have my neighbor and his sons come over."

"Well, let me give it a try."

Carson approached the heavy bough, slowly taking hold of it. He pulled with all his might but made no appreciable progress. He stood up to relieve the strain on his lower back.

"Hey, let me try something from here," she called. "Now, give it another go if you can."

She began singing. He faced the heavy obstacle again, leaning his weight back as he lifted. Rhiannon shouted out something and clapped her hands loudly three times. The heavy branch suddenly surged at him, landing on top of him as he fell backwards. It continued moving under its own momentum, rolling over his body as he clung to the roof. The bough tumbled on, all the way to the roof's edge, and then crashed to the ground. Pulling himself up, Carson looked down at Rhiannon. She was laughing hard. He was just thankful to have the task completed.

"Well, that seems to have worked quite nicely," she said.

"Next time, get the neighbors."

"Bravo for you. Come on down. I'll let you have the rest of the day off."

"That's very fucking generous of you."

"Now, now, a little exercise is a good thing to restore the mind's clarity. Besides, you didn't really hurt yourself, did you?"

"Frankly, I don't know yet. But thankfully, there're no broken bones or bleeding as far as I can tell. But that was no small piece of timber to have roll over me."

"Sounds like I may have to give you a thorough medical examination," she teased. "Wouldn't want you suffering."

Carson climbed down the ladder slowly, feeling some tenderness in one knee. They retired to the house and Rhiannon put on water to make tea.

"So, what was that little ditty you were singing that caused the bough to move?"

"Oh, it's a Romanian folk song I learned years ago, while traveling there. Out in the fields, the women would sing it while the men were lifting heavy bales of hay up onto their wagons. I never thought of using it for any practical purpose until this afternoon. Seems to work."

"Next time, you pull and I'll sing."

"Oh, poor baby," she teased, patting him on the back. "After some tea you should take a nice bath and then just rest up for tonight."

Carson got up, marched into the bathroom, and began filling the tub. He threw his clothes out the door.

"Would you mind sticking those in your washer?" he yelled out. "And if it's not too much to ask, could you bring my tea in here?"

He climbed into the hot water, generously adding an assortment of bath soaps and creating clouds of thick bubbles. Looking up at the skylight, he could see the sky was darkening with the approach of evening and another weather front.

A few minutes later, Rhiannon appeared, carrying a small tray with two cups of tea. She placed them on a shelf and lit several candles before settling on a small stool alongside the tub.

"Plan to stay for a while?" he asked.

"Well, I believe I owe you," she said mysteriously.

"Oh, and just what does that mean?"

"I'm going to shampoo your hair."

Rhiannon reached over and selected some items from a nearby shelf. She began gently cupping water over his head, then sensuously massaging shampoo through his scalp. He closed his eyes, surrendering to the pleasures of her touch. She repeated the process several times and then rinsed his head with clean water. As he was about to thank her, she placed her hands on the back of his neck and tilted his body forward. He yielded to her silent directive. Without a word, she began scrubbing, working from his shoulders down to the small of his back. The motion of water was the only sound in the room. When finished, Rhiannon gently pulled him back to a reclining position. She rose, leaving a plush bathrobe for him on the stool.

When he came out to the living room, preparation for the night's agenda was underway. Rhiannon sat before her altar in a meditation pose, with the candles already burning. His brief indulgence in sensual pleasure was obviously over.

He quietly went about putting on sweatpants and a sweat-shirt in preparation for the forthcoming journey, trying to focus on the impending session, but his thoughts seemed captured by the delicious experience of the bath. His libido churned with need. He stood by a window for some time, vacuously watching the soft, misty rain cover the windowpanes in a wet fog, pondering what he would do about his feelings.

"Come over here, Carson. We've much to do and need to get started."

Her calling jarred him back. He was glad she was finished with the meditation; he needed to speak with her. Walking into the living room, he sat down on the mat next to her.

"Rhiannon, before we get started, I think we need to talk."

"I know, I shouldn't have bathed you," she said quickly. "That was stupid of me, allowing myself to be human for a moment." She paused, selecting her words with caution. "It wouldn't be right; it would make us both too vulnerable, too distracted. This just isn't the time."

He realized there would be little chance of persuading her otherwise. Despite the anguish of wanting her, he knew she was right. If their relationship were to boil over into a romance, sexual pleasures and emotional bonding would subsume their attention and focus.

"Well, this sure ain't easy," he muttered, shaking his head. "I'm sorry that I haven't been able to do a better job of keeping my heart in line, but it seems I've gone and fallen in love with you."

"It might be mutual," she whispered without making eye contact.

Carson felt his heart leap. "Well, if we're gonna get killed by doing this stuff anyway, I would sure hate to die without, you know, us having—"

She looked at him with a warm smile. "Listen, it's not that one is forbidden to have a relationship during such times, it's that you and I shouldn't! Getting involved in that way, with all its intimacy, would seriously affect our capabilities. Not to mention that it would make us easier targets than we already are. It's not that we must remain pure and chaste because we're on a holy mission or something. I, for one, think chastity is way overrated." She laughed. "If we weren't dealing with this work, it would be quite different. But then, if we weren't caught up in this situation, we probably would never have met. Another irony, I'm afraid."

"I wish you weren't always right. It's damned annoying."

"I shouldn't say this, but I'd love to give in and take you to bed. We can't though. Not yet, anyhow. You have some very serious work ahead. Much is still required, and it may mean your going away from me. Don't get pulled in by me, really. Developing strong attachments is a by-product of undertaking medicine journeys together. One comes to know the other's soul in very profound ways. And I, too, need to maintain a certain distance. We both have plateaus to reach and we won't get there if we become lovers."

"And what would happen if we reached those plateaus? Where would that put us?" he asked, reaching over to hold her hand.

"Let's try to focus on what's needed now," she said evasively.

"But just for the sake of argument, say things looked pretty good for our side?" he pressed.

"Then I'd have to stock up on certain vitamins for you." She laughed. "I've some catching up to do."

"I don't know if I feel better or worse hearing that."

"Well, maybe knowing this will now inspire you to work harder."

"If I can concentrate!"

"We mustn't feel sorry for ourselves," she teased, giving his hand a squeeze.

"Do you have any idea how badly I want to kiss you?"

"Yes! Yes, I think I do," she said. "But let's not go there. Confession has its place, but I can feel this conversation starting to slide into runaway seduction. That'll only make it harder—and please, no jokes about it being plenty hard already. Come on, Carson; try to keep things within the necessary boundaries. Be fair. I sense your feelings; I understand your frustration. Believe me, I have needs too, but we must maintain our relationship as it is. Help me with this, won't you?"

Carson sighed in resignation. In truth, it was his growing love for her that rallied him to her position.

"Funny," he said. "I can't help but notice how many times I never really have a choice about anything. Whatever comes up, I keep having to go along with something other than what I want. I know it sounds like me carping again, but it's really most unusual."

"Perhaps that'll start to change when you locate your source of power."

"Oh, you diverted me skillfully with that line. Time to go to work, is it?"

"Yup, we need to get back to matters at hand."

"Very well, into the fray," he said.

The confession over, they turned their attention to the night's work. Rhiannon prepared the medicine, while Carson loaded the iPod with the music she had selected for the journey. They secured the doors and windows, stoked the stove fire, turned off the lights, said prayers for guidance and protection and took the sacramental medicine—a deep purple brew that she had specially made for this night. Its taste was initially sweet, with honey masking the pungent flavor of its potent ingredients.

Sitting on the mats, waiting for the hallucinogenic effects to begin, Rhiannon instructed him again as to the intentions of his journey, suggesting that he might imagine transforming himself into a great bird. This bird would fly high above the world, eventually landing amid those great mountains he had viewed in the book. To accomplish this, she guided him through a short meditation, suggesting images and thoughts he could use to transport himself to the Himalayas. Then, she gently guided his consciousness back to the confines of her cottage, grounding him in the place from where he must begin.

She took his hand in hers and began the ritual for sending protection to their comrades.

"While I was in meditation, I saw the person in need tonight. The vision was quite lucid," she said. "It's a Yoruba priestess, somewhere in a Louisiana bayou. This person and a group of her followers are in a small house, gathered in a circle, raising spirit energy, calling upon their ancestors and guarding spirits of their West African religion. There's a narrow river that runs beside the house, with a weathered shrimp boat moored across the river. The manifestation of a large Visitor is hovering over the boat's deck, directing its power against those inside the house. Sometime tonight, it will unleash its attack."

"Jesus, you were able to see that?" he mumbled, his mind starting to fall under the influence of the medicine.

"The more exposure you have to the Visitors, the more ability you gain to see what they are doing," she answered. "Now listen, we need to send help to this gathering. Ask your allies to go on this mission, bringing their powers and protection to these people. Envision your strength swirling into a bundle with that of your allies and form a column of energy. Make it intensify. Then send it out to those people."

He directed his mind to assemble his allies, building the swirling column of power she suggested. When he sensed his energy had peaked, he commanded it to go to those tucked away on the edge of the bayou on a night that would test their capacities beyond measure.

"May they be strong and safe," he whispered.

Sending her energy out to the Louisiana group, Rhiannon muttered a prayer under her breath.

"Carson, we've done all we can for those people. Their fate is in the hands of the medicine now. We need to focus back on our own journey, which will begin intensely at any moment. May you find what you seek."

She lay back on the mat, leaving Carson to his own journey.

The familiar sensations arose throughout his body. Departure was only minutes away. Again, he stood poised on the threshold of unimaginable realities. He eased down on the mat, pulling a blanket over himself and closing his eyes.

Chapter 12

Contact

The journey swept over Carson, his mind spiraling through myriad geometric patterns that swirled in kaleidoscopic display—a continuous visual of colors afire with super-electric hues and shifting forms. A constant parade of demigods and otherworldly beings floated through his consciousness; many resembling hybrid crossbreeds of animals and humans. Others appeared more representative of insect or reptile gods. This entire host proclaimed the same message; they were the gatekeepers of high, hidden realms, where one might find the codes that control the universe.

Emerging from this entry phase, he followed Rhiannon's suggestion to imagine becoming a great bird, allowing the experience to spirit his mind all the way to Asia. Soon he found his consciousness gliding at a great height, feeling the wind flow over his glistening feathers. Far below, he viewed the ocean's expanse, observing the thin curving line that separated it from the sky along the edges of Earth's curvature.

But the magnitude of the vision was overwhelming; he lost focus of his Himalayan destination. Instead he found himself wandering through what appeared as a mythical medieval city on the Asian continent. The streets were not much more than alleys, the houses modest and crumbling. The smoke of charcoal filled the air, combining with the stench of rotting garbage and dung. The inhabitants were thin and poorly dressed, their faces sullen. Everywhere he looked, people were suffering from sickness, poverty, and social exploitation. An old woman with a child reached toward him for help while others, apparently too weak or weary, stared at him with blank faces. A group of soldiers in silk uniforms, sporting turbans and armed with curved swords, dragged a man from a house, striking a pleading woman to the ground in the scuffle.

Instinctively, Carson realized that something evil held this realm locked in its grip. Suddenly compelled to look up, he spotted the source of the malaise. There, floating high above, was a macabre presence—a monkey riding a bicycle, suspended in midair. He studied the morbid scene intently, the medicine informing him further as to the nature of the monkey god. He grasped that this deity reigned over all below, sucking up the energy emitted from the suffering.

The sky, an ominous blood orange, was streaked with wisps of dark purple clouds. The monkey peered out at nothing, making no eye contact with anything in its domain—a blind parasite. Skeletal wings jutted from the monkey's back. The oppressive demigod held a parasol over its head, its only purpose to serve as self-adornment.

The monkey god slowly pedaled, as if in a trance, occasionally turning casually to go in the opposite direction. Yet it never really went anywhere, only circled endlessly over the tormented world upon which it fed.

Suddenly a gregarious guide appeared alongside Carson. This being was short and stout, a dwarf-like figure with a humped back and badly pocked skin. He jovially explained telepathically that not all experiences were like this place, that many kinds of domains existed; most were not of this nature, but on the contrary, were rich with pleasure and joy.

"Isn't this one glorious, though?" the guide said exuberantly. "I mean, if you want to experience suffering, you can't do much better than this place!"

"But why have this?" Carson asked. "Why would you want to maintain a place like this?"

"Why? Because, my dear fellow, it simply is," the guide said, shrugging his shoulders as if the question were superfluous.

"Where does all this misery come from?"

"Oh, I was hoping you would ask that one. I always love showing guests the machine."

Leaving the grim scenes of the maze of narrow streets, the guide led him down into a dungeon complex, passing people awaiting the most hideous forms of torture and execution: drawing and quartering, disemboweling, burning, and impaling. They moved on, arriving at a small chamber. There, mounted on a simple wooden table, was a dynamo-like mechanism, spinning away.

"Isn't that a beaut!" the guide exclaimed.

"What exactly does that do?" Carson asked.

"This wondrous apparatus, my dear fellow, generates the energy required for sustaining the misery unleashed on all life."

Carson was mesmerized by its spinning action.

"It's pure energy," the guide went on. "No soul, consciousness, spirit, or god owns it. It merely cranks out the power. By whom and how that power is used is not its concern."

Carson's mind suddenly began whirling, only to be pulled into the very core of the machine's vortex, sucked through a wormhole. Through this tunnel, he was carried across an immeasurable distance and spewed out the end of a giant phallus. He had barely begun to ponder where he had arrived when he was again carried off, this time up through a tissuey cavern. A growing feeling of insanity tore at his mind.

Then the entire episode dissolved in a silent explosion of golden light, accompanied by melodic laughter. Before him radiated a great and exquisite goddess of unspeakable power and beauty. He fumbled to acknowledge her with signs of homage, bowing his head and folding his hands in a sign of adulation, but he was too staggered by her breathtaking radiance to be effective.

"Why, you ask, my son?" the goddess spoke with unquestionable authority. "What you've just witnessed was but one ten-millionth of a hundred thousand worlds that I bring in and out of existence a trillion times a second. Why? Because it pleases me to do so, to create and destroy. Besides, you children would not like it if I became bored. Now, go. You've been in my presence long enough. You'll never know the vastness of my love for you. You call me Mother!"

Carson found himself back on the mat. He was sobbing heavily, overwhelmed by the contact with the goddess, by the awe and majesty of the encounter.

"Carson, Carson?" Rhiannon called. "Hey, can you hear me? It's all right."

She held him tenderly, allowing him to weep unabated. When at last his emotions were stable, she spoke gently.

"I believe you went somewhere off your map. Did you lose your focus for a while?" she asked. "I think you may have wandered into my journey's field. I felt your soul in my presence. I suspect I may have pulled you over to where I was traveling. What happened?"

Carson tried as best he could to explain the sequence of experiences, but when he got to the part about the goddess, he again broke down.

"She was so, so beautiful, and in a way that was both terrifying and yet completely nurturing."

"Her name is Kali," Rhiannon said. "Luckily you met her when she was in a mood to tolerate the uninitiated. Later, you'll have to do some puja to her for showing up like that. And yes, she's all you say and plenty more—believe me. But now you need to get back to where you're supposed to be journeying. Keep your intention before you. Don't get distracted again. And don't make me come rescue you. I've got my own work to process."

Carson lay quietly alongside Rhiannon, psychically singed by the encounter with the aulic goddess. Gradually, he brought himself back to focusing on his original quest. Images from the Himalayan photo book floated through his thoughts, teasing his mind to a place of remote villages with wind-torn prayer flags, raging rivers, and glacier-topped granite walls that soared into the stratosphere.

This time his journey carried him through a vast mountain terrain with towering peaks. The cry of distant birds rose on the wind, merging with the sound of rushing streams from somewhere far below. Vegetation was limited to sparse patches of lichen and occasional thistles, strewn among banks of snow and rocky outcroppings. This was a landscape of pristine beauty, but it conveyed foreboding, withholding the necessities for survival. A land of extremes, it was not meant for humans. It was a place only for gods.

Finding no connection with his sought-after power source in this harsh and mountainous environ, he shifted his focus. His eye was suddenly drawn to a dark opening in a rock wall. Unavoidably, he was pulled to the cave's entrance. Something bade him enter.

He found himself wandering down into the bowels of the mountain. There was no light in the normal sense, yet the medicine empowered him to see. He moved deeper into the vast cavern, passing piles of ancient relics. Some were Buddhist religious artifacts: sutra scrolls, bells, statues, and prayer wheels. Other piles contained assortments of weaponry: spears, swords, arrows, shields, armor, bows, flags and antique guns. Mounds of bones, both human and animal, were stacked up everywhere; varieties of skulls lined the corridors like trophies. These bizarre collections might have been a warning, yet he seemed unable to retreat.

Realizing he had entered a domain in which he was completely out of his league, he prayed for protection.

As if locked in a bad dream, he proceeded, wandering deeper into the cavernous world. The relics became more baffling. The medicine informed him that the stashes of battle standards he was viewing came from the armies of Alexander the Great and

Genghis Khan. He next came upon an enormous collection of huge animal skulls from the Pleistocene Epoch. Other items were easily identified, such as the twisted fuselages of crashed twentieth-century aircraft.

He wandered into a large, cathedral-size chamber. The chamber's periphery was cloaked in darkness. At first, it was oddly reassuring to be there, as if he had got to a final destination and could now start toward home. He studied the enormous interior, hoping to spot an exit.

Carson froze. Every fiber of his being stood on edge. Through primal instinct, he realized that he had stumbled into the presence of a force of immense power. Worse, he was aware that his own thoughts and feelings were being echoed back at him by this force, colliding with the beginnings of each new thought— his mind was being read. He had no place to hide.

The air around him moved with the breath of an unseen being. He was totally exposed, completely at the mercy of an unknown spirit that emitted waves of pure hostility. Immediately, Carson turned to the one practice that had sustained him before at precarious moments in his journeywork; he fell into a state of utter surrender.

But whatever loomed in the dark made no response. Only voluminous, deep breaths emanated from a vast shadow, sending waves of warm, moist air over him, making the hairs on his arms tingle. For a seeming eternity, he waited in silence.

All at once, a great voice boomed, "The thing I resent most about fools is the lack of flavor in their meat. Even their livers leave me disappointed. That much I can credit to the monks; at least their flesh is sweet."

He struggled to redirect his mind, trying to speed his journey to another realm.

"But you are neither a fool or a monk," the voice declared. "No, I know your type well enough."

Carson had no concept as to what type of spirit addressed

him, only recognized that it was of a magnitude of danger far exceeding anything he had ever encountered. In his last months with Wounded Paw, he had been warned profusely about the dangers of encountering certain extreme forms of spirit. With no known escape, he dared to engage the spirit in telepathic dialogue.

"I beg your indulgence, Mighty One; I meant no disrespect by entering your realm without permission. I ask—"

"Silence! Spare me your pathetic prayers and apologies. For the moment, you shall remain unharmed. But know this: had this encounter occurred under traditional circumstances, my retainers would have slaughtered you long before you gained access to my presence. Beware, adept."

"I heed your warning with the deepest gratitude," he stammered humbly. "And I'm far from attaining any status that would be worthy of classifying me as an adept."

"I see your miserable status all too clearly, but your manners have kept you in good stead. Fools who know me not—or worse, lack appropriate respect—swiftly meet horrific fates, while those who know my ways may on occasion be granted blessings."

Struggling to contain his fear, Carson dared ask, "Great One, if I may be permitted, may I have some knowledge of whom I am honored to be addressing?"

"My names are many. It would behoove you not to carry the burden of knowing them without appropriate initiation, adept. But you may know of my type; I come from a class of Great Lords who reign over all the lands of the Himalayas. You humans have known and feared us for millennia. We are the great original gods who sustain all that dwell within our domain." The being paused, lowering its great voice. "And I must say, it is of some curiosity as to how you gained this audience. It is only through this curiosity that your life is presently spared."

"Great Lord," Carson stuttered, his thoughts racing, struggling to communicate appropriately in the telepathic dialogue. "I cannot with any certainty explain how I came to be in your presence. I was journeying, seeking a source of power. Something must have misdirected me into this realm."

"There is little that occurs in these realms that is the result of misdirection. No, you were sent here, but by whom and why is what I ponder. I must smell you," the dark presence communicated, moving closer, its breath blowing hard against Carson's body, amplifying his terror.

Carson remained perfectly still, imagining how it must feel for a wounded animal to lie beneath a predator while having its scent relished by the dominant beast. He still could not see the spirit in a true visual sense; it remained a brooding shadow except for the eyes. They glowed with a fierce and eerie red light that was not of the ordinary world.

Despite the darkness, Carson was keenly aware of a three-dimensional quality to the spirit. In contrast to the diaphanous, ghostly spirits that he had often encountered through his medicine journeys, this entity seemed to be composed of highly dense matter.

"Very well, at least I know you have not been sent by her," the Great Lord mumbled. "And neither are you one of those pathetic vegetarians who served me for centuries. If they only realized how much their scent was similar to creatures I love to devour. Do you know the delicacy of properly butchered rhino? No, I needn't bother to ask."

Carson's mind raced to recall what he had read about the gods of this region. Despite the terror of his situation, he surmised that he might have a clue as to this type of spirit.

"If I correctly understood what you told me, then are you possibly what is known as a wrathful deity?" Carson asked cautiously.

"Yes, your species describes my type with such words. I see you are familiar with the term. And never for a moment discount the treacherous quality of our wrathful nature. Wrathfulness is not a simple matter to comprehend; it has many manifestations, often contradictory ones. It's one of the finer qualities of our class."

Recalling more from his readings, Carson dared to ask another question.

"Then, would that not make you what is also called a Dharmapala?"

"Dharmapala!" the Great Lord boomed in anger. "Bile boils in my heart at the mention of the word. Speak it again without my permission and I will rip your intestines out through your throat."

"My deepest apologies, Great One. In no way did I mean to offend you," Carson blurted telepathically.

"What would you know of that tragedy? You are not of the lineage," the Great Lord said dolefully. "At least you have heard the term, though it sickens me to imagine the meaning you have taken it to signify. Further, it saddens me to sense that you're shocked by my response. Those Buddhists have you all believing we are something that belongs to their faith. Ten thousand hells on the lot of them."

Carson was completely baffled. Not only was he struggling to accept that he was in the presence of a wrathful deity, he had never considered that these spirits might hold dissenting opinions about what was popularly presented through Buddhist teachings. Nevertheless, he was caught in the presence of this treacherous entity and he had no doubt that he was dealing with a bona fide deity.

"Trying to do what you call a 'reality check,' pilgrim?" The spirit gruffly laughed. "If I chew up your spleen before your eyes, would that convince you? You damn well better believe that I am real and pay utmost attention, or you will for sure perish from some clumsy mistake. I believe you must realize the ramifications of being in this arena, adept."

Carson careened into a fuller sense of terror. There had been occasions in other sessions when he had encountered difficulty, but never of this magnitude. He had made a grievous error with his journey and was tottering on the brink of death.

"Oh, come now, adept. You disappoint me." The wrathful deity chuckled. "Don't give in to the terror so easily, although your fear is well founded. Gather yourself. I sense you have enough experience in your work to know that your only option is to walk directly into the eye of the storm. If I choose to consume you, as I do most who enter my presence, you should consider your demise a great honor. There have been many who gladly forfeited their miserable lives for the opportunity to have such a sacred death. And since you have no control over your fate here, you may as well relish the outcome."

The deity laughed again, amused by his power.

"No, for the moment, I am bored and need company. And perhaps it is that you were meant to come here, to receive the blessing of my audience. You see, I know the nature of your work, this struggle you are in with those foreign spirits who intend to colonize our small planet. Yes, I know about them. As you may learn, I am very sensitive to such matters. To grasp what I mean you must hear about some things that occurred long ago. Who knows? This may prove of some use in the time ahead. Listen well, for your chance of survival may be in this teaching."

Carson could only submit and hope to assuage the deity eventually to grant him a safe departure. He focused his mind on engaging with the wrathful deity, knowing he needed to maintain decorum and utmost respect.

"As you wish, Great Lord; I am honored to learn from you. I will attempt with all my human limitations to comprehend your teaching."

Chapter 13

A Teaching

"The past is not as it has been told," the Great Lord began slowly. "Contrary to much of what passes for history, there are other truths by which to interpret the events of time. We, the Lords of the World, were different beings in our early days. It was a simpler time. We considered ourselves omnipotent, yet we lacked what might be called sophistication. Perhaps we were blinded by arrogance. Arrogance is a most dangerous commodity for young gods.

"We were once the reigning gods of all the lands we surveyed, although we paid homage to the greater entities who ruled over the entire planet—the Great Mother and Her court, and the forces who press down upon the planet from the cosmos. Still, we were lords and masters of our dominion. Our home, that mighty wall of stone and ice, was the highest mountain range on the planet. We believed that meant that there could be no greater lords from other mountain lands. And adept, great we were!"

As if Carson were nothing more than cloud vapor, his mind began drifting over the lofty Himalayan peaks, viewing with awe the landscape's forbidding grandeur.

The Great Lord went on. "For millennia, all was as it should be. Then humans began to arrive in our domain. They were a miserable, crude lot. Still, they had a way of knowing. They recognized our presence and made offerings to us, asking to be granted permission to live beneath our peaks. We killed some of them, of course, as is our pleasure, but many others we allowed to exist with our blessings. Survival in these lands has never been easy, regardless of one's form. Life is harsh here. Yet it is through such harshness and extremes that greatness emerges. Extremes always bring forth advancements, just as death does. Even gods eventually die, adept, but this is a good thing, as death produces a more evolved version of ourselves when we are reborn. Complacency and status quo produce little, if any, development."

The Great Lord peered at Carson pointedly. "Yet we, too, had unwittingly become victims of complacency. And consequently, we were vulnerable to the power brought by a new extreme. One cursed day, that extreme entered Tibet."

Shivers ran through Carson's body. He was certain that he should not be privileged to hear such esoteric information. He wished the deity would stop. His heart longed for the sanitized world of myth.

"Great Lord, I fear I may not entirely grasp your story," he stammered.

"Story! Do you imagine that I am babbling about some silly myth, some adventure tale permeated with hidden meaning? Listen, adept; what will be exposed to you in this teaching is how the world *was*.

"Now steady, pilgrim. I see that trying to comprehend in this manner is pushing the limits of your wretched human mind. Perhaps it is better that I use another method, so you may truly comprehend my great words. I will grant you this learning through the experience of direct viewing. Now, my worried scholar, shall we continue?"

"As you wish, Great Lord."

Carson's consciousness was suddenly swept away into an expanded perception. He was transported across the ages, carried back in time. He braced himself as the wrathful deity began altering his cognitive faculties. A warm energy spread throughout his being. An exceptional sense of clarity arose in his mind as his anxiety gradually dissipated.

"Better now?" The deity laughed at him. "You see, you only needed to trust me."

"As you well know, Great Lord, my needs are many in your

presence."

"Let us proceed, adept. There is much ground to cover."

With Carson's consciousness tumbling away in the altered state, he found himself moving through the Tibet of eons ago, to a time the deity called the "classical days." Nearly all the people were living as nomadic herders. Carson could see that despite their ignorance, they knew certain things well enough, especially to heed the gods at every moment and occasion. As he moved about, flying with the vision, he saw that it was a hostile, aggressive land—fostering hostile, aggressive people. Formal education, though flourishing in many adjoining countries, was completely absent. These people were more or less barbarians.

He wandered through a crude mountain hamlet. A tribe of nomads were guiding yaks past humble huts, the animals bellowing into smoke-choked air. Rag-clothed children scurried to hide behind mothers, while the local village men remained at the ready. A long established uneasiness between the villagers and the nomads charged the moment, each side suspicious and fearful of the other.

"These nomads smell worse than their filthy yaks," a village woman whispered to her husband, spitting at the herders as they passed through. "Make sure they don't camp near here. They breed with their animals and produce demons."

"Quickly, boys," a nomad leader called. "Move the herd through this cursed village. These villagers live like vermin, and the place breeds disease. And don't look at their ugly women, as it's said they're all witches."

His mind journeyed on, observing the people in early Tibet. They paid a heavy price to live in such a challenging and remote land, yet they were compensated for this by being able to develop exceptional shamanic skills. While other cultures were busy developing mathematics and philosophy, measuring the stars and learning to navigate oceans, the people in the land of snows continued to advance their ancestors' old magic ways. He saw that it was through their isolation and struggle that their spiritual powers grew to extraordinary levels. It was the key for the Tibetans' existence in this harsh land.

As this vision swirled in Carson's mind, the deity's voice returned. "And so it was for many centuries in our land, a place of wildness, mystery, cruelty and great beauty. I loved it completely," the god said, his great voice seemingly charged with longing and melancholy.

"Great Lord, do you wish to stop with this account?" Carson asked, feeling a curious empathy toward the menacing deity.

"You believe me wounded, don't you, adept?" The deity laughed. "Good perception for a human. It is true; the wound is old and deep. But that is not your concern. There is still more for you to learn."

Carson swooned into yet another state, entering a crude fortification constructed of large stones and heavy timber. He found himself in a big room with weighty silk banners hanging from beams, their golden threads glistening from the light of large torches. The king and his attendants were arguing, preparing to greet a foreigner at the Tibetan court.

"Watch closely, adept. This one's a master of deceit."

"What's happening, Great Lord?" Carson asked.

"Now that you have seen this man, I must take you back further and show you how he got here," the god said.

A sequence of scenes from yet an earlier time began unfolding in Carson's mind. The strange man seemed to float over a rugged mountain pass, his dark eyes burning with determination, making his way into Tibet. A small entourage followed.

"Yes, there he goes," the deity said. "He is rumored to come from India, or perhaps Sri Lanka; his type has been seen here before. He appears to be just another Buddhist missionary, come to waste his efforts on attempting to convert the local inhabitants from their old spiritual practices. Many of his kind have come before, both from China and India. These countries competed to win favor here, hoping to gain a handle on civilizing the fearless barbarians of Tibet. This one, too, should surely fail, just another itinerant monk who could not make it in his own land."

Carson could not take his eyes off the monk, who moved along the ground as though he were gliding. This was no ordinary missionary. Carson sensed that this man was a sorcerer of extraordinary talent, as close to a god as a human could be.

"His name is Padmasambhava," the deity hissed.

Carson found himself suddenly transported to the court of the Tibetan king, now listening to the strange monk as he offered a seemingly impossible proposition.

"Your Excellency," Padmasambhava said. "Allow me to entertain your court with a simple proposition on behalf of Lord Buddha. I will call out these wild mountain gods who hold your land under their capricious power. Yes, I will challenge them to submit to the Buddha, and thereby bring them into line. And you, sire, will thus become a true ruler of this land, no longer susceptible to these rough gods."

Laughter broke out among the king's attendants. These people knew full well that this magician from the south would be dead upon his first confrontation with a wrathful deity.

Amused, the king responded. "And tell me, my ambitious petitioner, what favor would you wish granted if you were able to achieve such a preposterous feat?"

"My reward is quite a simple matter. In exchange for rendering these wild gods under control, Your Excellency will make Buddhism the state religion of your kingdom."

"Very well; if nothing else," the king proclaimed, "this monk's demise will provide another interesting anecdote about the absurdity of such foreigners coming into our land, with their ridiculous notions."

Chuckling erupted in the court. The monk, unaffected by the cynicism, bowed in silence and withdrew. He was off to encounter the local gods.

The Great Lord paused, allowing Carson's mind to fully absorb the vision.

"But as is the case sometimes, the cleverest ones come in the guise of fools," the Great Lord said. "Now in those days, we deities in Tibet held ourselves apart from one another. Each of us gods had his own distinct dominion and there was virtually no communication among us. With the exception of our consorts, we tended to ignore the others of our class of gods."

Carson's mind drifted along the high mountains, coming upon a group of people engrossed in ritual at the base of a soaring peak. Adorned in magical costumes and to the beat of cymbals and drums, they performed a sacred dance.

A man wearing a crown-like hat, spiked with upraised feathers, and a long coat covered with metallic objects and crystals, spoke from a trance. "Mighty spirit, one and only great god, whose terror and blessing are beyond measure and under-standing, you who hold right over all life and death, one without comparison, one without equal, one beyond all knowing, we ask you to grant us your blessing. Permit us to live and travel beneath your great domain. Protect us from demons, thieves, avalanche, blizzard, hail and hunger, as only you, the one and only great being, can deliver. Your beauty is beyond compare, your wrath beyond measure, your glory beyond praise—you, the greatest of all gods."

"Thus as you just witnessed adept, we existed for ages, basking in our glory, basking in isolation," the wrathful deity said. "Isolation has always been the blessing and the curse of Tibet, protecting it, yet making the land unprepared for things brought from the outside. Consequently, we were ready victims."

Again the deity paused. Carson felt the god's revelation contained an odd mixture of remorse and pride.

"This devil magician from the dusty plains of India was only too aware of our weakness. Padmasambhava, to his credit, had mastered great abilities with his sorcery. To this, he added the services and powers of numerous gods from other lands and dimensions, as well as the gods of the ocean and the air. Legend will tell you that he could fly, but in truth he rode through the sky on a great, invisible dragon."

Carson watched as the sorcerer monk prepared to confront the wrathful deities, uttering prayers and mantras while marshaling legions of deities to his ranks.

"In hindsight, we were little more than country bumpkins compared to the sophisticated force he mustered against us," the Great Lord admitted.

Carson was immediately pulled in to witness a horrific confrontation. The monk, standing before a great mountain, taunted the local god, daring it to appear, demanding that it surrender independence, acquiesce, and serve the Buddha. Suddenly, a giant, demonic being emerged directly out of the mountain walls, moving toward the monk with the fury of a wild storm, whirling multiple weapons in its many arms, roaring with terrible rage. In moments, the once terrifying deity lay prostrate, unable to move under the sorcerer's power.

"My god, this is so amazing," Carson muttered, stunned by the intensity of what he was witnessing.

The Great Lord laughed. "Surely, you don't still believe the limited existence you humans live is the sum of reality? Come, there is much more to see."

Again the powerful teaching swept Carson away, carrying him along with Padmasambhava's entourage as they moved around the country, to the sacred residence of each wrathful deity. Inevitably, the local god would rise to meet the sorcerer's challenge. Through uniting the power of a host of gods into a single field, Padmasambhava generated a vast standing wave of energy into a single thought of stillness, one that would subsume all the power of the wrathful deity, leaving it utterly helpless.

Unable to turn away, Carson watched in horror as, one by one, the wrathful deities fell before Padmasambhava. He could hear their mighty groans and smell their spilled sacred blood. Each wrathful god fought to the brink of its great death. But the brutish strength of the Tibetan deities was no match for the tactics employed by the foreign monk.

As the sorcerer's power held each wrathful deity in the dust, choking the last of the life force from its mighty being, the crafty wizard strolled over and offered terms of surrender.

"Listen well, my friend," Padmasambhava said. "I will grant you back your life, even allow you to continue in your rule of this domain, but you must swear to me your allegiance to defend the Buddhist Dharma over all else, even over the sacred land itself."

"Protect the Dharma, the teachings of a dead man from somewhere in the cursed hot land of India!" the Great Lord mocked bitterly. "In that foreign garble called Sanskrit, 'pala' means protector. Thus we lords, once feared to cause avalanches at our slightest whim, came to be called Dharmapalas, protectors of the Dharma. Under this Buddhist colonialism, we wrathful deities became conquered subjects, reduced to deified guard dogs!"

Carson continued watching Padmasambhava as he went about his task of converting Tibet to Buddhism, ever mindful that he had discovered the perfect strategy for harnessing the inimical native gods. The shrewd sorcerer gave each wrathful deity a new name from India, yet allowed the gods to remain in control over their lands in exchange for protecting the Dharma — and Tibet. Yet it was an uneasy agreement. Who could have known it would last so long?

The god's terrifying eyes burned menacingly as they looked into Carson's awestruck face. "And so Tibet started on the tragic road to becoming Buddhist. The old ways of shamanism began to subside or fall under the directives of the Buddhists. Gradually, the country was becoming civilized. And so it remained for twelve hundred years.

"It was not an easy peace," the deity continued. "Making a pact with a deity is always more cumbersome than humans imagine. We old gods are shifty beings, after all, as is our nature, with little reason to want to abide by the terms of our surrender. The Buddhists, however, well understood the tenuous nature of this accord and undertook great measures to see that the alliance held."

Now Carson found himself standing in a monastery chamber, observing a class of Buddhist monks undergoing extreme esoteric training for managing the tenacious Dharmapalas. Light from butter lamps flickered on the massive stone walls as an old abbot, reciting a shamanic mantra, guided the students in their ominous work. These men had dedicated their entire lives to holding the wrathful deities in alignment—the equivalent of holding a cork in a volcano.

He noted that these monks in fact treated the Dharmapalas with great adoration. They had built a special enclosure underneath the monastery, where they conducted dangerous ritualistic work to hold a specific wrathful deity to its sworn oath—to protect the Dharma, to maintain the allegiance.

Carson was directed to explore one such temple dedicated to a Dharmapala, a macabre subterranean chamber called the mGon Khang. His mind's eye wandered through the bizarre, cave-like chamber, witnessing the ceremonial activities performed within. It was dark, lit by only a few butter lamps—not a place one would associate with a serene Buddhist monastery. The room was more akin to a dungeon. It was a place designed to contain an ambivalent, terrifying energy.

Weapons, fashioned after the ones the deity itself had once wielded, hung on the walls, their edges stained with the human blood they had drawn. Various tankas depicted the Dharmapala in its wrathful mode, its multiple arms brandishing an assortment of weapons, while it simultaneously engaged in sexual union with an equally fierce female consort. Stuffed bodies of great beasts stood throughout the chamber—bear, tiger, leopard, and eagle. Human skins, painted with sacred symbols, covered the walls. Incense burned constantly. Sacred songs and dances were continually performed to honor and gain the favor of the Dharmapala. Monks were making offerings, reassuring the god that as long as he adhered to the oath to protect the Dharma, no other god would be allowed to take his domain. A bowl made from a human skull was filled with human blood in honor of the deity. An old monk, crippled with age and missing a leg, explained more to Carson.

"Given that this is a special day for honoring," the old monk said, "we are serving the deity a delicacy that is one of his favorites—a platter of rhinoceros. On certain occasions, the god will feast upon some of the monks themselves, granting them great merit. As you can see, I have been so blessed, sacrificing one of my legs."

Carson could see that despite being vassals to Buddhism, these wrathful gods thrived on the attention.

Slowly regaining control over his consciousness, Carson engaged the wrathful deity in telepathic conversation.

"If you will allow me to say so, Great One, it appears that you were well treated by these monks," he said hesitantly.

"Oh, adept, that would be an understatement," the deity said. "The monks kept up this practice every minute, day and night, year in and year out, no exception. It never stopped. And adept, they had to! They understood us only too well. If they had relaxed the energy field that confined us, even for a moment, we would have eluded them and been free. To our amazement, these monks were able to sustain this extraordinary practice for twelve hundred years. That has to be one of the most noteworthy accomplishments in the brief, miserable history of humanity. I must say that through this experience, I gained some moderate respect for your kind.

Carson was drawn back to the same mGon Khang, noting that

while prayers and acknowledgments poured forth to the wrathful deity, these were always accompanied by references to the obligatory oath the god had made to protect the Dharma. The deity was constantly reminded that superior forces once had overcome him, that his current existence was due to the benevolent compassion of Lord Buddha, and that he had been subsumed into the Buddhist pantheon.

"Some deities might find all this conducive to their nature; perhaps it is more suitable for those gods of India. But such was not the way with us. We are cut from a different part of divine cloth," the Great Lord boasted. "While honoring an oath is highly meaningful in our tradition, independence is paramount. A deep unrest prevailed with this entire arrangement; we were only waiting for an opportunity to arrive."

"Great One, I have one question, if it may be allowed."

"Only one?" The deity roared with laughter. "After all I have just revealed, you have only one question? Curiosity is fed by knowledge, not ignorance."

"It isn't that there aren't many other questions, Great One," Carson hastened. "Forgive my cumbersome use of language. Of course, there are many things from this teaching that flood my curiosity."

"Come, adept, I know your mind here. I feel your question and your consternation about posing it. I will not be offended."

"Very well," he began. "If death isn't feared by gods, meaning that you can die but know you'll be reborn, why did you not fight to your death?"

"You want to know if I lacked the courage to fight to my death?" the god said menacingly.

Terror swept over Carson. He had grossly overstepped the line. How could he have allowed himself to make such an egregious error, blatantly offending this god?

But the wrathful one seemed more intent on finishing his tale.

"If a god is going to die, he does so for a reason," the wrathful deity declared imperiously. "There must be something of enormous consequence at stake; otherwise, death has little significance. This foreign conquest was an aberration and thus failed to have any meaning for us. It held no significance— nothing for a god to die over!"

Again Carson found himself wandering in a bewildering realm, observing the thoughts of the great gods of the Himalayas. He understood that it was their unwillingness to surrender their dominion over the sacred lands that so completely shackled them. With death, there would have been no assurance of returning to their previous holdings—to their birthright. At least by agreeing to Padmasambhava's terms, they would be assured that no foreign deity would usurp their place.

"So, we lived on," resumed the Great Lord. "And despite this new Buddha business, we remained active in our old ways, all the while learning from these new ones, the monks. They were not like the old shamans with their simple, honest ways. No, these monks had systems and processes.

"Still, there was always much to attend to. You have no idea how demanding it is to be a god. One's attention is constantly needed. Prayers and laments must be heard continuously—and sometimes answered. Lives must be given and taken. And in the midst of all of this, one's consort must be attended with perpetual fornication. With so much responsibility placed upon us, the task of the monks to keep us distracted from planning to break free was greatly aided. And those monks rewarded us well for the protection we provided. It was a theistic business contract."

"And now?" Carson asked. "Are you no longer under that oath? Are you free?"

"Indeed!"

Stunned, he couldn't stop to consider the appropriateness of asking, "How did you gain your freedom? What happened to the oath?"

"I was wondering when you would get to that." The wrathful one laughed. "We waited. We waited a long time even by our standards. Finally, we began to notice a shift in the quality of the monks' work. As you will see, pilgrim, even in a land renowned for its mystery, there were those who championed the rational mind over all else."

Again Carson was transported back to old Tibet, this time to a large monastery with thousands of resident monks, most of whom were still students. He found himself inside a large room, listening to a great debate.

An old lama protested, "Throughout our long tradition, we have always given priority to our duties with the Dharmapalas. Nowadays, you young abbots want to give more preference to the ascetic attributes of meditation and less to the shamanic practices required to maintain the wrathful ones in place. We have always selected and trained the best and brightest monks from our ranks to conduct the Dharmapala practice, but now that policy has changed. Today, more and more of these men are directed into scholarly pursuits."

While the assembly waited for the presiding lama to address the issue, some of the abbots and high lamas scoffed at the old monk's remarks.

"Dear Rinpoche," the presiding lama began, patronizing the old monk. "The Dharmapalas in our tradition will always receive the highest degree of respect. However, these are different times we live in. We are in the twentieth century now. The world is changing. Our teachings have always evolved toward enlightenment through knowledge and meditation. We cannot remain crippled by the myths of the past, which many now consider to be mere figments of superstition."

"I beseech you to consider my words," the old monk pleaded. "As this trend continues, conditions down in the mGon Khang chambers are becoming progressively weakened. Today, only a handful of us old monks conduct this work. We are what's left of those who have always held the Dharmapalas in place. As we die off—and these deities are directly hastening more of our deaths, I might add—the old gods are plotting to smash the vessel that has held the sacred oath. One day, when the power of the lamas is sufficiently weak, the Dharmapalas will break free!"

Laughter at the old man's warning erupted from back areas of the chamber. The presiding lama, seeking to restore decorum and assuage the old monk, called for silence.

"We will take Rinpoche's council under advisement," the lama said.

The old monk glared at them all. Slowly, he turned to leave, but then he stopped.

"There will come a day, and it won't be long. You so-called men of knowledge don't realize what you are dealing with."

The scene faded and Carson found himself back in the presence of the wrathful deity.

"That old monk was correct, adept," the deity said.

"What exactly did you do?" Carson dared to ask.

"We fed ourselves on their blood," the deity responded coldly. "We had the Chinese invade the country!"

Carson was stunned. How could these protective deities allow such a tragedy to fall upon their own land? Was there no limit to their cruelty? He suddenly tried to check his thoughts, remembering the lord could read his mind.

"We have no shame here, adept," the god spoke. "Yes, great suffering has fallen upon the people and Tibet has been grossly violated by the Chinese. But the monks, above all others, have gotten the worst of it. This was our way of showing them what our protection had meant. But more to our purpose, it served to purge the land of their dominance. Now their power has been expunged from the land and we are free to reign without the yoke they placed upon us."

"But what about the Chinese takeover?"

"Oh, we will get to them in due course," the god mused.

"They will provide us with copious amounts of flesh when we are ready to assert ourselves fully again."

Carson was carried off to a future realm. He watched masses of Chinese as they struggled to escape the onslaught of a monstrous death.

"Yes, moats of blood will flow around my temple at that time," the deity mused contentedly. "There are so many of them; the feasting will be most bountiful."

"And the Tibetan people, so many had to flee and are now scattered around the world. What about them?" Carson pressed.

"Well, adept, gods cannot predict everything that might happen," the deity responded indifferently. "We had not anticipated that result. Yet in the end, it may serve us all. Our people are learning more of the world this way, and this will serve them well when it is time to bring them home. Even the great Lord Buddha is gaining a boon through this process. Since those lamas were forced from Tibet, they've set up operations all over the world, hawking their faith and gaining many converts to their precious Dharma. I have seen them in many lands during my travels. All of this will be mended in the near future."

"And when the Tibetans are able to return to their homeland, won't you have to deal with the Buddhists again?"

"Of course. It's not that we forbid their presence. In truth, there is much to their system that we admire. What you must realize, adept, is that when the Tibetans get their homeland back, the wrathful deities will not be under any oath of obligation. Do you understand? We are obliged to no one now. And further, of those humans who will have the best chance of gaining our favor, it will be those skilled in the old shamanic ways with whom we will deal. Want a job, pilgrim?"

"Great Lord, bear with my ignorance. I humbly ask your patience with my questions."

"You may beseech for all of eternity; it matters little to me. I will do as I will, regardless. But since your life hangs in the balance either way, ask your questions."

"If I understand your words correctly, it sounds like you've traveled the world yourself. Or does it only mean that you are capable of being in more than one place at a time?"

"Let it be understood that my presence can participate in more than one location at a given moment. And it is true that these days I am often in places other than my traditional home. I have chosen to avail myself of other realms, expanding my own ways of knowing. Such are the demands of these times. The world is not as it used to be, adept. Gods, as well as other beings, must grow with the times."

"Can you share more about this with me?"

"After the Tibetan diaspora, most of the Great Lords were happy with simply reclaiming their autonomy and reinstating themselves over their traditional Himalayan dominions. An unfortunate few had become so used to captivity that they simply returned to mGon Khang chambers that existed in other lands. However, some of us began to roam the planet as itinerant gods, gathering manna where it could be obtained and forging new alliances. I have been in many places, garnering a great concrescence of my powers. This I will ultimately dispense from the place of my birthright."

Carson took a moment to reflect on the god's words then asked, "Were you actually born, that is, created through a birthing process?"

"Not as you know that process. Originally, we emerged from a concentration of energy that was held within bodies of matter at the planet's surface. Such energy occurs in numerous manifestations, such as oceans or deserts or forests—in our case, a great mountain range. As a result, deities or spirits reside in such places," the Great Lord explained. "There's an intelligence in matter, adept, a telos. Certainly your studies should have taught you that much."

Again, an unseen power pulled Carson into another vision.

Fast-forwarded sequences revealed the evolution of matter concentrated within the granite walls of a soaring mountain. At first, the mass of stone was nothing more than a potential. As the centuries hurled past as if seconds, he observed a consciousness begin to emerge from it. He began to weep in wonder. He was beholding the birth of a god.

"That is how the older ones of our type were born," the deity explained, momentarily impressed with his pupil's emotion. "Much later, we procreated as other beings do, mating with consorts."

Embarrassed, Carson struggled to regain his composure.

"How old are you, Great One?"

"We do not count time as you do. Though not timeless, I am both ancient and young. If you must measure my existence, I will simply say that my type has existed long before human time and will do so long after your species is extinct. Your wise ones understand this. Fear me well, adept."

"If it is permitted, I would like to learn more about the process whereby matter becomes infused with consciousness. How does a mass of Earth's matter evolve into a consciousness—become a god?"

"There is much to my wisdom that stands outside the limits of human language."

"Yes, I acknowledge that, Great Lord. Still, could I be permitted to experience some way of knowing how matter turns into consciousness?"

"Very well, this may amuse me." The deity laughed. "So granted."

Carson's skull was suddenly pulled back under enormous pressure. He lay paralyzed, though fully aware of his entire physicality, his body undergoing something akin to petrification. Gradually, he recognized that he had transformed into a giant layer of stone, one that topped a soaring mountain peak.

From above, forces of gravity pressed down upon every

particle of his body, while from beneath, an endless pressure pushed upward from subterranean forces needing release. Far greater forces, greater gods, competing causes and distant cosmic energies bore down with their conflicting needs. Squeezed between these forces, impregnated by their energies, the once dormant, inert matter that now composed Carson's mind began the process of self-organizing. He was radically transforming from mere physical substance into a divine consciousness.

He was atop a great mountain; he was the mountain itself. The scars of the planet's birth and growth were imprints on his soul. Here, in this place of awe and hostility, he was master. Nature herself had transformed him, granting him place and privilege as a great feudal lord, encased in trillions of tons of solid stone, a sentinel standing among snows, wind, and sun. The rocks and dirt strewn over the surface constituted his after-birth. Far below, in the remote valleys, lesser forms of his being expressed themselves as raging streams and windswept ravines. A variety of fauna and flora struggled to eke out an existence upon the rugged surface of his being.

For a few brief moments, Carson held the full manifestation of this condensed state of matter and energy. But the enormity of the teaching soon overwhelmed him. It was beyond human limits to continue. He began to swoon, releasing the experience.

Carson fought to retrieve his soul from petrifaction, to stay human. A keen sense of fear implored him not to lose consciousness.

The Great Lord jarred him fully back. "Well, adept, did your curiosity find satisfaction?" He laughed. "You did well. Not many practitioners of your art have ventured into such realms, and among those who have, not all have returned. Peril waits on the path to paradise. Always beware."

Carson listened through a fog of exhaustion. Yet one more question still urged him on.

"Great Lord, what about those known as the Visitors?"

"We shall not speak of this now. Go elsewhere, adept; I will allow your departure. I have other matters to attend to. Perhaps we shall reconvene sometime—if you live long enough. In the meanwhile, I shall absorb your prayers."

The deity withdrew.

Carson lay silent upon the mat, his body trembling. He was back. Slowly, he opened his eyes; Rhiannon lay beside him.

Chapter 14

Blood on the Tracks

"How's the sound reading, Lucas?"

"I'm set; everything's coming in fine," Lucas replied over the two-way radio.

Carson was glad to be back in the field. While under Rhiannon's tutelage for months, he had confined his work to the editing room. Now that he'd finished the final edits on the documentary about women truck drivers, it was time to get back behind the camera.

He had accepted a commission from Charles Landon, a self-obsessed electrical engineer who had made several fortunes in the early years of the Internet boom. Now sixty-one and semiretired, Landon had turned his attention to his lifelong passion—model railroads. Landon wanted a documentary that would capture the model railroad world—not only the elaborate electric train layouts but also the people who lived and breathed the stuff. Charles Landon expected much of the documentary, including its eventual broadcast on PBS. He was more than willing to put whatever money was required into the project.

For Carson, this was an opportunity to make some much-needed income. His business had suffered over the last three years. Believing the world might be coming to an end had not inspired him to be proactive in commerce.

Having only just arrived in Seattle, they were already filming at the annual convention of the National Model Railroad Association. This event would showcase the scope of the model railroad world. As the association's current president, Landon believed his keynote address would be particularly appropriate as the documentary's opening monologue. In fact, much to Carson's concern, Landon had many ideas as to how the documentary should be made.

While Carson and Lucas joked about Landon's ego, the retainer they had received allowed them to purchase state-of-the-art equipment and the generous expense account meant they would not have to live out of cheap motels and eat in bad restaurants. Landon was seeing to it that everything about this project was done first-class.

"Perfect, Lucas, the sound's a go. I'm all set, too," Carson said. "We have about two hours before his speech tonight. Let's get some dinner and come back here fifteen minutes before he's scheduled to start."

"I was hoping you would remember that I need to eat," Lucas said. "There's a little bistro just off the lobby that looks promising."

"Okay, tell you what," Carson said. "Let me make a couple of phone calls and I'll meet you there in thirty minutes."

"Catch you then."

Up in his hotel room, Carson grabbed his phone and walked to the large window that overlooked the lighted cityscape. First he phoned Ben. He had wanted to bring his son along, but the dates conflicted with Ben's school calendar. Their time together had become more precious in these last few years; everything had become more precious.

"Hey, buddy, how's it going? Is your mom making you something decent for dinner? Got your homework done?"

"Hey, Dad, slow down." Ben laughed. "Yeah, everything's great. How 'bout you and Lucas?"

"Seems to be going nicely so far. Or, as Mr. Landon would say, 'All aboard, the train's leaving the station.'"

"Dad, that's so corny. Hey, you gonna bring me something cool?"

"Maybe! What do you think that ought to be?"

"I don't know, but not an electric train, okay? I'm too old for that stuff."

"Or way too young, judging by this crowd." Carson chuckled. "Hey, buddy, I'll catch you later. Just wanted to check in, but I gotta go meet Lucas for dinner."

"Talk with you later, Dad."

Rain droplets snaked down the windowpanes. Carson peered into the night, wondering if he would be safe on this, his first road trip since his encounter with the Dharmapala that weekend at Rhiannon's.

He had left Rhiannon's the following day, later than he had anticipated. She was deeply distressed by his encounter with the wrathful deity, adamantly insisting that he follow through with the prayers and offerings he had promised to the Dharmapala. Whatever the source of this dark deity, Carson could not dismiss his obligations to him.

She made him give an offering to the Hindu goddess Kali, as well, thanking her for the unscheduled audience and asking forgiveness for his intrusion into her realm. Before allowing him to drive off, she uttered a protective mantra over the hood of his Cherokee.

Then, as Carson was about to pull away, Rhiannon quickly stuck her head through the driver's window and kissed him deeply. She abruptly turned and walked back to her cottage. That kiss burned inside him all the way back to Santa Cruz.

Pulling up to his house, Carson spotted her—Allison. She was sitting on his front steps with a stern expression.

"I guess I was worried, or maybe I'm just damn stupid," she began. "You said you would be home yesterday. I took a flight back from San Diego just to be with you, and you weren't here."

"Hey, I'm sorry. I know I said I'd be back yesterday, but I didn't know you were coming."

"Well, you could've called to let me know you had a change of plans. Has it ever occurred to you that I might be concerned? You could have had an accident or something."

"I almost did," he replied casually, recalling the logging truck encounter.

"Really! Well, you don't look much the worse as far as I can see. So what was it that kept you up there so long this time?"

"It's pretty complicated," he replied.

"Oh, let me guess; I could think of a few things. Are you going to make me have to spell it out or are you man enough to tell me?"

She got up and walked into the yard toward her car, throwing her hands up in the air.

"Allison, please. I know this work of mine is very demanding on our relationship, but if you would just—"

"Just what, Carson?" she said, turning to face him, her face flushed. "Do you really think I can go on like this? You go away every other weekend, sometimes more, to spend time alone with another woman on some magical mystery tour. What kind of idiot do you think I am?"

"Me? You go away more than I do, and spend lots of time with other men at those seminars. And a good chunk of that takes place in social settings, I'm sure. You aren't holding any moral high ground, from my perspective."

"Well, at least I'm not taking drugs with them," she fired back.

"Oh, that's right, you only do alcohol with them. Like that's never caused people to end up in the sack together."

"Fuck you!" she shouted, stepping toward him and pointing a finger at his head.

"Look, I'm not saying I've been the most doting boyfriend lately. I just want you to see your part, too. You aren't exactly there for me that much these days either."

"Fair enough," Allison conceded. "I know I've developed a more demanding lifestyle; my career's taken off, and I've started to really come into my own. I suppose I believed you would be happy for me, encouraging my professional achievements. How was I supposed to know my success would freak you out and you'd end up running off to hang out with some New Age witch?"

Carson struggled to remain composed, setting his overnight bag down on the steps.

"Allison, I don't resent your success, really I don't. But I can't help it if we've developed different interests. I can understand that what I'm doing must seem pretty weird; hell, it's weird to me. And as for your career, well, I'm glad you're happy with it. But frankly, I don't give a tinker's damn about whether a chunk of real estate gets turned into condos and some developer ends up making a fortune. I mean, to me, that seems trivial. I realize that's judgmental on my part, but honestly, what you do bores me to no end. We're just not on the same page anymore."

Allison stared at him icily. "Just tell me one thing. It would really help at this point," she said. "Have you been sleeping with her?"

"No. It's not like that." He paused. "But, I may have fallen in love with her."

"You're a jerk, Carson," she said, walking off to her car.

Rain continued to pepper the hotel window. Carson picked up the phone again.

"Hello," Rhiannon answered.

"Hi, just checking in."

"Oh Jesus. I'm so glad to hear from you. Is everything all right?"

"Well, if we don't hurl tonight during Landon's big speech, we should be okay. How about you?"

"I wish you had waited a bit longer before going back on the road."

"Hey, did you ever consider that the real strategy of our Visitor friends might be to just starve us to death? That's what would happen if I didn't do this film."

"Listen, you really need more time to come into your power.

I trust you're keeping up with the practice we mapped out for you? It's critically important."

"Oh yeah—what was that again? Something about putting your left foot in, then your right foot in, doing the hokey-pokey, and shaking it all about? Hope I didn't leave anything important out."

"I see your sense of humor's returned. That sure isn't how you sounded when you left here."

"I'm being careful, honest. If not for myself, I've got Ben to think about. He's been the real motivation throughout my medicine work," he said, suddenly moved by thoughts of his son. "But you haven't told me what's going on with you."

"Carson, don't try to change the subject. You can't afford to fuck around with things now. You're out there on your own, and with travel, and all the distractions, you have to be extra diligent. It's a more open environment; you have less control."

"I know, I know," he said. "Don't take my smart-ass remarks as a reflection of where I'm coming from. For God's sake, I'm caught between hostile alien energies and some ambivalent god who would just as soon eviscerate me as swat a fly. Given that situation, a person might not want to take things too seriously."

He didn't like the tension that had crept in between them.

"Just please don't assume that by being back at work it makes all this stuff somehow less potent," she said curtly. "On the contrary, the constant changes make you more vulnerable."

Carson felt miserable. All he wanted to do was climb through the telephone and hold her. The very thing she had warned him against was happening; he was becoming preoccupied by his desire for her. And it was making him less attentive.

"So, you gonna tell me what you're up to or is it a secret?" he asked again, trying to muster his wits.

"You're persistent tonight. Well, that's a good sign, I believe. You're at least trying to exert some power."

Carson wondered why she was being so evasive. Could there

be someone else—a lover? She had implied that she was alone, but perhaps he had misunderstood her.

"Well, it seems you would rather not share with me whatever it is you're up to," he said, a twinge of irritation in his voice. "I suppose it's none of my business, really. I mean, we both have our private lives out there on the side somewhere."

Rhiannon was silent, then laughed. "Carson, Carson. I warned you about where this kind of thing would lead."

"What does that mean?"

"Okay, I confess, I was planning to invite a gang of sailors over for the weekend and screw my brains out, but at the last minute, I decided to hold a quilting bee with some ladies from the local nursing home. Too bad you won't be able to drop in."

He laughed, in spite of his embarrassment.

"So, you want to know what I'm doing?" she continued.

"As long as it doesn't involve a bunch of quilting sailors," he replied dryly.

"Well, there are some people here," she said. "Don't believe any of them are sailors, unfortunately. And if you must know, we're doing a ritual that uses our menstrual blood. Now, aren't you glad you asked?"

"Okay. Maybe I don't need to hear about this."

"Hey, you've gotten yourself into this," she teased, "too late to back down now. But maybe you're one of those men who were not conceived in a woman's womb. I trust you did have a mother?"

"Guilty! I did have a mother, despite the rumors spread about me."

"Pity." She chuckled. "God knows the poor woman deserved better."

"You're really enjoying this, aren't you?"

"Just a little."

"All right, tell me about your ritual," he conceded reluctantly.

"Well, in numerous cultures, a woman's menses was understood to be an extremely powerful essence. It was used to make all kinds of potions and offerings. It was from this tradition that later blood sacrifices were derived, when men decided to take over the show. But I'll leave the politics of patriarchy aside and get back to what we're doing. We're working on recovering the power contained within our blood, to harness its healing and protective qualities. We're also trying to think of more contemporary applications."

"So, without going into the full-blown details, if you don't mind, just how do you intend to use it?"

"In all kinds of ways. But one just doesn't go and pour blood over something and that's it. That would just be a lazy form of superstition. First, it has to be infused with prayers and mixed with appropriate intentions. I may use it on my altar as an offering, out in my garden as a sacred fertilizer, around my doors as a protective ointment, or as a kind of baptismal elixir for amulets."

"Wow!" he said, uncertain as to how he should respond.

"Yeah, you should know there's a bit more to women than just something nice for sex," she said.

"Seems I wouldn't know much about that these days."

"Are you trying to make me feel sorry for you?"

"Maybe."

"Well, just let me tell you a little more and then I'll let you go," she inserted, going back to her description. "There are three very interesting women here with me, each with a different spiritual orientation. My friend, Suzanne, is a longtime devotee of Isis and knows a great deal about how Egyptian women conducted menstrual rituals to Isis and, before that, to Hathor. She's brought her friend, Anna, whom I've heard about but never met until now. Anna's been working with a number of Buddhist women, including a female lama. They use their blood in a ritual to honor Tara. And an old colleague of mine, Zinna, is here as well. We met in a little shop in Paris about fifteen years ago; she's originally from Algeria. Ethnically, she's a Berber. Her family's been practicing alchemy for generations. She uses menstrual blood as one of the ingredients for her alchemical alembic. She's been describing the most amazing stories around this. And I'm contributing my knowledge of female blood rites from the Celtic and Hindu traditions. Naturally, I'm hoping this will help provide additional protection against the Visitors. Doubt if they've ever run up against menstrual blood shielding."

"What ever happened to Tupperware parties?" he said ruefully.

The two of them laughed, their tension temporarily abated.

"It sounds fascinating, really," he said.

"Thanks," she said. "Thanks for letting me share my enthusiasm with you."

There was a pause. Carson wondered whether he should say more. Much more. But Rhiannon breezily shifted the mood.

"Well, I won't detain you any longer. Give my regards to Lucas. Would like to meet him someday."

"I'll do that. I'm late to join him for dinner right now," he said, rousing himself back to the outside world.

"Hope this little talk hasn't spoiled your appetite," she mused.

"First thing I'm doing when I get downstairs is order a Bloody Mary in your honor."

"What a man!" She laughed.

"Talk with you later," he said, not wanting to hang up.

"Carson, keep safe."

After dinner, Carson and Lucas had time to wander the expansive trade show hall. Exhibitors were still putting the final touches on their displays. He wished they could be filming this instead of having to record Charles Landon's speech.

Carson climbed up on an abandoned stepladder for an overview of the hall. All about him were collections of miniature worlds. The major displays contained large layouts with dozens of trains simultaneously threading their way through mazes of cities, towns, and villages with miniature factories, mines, and shipyards. The level of authenticity and detail was remarkable. The hum of conversation melded with the clacking of model trains, punctuated by the occasional lonely call of a shrill whistle.

He suddenly felt dizzy. Steadying himself, he descended the ladder. For a moment, he questioned whether he was in danger.

"You all right, man?" Lucas asked, appearing close behind, wearing a souvenir railroader's cap backwards.

"Yeah, fine," he replied. "We better get back to our equipment."

As they started to leave the hall, a voice called out. "Carson, you and your friend come over here a minute," a man commanded.

It was Charles Landon, standing near the doorway of the trade show hall. The filmmakers strolled over.

"I want you to meet the Richardsons. They're from Fort Worth—big buffs of the Santa Fe road. This is Carson Reynolds, our filmmaker, and his associate—I'm sorry, Lucas, but I can't remember your last name with all these people."

"Wills. Lucas Wills," he said, extending a hand. "Nice to meet you both."

"Hugh here was a Lionel man when I first met him years ago, but he soon came around to HO gauge."

"I also run some N gauge," Hugh Richardson replied proudly, sporting a cowboy hat emblazoned with the emblem of the Santa Fe Railroad. "But I still have my old Lionel table. Part of my childhood that I can't give up."

His wife looked on with a seemingly reassuring smile, her hands laden by a showy display of diamond rings.

"You'll want to film Hugh's layout for sure," Landon directed, giving his friend his blessing with a slap on the back. "And be certain to work in a nice interview. He's one of our best members and a hell of a railroad historian."

"Wonderful," Carson said. "We'll look forward to that stopover when we get down that way. Mr. Landon's laid out quite an expansive travel itinerary for us after the convention."

"We're delighted to have you coming to see us," Mrs. Richardson said. "You'll love Fort Worth. It's a terrific place, and we have a wonderful art museum."

"I'm sure we will," Carson replied. "But you'll have to excuse us now if we're going to get Mr. Landon's address on film."

"You see!" Landon exclaimed to the Richardsons. "These boys are top-notch professionals. Would've made damn fine railroad men—probably Union Pacific, I'd say." Landon and Hugh Richardson laughed.

After the long day, Carson was grateful to retire to his hotel room. With the day's filming completed and their gear stashed away, he could turn his attention to more serious matters. He sat on the floor and allowed his thoughts to turn inward. Outside, the sound of cars slogging through rain-soaked streets gave the night a veneer of white noise.

A small votive candle burned before him, providing the room's only illumination. Next to it stood a small, toy action figure. With no idol to represent the great and terrible Dharmapala, he was using the only image he had thus far been able to find that conveyed even the slightest similarity to the wrathful deity. He had discovered the object quite by chance, while packing for this trip. Reaching for a suitcase on a closet shelf, he had knocked over a box of his son's old toys. Glaring back at him from the closet floor was the toy action figure of the cartoon character Taz—the Tasmanian Devil.

Rhiannon had assured him that Taz would serve as an acceptable facsimile for now, as long as he treated the object with full respect. "It's the energy you connect with through viewing an image that counts, not the actual item," she had explained.

Now he sat alone in a sterile hotel room, in the middle of a major American city, in front of an action figure. His spiritual journey had come to this—praying to a latex toy. Absurdity's rule was now complete!

Carson closed his eyes and prayed to the Tasmanian Devil.

Chapter 15

The Haynesworths

"You know, man, I could've slept another hour or two. Did we really have to hit the road so early?" Lucas grumbled. "We're gonna make Portland with plenty of time."

"Just a hunch that we needed to get off, that's all," Carson responded evenly, feeling it was important to avoid being late. "Can't give you much more of an explanation than that; sorry."

The windshield wipers moved effortlessly across the damp glass. After three days of filming at the convention and meeting an assortment of model railroad enthusiasts, they were on the road. Interstate 5 stretched before them as they motored south for their first interview.

Landon had leased a new Range Rover for their use. He wanted his boys to ride in what he considered to be style. In fact, Landon had made arrangements for everything, selecting the locations and people to be filmed and setting it all in a tight production schedule.

The first leg of their itinerary immediately followed the convention, with a swing through a number of western states. The stops were intended to capture a spectrum of railroad buffs through interviews at their homes or at club functions. Some filming was scheduled at actual rail yards and railroad museums. The final filming sequence was planned for Landon's home, where he would unveil his own model train layout and provide the film's closing commentary.

All the while, Carson debated as to whether or not he should tell Lucas about what his life had become. He owed it to his friend; after all, he was in no small way putting Lucas' life in danger now. But how could he rationally convey any of this? *"Oh, by the way, Lucas, there's a slight additional factor you may have to deal with on this project. You see, I'm helping ward off an invasion of hostile alien spiritual energy and things might become problematic at some point."*

No, he was having enough trouble convincing himself that he was, in truth, sane. It would be best to say nothing—at least for now. Whatever angels watched over the innocent would just have to step it up a notch for Lucas.

"Okay, I don't mean to sound like I'm bitching," Lucas continued. "You know I'm no slacker, but I was having this really delicious dream when the goddamn wake-up call came—I hate that!"

"Sorry about that," Carson responded. "By the way, you better be careful about what you dream; sometimes that can lead to some pretty weird stuff playing out in your life."

"Well, I sure wouldn't mind having this one come true."

"That good, eh?" he asked.

"Oh, yeah."

"Well, sorry, Lucas, but we needed to get off early. For all I know, Landon has some global positioning bug on this thing, so he can monitor our whereabouts."

"That wouldn't surprise me one bit. Whoops, better not say anything; he's probably listening, too."

They joked more about Landon and continued cruising toward Oregon under the snarling gaze of Taz, who was proudly mounted on the dashboard by a suction cup attached to his base.

The Portland stopover entailed filming at the home of Colton Haynesworth, a retired lumber industry executive, who now divided his time between serving on the boards of civic organizations and running his model railroad. The Haynesworths lived in a wealthy community on the northwest side of town.

Two large, stone columns flanked the entrance to a long curving driveway at the Haynesworth home, a large, two-story Tudor graciously stationed atop a sprawling wooded lot. Carson slowly motored toward the front door; curious as to whether Lucas' dreadlock-covered head would in some way disturb their hosts.

"Come on in, gentlemen, been expecting you!" Colton Haynesworth exclaimed, opening the front door. "Landon phoned just a while ago and said you might be arriving about now."

Lucas and Carson gave each other a quick glance, wondering if it might not be true that Charles Landon had indeed installed a tracking device on their Range Rover.

"Beautiful home you have here," Lucas said.

"We're comfortable in it," Haynesworth said nonchalantly. "Can I offer you something to drink?"

"Perhaps a little later, thanks," Carson said. "We'd like to get set up if that's all right."

"Certainly, by all means, yes indeed," Haynesworth said. "I'll have Caesar Chiang give you a hand."

Haynesworth called to the rear of the house. A small Asian man wearing a white housecoat appeared.

"Caesar Chiang, would you please escort these gentlemen around to the garage and give them a hand getting their equipment up to my studio? I'll meet you boys out there in a few minutes."

Carson and Lucas retuned to the Range Rover, hopped in, and started the engine. Caesar Chiang walked silently in front of the vehicle, guiding them along the driveway as they maneuvered around the house to a large garage complex with four bays and what appeared to be servants' quarters along the second floor. There, the Asian man walked around to the rear of the Range Rover and waited while they began unloading.

"Follow, please," Caesar Chiang said, picking up a box of their gear and walking around the side of the garage. He disappeared inside.

Carson and Lucas followed. A set of stairs led to the second floor, where they came to a small workroom. Model railroad cars sat on shelves in various states of construction. A workbench that might serve a jeweler was well equipped with all the paraphernalia needed to work in miniature: small pliers and vises, a Dremel tool outfit, tiny paintbrushes and an assortment of electrical tools for wiring and soldering. Large photos of real trains adorned the walls.

"This is going to be pretty cramped for filming," Lucas said.

"No, no, follow please," Caesar Chiang insisted, leading them on into a dark room.

They entered a large space that ran the length of the garage's second floor. Caesar Chiang hit some switches and slowly the ceiling illuminated, starting at the far wall and progressing across the entire room. Small clouds, along with an airplane and a flock of migrating birds, were painted overhead. The three men walked out into a kind of maze that twisted through the entire room. Surrounding them on all sides, stretched a miniature world of hills and forests, small townships, lumber mills, and bucolic farmlands. Across this enormous layout ran a network of miniature railroad lines that spanned rivers and canyons with realistically constructed trestles and bridges. Tunnels bore through mountains and hills. No quarters for servants here; only model trains lived within Colton Haynesworth's private fiefdom.

"Goddamn, I just love it up here!" Haynesworth exclaimed, suddenly appearing behind them. "Haven't been able to get up here all week. Damned committee meetings and the like."

"This is incredible," Lucas said.

"Yes, quite amazing," Carson added.

"And don't worry about room to shoot in here, boys. There are some extensions that swing out from the walkway that allow access to most of the layout. Underneath it all, there's also a four-foot crawl space complete with creeper carts that can get you anywhere. Certain sections will hinge up to give you access to the surface."

"Jesus!" Lucas exclaimed.

"Don't take the Lord's name in vain, son," Haynesworth said soberly.

"Yes, sir," Lucas replied.

"Well, we'd better get busy hauling the rest of our gear up here," Carson interjected.

"Right; Caesar Chiang will give you all the help you need. I'll be in my little workroom until you're ready. Now I hope you men will stay for dinner. Want you to meet the wife."

"Well, thank you, but no. We wouldn't want to impose and we haven't checked in at our hotel," Carson said.

"Mr. Reynolds, when I invite someone to dine with me, I expect them to do so. Am I making myself clear? Your rooms have already been booked and confirmed, I can assure you of that."

"We'll be delighted to accept," Lucas replied.

"I like this man; he has good manners," Haynesworth barked, giving Lucas a slap on the back. "Caesar Chiang, these gentlemen will be dining with us this evening. Make one of your special dishes for the occasion."

Haynesworth withdrew to his workshop in regal fashion, leaving the three of them to unload and set up all of the gear. When the last case of equipment was upstairs, Caesar Chiang disappeared.

"Mr. Reynolds," Lucas whispered to Carson. "When I say 'jump,' you better ask how fucking high. You got that?"

They continued to exchange private Haynesworth jokes while they worked out the filming options. They would need a number of close-ups, both of Haynesworth and the trains themselves. Sound and lighting would not be easy, particularly given that Lucas wanted to record the model trains in a way that simulated the Doppler effect of real trains. Haynesworth's commentary would also have to be woven in among the sounds of the trains.

"Now, my railroad, like all my businesses, is run according to a tight schedule," Haynesworth warned when they were all set up. "It doesn't go backwards, meaning neither it nor I do retakes. So better get it right the first time."

"We're ready," Carson said. "We just need a run-through to know what your trains will be doing. That's how I run a tight filming schedule."

Haynesworth shifted, his body language signaling that he was pondering whether or not to take umbrage at Carson's comment. "Sounds reasonable, I suppose," he finally declared.

Like a CEO at a board meeting, Haynesworth gave an exact account of each train's route and intended performance. Carson was satisfied, and things seemed to be back on a friendly footing. They began filming.

"Now, my family had come out here as pioneers in the mid-1800s," Haynesworth began, sending the toy trains through their maneuvers. "We weren't ranchers though; mercantile and banking services were how we established ourselves. Soon that extended itself to the growing timber industry, and one of my grandfathers was among the initial investors in the Northern Pacific Railroad. But a little thing called the Great Depression forced the family to sell off its railroad shares. The timber tracks we owned weren't worth that much then, so the family just held on to them, thank God."

Haynesworth waxed appropriately sentimental. "Perhaps my little hobby is a way of regaining my family's lost railroad heritage; at least that's what my wife's therapist says. But it's more than that to me, much more."

Electric trains snaked across Haynesworth's empire, hauling boxcars with hidden content, gondola cars filled with coal, and flatcars piled with logs and timber. A pair of diesel engines, typical of the streamlined design of the early '50s, with the markings of the Great Northern Railroad, pulled an impressive line of passenger cars. Drawbridges lowered and rose. Overhead, the ceiling gradually dimmed to night as the miniature world came alive, with streetlights and lighting inside dozens of model buildings. Miniature headlights illuminated the paths of toy engines as they rushed through the simulated evening.

Not having been informed of this change of lighting, Carson stopped filming. This allowed him to simply enjoy the extravagance of Haynesworth's creation. It was a secure, predictable world, so unlike his own, he thought. As the room began to lighten some ten minutes later with the arrival of Haynesworth's timed dawn, Carson's attention returned to the camera's eyepiece.

Haynesworth changed eras by flipping over sections of the layout. He dismissed all the diesel locomotives into a tunnel that hid them from view. Then, from a mountain tunnel on the opposite side of the layout, he sent forth a fleet of 1930s steam engines. All the while, he rambled on about railroads, his family's history and pioneer philosophy.

They filmed for nearly two hours, mostly close-ups of Haynesworth talking, but also numerous segments of the trains in action.

"Well, that's about it, gentlemen, unless you want to shoot me working at my studio bench. But maybe we better not; some of my techniques are still secret," Haynesworth said, shrugging his shoulders in mock modesty. "When you get your equipment packed away, come on over to the house and we'll have something to drink before dinner. Sorry Caesar Chiang won't be able to give you a hand, since he's busy with the dinner preparation."

With that pronouncement, Haynesworth withdrew to the house.

"Well, you heard the man, Carson," Lucas said, suddenly assuming the gruff voice of their host. "Better pack these things up and get our asses over to the house. When he invites someone to dinner, they better show the fuck up or there's gonna be hell to pay. Don't make me have to come back out to the garage and—"

"Enough, Lucas." Carson laughed. "Listen, you better help me make it through dinner. While he may make for some interesting footage, I don't know if I can take much more of his, 'how my family won the West and made a fortune by raping the forest of all the virgin timber' stuff. But Jesus, I'm looking forward to whatever he has to drink."

"And you better not let me hear you use Jesus' name like that," Lucas mocked.

When they'd finished packing the gear back into the Range Rover, they headed for the house.

"Wanna lay a bet on what the wife is like?" Lucas mused.

"I just want to get through this as quickly as possible and then get over to the hotel."

"Okay, here's the wife, now check this out," Lucas began, stepping in front of Carson to get his full attention. "She's going to have one of those rich women's hairstyles, with the silvery-blonde highlights, and she'll tell us how interesting she thinks our work must be. The type who likes to bring her cocktail to the dinner table with very dramatic flare but never touches it again because she's on to the wine; probably has a couple of little stoopsy dogs she constantly scolds for begging for food, while feeding them prime cuts off her plate. Wears heavy gold jewelry but in a casual style, of course, as if she was born with it on, and will excuse herself immediately after dinner while exclaiming that this has been the most fascinating evening and we simply must come back because she feels like we're now almost part of the family."

"Christ, do I need that drink now," Carson said.

"Ah, there you are," Haynesworth boomed at them. "Come in, gentlemen, and step right this way. I have a little bar back here just off my study."

They walked down a baronial hallway with dark paneling and came into a room that exuded wealth and station. The windowpanes were leaded glass, cut in the diamond pattern typical of Tudor houses. Large bookshelves ran from floor to ceiling. Clusters of photos hung from the mahogany walls, displaying various family gatherings. Large vintage photographs of railroads and logging operations complemented them. Carson spotted one of Haynesworth and Ronald Reagan shaking hands in the White House and another with George Bush, Sr.

"So, what's your pleasure? I've got about everything here. If you prefer beer, I have an excellent local brew on tap. My grandson and his friends really love it. There's wine, of course, along with a variety of nonalcoholic beverages, too."

"Well, what are you drinking?" Carson asked.

"I'm a Scotch man, mostly," Haynesworth responded.

"I'll join you then, if I may."

"I'll try one of those beers, thank you," Lucas said.

"Very well, very well indeed," Haynesworth said, pleased to be in charge.

"I'll have my usual, darling," came a female voice from behind.

A tall, attractive woman with graying black hair stood in the doorway. She wore a tasteful, long, sheath dress, complemented by an elaborate necklace made of ethnic beads and turquoise.

"Hello, I'm Connie Haynesworth. Delighted Colton could persuade you to stay for dinner. He seems to have a gift for doing that," she said, giving her guests a wink.

Lucas immediately stood up and shook her hand.

"Pleased to meet you. I'm Lucas and this is Carson, of course."

"I told you this one has good manners." Haynesworth laughed, handing Lucas a tall, chilled glass of beer.

Connie Haynesworth warmly shook their hands and settled

on a small sofa while indicating to her guests to sit as well. Carson immediately liked her; there was no sign of pretentiousness in her demeanor.

"So, Charlie Landon has secured your professional services for quite a project, I understand," she began.

"Evidently," Carson said.

"Oh, he's not such a bad sort," she said. "We all have our indulgences, I suppose. One thing for sure, you're going to meet some characters doing this documentary."

"What my darling Connie is trying to say, in her graceful manner, is that there are some eccentric types out there." Haynesworth chuckled.

"Makes good subject matter," Lucas said.

"Of course, as you can tell, my darling husband is not the least bit obsessive about his railroading." She laughed.

"No more than you about your art, sweetheart," Haynesworth countered.

"It's true, gentlemen; we each have our little obsessions," she said. "But we're very tolerant of the other in that regard, and it's probably helped us maintain a happy marriage over the years. However, we've had to implement some rules, of which you'll be among the beneficiaries. When we have guests for dinner, we don't allow discussions of railroads or art."

Colton Haynesworth made certain that their glasses were kept refreshed for the next half hour, while they engaged in light conversation.

"Dinner ready, madam," Caesar Chiang announced from down a hallway.

"Thank you, Caesar Chiang," Connie Haynesworth called back. "Let's go in, shall we?"

They followed Mrs. Haynesworth into a large, formal dining room. An elegantly appointed table was set with expensive china, heavy silver flatware, crystal wineglasses and linen napkins. Tall candles burned in large silver candelabras. Carson reflected that nothing about the setting was in excess.

"Carson, you and Lucas have a seat on either side. I have to sit up at this end to keep myself out of range of kicking Colton if he gets out of line," she said. "Lucas, we aren't into being overly formal here, so please help yourself to either of the wines, or if you prefer, I can have Caesar Chiang bring you another beer. Charlie Landon informed us that you two are omnivores, so I didn't have Caesar Chiang make anything out of the norm. I trust that information was correct."

"We've never met a meal we didn't like," Lucas said.

"Good man," Haynesworth replied.

"I'm curious, if I may ask," Carson said to Mrs. Haynesworth. "Why do you call Caesar Chiang by his full name instead of just Caesar?"

"It's a form of respect in his culture," she replied. "It would denigrate him if we called him only by his first name. He got the name Caesar from the Jesuit priests at the school he attended as a boy. Evidently, the priests gave each child a Western first name from classical times. This helped the priests distinguish the students, as many children were orphans and went only by generic family names. Apparently, because his family was part Chinese, they were subject to persecution in Burma. While just a boy, he fled to Thailand with only the clothes on his back. That's when he was placed in the orphanage."

"So, how did your paths cross?" Lucas inquired.

"About fifteen years ago, I was on an art safari in Southeast Asia," Connie Haynesworth said, gazing at the burning candles through her wineglass. "We hired some men in Thailand as porters and cooks. Caesar Chiang was one of them. Besides being a skilled cook, he spoke fairly good English, along with Thai and some French. I was very fond of him from the outset. We got into a serious jam in a remote part of Thailand, with some regional bandits. Most of our hired crew disappeared into the bush. But

Caesar Chiang stayed with us and cleverly helped us slip away on the river that night, at no small risk to himself. Needless to say, I believe all of us on the outing owe him our lives. When I got back home I pulled a few strings, with old family connections at the State Department, and we were able to facilitate his immigration here."

The filmmakers were rewarded for having stayed for dinner. Caesar Chiang demonstrated his mastery of both Oriental and Occidental culinary arts. His first course was an Asian-style dish composed of Mahi Mahi, lobster, and Alaskan king crab. A perfectly cooked rack of lamb, complete with roasted parsnips, followed.

"Anyone care for coffee or brandy—or both?" Haynesworth asked, indicating that he planned to imbibe.

"Not for me, darling," Mrs. Haynesworth answered. "And if you start in on the brandy, remember our guests still have to drive over to their hotel. Better to give them a bottle to take back with them."

"Yes, yes, I won't pour long ones," he said.

"Wow, a spot of brandy sounds wonderful," Lucas replied.

"Good man. How about you, Carson?" Haynesworth asked.

"Well, last time I tried to refuse you it got me in trouble. But if it's all right, I'll let Lucas do the drinking for both of us for the rest of the night. Thank you anyway."

"Fair enough." Haynesworth chuckled. "Come on, Lucas; let's retire to my study where we can better relax. By the way, do you like a good cigar?"

The two men excused themselves, withdrawing from the dining room.

"Please don't feel obliged to stay up on my account, Mrs. Haynesworth," Carson said. "I can entertain myself plenty just looking around your home. You have such an amazing collection of art everywhere."

"Carson, please stop calling me Mrs. Haynesworth, for God's sake. It makes me more self-conscious about my age than I already am. Besides, if you were really interested in my art pieces, I'd love to show them to you. But be forewarned, I can be more pedantic about my art than Colton is about his damn trains. So you must promise to stop me when you can't stand hearing any more."

They wandered the house with Connie acting the role of docent, expounding upon her collection of sculptures, paintings and folk art. All of the pieces were from Asia, her specialty and passion. As a girl, she had lived in a number of Asian countries while her father had served as the Undersecretary of State for Southeast Asian Affairs. She had combined this background with a graduate degree in art history, to become a recognized authority in the field, serving as an advisor to curators at various major museums.

"This is certainly a contrast to your husband's interest," Carson dared comment.

"Rather." She laughed. "Colton, bless his heart, tolerates my art taste, although it's quite contrary to his. He likes some of the European masters, but if he could replace all my collection with Remingtons, he'd be far happier. It's the culture, really, that stumps him. I got him to go on one trip to Asia, but that was enough for him. In fact, he hasn't even cared too much for Europe the times we've been there. Although he loves their rail system."

"Well, seems like you get to say what goes in the house and he gets the garage and his study," he observed.

"I suppose it seems unfair of me." She smiled. "But he does make me compromise with some things. We keep the upstairs fairly devoid of my collection, except for my study, which he never has to go into. And I keep some of my favorite pieces down in the basement, where he doesn't have to see them. Those pieces upset him."

"Oh, what are they?"

"I can show you if you wish. Follow me."

She led him to a door that opened to stairs covered in Berber carpet. They descended and walked through a dimly lit hallway, stopping by a small room that had been set up as a shrine. Inside was a large stone Buddha. Carson paused to take in the ambiance. It reminded him of Rhiannon's place. Candles burned along an altar, and the smoke from incense curled around a human form. Caesar Chiang slowly turned from his meditation pose and returned Carson's stare.

Pulling Carson away from the altar room, Connie led him further along the basement hallway to a heavy, fireproof metal door. There they entered a large room with glass cases, flat files and wall-mounted displays. She turned on a bank of ceiling-mounted spotlights.

"It's mostly Tibetan art," she began. "The room's hermetically sealed to protect the work. Most of these pieces are quite old, many of them smuggled out during the Chinese takeover. Are you familiar with the term *Dharmapala*?"

Carson's throat tightened. An urge to flee surged through his body, but he was too stunned to move. Until now, his exposure to images representing the Dharmapalas had been limited to the pictures he had seen in Rhiannon's books. Now he was coming face to face with original artwork, created by the very people who had lived and breathed the reality of these wrathful gods.

"Well, come on. You can't see much just standing at the doorway."

He woodenly moved toward Connie's side. She began describing aspects of the various artifacts in her collection, eventually coming to the tankas, the painted banners on which the wrathful deities displayed fearsome might and scornful expressions. As in his visions, multiple arms brandished an arsenal of weapons as the wrathful gods rode upon wild animals or danced over corpses. Human skulls adorned their headgear and girdles. Many of the images depicted the deities in the midst of sexual union with their consorts. The faded colors gave the images a sense of timelessness. He was entranced, caught somewhere between fear and awe.

"You seem very taken by these, Carson," Connie said, as if she were trying to draw some response from him as they moved slowly from image to image.

"Quite."

"Are you Buddhist or a student of Tibetan art?"

"Neither, really."

"My, I don't recall ever seeing anyone so engaged by these who wasn't a connoisseur of them already. Would you like more time here? I can leave you alone for a while if you wish."

"No! No, don't do that," he exclaimed, grasping her arm for reassurance.

"Very well. Are you all right?"

Carson was suddenly embarrassed. "I'm sorry. Something about these images seems to affect me deeply. Art does funny things to some people, right? And it's been a long day, as well," he explained lamely.

"Yes," she said. "Perhaps you should come back in the morning, when you're more rested and have another viewing then."

"No, no thanks, I don't think that's necessary," he quickly answered, panicking that he was somehow back in the session with the Dharmapala. "I've read a little something about these gods, but this is the first time I've actually seen any of the genuine indigenous art that represents them."

"Oh, then you know how ominous they are," she said with a knowing smile. "Colton doesn't like coming in here at all. Gives him the willies, but he'd never admit it. Caesar Chiang only comes in here after he has made rather lengthy propitiation to these beings. He understands something of the culture from whence they come. I must admit that some weird things have happened down here when I've been alone. But since I'm their caretaker, I think I'm safe. At least they know I marvel at their beauty. Plus, I've listed in my estate a condition that specifies that when the political climate in Tibet is restored, these pieces are to be returned."

She waltzed Carson slowly on through the gallery's collection. From every direction, the eyes of the fierce gods burned into his soul, seeming to infuse him with a paradox of blessings and threats.

Carson and Connie returned to the main floor. From down the hallway came the inebriated laughter of Haynesworth and Lucas.

"Sounds like they've been having fun together," she said, shaking her head as she led Carson back toward the study. "Colton, darling, would you be so kind as to escort Lucas out here? Our guests need to get to their hotel and we have a 9:30 meeting with the Rose Festival committee in the morning."

"My apologies for staying so late," Carson inserted.

"Nonsense, we've both enjoyed having you here," she said. "He hates the damn Rose Festival, but it's important that he has something to do with his retirement time, besides watching sports and playing with electric trains."

Lucas and Haynesworth emerged together with smiles and flushed faces. After their good-byes, Carson helped Lucas into the Range Rover. They circled back down the drive.

As they came to the columns at the driveway's end, Caesar Chiang suddenly stepped out of the dark. Carson slowed to a stop and rolled down the window.

"I make something for you," Caesar Chiang said.

The man's face remained expressionless. Carson waited, wondering what this was about. Lucas had already fallen asleep. Slowly, Caesar Chiang pulled something off his neck and handed it to Carson.

"You and your friend must be very careful. Please wear. Good protection," he said.

Carson held the gift against the dashboard lighting. As best he could tell, it was some kind of amulet. He pulled it over his head and turned to Caesar Chiang.

"Hey, thank you very—"

But Caesar Chiang had vanished into the night. A keen sense of vulnerability pierced Carson. He turned onto the street, heading toward the hotel, trying to grasp the meaning of having met Connie Haynesworth and her art collection.

Chapter 16

The Big Boy

The Spike & Rail squatted among shabby warehouses, with long-forgotten purposes, alongside the large rail yard in Ogden, Utah. As Carson had discovered, Ogden was a major destination on any railroad buff's map. Union Pacific operated a major rail center here and the city was the home of a renowned railroad museum. But perhaps most meaningfully, Ogden had the Spike & Rail, a railroad café that was a throwback to another era, a living museum for people who loved railroading. For such people, no trip to Ogden was complete without a meal and a prolonged visit at the famed café, especially if Angel McBee, its legendary proprietor, was on duty.

Earlier that afternoon, Carson and Lucas had shot a lengthy interview with Angel, who provided them with engaging yarns from both railroading and her own life.

She was the only child of a family with a solid railroading pedigree. Her father and uncles, following their father, had worked for Union Pacific all their lives. For many years, Angel's mother had run a boardinghouse for railroad men. The boardinghouse was long gone. The café was now the only vestige of the family's proud heritage, running on a 24-hour schedule and closing only on Christmas Day. The aging café remained a viable operation, mostly due to the fact that Angel knew railroads and she knew people; everyone loved her.

The men who had frequented her mother's boardinghouse had given her the nickname Angel as a small child. Now, in her mid-seventies, Angel continued to work with verve, barking out commands to her staff and advice to her customers.

Railroad memorabilia hung from the café's walls. A gallery of deteriorating sepia photos recalled the once proud machines and the men who operated them. One entire wall was dedicated to train wrecks, each annotated with date and location; number of cars and locomotives derailed; length of time required to restore operations, and, lastly, number of deaths caused.

"You boys need more coffee?" Angel asked, a cigarette dangling from the corner of her mouth.

"No thanks," Lucas replied, trying to warm his hands around a heavy coffee mug stained by use.

"I'm fine, too, thanks," Carson said.

Until now, they had been fortunate with the weather. Roads had generally been clear of snow except at some of the higher elevations. And all their filming so far had been indoors. But tonight they had been thrust against the elements with little mercy.

"These Hollywood people can take forever, it seems," Angel said, coughing and laughing simultaneously. "Bet they're freezing their little L.A. asses off."

A Hollywood film crew was in town for a movie, set in the 1930s, which would include vintage railroad scenes. This required staging the rail yard to fit the period. Tonight they were coordinating filming sequences with the movements and sounds of period locomotives, so no actors were involved. This created an ideal opportunity for Carson and Lucas to come onto the set and film, a privilege negotiated by Charles Landon, who was old chums with the producer. Carson and Lucas had been on the set earlier that day, setting up their own cameras and sound equipment. The professional lighting provided by the movie company was a fortuitous coincidence.

But the main attraction and impetus for Carson's presence tonight was the appearance of one of the world's most famed steam locomotives, a recently fully restored Union Pacific 4-8-8-4 Big Boy, one of the largest steam engines ever built. Landon was thrilled that the Big Boy had been requisitioned from the

Ogden museum. This was made possible through a sizable contribution by the film company's producer, to assist in completing the locomotive's restoration. Landon, much to his frustration, could not be there. He had previously committed to speak at a conference in Prague.

The filming agenda was supposedly known only to those connected with the film, but word had leaked out. Railroad buffs surrounded the yard, waiting for the opportunity to see the famed engine in action. Soon the behemoth would huff and puff its way into the yard, pulling a full contingent of period cars. The Spike & Rail was electric with anticipation, awaiting the arrival of the storied iron monster.

Carson glanced at the old clock hanging askew on the wall, its black hands indicating 11:25. They had been in the café for over an hour now, waiting along with a host of others, enjoying the seedy warmth of the Spike & Rail on a bitter night. Even the catering crew had sought shelter inside. Naturally, things were behind schedule with the Hollywood production company.

"Gonna have a real train in the yard tonight, children, oh Lordy, yes," Angel proclaimed as she made her rounds through the café. "One that eats black dirt and snorts out holy hell."

The crowd cheered Angel's every exclamation.

"Now, you young people wouldn't know anything about what railroads were like back when I was a child," she said, pausing to exhale cigarette smoke. "Yes sir, back then the trains had to be really fast to get away from them dinosaurs!"

Angel laughed heartily, giving a wink to one of her waitresses, who was flirting with an out-of-town patron.

"I've seen 'em all come through this yard," Angel boasted. "Been watching them trains all my life. Yes sir, I have. But the Big Boy, oh, now that was a locomotive! She's a battleship that sails on steel wheels, pulling the world behind her without a care."

"You must have witnessed some big changes," Lucas said.

"Sonny, I've watched it all. I thought the worst was when they brought in them diesels. I kind of liked 'em at first; they were real pretty and so modern looking, and all. Thought it meant Ogden was turning into something important when they got here. Never realized it was the death knell for the old steamers. No sir."

"When was that?"

"Started soon after the war. My husband, Floyd, never came back from the fighting in the Pacific, and then the old steamers were next to go. Things change; that's the way of the world, I figure."

"Wow, I'm sorry," Lucas said.

"Oh, don't bother none." Angel smiled. "I went through worse and got by, I reckon."

"Well, your café doesn't look like it's had to change much," Lucas added. "This is a great place you've got here."'

"Now listen to him. I think that boy is trying to flirt with me." Angel laughed, lighting another cigarette. "I know this old place ain't like one of them fancy eateries out in California. Hell, I hear they'll charge a person damn near twenty bucks just for a plate of cheese grits 'cause it comes with an Italian name."

"No, I mean it, really! Don't change a thing. Everything here's wonderful," Lucas insisted.

"Would you listen to him carry on?" She laughed again. "I better tighten my corset or I might be finding him in my bed come morning."

Lucas blushed while the café's patrons hooted and made catcalls.

"And you might better bring a friend along," Angel added. "'Cause, honey, you don't look like no railroad man."

Carson sank back in the café booth, allowing his mind to wander for the first time in days. Since leaving Portland their time had been filled with either driving or filming, following Landon's itinerary that included their now being in Ogden.

Their second interview had required a day's drive to Missoula. Dr. Haze was a professor at the University of Montana, whose specialty was the history of the economic development of Montana. He was the antiquarian type, happy with all things not of his own lifetime.

Though Haze's train table was not as impressive as Colton Haynesworth's, he spoke eloquently about the role of railroads in the expansion of the West. Carson wondered how his Indian friends would have interpreted the same information. Nevertheless, the footage was successful.

Upon leaving Missoula, Carson and Lucas had headed back into Idaho and down to Pocatello to interview a retired military man, General Mitchell Lynch. The general lived just outside of town in a large, comfortable house. In the basement, he had created a rambling layout, featuring model locomotives with the markings of the Burlington Northern. His model featured rows of flatcars loaded with miniature army tanks, assorted armored vehicles and camouflaged trucks. He was a serious man and took his model railroading seriously. Carson had felt the general's aloof persona did not play well to the camera and questioned whether the footage would make it past the editing room.

After that, discovering Angel McBee was a delight.

"Yes sir, when that old Big Boy comes down the tracks tonight, it'll give off the most god-awful racket, cursing out steam and coal smoke. Makes every fiber of your body quiver," Angel declared, turning to a young woman from the Hollywood film crew who had stopped in to get warm. "Honey, it's just like being under a good railroad man, if you know what I mean!"

Angel coughed and laughed simultaneously, shuttling through the café to entertain other patrons. Carson glanced at the old clock again; it was nearly midnight. He wished he had time to phone Rhiannon, but the Big Boy's arrival could happen at any moment.

Besides missing her, he needed to talk with her about another matter—he was starting to doubt his ability to sustain his connection with the Dharmapala. While continuing to say prayers and make propitiations, he was experiencing less and less charge from these spiritual exercises. It was as if he were being reabsorbed back into the ordinary world. Even Taz's menacing glare had lost its meaning. Yet he knew only too well the dangers of becoming lackadaisical. In the midst of the café's chatter, he closed his eyes and prayed for guidance.

A shrill whistle blast cut through the night. The café fell silent. It blew again—the call of a leviathan.

"It's her! She's coming!" Angel yelled.

The entire crowd of the Spike & Nail poured out, spilling into the rail yard. Carson and Lucas fumbled to zip up their coats while running to take position behind their equipment. From out beyond the dark perimeter of the rail yard, a low rumble was growing with intensity.

Carson had set up two cameras, the first with a wide-angle lens to capture the Big Boy at a distance, as the train pulled into the expansive rail yard. The second was to be handheld, allowing him to film the locomotive up close as it rolled past at the track's edge. Lucas had stationed a network of mics at various locations, to capture an assortment of the train's sounds at different places as it came into the yard.

The mournful whistle blew again, now accompanied by a rhythmic chugging. From around a line of parked boxcars at the yard's far end, a great beacon emerged. The train rounded the curve, its powerful headlight illuminating the track. Spontaneous cheers went up across the yard. Carson, too, felt the electricity.

The giant engine came into view. Smoke belched from its stack, while its lower quarters hissed out pristine clouds of steam. Carson guided the camera's lens, absorbing the nocturnal spectacle, while calculating the moment he would have to abandon the first camera and race to pick up the second one beside the tracks.

The whistle again tore through the night, accompanied by the sound of a clanging bell.

"Now!" he yelled to himself, hopping over rows of tracks to get in position.

Skillfully grabbing up the second camera and lifting it to his shoulder, he stood facing the oncoming giant within feet of the track's edge. He had never been so close to something this massive in motion. The locomotive rocked from side to side as it slowed under a frightening squeal of brakes. Another deafening blast from the whistle penetrated him. The great metallic machine overran his consciousness, as if the beast were sucking him up into its enormous body. He was petrified, consumed by a moment of exhilarating terror.

"Good evening, adept," a familiar but haunting voice said telepathically.

Carson jerked the camera from his eyes and wheeled around, but only the train was there.

"It would behoove you to make a better greeting than that, pilgrim." The Dharmapala laughed, his voice coming out of the enormous steam engine. "What's the matter? Not expecting me? It would serve you well to realize that when you pray for my protection and blessings, you may receive them under circumstances not of your choosing."

"Great Lord, is it really you?" Carson sputtered mentally, peering at the steamy, dark locomotive.

"Why? Were you expecting someone else?"

His head swirled. How could this be happening? He hadn't sought an audience with the Dharmapala. Nor had he taken any medicine.

"Come, come, adept. You give your skills little credit. Or is it mine that you insult? You have been beseeching my assistance since our first encounter, and wisely you have continued to pay homage to me—a practice more necessary than you might imagine. But now, is this any way to respond when I make an appearance?"

Carson was numb, oblivious to the night's harsh cold, the camera hanging limp in one hand. He struggled to regain his thoughts.

"I had no idea that you would come into my ordinary world," he responded through the telepathic dialogue. "Great Lord, I'm utterly sorry to have disturbed you with my—"

"Don't further insult me with these idiotic apologies. If you are going to obtain power through me, adept, I expect to be well treated. I won't have pathetic weaklings feed off my energy. Do you fully understand?"

Carson nodded in silence.

"Now, approach closer; I need to examine your scent."

He staggered toward the side of the giant locomotive. Its boiler continued generating voluminous clouds of steam. It was alive. Again he sensed the heavy, dark breath from that first encounter with the Great Lord.

"Very well, you've not been in her presence. We may continue to speak."

"Whose presence, Great One?" he asked, further bewildered.

"My consort, of course!"

"I don't understand; how would that be?" he implored.

"Oh, adept, you are indeed naïve. I see I have more to teach you than I thought. But first, what do you think?"

"I humbly beg your pardon, Great One—think about what?"

"The train, pilgrim, the train!" The deity laughed. "I've been curious about manifesting as one of these things for some time now, and tonight I have done it. Am I not glorious and mighty in this form? Perhaps I should take one of these back home with me."

Carson felt his knees start to give. He cursed the insanity that had come to reside within him. Here he was, standing in a rail yard on a bleak night, engrossed in a telepathic conversation with an ancient deity from the Himalayas, who had embodied himself in a steam locomotive. Of all the spirit forms in the cosmos, why was it that he had come to connect with this one?

"Do you suspect me of being vain and silly, adept?" the god snapped. "And don't bother trying to hide your thoughts; I read your mind well enough."

"Deepest apologies, Great One. It's only that I don't have enough training to understand your complex ways. I fail due to the limitations of my simple human mind, or the madness that seems to plague it."

"You cannot afford to make many failures in this realm, adept. I have warned you of this before. What I choose to do and how I do those things is not a matter that need fit your understanding, much less your approval. You may regain some merit by showing much adulation. Come, adept, walk around my form and allow your admiration to fully flower. And by all means, use that instrument of yours to record my glory and might."

Carson pulled the camera back up to his shoulder, moving as if guided by hypnotic suggestion. He filmed in close, moving around the giant locomotive, stepping across the steel rails directly in front of the idling steam engine and then down the other side.

"Well, adept, are you mute? Must you humiliate me by more withholding? I require your compliments on my manifestation. When have you ever seen such a stunning avatar, especially one pulling a legion of heavy chariots behind? Is my wrath not awesome? Is my breath not charged with terror? Is my strength not worthy of legend?"

"Yes, Great One, it's as you say."

The wrathful deity whispered telepathically, "Adept, it would be wise to find the words yourself; I enjoy hearing them. It is beneath me to have to coax them from you. Do you understand?"

"I will strive to render more appropriate adoration, Great One. As before, I am overwhelmed by your presence."

"And strive you must, if you are to obtain from me what you seek," the god said, pausing to allow the weight of his words to sink in. "Now, hear me well, I didn't bother to confer with you tonight for my benefit. You have made propitiation to me and it has gained you some favor, but only some; enough for me to take a minor interest in your fate. You have asked for powers, powers to enable you to further your spiritual work. And soon, adept, very soon, you will need a bounty of such protection. A growing danger awaits you; this I have foreseen. Those you call the Visitors are seeking you. Do you understand?"

One fear replaced another. Instinctively, Carson jerked his body around to face an attack. The large bank of camera lights aimed on the locomotive blinded him. Carson was in a panic. Were they here now? Could he quickly surround himself with enough shielding? Would any spirit helpers be coming to protect him? Where could he hide?

"Good reflexes, pilgrim, but save them for when you need them." The deity laughed. "This encounter will not occur here, at least not while I am present. They don't want to incur my fury, I can assure you. If your life is to be taken tonight, it will be at my pleasure, not theirs. I will not have them usurp what is mine to have, be it steel machines or herds of yak, mountains or men."

Carson turned back to the train, washed in a malaise of foreboding. "Great One, perhaps you should kill me now and be done with it. I don't want to do this anymore."

"Don't disappointment me with your weariness, pilgrim. I have made an investment in you. I expect you to hold up your side of our little arrangement. I have instilled in you portions of my power; I require that you make a good showing, not some doleful display of surrender. You had better honor me by using my gifts well, or something worse than death at the hands of the Visitors may find you."

"Yes, Great Lord," he replied numbly, flooded with hopelessness.

"I have other matters to attend to and must now leave. It is best that I not stay in one place too long, because of her. Farewell, pilgrim, and send more offerings to me. I delight in such bounties."

The giant locomotive emitted a sudden whistle blast and lunged forward. With a banging domino effect, the railcars locked their couplings. The enormous engine rolled on down the tracks, bellowing out thick puffs of coal smoke. Carson stood motionless, watching as it moved to the end of the rail yard.

"Well, that was some cool stuff, all right," Lucas said, running up to Carson for a congratulatory high-five slap.

Carson remained unresponsive, gazing in the direction of the train.

"Hey, man, you all right?"

"Huh?" Carson responded.

"Are you okay?" Lucas insisted.

"Maybe, I suppose so."

"Well, you were sure moving nifty with the camera. I mean, that mother only stopped for a few seconds but there you were, right on it, moving in close. And then you did that little dance across the tracks right in front of it. Christ, I was scared shitless watching you. The film crew were yelling for you to get the fuck away from it. Shit, man, the engineer up in the cab couldn't see anything with all the lights they had shining on the train. But you were like this fearless son of a bitch with the handheld. I mean, that footage is going to be fucking incredible."

"How long did the train stop beside me?"

"It could only have been a few seconds. And the film crew people were telling me it wasn't supposed to do that. They had one of their guys inside the cab with the engineer on a radio. Seems something weird was happening with the engine for a minute there; the pressure gauges were saying the old mother was gonna blow. They thought the whole goddamn locomotive was about to explode, like some giant energy ball had gotten inside the fucker. I was seriously freaked. You were going to be history!"

"Lucas, my feet feel frozen. Let's get out of here."

Chapter 17

Memphis

Predawn washed the motel parking lot in chilly, gray light. Carson felt exhausted. Sleep had only made him feel worse. Troublesome dreams had awakened him, covered in sweat and panicked because he could not remember who he was. The previous night's encounter with the giant steam engine god continued to shred his already fractured psyche. He was left with two deeply troubling realizations: first, his relationship with the Dharmapala was indeed real; second, he had assuredly lost his mind.

He lay in bed waiting for a reasonable hour to call Rhiannon. He pondered how he might describe the rail yard phenomenon, reflecting on how preposterous it would sound to anyone but her.

The phone jarred him from his reflections.

"Carson!" a familiar voice yelled.

"Yeah."

"Thank God I caught you," Landon barked. "Something's up, and we have to make a change in your schedule. I need you boys to get over to Memphis pronto, or we'll miss Sugar Wilson's layout. He's got some troubles with the Securities and Exchange Commission and word is that he's about to take a little trip out of the country for a few years, while his lawyers do some negotiation. Not having a man of his stature in the documentary would be a pity. He's a major player in our community, you know."

Carson struggled to focus on business. "Sugar who?"

"Don't let the name mislead you. Sugar Wilson is an MD with a PhD in molecular biology, and one of the world's leading pharmacological researchers. Besides that, he comes from old money—the kind that built this country and its railroads."

"Got it, solid railroad stock," Carson responded, trying to

muster enthusiasm. "But what about the people we've already scheduled?"

"Don't worry about them. I'll work things out for you. Just you and what's-his-name get over to Memphis now. Drop everything else. From what I hear, poor Sugar isn't going to hang around for more than a couple of days. He's got friends in South America so there's a safe haven waiting for him there. Of course, I made calls on his behalf, but when the damn Feds indict you, man, you're screwed unless your guy is sitting in the White House."

"What did this man do to bring the SEC down on him?" Carson asked, trying to hide his annoyance.

"Never mind that; just get over there fast."

"So, let me get this straight," he said stiffly. "We're now to head out immediately for Tennessee and just drop everything else as planned until further notice?"

"You boys are pros; you know how these things go. By the time you're done in Memphis, I'll have a new schedule put together for what's next. Now, tell me—how did it go last night with that sweet monster pulling into the Ogden yard?"

"Fine, I expect. Of course we haven't viewed the footage yet, but it should be good."

"Fine? It damn better be terrific!" Landon countered. "If that footage is missing or not right, you're going to have to go back there and get something on that Big Boy engine. No way am I not including it."

An awkward silence hung over the telephone line.

"Carson?" Landon snapped.

"Yeah, sorry, just doing some calculations on this end."

"You can calculate on the road. Now get your asses moving, for Christ's sake. The train's leaving the station, man!"

"Right, we'll be rolling within the hour."

"I'll have someone from my office phone you with details on where you're to go in Memphis. I'll be in Europe another week at least."

"So, how's Prague?"

"Delightful," Landon replied. "I just might buy part of the fucker. Now get moving."

Traffic along I-80 was slow due to a snowstorm that had generously blanketed Wyoming. Despite the efforts of snowplows working through the night, certain parts of the highway were still clogged with cars.

"Where are we, man?" Lucas asked, rousing himself from a prolonged nap.

"We're about sixty miles west of Rawlins. Just crossed the Continental Divide a few miles back."

"Oh, that's good," Lucas mumbled, squinting from the glare of the snow-covered landscape. "Guess that means it's all downhill to Memphis."

"Hope you're well rested," Carson said. "If we can't make better time than this, we're going to have to drive through the night taking shifts. I've a strong hunch that when Landon's office phones, they're going to have us scheduled to be filming this upstanding citizen sometime tomorrow. Wouldn't want to delay a would-be felon from sneaking out of the country, especially if he's a great railroad man."

"Hell, I'm looking forward to meeting this one—Dr. Sugar Wilson! Wonder how he got that name." Lucas laughed. "Hey, maybe we could do a documentary on America's greatest white-collar criminals, a sort of Who's Who; get them all bragging about how they pulled off their scams. Now, that would make for some killer footage."

"Lucas, pull out the maps; we need to figure out our route. Given the chance of more snow and ice, I think we need to head south when we get to Cheyenne and go down to pick up I-70, working on down to I-40."

"I still don't understand why we just didn't fly. This is crazy,"

Lucas whined.

Carson had convinced himself that it would be best to drive, not knowing what Landon might plan next with their filming schedule. But in truth, Rhiannon had warned him to avoid air travel during these times. Maintaining contact with the Earth provided more protection, she said. Despite the distance, if they pushed hard, they could be in Memphis sometime the next day—barring the unforeseen.

By late afternoon, they were navigating their way around Denver. They decided to stop for their first real meal of the day while the rush hour traffic thinned. It was going to be a long night, pushing halfway across Kansas and then down into Oklahoma.

Landon's office had phoned midday with the contact information for Memphis. As Carson suspected, they were indeed scheduled to film at Sugar Wilson's home the following afternoon. It was now certain that they would be driving all night.

He pulled out his cell phone to try Rhiannon again, having made numerous attempts to reach her throughout the day. Once again, he was greeted by her voice mail. He left another message, asking her to call him.

Lucas took the wheel when they left Denver, driving east into the oncoming night. He planned to make his shift last to the junction with I-35.

All seemed to be going well as they pushed across an expanse that had once been the domain of great herds of buffalo. Still, many miles remained before Memphis. From his post on the dashboard, Taz snarled at the oncoming traffic. Carson drifted off to sleep.

Hundreds of miles to the southwest, Luther Redbone and other medicine workers on the New Mexico reservation were climbing down into a kiva, the round chamber used for their spiritual ceremonies. There was work to do—it would be another difficult night.

"Hey, that's for you, man. Wanna get that?" Lucas said, shaking Carson from his sleep. "Your cell, man; answer the fucker or turn it off."

"Hello?"

"Did I wake you?" a welcomed voice asked.

"Hey, where've you been?"

"I was staying over at a friend's. There've been some developments," Rhiannon began. "How are you?"

The cell reception was spotty; their words were broken.

"I wouldn't know where to begin, but for starters, we've had a change of plans and we're on our way to Memphis—nonstop."

"Where? I missed that."

"Memphis. Memphis, Tennessee!" he yelled.

"You're driving tonight?"

There was a long pause. Carson couldn't tell if Rhiannon was pondering the implications of his being on the road or if the connection was cutting out. Hoping she was hearing, Carson continued. "Yeah, thanks to Charles Landon, we don't have a choice in the matter. Besides, this feels about as safe as being anywhere else. Listen, I'll call you later when I get better coverage. I need to tell you something."

"Carson? Carson, can you hear me?"

"Sort of. Rhiannon, what's up?"

"I'm afraid to tell you this, but I'm leaving for a while. I'm at the airport. Seems we've both been forced into unplanned travel. If I can reach you, I'll phone you from London. I'm changing planes there."

"What? You're going to London?"

"Not exactly, I'm on my way to a rural part of southern Turkey."

"Turkey!"

"Carson, you're breaking up; I'll phone when I can—"

"Wait, I gotta talk to you."

The cell phone was dead. No Service, the faceplate announced.

"Lucas, when do we get into a town?"

"Well, let's see. Wichita is several hours ahead. I've heard that they've got electricity and running water there now, but I don't know if it would qualify as a town, really."

"If you see someplace, an exit with a filling station or whatever, pull in. I've got to get to a pay phone."

"Woman problems, hombre? No matter where you go, there's always woman problems. You should take a nice, deep hit off that bottle of port Mr. Haynesworth sent us home with and go back to sleep. Whatever she's up to, you can't do anything about it way the fuck out here."

Lucas' teasing loosened him up; there was no point in working himself up more than he already was. He began calming down.

"Maybe you're right, my friend. Never mind the stop; just drive on."

"So, if I might be so bold as to pry into your private life, who is this woman anyway? I know it ain't Allison."

"No, it sure as hell isn't Allison. I'm not sure who she is, actually."

"I know one thing for sure—seems she's got under your skin. I believe you've gone and fucked up big time and fallen in love."

"Perhaps so. If only it were that simple."

"Don't tell me. She's married with six kids, and her husband's a jealous, homicidal maniac who's stalking you at this very minute."

He'd gladly exchange an enraged husband for the ever-present threat of the Visitors.

"No, this is different," Carson mumbled.

"Thanks for that penetrating insight."

"It's just too complicated to explain."

"Whatever," Lucas said impatiently. "You know, man, you've been a little weird this trip."

A silence descended upon them. Carson peered ahead at the vacuous highway. Embarrassed, he reclined in his seat. Lifting the bottle of port to his mouth, he took a long, slow sip of the velvety juice.

"Yeah, I know," he admitted softly.

Chapter 18

The Oracle of Tarsus

Joe Buck and Sydney sprinkled sacred water over the smoldering embers of the previous night's vigil fire, sending the last of their prayers into the ether. Inside the dilapidated cabin, Wounded Paw remained in a trance before the skull of the giant bear. Bittersweet tears rolled down his wrinkled face. Last night he had made contact with the spirit of his great-grandfather. The Ghost Dance, that great nineteenth-century movement, had been created through his great-grandfather's visions, spreading messianic hope among Native Americans for their liberation from white domination.

Matching the pace of the faster semi-trucks, Carson and Lucas drove with little concern for speed limits, motoring east into the first light of dawn. With one driving while the other slept, they had made excellent time through Kansas and across Oklahoma. Perhaps the Dharmapala was watching over them; perhaps it was the amulet Caesar Chiang had given Carson and Lucas. Whatever contributed to their well-being, Carson felt buoyed that the long night had passed.

At a breakfast stop in Tulsa, they filled their thermos with premium, high-octane coffee. Then at lunchtime, at a refueling stop outside Little Rock, they lucked upon a roadside stand with exceptional down-home barbecue.

The signs seemed favorable, especially the change in climate. They had driven out of winter into a Southern spring. The soft, fresh colors of flowering trees ornamented the landscape with the life-renewing forces of April. The air was laden with warmth and moisture. They would be in Memphis by midafternoon.

Thousands of miles to the south, Sabina scurried through the narrow alleyways of the hillside village, clutching her medicine bag, knowing that the others were already preparing. An icy wind off the surrounding peaks of the Andes punished her old body. She stopped occasionally, cautiously checking over her shoulder, assuring herself that she was not being followed.

Inside the house at the edge of the village, the small group of medicine workers said little as they prayed and meditated in preparation for the coming night's work. Fondling the rosary that had once signified salvation through the Church, Father Clemente whispered a prayer asking for strength through the true blood of Christ.

Following that horrendous day when he had discovered the destruction of the pagan commune, Father Clemente had sought answers within a spiritual network that practiced ways outside the confines of the Church. And consequently, he had been summoned before a council, for refusing to cease his unorthodox spiritual work with those deemed unholy by certain authorities within the archdiocese. A colleague had warned him that the council had predetermined its finding. Two men from a special agency within the Vatican were planning to escort Father Clemente to an unspecified sanatorium.

It wasn't the threat of censure or even defrocking that caused him not to appear. No, he had become fully engaged with a group of Chilean spiritual workers, who employed a mixture of early Christian mysticism and old indigenous shamanism. Their work was far too critical to be interrupted by Church authorities. And having failed to appear before the council in Santiago, he was now no more than an outlaw in the eyes of his archbishop.

Cautiously opening the heavy wooden door, Sabina quickly slipped inside the makeshift sanctuary. Another encounter with the Visitors was imminent. Their last one had taken them to the brink of annihilation, requiring every ounce of their collective strength just to hold on. Don Arturo, the senior member of the group, moved silently among them, anointing each one with a protective holy oil.

A soft rain drizzled against the windowpanes of her departure gate at Heathrow airport. Rhiannon stood anxiously. Her connecting flight to Istanbul was already boarding. Still, there was no sign of the person for whom she had journeyed so far—the Oracle of Tarsus.

She had been told there would be a chance that the Oracle would have to cancel her plans at the last minute. There were many dangers that had to be taken into consideration; some recent, like the Visitors, and others ancient and perhaps even equally sinister. After all, it had been three millennia since work like this had been orchestrated.

"Shouldn't you be boarding, madam?" a tall man in a British Airways uniform asked.

"Yes, but I'm waiting for a colleague," Rhiannon replied.

"Perhaps that person has previously boarded, madam," the agent said in a calm manner. "Due to certain security precautions, a particular person and her entourage were allowed to board separately from the regular passengers. We do this occasionally—a sort of special diplomatic procedure, you might say. She wishes that I inform you that she will speak with you onboard after the flight has departed."

While sensing the man to be telling the truth, Rhiannon remained apprehensive. As the last of the passengers moved through the jetway gate, she had little choice but to board.

The flight was full, and Rhiannon's seat in the middle of a row didn't allow her much of an observation point to study the other passengers. She had been given no description of the Oracle's appearance. After all, her identity was a closely guarded secret. Rhiannon could only wait until this mysterious person made contact.

All this had happened suddenly. When Gwenllyan, a mentor

and longtime friend, had phoned from her retreat in Wales and asked if Rhiannon would be willing to participate in an epic undertaking, she was initially elated. She had long ago heard of the Oracle of Tarsus, but the true nature of the Oracle's work remained largely unknown. The accounts she had heard were filled with occult legends of political power and international conspiracies. Some people questioned whether the Oracle even existed today. Now, alone on the flight, she began to doubt her decision.

Outside, the sky was rapidly darkening as the jetliner raced eastward into the night. It had been nearly two hours since she'd departed from London and her concern grew as the minutes passed.

"Excuse me, miss, but I'm afraid you're in the wrong seat," a flight attendant said.

"Am I?"

"Yes, would you please follow me and I can correct the matter?"

Rhiannon gathered herself and followed the flight attendant toward the front of the plane. Upon entering the first-class cabin, the flight attendant pointed to an empty seat next to a small woman in conservative attire. The woman, who appeared to be in her early seventies, peered out the window as if she were looking at something below.

"Here you are, sorry about the mistake," the flight attendant said and walked away.

Rhiannon sat down slowly, not wanting to disturb the small woman.

"So nice to meet you, my dear," the woman said, still peering out the window. "I don't like to be on these things, but sometimes it's necessary."

"Yes," Rhiannon answered.

"Oh my, you do have such delightful energy," the woman continued, still looking away. "I see Gwenllyan was most correct in recommending you."

Rhiannon felt a sudden sense of relief. "Thank you," she replied. "And are you the—"

"Yes, dear," the woman interrupted, turning to face Rhiannon with a warm smile. "I am the one."

"I'm afraid I didn't know what to expect."

"That's the idea, my dear," the Oracle mused. "Well, part of it these days, I'm afraid. So lovely of you to come."

She had half expected to meet someone dressed in medieval garb, perhaps even wearing a veil. Instead, she was encountering a woman with the dress and demeanor of a refined English lady from St. John's Wood. Only her accent was slightly affected, a veneer of privileged English finishing schools that had been placed over an ancient tongue.

"I'm honored to meet you. And to be joining you," Rhiannon said warmly.

"Yes, my dear, I see that."

"How should I address you? Do I call you Madam Oracle, or do you have a name?"

The Oracle laughed. "Simply call me Priestess; I've got so used to it that I don't think of it as a title anymore. It's just who I am. I've not had a personal name since I was a small child."

"I hope I may be of service," Rhiannon said. "However, Gwenllyan told me nothing more than that we'd be going to a rural part of Turkey. I don't even know what's supposed to happen once we get there. And I'm embarrassed to say, I don't have much real knowledge about you. I've heard of you for many years, but you've always been a great mystery."

The Oracle chuckled. "Yes, it's been necessary that the work of the Daughters remains secret. But now times allow that we might somewhat resurface from our hidden sanctuaries."

Rhiannon glanced about at the nearby passengers, wondering who among them made up the Oracle's entourage, her mind churning with curiosity as to who the Daughters were. No one seemed to stand out.

"Priestess, is it permissible for me to know more of what you intend to do once we arrive at our destination?"

"But of course, child. That's why I sent for you now. There's much you need to know. There will be little time once we get there, and you need to prepare yourself. But before I tell you about what we'll be doing, you need to know some of the history behind the Daughters."

Rhiannon felt a chill run up her spine, realizing something extraordinary was about to be revealed. Again, she glanced around the cabin, nervous about their security.

The Oracle began, "We go back a long time, my dear. How long, we ourselves don't really know. But earlier than the times of kings. The Daughters came out of Egypt—old Egypt. We were there long before the pharaohs. We were an order of priestesses who served the Great Goddess. Of course, the world knows Her today as Isis, but Her names have been many, as you well know.

"Our temple was on the island of Quadjet in the Nile Delta. Millennia later, the island's name was changed to Buto when the Greeks took over Egypt. But throughout all this time, it was our task to sustain the world in accordance with the Great Goddess and to keep all in harmony for the greater good. I know you well understand such things."

Rhiannon nodded.

"Troubles eventually came in those ancient times. A new epoch was emerging and with it, a new political order. Men, acting as kings—and even gods—claimed their right above all others. Even the status of the Great Goddess Herself was challenged. Her consort, Ra, was promoted to become Her lord. Naturally, this new political structure sought to demote Her priestesses, as we posed fierce theological and political opposition to this change.

"Fortunately for us, we had foreseen much of this coming. Through a revelation, we were instructed to leave Egypt and seek sanctuary in a land beyond. So, one night, beneath the darkness of a new moon, the Order slipped away and sailed to Crete. There, we established a new center and continued our work.

"However, another revelation came to us within that same year. Our mission was not complete. We were to expand further and, oh my, at what great cost. The Order was divided into seven cells and instructed to disperse across the ancient world. We were to create a chain of seven sites, spanning much of the known world at the time. And so it was done.

"With the first cell established in Crete, the others set off the following spring. Two sailed west, the first stopping in Sicily and founding a site and temple in the middle of the island, at Lake Pergusa. The other went on, arriving at the coast of Spain. That cell built a temple in the coastal mountains above current-day Cartagena.

"The four cells assigned to go east first traveled together to Anatolia, ancient Turkey. There, one cell settled above the coast at what later became known as the city of Tarsus. It's from this cell that my lineage comes. The next spring, the remaining three cells moved on, one stopping in the hills outside of what today is Mosul, in northern Iraq. The other two continued on to northwest Afghanistan, near what later became the city of Herat. Here, one of the two cells remained. The following summer, the last cell made an arduous journey over high mountain passes, finally settling in the area we know today as Ladakh, very near the present-day Tibetan border.

"And with that, our seven sites were founded and the sacred chain was complete. If you take a world map and mark these locations, you can trace almost a straight line from Ladakh to Cartagena. Imagine accomplishing such a geographic alignment at that time! But oh my, many died through those ordeals. Our Order was greatly weakened; yet we had accomplished what the Great Goddess had told us to do. And in time, we grew strong once more. And the sacred chain allowed the Order to greatly amplify its skills and power."

"Incredible!" Rhiannon whispered. "I've never heard anything of this. Nothing. I'm stunned."

"It's a history whose suppression has suited both sides," the Oracle said. "For us, it's meant more security."

"So what happened after the seven centers were established?" Rhiannon asked, her mind flooded with questions.

The Oracle smiled, as if recalling pleasant memories from her childhood. "All the centers taught and practiced many kinds of knowledge, yet each emerged with a specialization in a particular field. To this day, we don't fully understand why it happened that way; perhaps it was planned. Crete developed as a center for the arts—painting, sculpture, dance, and architecture. Mosul made great advancements in astrology and astronomy and later taught the Chaldeans all they knew. Herat became renowned for its healing arts and knowledge of medicine and pharmacology. Far to the east, nestled in the Himalayas, the Ladakh cell produced astonishing breakthroughs in consciousness and philosophy. Cartagena, on the western extreme, specialized in natural sciences, acquiring vast knowledge about communication with animals, plants and minerals. And Sicily learned all about the sea, of course, her life forms and temperaments, how to navigate upon her and live from her bounty."

"What about Tarsus?" Rhiannon asked, spellbound.

"Now, Tarsus. Well you see, my dear." The priestess paused. "Tarsus was in the center, the keystone for all the others. Given the necessity of maintaining communication across such a vast area, it was only natural that it evolved as the center for psychic science. Messaging was telepathic and sent from one cell to another through the priestesses at Tarsus. Given the nature of their work, it was only fitting that the Order's most esteemed oracle would reside and work there.

"And so our Order continued throughout the centuries while what would later be called civilization, meaning empires and patriarchal domination over the world, grew and spread. In hindsight, I can proudly say the Order managed to sustain itself with exceptional endurance, given the violent forces that rampaged across the lands. Perhaps we couldn't imagine a world existing without us. After all, we had been there holding the planet together from the time before history began."

Tears rolled down Rhiannon's cheeks. She was overcome with feelings of gratitude and loss for these ancient women and their secret history.

Patting Rhiannon's hand, the Oracle spoke gently. "I know it is not easy to take all this in. It comes with such beauty and sadness, such love and such suffering. Shall I continue?"

Rhiannon nodded, longing to hear more despite the bittersweet pain it triggered.

"Danger was constantly around us," the Oracle went on. "Still, we did what we could to protect ourselves. And fortunately, we had allies from time to time, especially among the local peasant folk. For centuries, the famed Amazon warriors protected Tarsus and our center at Mosul. But our time was drawing to an end. There were simply too many struggles and threats to continue as before. By the first millennium BC, troubles had grown to the point where we could no longer operate openly. One by one, the centers closed down and went underground. Over time, most ended up having to relocate to other parts of the world. The sacred chain no longer existed.

"Those who know of us today, which thankfully are few, usually consider us only some obscure occult sorority. Secrecy has served the Order well, though it hasn't been easy to function under such conditions. And somewhere in the midst of all this time and chaos, the Order was given the moniker that it has gone by ever since—the Daughters of Isis."

"You mean the Order still functions today? I'd heard there were only you and some followers. I had no idea."

"Yes, though we were almost exterminated or nearly died out

many times."

"May I ask how many make up the order today?"

"You may ask, but this information is best not shared." The Oracle smiled.

"So, about the other cells, some have survived besides yours?"

"They all have, that I can tell you. This is critical to our journey. Still, we must be cautious with what's known about us; knowledge is power and can be turned to many purposes."

"Besides secrecy, how else has your Order sustained itself over the ages?" she asked, wanting to learn all she could while the plane raced toward Istanbul.

"Well, my dear, despite our sufferings over the centuries, we have always dwelt in the bosom of the Great Goddess Herself. That, indeed, is protection beyond our understanding. Still, we strive to do what we can to sustain ourselves. Also, the Daughters learned long ago the benefit of having friends in high places, as we can often provide them with protection and information that isn't within the domain of their mundane powers. We establish allies."

"That sounds possibly political," Rhiannon injected.

"Politics in its purest form is spiritual work, a directed application of energy," the Oracle explained, suddenly speaking in a powerful voice that came from beyond the small woman sitting next to Rhiannon. "Politics without an awareness of spiritual connection is blindness. Unfortunately, for too long, this age has been foolish enough to think that humankind alone is master over this realm."

"But don't these people you help try to take advantage of your powers?"

"Well of course, that's always been the dilemma, you see." The Oracle laughed softly. "Inevitably, those we have befriended come to some crisis in their lives and turn to us to intercede with something *magical*. And while we may wish to help, it doesn't mean that we can or even should—or that they'll like what we tell them. Such situations are quite complicated and can require delicate diplomacy. And sometimes they simply forego our warnings in the confusion of the moment, as was sadly the case when we lost a dear friend in a Paris tunnel some short years back."

Rhiannon leaned back in her seat, closing her eyes. "Oh my God, Princess Di."

The Oracle shifted abruptly. "But now, enough talk of the past. I must prepare you for our mission," she said.

Rhiannon suddenly felt a wave of alarm run through her body and again she scanned the cabin's passengers. She was certain that the large man sitting two rows back and across the aisle had been watching them.

"Priestess, I'm getting strong readings off a man two rows back. I'm sure he's been observing us."

"I'll have to tell Salamon that his skills are slipping. He's not supposed to be so easily detected." The Oracle smiled again. "You're gifted, my dear. I'm sure he has been observing us, and hopefully everyone else onboard. That's part of his job. He's one of my bodyguards."

"Oh, I see," Rhiannon replied, calming down.

The Oracle leaned closer and took Rhiannon's hand.

"But let's turn to the matter at hand. If need be, let all that I've said up until this moment fall away, and let's focus on what's before us. You see, the Order was among the earliest to detect the coming of the alien spirits; nearly seven years ago, we got indications of their intentions. And like other groups, we've been targeted by their attacks. About six months ago, two women from the Sicilian cell were killed by a completely unexplainable accident. This was on a morning after that cell had fended off one of the Visitors' assaults. The women were sitting in a street café in Palermo, no doubt exhausted from the night before, when a bus jumped the curve and crashed into their table. The authorities never found a driver nor were any passengers aboard. We need no proof as to what caused it."

Rhiannon felt a stab of grief. "Oh, Priestess, I'm so sorry. Of course, I hadn't heard of this. There've been so many who've been lost, ones we'll probably never know of. So, is the Sicilian cell still functioning there?"

"Amazingly, yes. That cell and the one in Spain never had to leave their homes, despite all the invasions and turmoil that took place over the centuries—Greeks, Romans, Moors, Catholicism, pirates, Christian witch hunts, the so-called Age of Enlightenment, Franco, Nazis. Oh my, what a list of ignorant brutes." The Oracle shook her head sadly. "But of course, these cells had to abandon their original temple sites long ago. They melded into the woodwork of the local culture, yet secretly remained intact. In the small villages nearby, they kept their lineage alive, continuing to practice our traditions and passing them down from mother to daughter for countless generations."

"And the others?"

"The others, too, still exist. Always have," the Oracle said. "And oh, what stories they each have about their many migrations and struggles. Today none of the cells are as large as they should be; less than a dozen priestesses comprise most of them. My own cell's been in England for the last 150 years, but before that we were safely operating in India for centuries. I'm afraid I can't reveal too much about those matters; forgive me."

"But of course, Priestess. I understand."

"Thank you, my dear. I know you can appreciate the delicacy of such things, especially in these times. Now, are you ready to hear what you're here for?"

"Of course," Rhiannon said, leaning closer to the Oracle.

"Remember what I said about politics? About being aware of its spiritual dimension? Well, certain conditions have changed that are allowing an unprecedented opportunity for our Order. You see, with both Iraq and Afghanistan possibly open, and the other original sites again accessible—"

"Oh my God!" Rhiannon exclaimed, feeling her throat choke and tears well in her eyes.

"Bless you, child," the Oracle said happily. "You grasp things so quickly. Yes, the Daughters of Isis are returning to restore the sacred chain. Each of the seven cells is reoccupying its original site. You see, dear, after three thousand years, we're going home."

Tears again fell down Rhiannon's face.

"With the chain restored, we can bring the Order's full power into alignment once again. It's always been our goal to restore the seven sites. And the timing couldn't be more needed, given the onslaught of the Visitors. Resisting them will be our first objective. But just to arrive at this point hasn't been easy, mind you. It's taken some extraordinary arrangements. And of course, the powers governing these areas don't know our true purpose. We'll operate covertly. We'll be seen as archaeologists or restoration artists, scholars doing research, what have you. That and some occasional donations to certain local authorities should do the trick."

"Amazing," Rhiannon whispered.

"These are amazing times, my dear."

"But why invite an outsider such as myself?"

"Warm bodies," the Oracle said. "There are simply not enough of us left in the Order to perform the ceremonies properly, especially those that'll be needed initially to align the seven sites, to reconnect the chain. Simply put, we needed to import women such as you, who can assist us with reestablishing our power. We don't have time to rebuild ourselves over several generations. I hope you don't feel taken advantage of. Gwenllyan seemed certain that you'd be an ideal fit for us. And if all goes well, I hope to have you home within a fortnight."

"So, we're going to Tarsus," Rhiannon said softly, sitting back in her seat. "Unbelievable!"

"Well, not far from there. Our temple was on a hill a few

kilometers outside where the ancient city was built. Today the ruins of an Eastern Orthodox church stand over it. It's also served many purposes over the centuries, as a small mosque, a shepherd's hut, and a hideout for young Turkish men wishing to avoid being drafted into the First World War. Of course, we don't intend to openly rebuild the temple at this time. No, we'll first purge the site of the years of accumulated abuse. Then we'll concentrate on rekindling its connection to the Great Goddess. When those steps are complete, linking to the other sites can begin."

"I can't express how deeply honored I feel to be asked to participate in this," Rhiannon said, her voice wavering with emotion.

The Oracle smiled back at her knowingly, patting Rhiannon's hand.

"There's much to do in little time," the Oracle said, her thoughts turning to the task ahead. "This moment is what the Order has lived for across these centuries in exile. Now that it's happening at last, we're nearly overwhelmed. There can be no failure, not with the Visitors pressing their agenda on the planet."

Silently, Rhiannon prayed in gratitude for what she had just learned, and in supplication for the success of the Order.

"I must rest now," the Oracle murmured. "Do continue to sit here beside me. Enjoy the remainder of the flight, my dear."

"We'll be there within an hour," Lucas said, tuning in to a Memphis classic rock station.

"Oh yeah, this trip hasn't been so bad at all," Carson replied, noticing a growing dark cloud in the side-view mirror. "If we can just stay ahead of this storm, we'll be at Sugar Wilson's in no time."

"Sweet," Lucas said, also noticing the rapidly darkening sky, patting the front console in rhythm with the beginning notes of the Rolling Stones' "Gimme Shelter."

Large hail suddenly pelted the highway, accompanied by strong winds. Lucas turned up the radio, the speakers blasting out the Stones.

A lightning bolt hit nearby and a wave of thunder exploded. Blinding sheets of rain suddenly turned into a barrage of giant hail, causing all traffic to come to a stop. Then, for a moment, the weather stilled, leaving the highway covered in hailstones and an uncanny calm under the massive, dark sky.

"Jesus H. Christ," Lucas whispered, allowing a nervous laugh as he turned to look at Carson. "That was weird!"

Carson relaxed for a moment, thinking the storm had passed. A large magpie swooped across the highway directly in front of them, no doubt seeking better shelter. He looked around and was about to start driving again when he saw it. There, standing on the overpass just ahead, was one of the large, robot-like Visitors.

A great, roaring wind swept over them, pushing the Range Rover sideways down the highway in total darkness; smashing it against something. Metal ripped and glass exploded in a cacophony of violence. Someone screamed.

Chapter 19

A Dose of Sugar

"Mr. Reynolds? Mr. Reynolds, can you hear me?" a voice called.

Carson's mind still clung to a muddled dreamscape. He slowly cracked open an eye, glimpsing an unknown, brightly lit room. He was in a strange bed. The place smelled vaguely familiar. His head hurt.

"Mr. Reynolds," the voice called again.

Carson felt his hand being slapped.

"Yes," he husked.

"Hello, Mr. Reynolds, do you know where you are?" the voice continued in a smooth Southern drawl.

"Where am I?" he asked, fully opening his eyes. "What happened?"

"Tornado, Mr. Reynolds. You were caught in a horrific tornado. You're lucky to be alive. Others weren't so fortunate."

Carson began to patch certain details together, darkness and a horrendous noise—someone screaming.

"Lucas, where's Lucas?" he asked, trying to bring into focus the face of a man behind a green surgical gown.

"Mr. Wills is recovering from surgery. He's going to be all right, I believe, but he'll have to stay in the hospital for a bit. You've suffered a concussion and sustained a nasty cut across the back of your left shoulder, but nothing serious, really. You're lucky you weren't decapitated. A flatbed truck loaded with heavy lumber had stopped on the westbound lanes across from your Range Rover. Its entire load was sucked up and spewed out like giant spears by the tornado's vortex. Four-by-four posts shot through the windows and door panels of your vehicle, I'm told. Could've easily taken your head off. If other vehicles hadn't also been struck, one might almost think that storm was intentionally aiming at you."

Carson's memory remained vague, something about sudden darkness and the deafening sound of a hundred freight trains.

"If you're not showing any danger signs, I think the doctors will discharge you sometime tomorrow. Your SUV is completely totaled, but somehow your equipment was spared. I'm sure Charlie Landon is greatly relieved." The man chuckled.

"Who are you?" Carson asked.

"A friend you don't know. I'm Sugar Wilson."

"I need to use a phone. And I want to see Lucas."

"But of course, I'll have the nurse come in as soon as I leave. It's convenient to have access to a surgical gown, given that I'm not supposed to be here. I must go now; it's best that I not stay too long. I'll keep tabs on you, though, and when I hear you're being discharged, I'll send a car for you. We have much to discuss, you and I, and time is of the essence."

"Dr. Wilson, I'm in no condition to be filming, especially without Lucas," Carson replied angrily.

"Oh, I'm not speaking of model trains and Charlie Landon's little pet project, Mr. Reynolds. No, that's of no concern at all. There're other matters that are far more important. It was a pleasure to meet you. And please, call me Sugar."

Dr. Wilson turned and left the room.

Waiting for the nurse's arrival, Carson tried to recall what happened. He remembered passing a freeway sign, Memphis— 49 miles. Running on rock and roll and double doses of caffeine, his attention had shifted from their safety to their next filming task. It all happened so suddenly: the barrage of giant hailstones, the crashing lightning, the rain slashing in horizontal sheets, a great rumbling noise accompanied by the sound of trees being ripped apart. He remembered the vehicle rocking violently and then being dragged sideways until it slammed against something. They could see nothing. Glass exploded, metal tore, a scream—the rest went blank.

The hospital door opened, and the nurse moved calmly to his bedside.

"Well, what have we here?" she began. "Chart says you are one, Carson Reynolds, with a shoulder laceration and a concussion. Let's see, CAT scan looks good, no hemorrhaging, no broken bones. I understand you want to see your friend and make some phone calls. And just as soon as I can get some information from you for our records and take your temperature, I'll be delighted to help you with your request."

"Thanks. How long have I been here?"

"Not long; they brought you in sometime this evening I believe. You were unconscious. I only came on duty about a half hour ago, so I haven't got all the details, but I understand you were caught in that killer tornado. You're lucky to be here."

"You mean someone was killed?"

"Nine dead, thirteen with serious injuries," the nurse responded. "I-40's still a mess with downed trees and all kinds of debris. Oh, I've got something for you; the emergency room people sent this up. Apparently, when the ambulance crew brought you in, you were clutching this in your fist. Maybe it's your good luck charm."

She reached into a small bag and handed over Taz.

Within a quarter hour, the nurse returned with a wheelchair and took him to Lucas' room. Lucas had two broken ribs, internal bleeding, a punctured lung, a fractured forearm, and a number of cuts from shattered glass.

"Hey, you miserable bastard, am I glad you're alive!" Carson said, smiling at his friend.

"What, no flowers?" Lucas whispered, trying to lift a hand.

"How you feeling?"

"I can't really tell, with all the drugs they've pumped into me," Lucas replied slowly. "Everybody keeps telling me how lucky we were. Jesus, they must have a different standard of luck around here. Lucky for me would be having a drink down about now on Beale Street, with a friendly local babe."

"Hey, you'll get there," Carson encouraged. "You got beat up pretty good out there, they say. Got to give yourself some time to mend."

"So, what happened to you?" Lucas asked. "You're wearing a hospital gown."

"Seems I got a big cut across my left shoulder, and something hit my head pretty hard. You seem to have got the worst of it."

"Carson," Lucas' voice trembled. "We were nearly skewered alive out there."

Back in his hospital room, Carson agonized over what he should do. Completing Landon's documentary had to be radically reconsidered. Withdrawing from the project would not be easy. Landon was not the kind of man to allow an *accident* to delay a production schedule.

One thing for certain, Carson knew he could no longer continue to endanger Lucas. When he had first recalled the image, he had attempted to dismiss it as a by-product of the trauma. But with each passing moment, his memory became more lucid, confirming the reality of what he had witnessed. Yes, it had been there, standing on the overpass an instant before the tornado hit—a being similar to the one he had seen that night outside Rhiannon's cottage. It had stood there, peering down at them.

The pain medication clouded his mind—if only he could talk with Rhiannon. On the table next to the bed stood Taz, looking fierce. Carson drifted into a dream-charged sleep.

The room was dark and he was still disoriented, yet he knew that sound—the breathing was unmistakable. The Dharmapala was in the room.

"Well, adept, you should know better than to be sleeping in my presence." The wrathful deity laughed.

"Oh Jesus," Carson whispered to himself.

"Best keep your gods straight and mind your tongue, adept—if you don't want to have it ripped out for bad manners."

"My apologies, I was not prepared—"

"Silence! Again your pathetic dribble of excuses," the god scolded. "Look at yourself; you're a fine sight. I thought you could protect yourself better than that. I shouldn't have bothered to save you two miserable creatures."

"You saved me?" he asked in disbelief, straining to see the spirit stationed in a shadowy corner.

"Well, you certainly did next to nothing, nor was that seraph you call Jesus or any other demiurge coming to the rescue. If I had not so enjoyed the opportunity to crush those alien parasites, I would not have bothered."

"Thank you for that most generous salvation," he said, trying to suppress his anger at the belated rescue. "It's true; I had let my guard slip. I'm indeed unworthy. Perhaps we should recognize my inherent weaknesses and dismiss me from seeking your esteemed assistance."

"This creature has become exasperated with his immortal superior; how disgustingly human. He's angry because he was nearly killed. If it weren't for me, you would be as the one whose body I now claim."

A huge male figure emerged from the shadowy corner of the room and stepped to the edge of the bed. It stood at least six-foot-five and easily weighed over three hundred pounds. Its striped work shirt was caked with dried blood. A nametag read Cecil. But the red eyes that glowed in Cecil's head were undeniably not human. Whoever Cecil had been, the Dharmapala now possessed his body.

"I have honored this human by taking his body, though he is

not worthy of such a gift. I entered this poor creature's corpse after my swift victory along the highway. He had been killed, of course. Those alien beings had pulled him out of his machine and flung him at me as if that might inflict harm. Perhaps this is not my most beautiful manifestation, but I was pressed by the moment. You see, since we last met, I have been in a state of constant sexual union with my consort."

"Mighty Lord, with all due respect, would it not be within your infinite compassion to return this man's body so that his family could bury him?"

"Compassion! When I give this poor being the occasion to have my breath move through his useless lungs, charge his blood with my glory? But not to worry, adept. I will not use this corpse for long. And when I am done, I will allow you to dispose of it as you deem appropriate. Now, let us go."

"Go? I beg your pardon, go where?"

"Between that skirmish and the constant copulation, I have developed an appetite. If that appetite is not sated, the ramifications may be displeasing to my devotees. Come, adept!"

"Great One, I can't go anywhere. I'm in a hospital gown. I have a concussion. And you, well—"

"I sense there is concern as to an unacceptable appearance. Very well, I shall alter you so that you blend in with me. Be assured you will receive appropriate respect while in my company."

"No, my Lord. It's your attire that requires the altering. Seeing someone in bloodstained clothes would greatly disturb people. And then there's the other matter—your eyes."

"Yes, my eyes are indeed magnificent!" The deity smiled, blinking his eerie red eyes with pleasure.

"Yes, Great One, but so marvelous as not to look human. Can't you temporarily change them somehow?"

Ten minutes later, Carson slipped through the stairwell doors of the hospital's ground floor. He had managed to lift an overcoat from a waiting room to cover his gown. The deity, now wearing sunglasses and a set of surgical scrubs stolen from a closet, walked alongside. Waltzing casually through the main entrance, they walked into the night.

The Sublime Steakhouse, a neon sign proclaimed. The odd couple strolled in and approached the maître d'.

The two sat down at a large table near the back. The main dinner crowd had finished for the night. Carson looked over the menu with little appetite. A waiter approached.

"Good evening, gentlemen. May I start you off with something to drink?"

"I don't think I'm allowed to drink anything yet," Carson answered. "My doctor here just snuck me out of the hospital to get a bite of real food, but I better pass on the alcohol."

"He can have whatever those creatures are swallowing," the wrathful deity said, pointing to a table nearby where the guests were imbibing a round of martinis. "Yes, bring us a bounty of those offerings."

The baffled waiter stood patiently, pencil in hand, waiting for the joke to be revealed and a genuine order given. In an effort to draw the stalemate to a close, the waiter decided to press the matter.

"Would that be gin or vodka?" The waiter smiled, enjoying his own humor.

"Bring both, and do so with haste!" the Dharmapala barked.

Carson felt his head starting to pound. His insanity had marched right out of his addled brain and was now walking around downtown Memphis on its hind legs.

In a few minutes the waiter returned, cautiously carrying a small tray loaded with eight martinis.

"I hope I have this correct, gentlemen. I brought four martinis with gin and four with vodka."

"Yes, thank you," Carson interceded. "I'm sure that'll be

perfect. You see, the doctor's just come off a grueling day of surgery."

"Of course," the waiter responded. "Are you ready to order some dinner, perhaps start off with an appetizer?"

"Meat!" the deity snapped.

"Why yes, did you have a particular cut in mind, sir?" the waiter said, trying to keep his voice composed.

"It smells as though it is from cattle, is it not?"

"Cattle? Why indeed, sir. We have exceptional steaks."

"Then bring them," the Dharmapala said, swallowing down his third martini. "And more of this libation."

"I think what the waiter would like to know is which type of steak you'd care to have," Carson said delicately, pointing at the extensive menu. "They have porterhouse, sirloin, New York, filet—"

"Bring them, I said; bring all of these offerings to me. If I have to say it again, I shall eviscerate all beings in this place."

"The doctor gets in a bad mood when he's this hungry," Carson said to the waiter, smiling. He slid two of his martinis over to assuage the ill-tempered god. "He'll start with one of every kind of steak on the menu. Keep them on the rare side and make it quick. Oh, better bring another round of drinks."

"Sir," the waiter said, a look of consternation on his face. "I'm afraid I'm going to have to ask you to leave—"

Instantly, Cecil's corpse began enlarging beyond human proportions as a great bellowing sound emerged from within. Carson leaned back in horror as ...

"Mr. Reynolds, sorry to wake you, sir," a nurse was saying.

Carson bolted violently from the nightmare, drenched in sweat, his breathing short.

"Got to take your temperature and give you another dose of medication. We have to check on patients with concussions regularly in these early stages. Best not to sleep too much," the nurse chattered, setting small paper cups with his medication on a table. "Oh my, are you all right?"

"Just a bad dream, that's all."

"You look like it. After what you went through, I guess that's pretty understandable. I'll bring you a dry gown, sweetie."

"Don't leave just yet, if you don't mind."

"All right, I'll stay with you a bit. But let me get a towel to dry you off," she said, stepping toward his bathroom. "Oh my goodness, that's odd. Now who would've been so careless as to drop surgical scrubs and sunglasses right here on your floor?"

Carson remained in a wheelchair at the hospital's curb. The afternoon sunlight felt warm and reassuring. His release from the hospital had come just as Sugar Wilson had predicted.

That morning he had phoned Landon's office, to explain further what had happened and to say that he was going to need some time to think about how to continue with the film. He was anxious to go through the Range Rover's wreckage, assess the condition of the equipment, and hopefully locate his cell phone, his only direct means of communicating with Rhiannon. He had managed to call in for his voice mail from the hospital, but there were no messages from her.

On his lap, he held a small paper bag containing his medications and Taz. A Lincoln Town Car with tinted windows pulled up slowly and stopped. A tall black man in a chauffeur's uniform emerged.

"Mr. Reynolds, I'm Joseph," the gentleman said. "Dr. Wilson sent me over to fetch you, sir. Let me help you into the car."

"Where're we going?" Carson asked.

"Well, that depends, don't it?" Joseph laughed, closing the car door.

Driving away from downtown, Carson expected to head for one of the city's wealthy residential neighborhoods while he mulled over Joseph's cryptic remark. Instead, the car navigated through the twisted backstreets of an old warehouse district, not far from the river.

"Joseph, where are we?"

"We're in Memphis, Mr. Reynolds. We're in Memphis, sir," he replied.

As they turned a corner, heading directly toward one of the aging warehouses, a large roll-up door opened. Joseph wheeled quickly into the building as the door closed behind them.

Sugar Wilson opened the car door. "Mr. Reynolds, I hope you're feeling better today," he drawled. "Please, come with me if you'd be so kind."

Carson followed, his curiosity piqued by the mysterious surroundings. The cavernous old warehouse appeared to have been unused for years. The building's creosote floorboards emitted the smell of forgotten decades of commerce.

"I thought it best to have you brought here," Sugar Wilson said. "Never know who might be watching the house. This place goes back to a time when my family was in the cotton brokerage business. As a child, my father used to bring my brothers and me here on occasion, and we'd play hide-and-seek among the stacks of cotton bales. So, you see, this place has a certain sentimental value. From time to time it still has its uses, I suppose."

Sugar Wilson stopped for a moment and peered hard into Carson's eyes. "Are you feeling all right? We're almost there; it's just around this wall," he said, leading Carson around stacks of wooden pallets and a group of parked forklifts. "Oh, here we are. I hope you'll find your belongings in reasonable order."

Carson walked over to a table. The cases containing all their equipment were neatly aligned. Even their suitcases seemed intact.

"How did you get these things?"

"Let's just say I have connections with certain people." Sugar Wilson smiled. "Would you like to see what became of your vehicle? The manufacturer could make a hell of a commercial from this. 'Range Rover even allows its occupants to survive the rage of a mighty tornado' —my, my."

Sugar Wilson nodded at Joseph, who walked over to the wall and removed the heavy canvas tarp that covered the crumpled remains of the Range Rover. The body's sheet metal was pierced with large, ragged holes. Of the glass, only the front windshield remained, though it was badly shattered. Both tires on the left side were flat. Carson peeked inside. The rear seat was torn and twisted. The right front door was missing. Both the driver and front-passenger seats were stained with blood.

"It took the rescue team quite a lot of work to untangle you boys from that mess. The worst, I'm told, was having to pull away the heavy lumber that had embedded in the sheet metal." Sugar paused. "Rather sobering, when you consider it all."

"Who are you, Dr. Wilson, and why am I here?" Carson asked pointedly.

"Gracious, such questions baffle even me." The doctor chuckled, taking Carson by the arm and leading him over to a group of worn, cane-back chairs. "Have a seat. And please, call me Sugar."

The two men sat down in the old chairs, Carson's patience rapidly wearing thin, while Sugar Wilson rocked back and forth on the chair's back legs in a prolonged silence.

"My, where to begin?" Sugar mused. "Well, Mr. Reynolds, I'm sort of a comrade of yours, not that you should take my word for it. You see, a very trusted source of mine informed me about you. Seems you had come into her visions. I know it sounds preposterous to some people, but I've always found her visions to be exceptionally accurate. The challenge is in interpreting them. Now, when she first sent word of you, I'll admit, it totally stumped me for a while. She only said:

A man with seeing machines is coming your way.
He wants to capture your toys.

Danger pursues his path,
Though a great shadow watches over him.

"Don't you just love riddles?" Sugar smiled.

"You're evading my questions," Carson shot back, irritated by the man's manipulative manner.

"On the contrary, Mr. Reynolds. I'm your friend, and friends should help each other, should they not? You see, I know about your work. Not the filmmaking, but the other work. I know what you are."

Carson stared in disbelief.

"Perhaps I should explain that I'm not one of you. That is, I'm not a worker of the medicine, but I do know much about its ways. And I know about the struggle you're caught in, the great threat that hangs over us all. As I say, I have connections."

Carson's mind madly questioned how this enigmatic man could know so much. Exactly whose purpose was being served through the doctor's supposed friendship? Was Charlie Landon in on this as well?

"Allow me to back up a bit, if you will, and perhaps that will answer some of those questions of yours. I've done some interesting things in my life. Most of which occurred around the edges of my work, so to speak. You see, my pharmacological research has taken me into some very intriguing worlds. I didn't achieve all my success by sheer science. I'm afraid I'm nowhere near that smart. But I am lucky, Mr. Reynolds."

Carson felt growing impatience. Would this guy just get to the point?

"My research in the South American rain forest, naturally led me to associate with the local people. Their shamans have knowledge of plant life that's just extraordinary, entirely different from anything Western science understands. It was through their knowledge that my so-called breakthroughs came. Otherwise, achieving success with my research would have taken millions of experiments over many lifetimes."

"So, you stole their medicine ways," Carson said brusquely.

"Well, that's a little harsh; I prefer to think of it as a cooperative exchange. But it's true that I didn't discover any new drugs. What I discovered was how to work with the people who already had the knowledge I was seeking. What I knew was how to take their amazing information back to a laboratory and reproduce it. I'm afraid the famous Dr. Sugar Wilson is really only a messenger, bringing back knowledge given out by the plant spirits themselves. That, Mr. Reynolds, is how I learned about the way of the medicine workers."

"Well, forgive my cynical attitude, doctor. But how does such a noble and modest man as you end up with the SEC after him? Seems somebody wants to nail you pretty bad."

"Somebody does, Mr. Reynolds. But not for the reasons you might suspect. That's just a ruse. I'm afraid things with our Visitor friends go far deeper than you might realize. While their attacks have been focused on the medicine workers, that isn't the full extent of their activity. Unfortunately, they've made alliances with certain human institutions and prominent individuals."

"What exactly are you saying?"

"The Visitors have made arrangements with certain sectors of government. They have alliances with various religious, financial, and educational institutions, as well as strategic controllers of major media. Apparently, a number of people have somehow been drawn to cooperate with them, perhaps naïvely believing their intentions will bring us world peace or the like. I don't know how or why it was done, only that the Visitors have established relations with human agents, who are already active on the Visitors' behalf. Now a sort of secret society is operating, composed of people with power and influence, who are definitely not on our side. Sadly, these people have made a sort of pact with the devil, Mr. Reynolds."

Carson felt stunned, uncertain as to whether to believe this man. How could Sugar Wilson know so much?

Sugar Wilson leaned forward, his eyes burning into Carson's. "You see, the people, the ones in alliance with the Visitors, are targeting those who might be helping you. In my case, someone got the SEC after me over insider trading. The charges are trumped up, of course, but it wasn't so hard to accuse me, given that my company's stock has had a record of stellar performance.

"And we had that success because we knew which drugs were going to succeed. It was through my shaman friends that I gained this edge, a very significant one in our industry. The plants themselves inform the shamans how to combine various substances to create a successful drug. Perhaps it could be said that I cheated, since I use such a talented group of analysts, people from the rain forest who can barely read or write.

"In exchange for all that they've shared with me, I funnel major profits back into rain forest preservation projects and the like. This has enabled the indigenous people to protect their land and culture. Needless to say, my successes have not made me popular with my competitors or with certain corporate interests who want to exploit the timber and oil reserves of the rain forest."

"How long do you think you can evade the SEC?" Carson said, beginning to soften.

"I don't really know. I imagine their strategy will be to smother me with legal actions, especially if they can seize my assets. But the real objective is to keep me from helping others who are doing the frontline work. Without the financial protection that's preserving these indigenous enclaves, these cultures—not to mention the work of their shamans—will rapidly diminish. The Visitors will have eliminated yet another source of resistance."

"What are you going to do?" he asked, now concerned for this man.

"That really needn't worry you, Mr. Reynolds. You have your

own hide to take care of. But from now on, I hope you'll keep in mind that certain agencies may be tracking your activity. Any use of phones, credit cards, e-mail, texting, or the Internet can disclose your location or where you intend to travel. I think you get the picture."

"Are you suggesting that I'm on some hit list or something?"

"I really couldn't say. But it's highly likely that people such as yourself are now, oh, how should we say it—more accident prone."

Carson felt chilled as he recalled the near fatal incident with the logging truck and glanced over at the wreckage of the Range Rover.

Sugar Wilson continued. "Keep in mind that your privacy may be seriously compromised already. For the sake of yourself and those with whom you work, I would advise using discretion whenever possible. In the meantime, you need some time to heal and regroup in a safe location. And I have just the place."

Carson wondered numbly where he would be shuttled to next.

"Oh, by the way, this package came overnight for you from Landon's office," he said, handing Carson a padded envelope. "Sorry we couldn't have met under more pleasant circumstances, Mr. Reynolds. I really was looking forward to showing you my trains. I have some stuff that would have made Landon choke with envy."

From a distant part of the warehouse, an engine started. A pickup truck rolled up. Joseph stepped out and began loading Carson's gear. He had changed out of the chauffeur's uniform into casual attire. Carson tried to inventory his belongings as Joseph finished and threw a tarp over the back.

Carson turned to ask Sugar another question, but the good doctor had already left.

"Well, sir, best hop in, 'cause we have some miles to make," Joseph said.

"Where are we going?"

"Home. For me, anyhow," Joseph replied.

"Home? And where might that be?"

"Mississippi."

"I'm going to Mississippi, to your house?"

"No, sir; I'm takin' you to my great-aunt's place."

"And who might she be?"

"She's the one who has the visions; she done seen you comin' for a long time already. Didn't Dr. Wilson say nothin' 'bout her?"

Carson wearily climbed into the truck's cab, resigned to meet Joseph's great-aunt.

Joseph pressed a garage door opener and drove the pickup out of the opposite side of the warehouse. Evening was setting in.

"Does your great-aunt have a name?"

"Course she's gotta name." Joseph laughed. "Lots of people know her. She's sorta famous 'round home. Yes sir, everybody down there knows 'bout Blind Mama Bauché."

Chapter 20

Edna's Juke

Night engulfed the land. Joseph's route consisted of a series of back roads that cut ever deeper into the heart of Mississippi. Several hours had passed.

"We be there shortly, I reckon," Joseph offered. "But I could sure use somethin' to eat. How 'bout you, Mr. Reynolds?"

"Carson. Just call me Carson, okay? And yes, I'm hungry."

"Good, 'cause there's always somethin' tasty to eat at the juke," Joseph said. "We can stop there and get some food before I take you to Blind Mama's. It's sorta hard to eat at her place anyway, 'til you get used to her some. At least that's how it is for most folks."

"I suppose if you told me exactly where in Mississippi your great-aunt lives, it wouldn't really do me any good," he said.

"Not less you's real familiar with Holmes County." Joseph laughed. "Blind Mama's place is a ways outside of a little spot on the road called Eulogy. Dr. Wilson put a small house trailer out back at her place for people to stay in. He comes down here and stays himself from time to time. That's where you'll be sleepin'. Now, Eulogy is 'bout halfway between Thornton and Ebenezer, but I doubt you ever heard of them places."

"No, I'm afraid I've never had the pleasure of spending any time in either of those metropolises."

"Well, you ain't seen shit, have you?"

The two men laughed together. Carson was starting to like Joseph.

Twenty minutes later, Joseph wheeled the truck into a sandy parking lot in front of a meager roadside store. He parked alongside an older Dodge pickup, with fishing rods hanging over the tailgate. Moths danced around the light bulbs that illuminated a rusting metal sign, identifying the place—Edna's.

"Hope you're gonna like the food. Don't think they make anything like this where you come from."

"Joseph," Carson said. "What about my stuff? I mean, it's just sitting there in the back of your truck."

"And that's exactly why you ain't gotta worry. Everybody round here knows my truck, and nobody's gonna mess with it. Not as long as Blind Mama's alive."

Joseph let out a big laugh and led Carson inside. The place smelled of stale beer, cigarettes, sweat, and honest food. A dozen or so people were sitting around tables, drinking beer and eating. He studied the place. It seemed to be part store, restaurant, dance hall, community center and bait shop— without giving preference to any one type of establishment.

"Well, if it ain't mister big city man himself. Welcome home, lamb," a large woman in her late fifties proclaimed. "Who's yo' friend?"

"This is Carson, come to spend a little time over at Blind Mama's," Joseph said. "Carson, this lady is Edna; this here's her place."

"Pleased to meet you," Carson said.

"Carson, huh?" Edna paused. "Well, Carson, welcome to Edna's. We don't get too many white boys in here on weeknights. I mean, after all, we got standards to hold up."

Edna laughed hard, giving Joseph a slap on the back.

"Now, what can I bring you gentlemen?"

"How 'bout a couple of cold beers and the house special?" Joseph said. "Carson here probably never had no down-home food."

"Sounds fine," Carson said amenably, trying to fit in. He had been told at the hospital to avoid alcohol but figured that he could manage at least one beer.

"Never been in a joint like this, have you?" Joseph said. "Well, this is what's called a juke. It's quiet in here tonight, but you come here most any weekend night and the place will be stompin' with the blues. Lots of local folk play here. Pretty good, most of 'em."

Edna brought the beers, two tall bottles dripping wet from the ice water used to chill them. She winked at Joseph and went back to the kitchen.

"Joseph, how did you come to work for Sugar Wilson?"

"Oh, his family and mine goes back, I suppose." Joseph laughed. "I've known the Wilson family all my life. Wouldn't wanna work for nobody else, 'specially with the job I got."

"Do you like being a chauffeur?"

"Chauffeur?" Joseph laughed again. "Well, it sure is a handy cover, ain't it? No, I do lots of special work for Dr. Wilson. Kinda secret stuff."

"Oh, I'm sorry to have assumed—"

"Now, you ain't insulted me none. It's all good. Folks is supposed to think that. I could've gone on to school, I reckon, but I jus' wasn't that interested. My sister, now she's jus' the opposite. Went to law school and all that. Now she's this big-time attorney in Atlanta, makes $400,000 a year easy—more when she wins some big case. But me, I guess I'm not made for stuff like that. Besides, ain't nothin' wrong with bein' a chauffeur for his company. They always got people comin' from and goin' to the airport. I get to hear lots of interesting things while they're ridin' in the back there, if you know what I mean. 'Specially late at night if I'm takin' 'em back to their hotel after they done drunk too much somewhere." Joseph gave Carson a wink.

"I'll try to remember that about you, Joseph."

"But that part is sorta my day job. I do special kinda errands that the doctor don't trust to nobody else. I go places for him, deliverin' things, pickin' things up, doin' stuff that he don't want nobody to know 'bout. That world of the drug manufacturers is some heavy stuff, man. You can't trust nobody. He's sent me all over the world almost. My niece is a flight attendant for Delta, goes to Europe and all; man, she's been next to nowhere compared to me. Nobody suspects some black man from the backwoods of Mississippi might be totin' the secret that's gonna cure cancer, or somethin' like that. And there's other errands, too, like bringin' you down here. You ain't the first."

Edna returned with a tray of steaming food. Carson's plate contained two large pork chops, a mound of rice, and a side of black-eyed peas. A heavy sauce spilled over the top of everything. Edna set down side dishes with coleslaw and a large basket of corn bread.

"Wow, this looks good."

"Well then, let's eat!" Joseph laughed, diving into his food.

Carson was ravenous; the rich flavors exploded in his mouth.

"What's in this sauce?"

"That's got tomatoes, okra, onions, garlic, Tabasco, maybe some crayfish or shrimp, and whatever they need to get rid of back in the kitchen. Sure is good!" Joseph laughed again.

Carson felt compelled to know more from Joseph.

"Joseph, who else have you brought down here?"

"Jus' a couple of others."

"Do you know why they were sent down here?"

"Same as you, I reckon."

"What do you mean same as me? And why did they come here?"

"You know, friends of Dr. Wilson. That's all."

"Well, do you know what happened, I mean, what became of them?"

Joseph looked away as if he hadn't heard, continuing to chew on a pork chop. Finally, he turned back to Carson.

"The first one was this rabbi friend of Dr. Wilson's. He's some kinda professor of ancient religions or somethin', at some university in Boston. Well, he seemed to be all right after his stay. I know this for a fact, 'cause I came down and got him when Blind Mama told me to. I carried him myself down to the airport in Jackson and put him on the plane. I reckon he got home safe enough."

Joseph paused, reluctant to continue.

"And the other?"

"Well, that would be this woman that Dr. Wilson worked with down in the Amazon, part of his research team. I drove her down here last fall." Joseph hesitated. "Nobody but Blind Mama probably knows what really happened. Some folks believe that it was jus' the old troubles again that's been a part of this area."

"Old troubles?"

"We better get goin'."

"No, wait a minute, Joseph. I need to know about this. Who was this person and what became of her?"

"Listen, I don't know that much. They don't tell me more than I need to know to do my job. And between all the weird shit that Dr. Wilson and Blind Mama deal with, well, that's jus' fine by me. There's enough strange things goin' on round here already, without it lookin' to find me."

"Joseph, you're holding out on me, man."

"Let's talk outside," Joseph whispered.

They sat in Joseph's pickup for several minutes. The music coming from the jukebox inside Edna's punctuated the silence.

Eventually, Joseph spoke. "Her name was Marianna, real nice lady. Seems she was in the same kinda trouble as you, but I don't wanna hear nothin' 'bout whatever that is, you hear?" Joseph said forcefully.

"Anyway, Dr. Wilson sent her here believin' it would be safe. But she must of not listened to Blind Mama, 'cause she ended up missin'. Sheriff's people did a big search with dogs and everything but never found no body. Dr. Wilson was real upset. He and Blind Mama, they talked for days 'bout it. All I know is that some body tissue and lots of blood was found back on the trail that leads into the woods, behind the trailer."

Images of a Visitor attack raced through Carson's mind. Suddenly the idea of staying at Blind Mama's seemed to offer no haven whatsoever, especially if he had to sleep in the same trailer that had served as Marianna's home.

"Did either Sugar Wilson or Blind Mama say anything to you about what they thought might've happened?"

"Nope, that's what makes me believe it's them old troubles come back."

"Joseph, what the fuck are the old troubles?"

Another silence came over Joseph. He breathed heavily, as if speaking would bring his doom.

Joseph looked around outside the truck to assure their privacy. Then he leaned over and whispered, "werewolf."

Chapter 21

Blind Mama Bauché

Leaving Edna's juke joint, Carson and Joseph rode in silence, both men engrossed in private thoughts. The narrow, two-lane road cleaved through dark expanses of pine trees. In vain, Carson checked for cell phone coverage, while the story about Marianna burned in his mind.

He had been too relaxed driving to Memphis and it had nearly cost his and Lucas' lives; it may have cost the lives of others. Now he prayed to his guardian spirits, especially to the treacherous Dharmapala. Inside the paper bag containing his medication, his hand clutched Taz.

"I know you be thinkin' old Joseph is jus' some ignorant country hick 'cause of what I told you," Joseph said at last, breaking the silence. "But it ain't jus' me that believes it. Plenty of people do, white folks included. They've been attacked, too. In fact, it was some white fellow out huntin' that got killed jus' a while back."

Carson's mind was on the Visitors, not lycanthropy, the myth of people turning into wolves. Joseph, however, was insistent.

"Jus' you mind," he continued. "You be out walkin' at night, or sittin' round on the porch, and all of a sudden everything goes dead quiet. All the crickets and frogs hush up; the dogs go runnin' under the house. Nothin's movin' 'cept the hair on the back of your neck. Then you know somethin' is out there!"

"Has this ever happened to you?" Carson asked skeptically.

"A couple of times, yeah."

"So what did you do?"

"Man, you learn to pray like you never have! And then, all you can do is wait 'til it done gone on to somewhere else."

"Really? Sounds awfully scary," he said unsympathetically.

"That's okay, you can think old Joseph's jus' a sucker for superstition and such," Joseph said. "That's what everybody thinks 'til they hear that howl come out of the night."

They turned off the road and onto a dirt strip that was not much more than an old wagon road, with low, overhanging trees. After driving through woods for nearly a quarter mile, they came upon a clearing. A mixed-breed hound dog circled the truck, barking. An old sharecropper cottage stood at the clearing's edge. Joseph maneuvered the truck closer and turned off the engine.

"Damn it, Frank, shut the hell up. You know me!" Joseph yelled at the dog.

Opening a creaky screen door and then a wooden one, Joseph led Carson into the home of his great-aunt. The room's only light was coming from the fireplace.

"Blind Mama, I've got a friend of Dr. Wilson's with me. This here is Carson."

An old woman sat in front of the fieldstone fireplace, her white hair pulled back in a tight bun. Carson moved slowly toward her.

"Hello, Ms. Bauché. Thank you for having me here," he said.

The woman turned in his direction. Her eyes were glazed over with a white membrane. Carson was taken aback. She was quite old. More than that, there was something about her appearance that suggested a person who was slowly morphing into something beyond human.

"Carson, is it?" she mumbled. "The man that captures with the seein' machines. Come over here and let me get a better look at you."

Blind Mama reached out and began tracing his face with her hands. Next, she moved her hands across his body. When she was finished, she spat into the fire.

"Joseph, honey," she said. "Did you bring me any pipe

tobacco?"

"Yes'um, you know I wouldn't forget." He laughed.

"And Dr. Sugar, he be all right?" she asked.

"Well now, you probably be knowin' better than me, the way you do," Joseph said. "But he looked fine when we left Memphis this afternoon."

"And this one," she said, pointing to Carson. "Awful close to being a shadow, he was."

"Yes, I was," Carson replied.

He glanced about the house. The furnishings were stark. It was hard to make out much in the dim light from the hearth. He wondered if she had plumbing or electricity.

"Joseph, go open the trailer for Mr. Carson. Make sho' things is workin' out there. Take Frank along with you in case they's snakes. Then you can go on home, and you tell yo' mama she better come see me soon."

"Yes'um. Carson, I'll put all your stuff inside the trailer."

"I'll come help," he said.

"Sit!" Blind Mama commanded, grabbing him by the arm and pointing to a chair with her cane.

Carson obeyed.

"I'm sho' you're tired, young man," Blind Mama began. "But we needs to talk a spell. I reckon you knows why."

"Sugar Wilson told me a little about you, and I gather you somehow know a great deal about me," he replied.

"Humph!" she said, and spat into the fire again.

"I understand that you're very gifted psychically," he continued.

"Is that what you folks call it?" She laughed.

"Well, I'm sure it could be described many ways," he said. "Were you born blind?"

"Honey, I ain't never been blind. I just see different than most folks. Guess I don't need no normal eyes. I was born with a caul over my head, you know; doctors call it a membrane or somethin'. Some folks says it's a sign of a witch." She chuckled. "My birth happened right here in this house."

"Were you able to see what happened to me a couple of days ago?" he asked.

"Sho' 'nuff; I seen that, and plenty more."

"Then tell me, did you see anything that was, well, real weird?" Carson probed.

Blind Mama laughed. "Carson, honey, if you mean did I see that mean old critter up on the overpass that nearly killed you, yes, I seen him. They been round here before. I seen 'em plenty, all right."

"Ms. Bauché, am I doing the right thing by being here?"

"How do one know what the right thing is in these here times?" she said, spitting into the fire again. "And don't be callin' me Ms. Bauché. Might make me think I'm somebody that gotta have respect 'cause she's an old woman. I wasn't born no Ms. Bauché. You just call me Blind Mama, or Mama, like everyone else, you hear?"

"Yes, Mama."

"I like yo' voice, son, they's some good in it. Any of yo' kinfolk black?"

"No, Mama, none I know about anyhow."

"Too bad. But you be here now, so I sees what I can do to help you," she said. But child its gonna take some work on yo' part. These is hard times. You gotta be very careful. I lost a sweet girl here a while back."

"Are you referring to Marianna?"

"Yes, child, God bless her poor soul."

"Yeah, Joseph told me about her; that was terrible. But he has some wild story about a werewolf."

"It weren't the werewolf, Carson. You know as well as me what got her."

Carson's thoughts sank into gloom. Outside, Frank barked as Joseph's truck pulled past on its way back to the highway and the ordinary world.

"Do you know what happened to her? Did she do something wrong, or was she just overwhelmed by too much of the Visitors' energy that night?" he asked.

"Hard to say. I think she just got weary with keepin' up the fight. That's how it is for some folk. She done lost some of her people down in that jungle she come from. Her husband and sister was among 'em."

"Well, if the same thing happens to me, I suppose that werewolf story will really take off," Carson joked.

"Wolf never bothered nobody round my place. You don't need worry there," she said seriously.

"Well, that's a bit of encouraging news, I suppose," he said.

"Listen to you! You the one that got a mighty big beast yo'self hangin' round." She chuckled. "I see his shadow all round you. Child, how'd you come across somethin' like that?"

Carson felt exposed. No one else had detected the Dharmapala's presence before.

"Can you see the spirit that I try to work with?"

"Yes sir, I do. And, honey, he's as ornery as a bag of bobcats. No wonder Frank didn't bark at you none."

"What do you mean? The dog was barking plenty."

"He was barkin' at Joseph, not you. That was his hello bark for Joseph. He knows the sound of his truck. But when you got out, he didn't bark none at you. I can tell. No, he didn't wanna say nothin' to you."

"I hope I didn't scare him."

"Frank don't get scared by much, not livin' out here with me. But he do know when to shut up."

"So, Mama, is there something in particular that I'm to do here? I mean, I'll be glad to help out, or whatever. But you know what I'm talking about." Carson paused. "I mean to be prepared for, you know, if they come back."

"Say it!" she snapped, striking her cane on the floor.

"Say what?"

"Say *when* they come back, not *if*," she demanded, spitting into the fire. "*If* is what nearly got you killed. *If* may be what tore poor Marianna to bits. No sir, there ain't no *if* at Blind Mama's place."

"Yes, Mama," he said obediently.

"They's plenty that can be done and needs tendin'. Beginnin' with you settlin' down with that demon that hangs round with you. Then you's got other things to learn."

Carson pondered her words, sensing their wisdom but puzzled as to what exactly they meant.

"All right, whatever it takes," he answered, accepting his situation for the moment.

"Carson." She sighed. "You best go get some rest. I can see you be tuckered out. We'll talk more in the mornin'. Go on back to the trailer. There should be a flashlight over on that table by the door. You just go on back. The 'lectricity's turned on and everything is supposed to be set for you. Frank'll guide you back there."

Carson stepped out into the night, perplexed to be dismissed so promptly by the old woman. Frank stood before him, frozen in anticipation, his eyes glowing in the flashlight's beam. The woods were filled with the sounds of crickets and frogs.

Frank trotted ahead, assured of every step. Carson welcomed the company. A light already burned inside the trailer. Frank sat down at the trailer's door. Carson stepped up and went inside.

All of his belongings were neatly stacked on the floor. He walked through the trailer, turning on lights and testing out the bathroom plumbing. He was relieved to find the kitchen stocked with an ample supply of food and drink. Silently, he sent thanks to Sugar Wilson.

He went back to the door and looked out into the dark. Frank was still there, staring at the door.

"Thanks for the escort, Frank. Would you like to come in for a nightcap?"

Frank stood up and trotted back in the direction of Blind Mama's.

Carson closed the door, making sure the lock was secure. He pushed the equipment cases off to one side, threw a couch pillow on the floor, and pulled a small votive candle out of his suitcase. Removing Taz from the bag with his medications, he lit the candle and called upon the Dharmapala for protection. He offered prayers for his friends and loved ones. He thought of Marianna.

Carson sprang from his sleep, his heart racing. Hammering blows struck against the trailer wall.

"Hey, you gonna sleep all day? No sir, you ain't!" Blind Mama yelled out.

Carson staggered from the bed and looked out the window. Mama and Frank were standing outside. She was preparing to give the trailer another series of blows with her cane.

"Good morning," he called hoarsely.

"Come down to the house, I fixed you somethin' to eat," she said.

"Wow, you didn't have ..."

But Blind Mama had already turned and was walking back to the house. Frank continued to stare at him for another minute then took off after his mistress.

Back in Blind Mama's house, Carson was amazed to find a full breakfast of eggs, bacon, toast and grits lay before him. He marveled at how she could manage so much by herself. By the light of day, he could see that the house had electricity. But other than a refrigerator and two hanging light bulbs, there were no other appliances.

"Mama, this is delicious," Carson mumbled between gulps.

"Them's real eggs, come from chickens, not no store." She

chortled.

"I sure didn't mean for you to go to all this trouble."

"This ain't trouble. You best have some food while you can. May come a time when you won't be gettin' any."

Perhaps it was the light of day, the comfort of food, or the reassurance of being with Blind Mama now, but the world seemed far less threatening this morning. Sugar Wilson's descriptions of dangerous human agents seemed more a paranoid fantasy than a bona fide conspiracy. After a few days of recuperation here, he projected that he would be ready to go back to Memphis, see Lucas, and hopefully go home. There was so much to consider, especially as to what to do about the documentary.

"Say, Mama, would you mind if I used your phone? The charges'll go to me."

"No, I don't mind a bit, 'cept I ain't got no phone." She chuckled. "They's a phone down at Moses' store. That's only 'bout a four mile walk, once you get out to the road. Or you can take the shortcut through the woods and probably save a mile or so."

"Oh, Christ. I really need to check in with my answering service."

"What you need to do is right here," she scolded, her voice sounding serious as she shuffled across the kitchen. "Here you been roamin' round the country with this powerful demon, like you some gangster that don't know he's his own worst enemy. Son, it may not be them from space that's get you but yo' own pet monster. Whatever that thing is, child, you better learn to do better by it or it's gonna be yo' end."

Her words cut deep. Mama, in her simple wisdom, had brought to the surface the matter he had been skirting since his first encounter with the wrathful deity.

"I know you're right, Mama," he began. "But I'm afraid I don't really know how to do that."

"Carson, you figure somethin' out," she said flatly.

Back in the trailer, he began storing away his things. His idea of staying for only a few days began to fade. He wanted to go home, to see his son, to sleep in his own bed, to reconnect with Rhiannon. But Blind Mama had laid down the gauntlet. He had to come to terms with the Dharmapala and the power offered to him through that relationship.

At the back of the kitchen counter, the overnight package from Landon's office sat unopened. He had little interest in seeing whatever Charlie Landon's people had sent as a "get well" gift. Out of obligation, however, he tore it open.

His name was elegantly written on a small envelope that was taped to a heavy, hardbound book in bubble wrap.

Dear Carson,
Thought you might enjoy this. Delighted having you and Lucas in
our home.
Best wishes,
Connie Haynesworth

He pulled back the bubble wrap, exposing the dust jacket: *Tibet's Sacred Demons of Enlightenment.*

Hours drifted by unnoticed. The book's words pulled at Carson's gut; the photographs moved off the pages to walk about in his head. The realm and reality of the Dharmapalas lived and breathed once more as the phantasmagoria of this ancient culture poured directly into him. He felt as though he was but fodder to these beings, yet blessed through their presence.

Only with the coming of night did he take a break, and then only to turn on a light, drink some water, and light the votive. The reading continued to consume him. With information gained from each new chapter, he would go back and reread previous ones, each time going deeper into building an understanding of these gods.

The process continued until he came to the chapter on chöd. Carson suddenly realized why this book had come to him. Here was the ancient teaching that could possibly bring him into some semblance of accord with the wrathful deity. He felt sick with fear.

Chapter 22

Chöd

Sitting on the trailer steps the next morning with a cup of coffee, Carson reread the chapter on chöd. He had thought its meaning would be less disturbing if he gave it more time, but he was mistaken. It was now abundantly clear; he was going to have to undergo this terrifying process with the Dharmapala. He was going to have to sacrifice himself to the Dharmapala.

Carson went over the text carefully. In its most ancient form, chöd involved monks and lamas undergoing lengthy training and then taking themselves out to a remote location, often smoldering charnel grounds where the dead had been recently burned. There, among the decaying corpses, they would sit through the night, sometimes many days and nights, offering their bodies as literal sacrifices to a wrathful deity or even a group of deities. The practitioners would viscerally undergo the experience of having their bodies torn to shreds. When the chöd was successful, it would bring them great advancement toward enlightenment. But not all practitioners returned alive.

In a kind of reverse Christian communion, chöd called for worshippers to give their bodies and blood as sacrifice to the deities. Carson knew only too well that his Dharmapala would accept no substitute of bread and wine; real blood would be required.

Carson spent the following days and nights mulling over what awaited. He slept little and ate practically nothing. During those days, he had no contact with Blind Mama, though he felt she knew that he was agonizing. Frank would come by in the afternoon and sit outside the trailer for a while. At the end of three days of isolation, he walked up to Blind Mama's house.

"Come in, Carson," she called. "I know'd you was comin' up."

"Hello, Mama. How you doing?"

"Me?" She laughed. "Child, I done had my days of initiation long ago. You be the person that gotta walk through that lonesome valley. You think you can make it?"

"To be honest, I don't have a clue."

"That's good. Bein' humble is bein' smart, if you ask me," she said.

"I think I have to undergo something here, Mama. I have to endure a kind of ritual process. And to tell you the truth, I don't know if I have much of a chance of surviving it."

Against his will, he began to weep silently.

"That's all right, honey. You need to cry some," she said gently. "Go on and let it out."

"I feel pretty ashamed of myself right now, especially when I think of what happened to Marianna," he continued. Composing himself somewhat, he asked, "Can you tell me where around here you think might be a good place, you know, where the energy is right for doing something like this?"

"You take that trail that runs on behind yo' trailer. It ain't too far a piece. You gonna come down to a swampy place at the back of the woods. As a child, I played there lots of times. The other chil'dren wouldn't go there; they got scared. Me, I always loved it there. Lots of my helpers come to me out there. They come out the water and the earth. That's where you ought to go."

"That sounds fine. But any sense that the Visitors might be returning soon?"

"Not presently," she said. "But that don't mean you be safe from 'em. No sir."

She spat into the fire and fumbled to find her pipe. "When you figurin' on doin' this ritual, Carson?"

"Tomorrow night, if I can bring myself to do it."

Mama lit her pipe and blew tobacco smoke toward him. "Tomorrow night's a good time. I be prayin' for you, child."

He walked back to the trailer. A soft breeze whispered in the pines. Frank moved ahead of him, the dog's nose busied by the night's scents.

Much of the next day was occupied by going over a checklist of what he should do and bring. With no training or preparation, he was going to have to improvise, and much of this was based on conjecture as to what was revealed in the book. He could only do the best he knew how.

While there were variations of chöd, most practitioners used a bell, a drum and a trumpet made from a human thighbone, to help summon the gods. Also, knives were used to symbolize cutting away the bindings of ignorance, or the flesh if need be.

An old shed just beyond the trailer became a resource for critical items. Inside, he found a rusting five-gallon can with no lid or bottom. It would serve as the frame for a drum. Nearby he discovered a roll of oilcloth that provided the drum's skin. Using an assortment of wire, plastic ties and tape from his film gear, he was able to stretch the oilcloth securely over the metal can.

In the midst of harvesting the drum supplies, it had literally fallen from the wall before his feet—a cowbell.

As that evening pressed in, Carson gathered up the necessary gear into a plastic tarp and headed off for the swamp. The fact that he was walking down the trail where Marianna had been killed made his task all the more ominous; fear swelled in his throat.

The trail was not well used; underbrush grew across it in many spots. He was pushing hard to get to the place Blind Mama had described before dark. Then, just when he was wondering if he had taken a wrong turn, he stepped out of the woods and into an eerie clearing. It smelled of brackish water; Spanish moss draped down from the trees. The light, already fading, mixed with a misty haze that hung in the bushes.

Carson found a spot where the ground seemed reasonably firm beside a pool of dark water. He spread out the tarp. Off to one side, he set out the flashlight, a bottle of water, and a supply of extra candles. Along the front of the tarp, he placed the drum, the cowbell, the votive candle, a kitchen knife, and Taz. Caesar Chiang's amulet hung around his neck.

Carson lit a candle and sat quietly at first, needing to gather his courage. Finally, he began calling out loud; calling the Dharmapala; calling for protection, guidance and mercy.

The swamp was filled with noise. The darker the night grew, the louder the sound became. Dragonflies zinged through the air. Birds called to one another as they bedded down for the night. Crickets sang and a great chorus of frogs echoed over the swamp. He had not anticipated this; he needed to meditate and found the wildlife activity distracting.

Abandoning any attempt to meditate, he reached for the drum. He began to play a slow, ritualistic beat. Instantly, all other sound ceased. Only the drum called through the darkness.

Gradually, his consciousness shifted, bridging the separation between himself and the swamp. Heat slowly built in his body, coursing up his spine and pulsing into his surroundings. As his energy grew, his playing became louder. He heard himself calling out sacred names he had never known. He reached for the cowbell, adding the sound of its dull clapper to the ritual.

He beseeched the wrathful deity to come forth. A sudden state of ecstasy overwhelmed his fear, allowing him to celebrate utter surrender through a sublime feeling of acceptance. His immanent sacrifice would become an ecstatic state of bliss.

Unable to continue drumming, he lay down on the tarp and waited. Breathing rhythmically as silence hung over the swamp, he waited for the divine moment. At any instant, it would begin. First would come the sound of that terrible, deep breathing; then the glowing red eyes would emerge out of the darkness. Carson was subsumed in awe—time was suspended.

First one frog started, far on the other side of the swamp, then a second, closer by. Within minutes, the swamp was a riot of sound as the frogs reclaimed their broadcasting rights.

The chorus of frogs pulled him back into his regular consciousness. No wrathful deity or any other spirit had come. He reconsidered his actions: What had he not done? Or worse, what had he done wrong? What an idiot; he obviously need to give the process more time.

Sitting back up, he made more propitiation to the Dharmapala, uttering prayers and giving praise to the Great Lord, begging that his offering be accepted. He concentrated on details in the book and images associated with the wrathful deities.

He swatted a mosquito and waited. Hours passed.

With his candle supply exhausted and disappointment setting in, Carson decided to return to the trailer. It was only then that he realized finding his way back through the overgrown trail would be tricky in the dark.

Suddenly, as he stood up, it tore through the night—the piercing howl of a wolf.

Everything in the swamp fell deadly silent. Time stopped once more. His earlier courage completely abandoned him. He couldn't think. Joseph's words about learning a whole new level of praying raced across his mind. He whispered for divine inter-vention, calling upon the absent Dharmapala, his animal guides from Wounded Paw, the help of Blind Mama, and the protection of Jesus. He knelt down quickly, feeling for the flashlight and the kitchen knife, as if either might provide adequate protection.

Suddenly a noise came from the brush directly behind him. It was heading straight toward him. He wheeled around, ready with the knife, aiming the flashlight.

Frank casually trotted out of the brush and sat down at the edge of the swamp. The frog chorus started again.

"Yeah, I sent old Frank down to fetch you," Blind Mama said as she poured him coffee the following morning. "I seen you was just mostly makin' the frogs miserable."

It was Carson who felt miserable. The only takers on his offer of self-sacrifice were the mosquitoes, which had gladly fed upon his blood.

"I feel like an idiot," he mumbled.

"That's all right." Mama laughed. "Sometimes it goes that way 'cause that's the thing you gotta go through before you can really do the next step."

"What do you mean, Mama?"

"Think 'bout it. Sometimes they's some other part of yo'self that be hangin' round over in a corner somewhere. When a body goes to do a ritual like you done, then that part that you ain't been payin' no attention to comes and jumps out 'cause it needs fixin' first. Maybe what you done had some reason it happened that way."

"Wait, are you saying I have to stop worrying that I might look foolish?"

"It ain't me saying nothin', but sound like somethin' might wanna tell you that," she said.

While Carson considered her words, Blind Mama shuffled over to the fire and loaded her pipe. "All I know is you ain't finished what you done come here for."

She turned and spat into the fire again. Carson suddenly realized that she uttered something under her breath every time she spat into the fire.

"Mama, what is that you're saying when you spit? Is it a curse, a prayer, or what?"

"It's what you might call a seal," she said. "I seal my words that way; that be my business."

"Sorry, didn't mean to pry."

"Don't matter none." She shook her head, laughing. "Ain't gonna say but what I wanna. You be curious all you want."

"Well, given that today I'm allowed to be curious as well as make a fool of myself, I've got to ask you about something else that happened last night. Does Frank sometimes howl like a wolf?"

Blind Mama suddenly turned away from him and puffed hard on her pipe. Her body language was clear. There would be no further discussion.

Chapter 23

The Magdalene

"Yes'um, I won't forget," Joseph called back to Blind Mama. "Get in the truck, Carson. If we don't get movin', she be givin' me orders all day and we ain't never gonna get to the store. Every time I come see her, she treats me like I'm six years old." Joseph shook his head ruefully, slamming the truck door.

Carson climbed into the pickup. It had been more than a week since he had arrived at Blind Mama's, and the sudden opportunity to make contact with the outside world was both exciting and unsettling. He had grown accustomed to the isolation. There was really no measuring of time at Blind Mama's, only the shifting pattern of day to night—and, for her, not even that.

The truck fought its way out to the two-lane blacktop and headed down to Moses' store.

"So, you been all right?" Joseph asked. "Look like you still alive."

Carson smiled, enjoying the wind in his face from the open window.

"If you need to do some big shoppin', I can drive you over to Eulogy, or even Ebenezer," Joseph said.

"As long as Moses' store has a working pay phone, that won't be necessary," Carson said. "How's Sugar Wilson doing?"

"Dr. Wilson is sorta hard to find these days, if you know what I mean," Joseph said with a wink. "But I reckon he's doin' fine, wherever he is."

A half dozen trucks and cars were parked in front of Moses' store. Paint peeled from the building's clapboard siding. Looking at the place, Carson guessed that it might have been built in the 1920s. A single gas pump stood alone in the dirt parking lot. Off to the right of the storefront, he spotted the phone booth.

"Joseph, I'll meet you inside. I've got to make my calls."

Phoning Ben came first. He had not spoken to his son since leaving the hospital. Next he called the hospital to check on Lucas. Then he gave an obligatory check-in to Landon's office, to announce that he was recovering nicely and hoped to soon have an estimate as to when he could continue with the documentary. Finally, he dialed his voice mail. There was only one message from her.

"Carson, hello, dear man. Sorry we haven't been able to connect. God, I hope this gets to you. Last I heard you were on your way to Memphis. Did I get that right? Anyway, I can't really tell you much about what I'm up to, but right now I'm in a little regional airport in southern Turkey. As soon as we claim our luggage, we're heading off to a kind of retreat. I think I'll be there at least two weeks and doubt I can phone once I'm there. If you don't hear from me for a while, it's because of what I'll be doing, okay? I'll check in first chance I get. Please stay safe. I miss you."

Rhiannon's words brought relief and longing. He walked inside Moses' store.

"You tell Blind Mama her time is running out," a large, fat man, wearing a brown pinstripe suit said while pointing his finger angrily at Joseph. "If she don't repent and come into the house of the Lord, it's gonna be too late to save her eternal soul. She's gotta stop all that devil worship mischief she's been carrying on all these years."

"Carson," Joseph called. "This here is Reverend Wilcox." He nodded toward the dapperly dressed man leaning against an ice cream cooler. "He preaches over at the Laurel Creek Baptist Church when he ain't busy messin' in other people's business."

"Nice to meet you," Carson said dryly, observing the large diamond stickpin strategically placed high on the reverend's bright lavender necktie.

"Don't tell me she done got another one over there," the

Reverend said emphatically, looking Carson over.

"You have a nice day, Reverend," Joseph said, turning away.

Carson and Joseph assembled several cardboard boxes full of sundries and food. All the while, Reverend Wilcox glared at Carson.

"Chlorese, you got them things from the slaughterhouse ready?" Joseph called to a tall woman behind the meat counter.

"Oh yeah, they back here waiting for you," replied the young woman.

Chlorese passed over a bundle wrapped in heavy butcher paper. Then she walked to the side of the meat counter and pulled out a lidded, five-gallon plastic bucket from the back of the refrigerated unit. She slid the heavy bucket along the floor to the side of the counter.

"Get that, would you, Carson?" Joseph said, taking the butcher-papered package to place with the other items.

Carson picked up the bucket. It was heavy, its contents sloshing inside.

"I hate to think what she gonna do with them slaughterhouse parts," Reverend Wilcox called over as they checked out.

"Reverend, when you find the verse in the Bible that says, 'Thou shall not feed thy hound dog,' you show me. Meanwhile, Frank—he gotta eat!"

They drove back toward Blind Mama's.

"Well, that was an interesting little confrontation," Carson said.

"That's been goin' on round these parts for years." Joseph laughed. "Reverend Wilcox ain't the only preacher that tried to mess with Blind Mama. She got herself a completely different way when it comes to Jesus and all that. Preachers, they don't like it none. Truth is, they all scared of her."

While they unpacked, Blind Mama queried Joseph relentlessly as to whether he had completed her shopping correctly. Next, she made certain that each item was stored away in a precise order. Outside, Frank gnawed away on a fresh bone.

"Say, Carson, you wanna go bass fishin' tomorrow?" Joseph asked.

"No, he don't!" Blind Mama injected, cracking her cane on the floor.

Carson sensed something was developing.

"No, I guess he don't," Joseph said, giving Carson a swift look.

"Hopefully another time, Joseph," Carson added.

"Now you get on over to yo' mama's and tell her I see her next week," Blind Mama said, officially dismissing Joseph.

She waited a few minutes after the last sounds of the pickup had faded down the dirt road.

"They be comin'," she said.

Carson's insides lurched.

"When?"

"Soon enough. You best be busy gettin' ready. Bring yo' spirit things up to the house. We gonna wait together."

Carson hurried down to the trailer and gathered the items he considered essential. It was already late afternoon. His mind raced. How was it that certain people could tell when the Visitors were coming and he couldn't? Returning to the house, he set his things down.

"Carson, come sit by me," Blind Mama commanded.

"How much time do we have?"

"Time?" She shrugged. "Me and Frank, we don't keep no time, but I know what you mean. They still be a ways off. Yo' head all better nowadays?"

"Yeah, my shoulder's still tender from the injury, but I'm pretty much back to normal. Why?"

"Gonna need to be strong when they come," she replied. "Make sho' we have plenty of firewood inside."

"Oh my God!" he exclaimed, remembering the wood stove at Rhiannon's. "They can come down the chimney."

"They can try, but they ain't gonna," she said, spitting into the fire and striking her cane. "You just make sho' you got that demon boy of yo's to be round a helpin' you. I take care the rest."

"Blind Mama, I was taught that when they return to a place, they always come back stronger than the last time and with different tactics. This Visitor attack will be much more intense than last time, with Marianna."

She gave no response.

"Carson, in a little while I want you to let Frank in and make sho' he got himself some water set out over in the kitchen."

They sat together, each preparing in his or her own manner. Carson stared into the small fire, praying and calling to his guides and allies. Again, he solicited protection from the wrathful deity, but given the lack of results from the chöd exercises, he was feeling less than confident.

"Did you make them phone calls down at the store?"

"Yeah. Should I not have done that?" he said, suddenly wondering if his calls had been the catalyst for bringing on the attack.

"I don't know, son. We see soon enough, I suppose."

"Some preacher down there seemed to be pretty upset about you."

"Sounds like that fool, Wilcox," she said, spitting again into the fire.

"Yeah, that was his name." He chuckled. "I guess he thinks you're going to hell or something."

"Honey, I been to hell plenty of times already. That's part of what makes them preachers so nervous. Ain't a one of 'em ever walked with the Holy Ghost, through the fire. No sir!"

A shiver ran over Carson as he suddenly grasped more of the depth of Blind Mama's spiritual path.

"These preachers round here, like that Wilcox, they don't care nothin' 'bout savin' my soul." She smirked. "And they sho' don't like it none when I ask if they ever been cooked in hell any. No sir, that makes 'em look at me like I be best friends with Satan."

"Joseph said something about you having a different perspective about Jesus. What did he mean?"

"Them preacher fools don't know nothin' 'bout sweet Jesus, child," Blind Mama declared. "Poor Jesus, he didn't die for our sins. He died to get rid of the bad spirits that was holdin' the world in misery. Back in them Bible times, them Nazarene folk, they done some powerful work. Jesus was one of 'em, but so was his woman—the Magdalene. All of 'em was workin' to break the stranglehold of bad spirits over the world—get folks to wake up and see they's another way to live. When you gets to the bottom of it, that's what them folks was 'bout."

"Say more, Mama."

"Jesus, he took on big stuff, more than the rest of 'em all put together. But he come to a crisis round shiftin' that mean ol' energy. I believe he figured he could get rid of the bad energy by takin' it away with him, through his own death process. That was the best that sweet man could do.

"And you gotta understand, workin' with powerful spirit energy like he done is more than a body can bear. Even the bliss burns you up in a terrible way. And if a man take on that much spirit energy, well, he might get by for a short while, but soon 'nuff, he gotta release it or be consumed by it. Them Nazarene teachin's was too much for the menfolk to be handlin' over long periods of time. Holdin' that kind of knowin' for long could only be done by a woman, 'cause they understand how to carry sufferin' in their bodies. His woman, the Magdalene, she know'd how to carry that kind of sufferin'."

Carson's thoughts journeyed back two millennia, as he reconsidered the work of Biblical shamans.

Blind Mama spat into the fire and went on. "And what Jesus and his lady was doin' was somethin' fierce. It was too much for most folk, 'specially for them rascals that put together what they called Christianity. They got the teachin's all wrong, so they made up their own version 'bout Jesus and all. Just tried to make theyselves look good, that's what. They wanted to sorta rub up against the Holy Ghost, but just take the safe parts where they's all filled with white light and bliss. But no sir, if you gonna walk with the Holy Ghost as truly righteous, you gotta go all the way. You gotta take that long road down through them hell places. You gotta suffer and know what that's all 'bout—fo' yo'self and all the rest. You gotta let them hellfires cook you some before you gonna get the salvation that be waitin' on the other side."

Carson pondered how many hells Blind Mama had endured in her long life of hardship.

"It was dangerous times, maybe sorta like now. And the Magdalene, she know'd she had to slip away from them Romans and all them apostles. She got herself on a boat to somewhere else and carried them teachin's and all, carried 'em away in her body. You see, child, the kind of knowin' what Jesus and the Magdalene know'd, well, it can't be just in yo' mind, or even in yo' heart. It only be held in yo' whole body! And honey, it ain't yo' fault, but men just ain't made to carry that much power. Not for long, that's for sho'."

Mama paused, her thoughts carried far away to a secret place. The fire in the hearth hissed softly. She wiped tears from her aging checks.

"Sometimes, when I be feelin' bad for myself 'cause my life be so alone, I can feel the Magdalene's fingertips just lightly brush over my veiled eyes. I love her so."

Chapter 24

Visitors at the Door

Something scratched at the door. Cautiously, Carson opened it partway, and Frank quickly slipped inside, disappearing immediately under Blind Mama's bed. Night had fully descended.

For whatever good it might do, Carson made certain the door was locked. He returned to the fireplace and turned his chair around to face the door. Taz stood on the mantle, also facing the door.

"Mama, do you think the Visitors have any understanding of compassion or love?"

After thinking for a moment, she said, "They might, but I ain't seen none of it. It could be that they do but it's only for they own kind."

"I still have trouble accepting that the sacred powers in the universe would allow this to be happening," he said.

Mama laughed. "Well, if you'd done gone bass fishin' with Joseph, maybe them fish would be lookin' up through the water and wonderin' why them men wanna put hooks in their mouths and take 'em home and throw 'em on a skillet. Ain't them men got no compassion?"

Her answer only made him ponder harder.

"You best make ready, son," Mama said. "It won't be too long now, I reckon."

"Is it all right if I play my drum and bell?"

"You do all you need," she replied.

Carson pulled the homemade drum between his knees and began a steady beat. He could feel energy rising through his body.

He suddenly decided to try the chöd exercise again. He beseeched the Dharmapala to come and be sated through the sacrifice of his flesh and blood.

He swooned under the mind-altering power of the drum. In a chair at the other side of the hearth, Blind Mama was softly singing a hymn: "What a Friend We Have in Jesus."

Beams of blue-white light swept across the windows. Carson bolted up to look outside. The light began scanning the clearing in front of the old sharecropper house. Within moments, the light was probing beneath the door and then piercing cracks in the old walls. Flashes of orange light washed across the walls through the musty windowpanes. The Visitors had arrived.

Using the handle of a kitchen knife, Carson beat upon the cowbell. He focused his breathing, exhaling waves of energy to build a protective field.

He prayed, "Great Lord of the Himalayas, come take of me, drink my blood, devour my flesh; may these please and nourish you. May my humble offering serve you with pleasure, bring healing to whatever may afflict us all and offer glory to your many ineffable names."

The boards of the house creaked violently as tenacious forces pressed upon them—the aliens' from outside and Blind Mama's from within. She threw more wood on the fire, chanting in a language that seemed imbedded in an unknown African dialect.

Sounds came from underneath the house; something was tearing at the old floorboards.

"Carson, get on the bed, quick! Stay off the floor!"

Automatically, he obeyed, his consciousness remaining focused on the chöd. He had become nearly oblivious to the attack. Frank scrambled from underneath the bed and leapt on top, nestling behind Carson.

Blind Mama stood on the stone hearth, shouting commands to her spirits in a tongue unknown to Carson. From a frayed silken pouch strung over her shoulder, she slung handfuls of dirt and cowry shells across the floor in every direction.

Everything fell back into silence.

The sudden calm caused Carson to return to partial consciousness. All appeared intact. The lights had stopped; the house was quiet. Blind Mama was standing motionless on the stone hearth.

"What happened? Why did they stop?" he whispered.

"They ain't stopped."

Carson got up and moved slowly toward a window.

"Watch how you step," she warned. "Probably lots of nail heads stickin' up through the floor after that."

Peering outside, he could see only darkness; all was still. Wiping a layer of grime from the windowpane, Carson leaned closer. He could detect neither lights nor movement in the field. Could they have left?

Another face, just on the other side of the windowpane, met his. He jerked back several feet, breathing wildly. The face was gone.

The encounter had lasted only an instant, but he was certain of one thing—the face appeared reptilian.

"They're still out there, Mama," Carson whispered.

"Course they is. Fixin' to come at us again."

Carson prayed, "Mighty One, bring your terrible wrath down upon these who seek to steal your domain and harm your servant."

Cautiously, he eased toward the window but could see nothing. Then, along the edge of the clearing beyond the house, a crackling sound began. An electrical phenomenon like slow-motion lightning sizzled horizontally across the clearing. A great thud hit the front door. Blind Mama yelled out curses and violently struck the floor with her cane. Out of the corner of his eye, Carson glimpsed a host of numinous forms moving about Blind Mama.

He prayed, "Do not let these, your enemies, take my life when I have made this offering to you, Great One. Do not let these colonizers, who serve you not, usurp your dominion over what has been yours from before time began."

Building in power and will, he stationed himself in a bold stance before the window. If necessary he would die meeting them head-on.

Outside, the sporadic electrical activity was coalescing, gathering in three separate bundles, one at each end of the clearing and a third in the middle. The bundles began morphing into recognizable forms, the same kind of being that he had seen at Rhiannon's and standing on the overpass before the tornado hit. Static electrical energy sparked around the tall, diaphanous entities. Long, tentacle-like appendages flowed from the backs of their trapezoidal heads.

Jagged strobe-light beams shot out from the appendages toward the sharecropper shanty. Huge, prehistoric-looking insects buzzed through the air, making choppy metallic sounds. Bizarre creatures, suggesting a cross between hyenas and giant spiders, their eyes afire from the light, scampered across the ground.

Carson yelled out, "Cut through my ignorance; break my blindness through your compassion!"

Something slashed at his throat; blood gushed down his chest.

Beams from the three large, robot-like beings converged on the house, causing everything inside to glow with a light that penetrated Carson's skin and reflected his skeleton against the walls. His consciousness exploded into oblivion.

I'm dead, am I not? Carson looked down on his body, lying on the kitchen floor.

All was quiet. There were no more Visitors.

Blind Mama's house still stood as before, only the door was wide open. His consciousness floated about, readily moving wherever his eyes focused. He felt oddly aloof from the intensity of the battle just fought.

"Well done, adept," a familiar voice said.

"Great Lord! Am I no longer of your world?"

"On the contrary, you became that much more of it tonight."

"Is that what occurs with death?"

"Under certain circumstances, yes," the deity answered.

"This state feels strangely familiar." Carson paused. "Will you guide me through my death passage, Great Lord?"

"Perhaps, in due course. But adept, you are not quite dead—not yet."

"I'm confused, Great One."

"Your training has not allowed you the benefits gained by years with the monks. You are merely experiencing an out-of-body state. Your body remains on the floor, yet lives. The real you has become free of it. Perhaps you will choose to stay free of it forever; perhaps you will go back to dwell inside it."

"But what happened? I mean, the Visitors were—"

"I unleashed my wrath upon them, adept. They're vanquished for now—those that could escape. They will seek other adversaries next time. Many did I smite with my terrible weapons. My victory was glorious. What a splendid legend I make."

"You came? You saved me?"

"Adept, need I remind you of your manners? Do you think I would suffer the insult of those leeches taking a life that is mine to have, especially when you had gone to such pathetic measures to offer it to me? However, through my magnanimous compassion, I allowed the blessing of accepting your unworthy gesture. I tore your neck and drank your unconsecrated blood!"

"And Blind Mama, what of her?"

"The old one? She lives. She has powerful guardians enough. Now, choose your path, adept: Go back to that carnal sack you inhabited or proceed in this new state. Either way, I must take my leave. I have begun to coalesce my energies once again within my mountain domain. Perhaps you will one day pay me homage there. Much work awaits."

"But wait. What about the Visitors next time? Will you be there to help?"

"Adept, has this night not shown that you have learned to invoke my power? Humans can be so dense."

"Great Lord, I don't know what I'm capable of."

"You have experienced much, thanks to my blessing, and now carry a sliver of my mighty wrath as your power source. Use it well, adept. The fight with these parasites is far from settled. I have instilled in you great power and I expect you to bring me glory in this struggle. Grow in your power and confidence; perhaps even learn a smattering of what that devil Padmasambhava knew. I will accept nothing less."

Carson felt a stinging in his neck; he raised his hand and discovered a soft cloth bandage wrapping his throat. He could smell blood and pine resin. As usual, the only light was from the hearth's fire in the living room.

He pulled himself up and went to find Mama. She was not there. The front door stood open. He found his flashlight on the table and stepped carefully outside. The sky was just starting to lighten with a hint of dawn.

He spotted a shape in the middle of the clearing and walked toward it. It was Frank, sitting as if frozen, staring at something directly in front of him. Carson switched on the flashlight, pointing at the object of Frank's obsession. It was Taz.

He gave Frank a few pats and picked up the toy figure.

A noise came from the side of the house. Carson moved in its direction, hoping to find Mama. There, halfway back along the side of the house, she stood with her back to him. Under one arm, she was holding the white plastic bucket that had come from the slaughterhouse. On her other side, concealed in the shadows, something large was slurping from the bucket.

"Carson, get back in the house. This here ain't none of yo'

business."

"Yes, ma'am," he said, retreating.

He sat down by the fire, adding wood to build the heat and light. His mind was spent, his body beyond exhaustion. It wasn't long until Blind Mama shuffled in.

"Gonna make some coffee," she announced casually, as if nothing had occurred.

"I'll help," he said.

"No, you just sit where you is," she insisted. "You and me, we need to keep apart just a little longer 'cause we got such different kinda spirits that works with us. That friend you got sho' be the gruff type."

"Yeah, that he is," Carson replied. "You doing all right?"

"Lord yes, I'm fine, I reckon," she said. "Just tuckered out. I put pine pitch on yo' cut, work just like stitches if you leave it alone for a while. How's yo' neck feelin'?"

"Fine, I reckon," he said, trying to imitate her.

They broke into laughter, releasing volumes of tension.

For a long time they sat, sipping coffee and appreciating the fact that they had survived the night. Blind Mama puffed on her pipe.

"Mama, I thought I got killed last night."

She shifted in her chair. "In a way, you kinda did. But it weren't them alien spirits that had hold of you."

"No, I suppose not," he paused, reflecting on the Dharmapala's presence. "But the Visitors came damn close!"

"Oh, they was tryin' somethin' awful. I had to plumb nearly stuff the place with angels."

"I have a suspicion they won't come back to your house for a good while," he said.

"Hope you right, child," she said, spitting into the fire, sealing a curse and a prayer. "I don't know if old Frank can stand another time."

They laughed more.

"Well, Carson, I hope you done what you needed to. You found a way to work with that demon you knows. I think you need to go back to yo' world now."

"Perhaps I do. I can't thank you enough for all that you helped me to achieve."

"That's all right. It's my job, I reckon. I'm gonna miss hearin' that nice voice you got. I figure I won't be for this world too much longer, but you ever back this way, you come see old Blind Mama."

"Mama, I'll make a point to come see you. In fact, if things happen the way I want, there's someone I want to bring here."

"Ah, yo' woman." She sighed. "I seen you be in love when you first got here. It had me mighty worried, seein' you all wishin' to be with her, not wantin' to take on this terrible work by yo'self. But you stayed."

"She's been the one who's insisted we stay apart because of all this. I don't know if that'll ever change."

"Well, you ain't gonna know 'til it happens, but I know she be thinkin' of you. I believe you be seein' her before long. And I think you be strong enough to leave here now. I'm gonna send word to have Joseph come fetch you. You need to go home, see yo' boy, and take that demon of yours away from Mississippi!"

"Thank you, Mama."

"Now, old Mama need to be alone. You go on down to the trailer and get some rest while you can; can't be lettin' yo'self get careless just 'cause you lived past last night."

Carson stopped at the door and turned back, his curiosity unbearable.

"Say, Mama, forgive me, but I've got to ask—this werewolf business?"

"Carson," she said, striking the floor with her cane. "That be no business of yo's."

Chapter 25

The Gala

She was late. A heavy fog had plagued landings all day at San Francisco International. Quickly clearing customs, with her baggage in tow, Rhiannon scanned the expansive terminal. If Carson was there waiting, she couldn't spot him.

She had phoned from Turkey and London, leaving messages as to when she would be arriving. She knew he was back in California through the messages he had left for her; however, his words had been unusually cryptic, alluding only to the fact that he was home and hoped to see her sometime.

An attractive Native American man approached.

"You must be Rhiannon," he said confidently. "Welcome home. I'm Luther Redbone."

"Luther?" she responded. "I'm sorry. Yes, I know who you are. Where's Carson? Is there—has something happened to him?"

"He's all right. Well, as much as any of us are. Given the circumstances, he couldn't get away to meet you and we thought someone should pick you up."

"What's happening, Luther?"

"Let's talk while we drive," he answered.

He took her bag and they walked outside. Immediately a van pulled up to the curb. Luther opened the front-passenger door for her before getting into the backseat with her luggage. Jimmy White Stone sat in the driver's seat.

The van maneuvered into the outbound traffic lane. Two hundred feet behind them, a black Chevy Suburban with dark tinted windows also pulled away from the curb, undetected.

"Rhiannon, nice to meet you. I'm Jimmy White Stone."

"Jimmy, good to meet you finally. Carson's told me much about both of you."

The Indians made no response.

"All right, so what's going on?" she implored, starting to sense something was wrong.

"Things have become possibly unsafe on a new front," Luther answered bluntly, leaning toward the front seats. "According to Carson, he's being watched by men in unmarked cars and the like. He suspects that his phones are tapped. Even if he could have met your flight, he thought it best not to expose you openly."

"Oh no! And here I was leaving Turkey with the first ray of hope I've had in years. Has something specific happened?"

"We're not certain what's going on," Jimmy interrupted, glancing in his rearview mirror. "Carson only got back several days ago. But he's suggesting that these people are somehow working with the Visitors. Last week, Charles Landon, the guy who's been financing the model train documentary, was arrested in Prague on some kind of money laundering charges. Someone tipped off Interpol that he was supposedly doing business with elements of the Russian mob. Federal agents have raided his offices and seized lots of records. And since Carson is working for him on a rather personal project, it may have drawn their suspicion. But Carson isn't buying it; he thinks those charges are only a cover. He met a man in Memphis that had something similar happen to him."

"So, why are you two here? I mean, what are you up to besides giving me a ride?"

Luther leaned back in his seat, watching Rhiannon's face for a moment, then explained. "Well, it's an interesting set of coincidences, but there's a national fund-raising event taking place here this week, for urban Native American health care centers. It's been in the planning for several years. All kinds of festivities have been occurring across San Francisco. Among the events is a screening of the medicine circle documentary, and I was asked to be one of the spokesmen for the film. It's been a pretty glitzy week, watching all the politicians and movie stars trying to out-empathize each other. Sometimes it's very baffling being a minority."

"And Jimmy, you're here because of your work on the documentary as well?"

"Yes, that and the fact I'm writing a couple of articles on the fund-raiser, one for *Native Peoples Magazine* and another for the *Washington Post*," Jimmy answered. "So we were already in San Francisco for this when we learned that Carson was back. Naturally, we invited him to be a part of the documentary screening. Tonight is its biggest showing. So while he's being lauded for his work, we came down to pick you up. And until tonight, we hadn't heard that he'd been injured."

"What?" Rhiannon interrupted. "Damn it, Jimmy—"

"Oh, he's fine now," Jimmy reassured her. "He was caught in a tornado and got banged up some. His soundman, Lucas, got the worst of it."

"When did this happen?"

"Over two weeks ago, just outside Memphis. They waited to fly home until Lucas was well enough to leave the hospital. Lucas is recuperating pretty well," Luther explained.

"Tonight's big gala is at the Palace Hotel," Jimmy continued. "Carson's there right now. He believes it should be fairly safe, given that he'll be too much in the limelight for something to happen. If some of these people are spying on him, they probably won't try anything tonight with all the media presence, not to mention the rich and famous folks wanting to shake hands with the filmmaker. I don't think this is exactly the kind of reunion he was hoping to have with you, but this is how it's working out."

Rhiannon stared out the window, vexed that people would be cooperating with the Visitors. Outside, the familiar sight of San Francisco's nocturnal skyline came into view. At least she would soon see Carson.

"And your time in Turkey, did it go well?" Luther asked,

watching her face closely.

"Beyond all measure. Perhaps the most powerful work I've ever experienced. These women are restoring an unbelievably powerful tradition. Their work's already affecting the impact of the Visitors. If we ever have the time one day, I want to tell you about it."

"That's welcome news," Luther replied calmly, moving a hand slowly across her suitcase. "On the Zuni Reservation of late, we've felt a decrease in the Visitors' threat level. At least enough to where I felt I could attend this thing in San Francisco without leaving my people too vulnerable. Perhaps it was because of what you accomplished."

"Oh, I would love to think so. But if it's working, it's all of us, Luther."

"But now, at least according to Carson, we have this new element to deal with," Jimmy said. "He wants to see you before we take him to a safer location for a while. He's trying to avoid being arrested or, perhaps worse, becoming the victim of an accident or something. And after what happened to Lucas, he's very concerned about others, especially his son. So, he thinks it best that he remove himself as soon as possible, limiting his contacts to only those directly involved with the medicine work."

"There's something else," Luther added. "He also needs some time to digest what he's been through and to figure out what to do next. Whatever power source you helped him connect with, well, it's apparently taken root. He walks with a powerful medicine now, yet one that's very different from our ways. I almost didn't recognize him."

"Oh my God, he pulled it off—" Rhiannon uttered, choked with elation.

"So, we're going to provide him with sanctuary for the immediate future," Jimmy said.

"Sounds like you're taking him to Wounded Paw's,"

Rhiannon guessed, turning around to face Luther while wiping tears from her face.

"Precisely," Luther affirmed.

"Then I'm coming, too."

Arriving at the hotel, Jimmy White Stone drove down the ramp into the underground garage. Seconds later, the black Suburban followed.

The three of them walked to the garage elevators. The door opened and Jimmy pressed the button for the mezzanine.

Having recently undergone a complete restoration, the Palace Hotel had become a popular venue for glamorous events, its understated grandeur nostalgically recalling the opulence of a bygone era, with it's vaulted, stained glass ceiling, oversized Victorian furnishings and mahogany paneling.

The elevator opened onto a balcony corridor enclosed by a Baroque iron railing and gilded light fixtures. The drone of a multitude of conversations nearly drowned out the piped-in music of the female group Ulali. A crowd of elegantly dressed people spilled into the corridor from the large reception hall. With the screening of the documentary already completed, the social business of the night was in full swing.

The threesome moved toward the reception hall.

"How is it that you can just waltz in here?" Rhiannon asked.

"We have passes to all the events this week. And we're allowed to bring any guest we think is appropriate for the fundraiser," Jimmy said.

Men in tuxedos or expensive black-tie alternatives laughed and slapped each other on the back. Elegant women adorned in cocktail dresses and sporting expensive hairstyles held champagne flutes as though they were trophies. Different tribal representatives, many clad in native clothing and accessories, were in attendance, scattered among the event's guests. It was a high-profile night for an odd mix of people—socialites and

Indians. Rhiannon searched for Carson Reynolds, buried somewhere in the midst of this crowd.

"They're on the mezzanine," a man reported into a radiophone. "We're standing by as instructed."

"Very good. Avoid contact at this time," the voice on the other end replied. "Remember, we want the woman as well as the others."

The reception hall was a large ballroom with polished hardwood floors and mirrored walls. Tables with mounds of decorative foods and well-stocked bars were strategically placed to keep the crowd in a festive and generous mood. The room was packed.

"Jesus, I feel so out of place here," Rhiannon confided to Luther.

"You!" Luther grinned at her.

"All right, you got me there." She laughed. "What I mean is I just crawled off an international flight after traveling thirty hours straight from a makeshift temple in Turkey, and now suddenly this! I'm thrust into a gathering of San Francisco's Who's Who, to find the man I helped teach the path of the medicine, while all bloody cosmic hell is still hunting us down. Well, it's just the slightest bit surreal. Gentlemen, I could use a drink."

"I thought you'd be knocking people over to get to the man of the hour." Jimmy winked at her.

"This reunion shouldn't be hurried," she said.

"I'll get you something," Jimmy said.

"If they have decent tequila, a glass of it straight, Jimmy," she said.

Jimmy disappeared into a crowd of people. Rhiannon immediately wheeled around to confront Luther.

"Quickly, tell me as much as you can, Luther."

"I've only seen him once since he got back and that was only briefly, so my knowledge is sketchy. But here's what I know.

After the tornado incident, he went and stayed with an old woman in the backwoods of Mississippi, evidently a medicine person herself. With her help, he finally learned to integrate his training. Apparently, he's gained skills in working with the spirit you helped him find. In the midst of an attack by the Visitors, he underwent an initiation with that spirit. I don't know much more than that, but he's different now. Carson can work the medicine."

Rhiannon rocked back, flushed with pride and curiosity.

Jimmy returned looking amused, carrying Rhiannon's tequila. "Sorry it took so long, but I ran into an editor from *Mother Jones*. Anyway, here you go, premium tequila, as requested—Patron Añejo."

"Wow, I really didn't expect they'd be pouring this," she said.

"For this crowd, they have all the good stuff. Perhaps it's a lucky omen," Jimmy said. "Hell, they wouldn't even let me pay. Some guy standing over by the bar insisted on treating me. Said he owed me at least a damn good drink."

"Beware of Long Knives offering fire water, my brother," Luther said deadpan.

"I'll try to remember that great wisdom," Jimmy fired back, adjusting his thick eyeglasses.

"Gentlemen, can we stay focused?" Rhiannon interjected. "Let's move on through the crowd, shall we? And I would prefer it if we could head to the side of the room and work our way along the wall."

Just as they started to move, an intoxicated woman approached. She was wearing an overly stretched gold lamé evening gown, accessorized by an assortment of gold bracelets, necklaces and rings, set off by diamond earrings that were garishly large.

"Oh, I believe I recognize you from the film!" she exclaimed, grabbing Luther by the arm.

Her speech was slurred. She needed Luther's arm to steady her.

"I think you people are just marvelous," she said in a dramatic manner, closing her eyes for a moment. "You know, sometimes I hear the Great Spirit calling to me. Perhaps I was a squaw in my last life. My family would never talk about it when I was growing up, but I'm pretty sure my great-grandmother was a real Cherokee princess. Are you Cherokee, by any chance?"

"Cherokee to the bone, ma'am," Luther replied, giving Jimmy a wink.

"Oh, I knew it when I laid eyes on you," she responded and turned to Jimmy. "Are you also Cherokee?"

"No, ma'am. I wanted to be but I didn't have the grades to get in."

"Oh, you poor dear," the woman said, reaching over to pat him on the arm.

"It was a pleasure to speak with you," Luther interrupted. "Sorry we don't have time to talk more about our family relations, but we're trying to help this lady find her husband. The poor woman says he gets terribly intoxicated at these things."

"Oh my, don't let me stop you another moment," she said, switching her grip to Rhiannon's arm. "Good luck, my dear. You deserve better."

They worked their way to the side of the room, easing through the crowd along the mirrored wall. Occasionally, people stopped Luther and Jimmy to comment on the film. Luther became momentarily engrossed with a group of his Zuni elders. Rhiannon used these pauses to scan for Carson.

Suddenly she caught a glimpse of him out of the corner of her eye. Turning rapidly, she stepped into the path of a large man in a dark suit.

"Excuse me," she said, looking up into the man's expressionless face.

"No harm," the man replied dryly and walked away quickly, disappearing into the crowd.

As he moved away, Rhiannon spotted the earphone, its cord

running down inside the back of his collar. Quickly, she pulled the Indians aside.

"They're here—in this room," she said urgently.

Luther stared hard into her eyes.

"Are you certain?" Jimmy asked, pulling his glasses off and nervously cleaning them with a handkerchief.

"Yes. I just bumped into one. He was even wearing an earphone."

"Rhiannon, there are lots of very powerful people in the room. There are all kinds of private bodyguards and security people mixed in among this crowd."

"This isn't paranoia; I read him clearly. No mistake! They're intending to do something tonight. And they mean to include us."

Luther's face tightened. "Go get Carson, now!"

"Thank you very much," Carson said, excusing himself from a circle of admirers.

He moved toward the side of the room, needing to find a bottle of water. It had been a good night for him, for the documentary, and for the fund-raiser. He was grateful to have his mind so completely engaged with the screening and reception. It was ironic, given all the anticipation he had expended over seeing her again, to know it was to happen in a room full of strangers demanding his attention. It had been so long, so much had happened. He tried to suppress the barrage of expectations rising within. Why should he believe there could be any possible future with her?

"Yes, sir, what can I get you?" a bartender asked.

"Just bottled water, please," Carson answered.

"Funny that I'm the one who's drinking the hard stuff tonight."

Carson turned to face the familiar voice standing at the end of the bar.

"Loved your work, Mr. Reynolds, simply brilliant." Rhiannon smiled and stepped toward him. "Whatever possessed you?"

"Why, thank you very much, madam. In hindsight, I suppose I could say this documentary was kind of a calling for me." Carson laughed.

Although he could tell she was exhausted, he was overcome by how wonderful she appeared to him.

"Seems I know that feeling." She smiled coyly. "Perhaps I should get some fresh air. I find that there are too many people of the wrong type in this room for my liking. You probably think I'm crazy, but if I don't get out of here quickly, I fear for my health."

Carson nodded and turned to the bartender, "Excuse me, but do you know a fast way out of here, so I don't have to fight my way back through this crowd?"

The bartender leaned toward him. "Well, you didn't hear it from me, but that side door over there will take you through the kitchen, and if you keep going, you'll come out down by the elevators."

They moved casually toward the side door. Carson stopped to look back over his shoulder. "Yes, there're some unfriendly folks in attendance. I find them easy to spot because they pulsate with a goon-like energy. There's not much independent thinking happening inside their heads, but they sure are tenacious."

"Wow, I'm impressed. You certainly didn't have that depth of perception last time I saw you," she whispered. "But come on, Jimmy and Luther are waiting down in the garage."

"This isn't exactly how I had imagined seeing you again," he mumbled under his breath.

Rhiannon flashed a quick smile. "I had envisioned something else, myself."

The elevator opened onto the garage level. Rhiannon expected to find the van waiting.

"Where are they?" she asked. "Carson, where are you going?"

"To my car. Come on!"

"But what's happened to them?"

"I don't know, but we can't stand here waiting."

They began walking along the rows of parked cars. From a lower level came the sound of an approaching vehicle. Carson quickly stepped behind a concrete column, pulling Rhiannon with him. A bright yellow tow truck rolled past, towing Jimmy White Stone's van. As the sound of the truck faded, they heard approaching footsteps.

"Why should I have to carry it?" Jimmy complained, struggling with Rhiannon's luggage.

"Because, my brother, you are not yet a Cherokee!" Luther said in a low voice.

"Luther, you're an ass."

"Quiet, the danger here isn't over."

Seeing that the two men were alone, Carson stepped out to meet them.

"What happened?" he asked.

"The goddamn hotel security reported my van as being abandoned in the garage. Had a tow truck haul it off." Jimmy cursed.

"Yeah, we saw it going by," Carson replied.

"When we got down here my van was already up on the hook. It was pointless to argue with the driver; he had orders that it was to be impounded," Jimmy continued. "Said my van had been parked here for over a week. At least he let us get our things out."

"Did the driver say where he was taking it?" Carson asked.

"No. Said I'd have to inquire with the hotel security people."

"This isn't good. Sounds like they may be trying to make it look like you were never here."

"What about your SUV, Carson?" Rhiannon asked.

"Let's find out," he replied.

It was there. They approached the vehicle cautiously.

The reception was ending. The noise level in the garage increased as people began coming for their cars. The sound of laughter, engines, and squealing tires created a chamber of echoes.

"What do you think? Should we try to drive out?" Jimmy asked.

"I suppose we have to," Carson said. "There's no point in trying to leave any other way. The hotel has security cameras all over the place, so I'm fairly certain we'd be seen trying any exit."

"I have an idea," Luther interrupted. "Jimmy, get behind the wheel. Rhiannon, Carson, get in and put whatever you need in your lap, now."

Jimmy started the engine and pulled away, driving toward the garage exit. The men in the black Suburban watched from their vehicle, parked at the end of the next row. When the Cherokee arrived at street level, exit signs pointed to the left, directing all traffic out a side alley to New Montgomery Street.

"Now, don't go left here; very casually turn right and go up the alley," Luther instructed. "Just up ahead there's another alley that runs into this one. Turn into it and slow down immediately. We'll jump out quickly. Jimmy, you keep moving. Drive directly over to the Mission District, where we were this morning, and park right in front of the Native American Center. Double-park, if necessary. Have someone else move the Cherokee later. Stay at the center until someone you trust comes for you."

Luther, Carson, and Rhiannon sprang from the SUV as it turned behind a building into the perpendicular alley. Luther quickly ushered them and their belongings into the shadows of a doorway.

"Negative. I repeat, subject's Cherokee has not exited," a voice from an unmarked Ford Crown Victoria on New Montgomery Street reported.

The black Suburban wheeled around and raced back up the alley, barely missing several oncoming cars and making the tight turn into the intersecting alley just in time to see the taillights of Carson's vehicle turning onto Mission Street at the far end. The Suburban rushed by the darkened doorway where Carson, Luther, and Rhiannon stood and was immediately followed by two other unmarked cars.

"Damn. Seems someone's called the cavalry," Luther whispered. "Wait here."

"Luther, how did you know about this alley?" Carson asked.

"Part of my task here has been to oversee security for my elders," he answered. "It's always good to study the terrain you must work in."

Luther disappeared around the corner and headed back up the alley toward the hotel.

Standing in the shadows, Carson and Rhiannon had their first private moment.

"I know I wasn't supposed to, but I've missed you," Carson confessed.

"Yeah, I know," she answered, leaning against him. "We have so much to share if we ever get the chance. I hear you're looking for a new soundman. Think you could teach me?"

"Well, it seems my filming opportunities may be curtailed for a while. I was kind of thinking of applying for a job as your gardener and roof repairman, provided the position still comes with bathing privileges."

"You'll have to fill out an application. But I must warn you, it comes with a drug test."

Struggling not to laugh, Carson pulled her close as if to muzzle himself with her body. She placed her hand over his mouth, whispering in his ear for him to shush. Suddenly, their repressed desire broke free. Carson pulled her mouth to his. They dissolved into the kiss.

A large car backed quickly into the alley. Carson and Rhiannon jumped back into the corners of the doorway. The limo's rear door opened, and Luther stepped out.

"All right, let's go," Luther commanded, waving his arm rapidly.

The three piled into the back of the elongated car.

Luther uttered something to the driver, and the limo started rolling.

"Rodney's not only Ashiwi, he's even from my clan," Luther said, pointing to the driver. "He works out here as a chauffeur. We contracted with his company to drive our elders around this week, knowing he would take good care of them. Seeing my elders tonight reminded me that Rodney would be somewhere outside with this limousine. Fortunately, they hadn't left yet and I was able to spot him."

"So, what happens now?" Carson asked.

"Well, first we have to go pick up my elders. It wouldn't be right to leave them without their ride. We'll take them to their hotel. Then Rodney'll have the opportunity to earn a little overtime."

"If you mean we're riding to Wounded Paw's in this limo, I'm all for it," Rhiannon said. "I'm dying to get some sleep, and that long side-bench looks wonderful right now."

Having deposited the Zuni elders at the Stanford Court Hotel, Rodney pulled the limo onto California, descending the steep street. At the bottom of the hill he turned right on Battery Street. But an unmarked Ford Victoria, with dark tinted windows, suddenly pulled up alongside as both vehicles stopped for the red light at Bush Street.

"Looks like we might have company," Rodney announced over his shoulder.

"I know," Carson said. "I'll try and do something."

He opened the limo's sky roof and stood up, directing his attention to the threatening sedan. He envisioned a wall of impenetrable energy around it.

A band of homeless people began crossing the street, pushing overloaded shopping carts. Two of the carts collided with each other just in front of the unmarked sedan, rendering the carts immobile while their owners argued with each other.

The sedan window opened on the driver's side. "Hey, get those damn carts out of the way," a voice yelled.

"What did you say, mister?" a crusty homeless man shouted back defiantly.

"I said move it, pops."

The remainder of the homeless caravan pulled to a halt in front of the Ford.

"Well, mister big shot, you wanna come out and make us?" one of the homeless challenged.

"Move or I will push you off the street."

"Is that so?" a rugged man replied, pulling a steel pipe from his cart.

As more of the homeless tribe quickly emerged from nearby office building porticos, the sedan became completely surrounded. Several individuals began angrily ramming their carts into the dark car, while others smashed the headlights and slashed the tires. A baseball bat shattered the front window as the car's airbags automatically inflated.

Rodney quietly eased the limo away.

Ten minutes later, the long, sleek car was cruising east over the Bay Bridge as it departed San Francisco, on its way to Nevada. Rhiannon had already fallen asleep. Luther sat up front with Rodney, chatting away in a mixture of English and Zunian. Mounted between them on the dashboard, in all his glory and fury, stood Taz.

Leaning back in the rear seat, Carson questioned how successfully they had evaded their adversaries. There was no point in guessing the future; far too much remained in question. Yet for the time being, the power of the medicine path was still holding. Only one thing seemed certain—the world would never be as he once knew it.

He sent prayers for the safekeeping of the many others he had encountered through the medicine work. Closing his eyes, he whispered to the wrathful deity, "Great Lord, may I continue to have your blessings. And may my work be powered through your terrible agency."

Epilogue

"How much longer do you think we'll have to stay here?" Rhiannon asked, panting slightly as they hiked up the mountain behind Wounded Paw's cabin.

"I don't know, maybe another week or so," Carson answered. "At least there's been no indication of Visitors showing up here. And Luther says Jimmy has a group of their attorneys working in conjunction with Landon's legal team. As soon as they can file some motions, we should be able to emerge from here without fear of an indictment. Jimmy's also cashing in some political favors with a congressman or two, and Luther's elders have gotten the support of a senator from New Mexico. There're at least a few national politicians watching our backs."

"Wouldn't you think someone in the government would be asking by now who these rogue agents are and what they're up to?"

"Apparently, some people have," he said. "Too many people in positions of power have been harassed. I think these guys have overplayed their hand."

"I thought you said Luther went straight back to the Zuni reservation from here. How's he sending all this information to you?" she asked.

"He passes it through channels. Sydney gets it and then tells me." He paused, repressing a smile. "Didn't you see those smoke signals this morning?"

"Very funny."

Carson winked. "We're almost there, come on," he said, reaching back to give her a hand climbing over a large boulder.

"I hope you know where you're going."

"Me too," he said, smiling at her as he wiped the sweat from his neck.

"I just want to take you back to my place and live like regular people for a while," she said, exposing the accumulating weariness of their ordeal.

"Yeah." Carson sighed. "Wouldn't that be nice?"

They hiked on, eventually arriving at the area with the petroglyphs that Carson had encountered, that fateful day with Wounded Paw, years before.

They stood in silence, taking in the stone images that peered out at them from the rock wall. Without a word, each reached out to clasp the other's hand.

"So, this is where it really began for you," she said, leaning into his shoulder with her head.

"Oh, there've been so many places of beginnings on this wild journey,'" he mused. "But this is one of them, for sure. Your place was another."

Rhiannon pressed her hand in his, wondering whether a future was possible for them.

"Let me show you something," he said.

He led her around some large outcroppings to a spot with relatively fresh carvings. There they were—new images of the Visitors chiseled on the mountain wall. But these showed the alien entities with shattered bodies, some of them pierced with magic arrows.

"My God, did Wounded Paw do this?" she asked.

"Yeah. He, Sydney and Joe Buck have been doing it, depicting the Visitors as wounded or dead, showing their defeat—trying to direct the future. But something unexpected occurred. Look up here, behind you."

Carson turned her around and pointed high above them. There, some twenty feet up on an opposing stone wall, was a large image of a being that closely resembled a Tibetan wrathful deity. The spirit was brandishing weapon-like objects in its multiple arms and riding a creature suggestive of a dragon. It was descending directly toward the Visitors' images on the opposing wall.

"Wounded Paw says there was a big storm recently, with tremendous thunder and lightning. When they came back up here they discovered that image in the stone."

Rhiannon squinted to get a better look at the figure, noticing that it had not been cut into the rock like the petroglyphs had. No, it looked more as if a layer of the cliff's surface had broken away, revealing the hidden image beneath.

Carson climbed up the stone face a few feet and reached into his coat pocket. He pulled out Taz and placed the toy figure in a crevice. Scuttling back down to Rhiannon, he clasped his hands together.

"Welcome home, Great Lord, both here and in Tibet," he said in prayer.

Rhiannon uttered a quick mantra.

They stood in silence, soaking in the blessings and struggles of the multitude of events that had brought them together.

He turned to her. "Just maybe, we're doing better than we realize."

COSMIC
EGG
BOOKS

If you prefer to spend your nights with Vampires and Werewolves rather than the mundane then we publish the books for you. If your preference is for Dragons and Faeries or Angels and Demons – we should be your first stop. Perhaps your perfect partner has artificial skin or comes from another planet – step right this way. Our curiosity shop contains treasures you will enjoy unearthing. If your passion is Fantasy (including magical realism and spiritual fantasy), Horror or Science Fiction (including Steampunk), Cosmic Egg books will feed your hunger.

If you have enjoyed this book, why not tell other readers by posting a review on your preferred booksite. Recent bestsellers from Cosmic Egg Books are:

The Zombie Rule Book, A Zombie Apocalypse Survival Guide
Tony Newton
The book the living-dead don't want you to have!
Paperback: 978-1-78279-334-2
e-book: 978-1-78279-333-5

Cryptogram, Because the Past is Never Past
Michael Tobert
Welcome to the dystopian world of 2050, where three lovers are haunted by echoes from eight-hundred years ago.
Paperback: 978-1-78279-681-7
e-book: 978-1-78279-680-0

Purefinder
Ben Gwalchmai
London, 1858. A child is dead; a man is blamed and dragged through hell in this Dantean tale of loss, mystery and fraternity.
Paperback: 978-1-78279-098-3
e-book: 978-1-78279-097-6

600ppm, A Novel of Climate Change
Clarke W. Owens
Nature is collapsing. The government doesn't want you to know why. Welcome to 2051 and 600ppm.
Paperback: 978-1-78279-992-4
e-book: 978-1-78279-993-1

Creations
William Mitchell
Earth 2040 is on the brink of disaster. Can Max Lowrie stop the self-replicating machines before it's too late?
Paperback: 978-1-78279-186-7
e-book: 978-1-78279-161-4

The Gawain Legacy
Jon Mackley
If you try to control every secret, secrets may end up controlling you.
Paperback: 978-1-78279-485-1
e-book: 978-1-78279-484-4

Mirror Image
Beth Murray
When Detective Jack Daniels discovers the journal of female serial killer Sarah he is dragged into a supernatural world, where people's dark sides are not always hidden.
Paperback: 978-1-78279-482-0
e-book: 978-1-78279-481-3

Moon Song
Elen Sentier
Tristan died too soon, Isoldé must bring him back to finish his job... to write the Moon Song.
Paperback: 978-1-78279-807-1
e-book: 978-1-78279-806-4

Origin
Colleen Douglas
Fate rarely calls on us at a moment of our choosing.
Paperback: 978-1-78279-492-9
e-book: 978-1-78279-491-2

Perception
Alaric Albertsson
The first ship was sighted over St. Louis...and then St. Louis was gone.
Paperback: 978-1-78279-261-1
e-book: 978-1-78279-262-8

Find more titles and sign up to our readers' newsletter at
http://www.johnhuntpublishing.com/fiction.
Follow us on Facebook at https://www.face-book.com/JHPfiction
and Twitter at https://twitter.com/JHPFiction.

Most titles are published in paperback and as an e-book.
Paperbacks are available in physical bookshops. Both print and
e-book editions are available online. Readers of e-books can
click on the live links in the titles to order.